Gold Coast Detective
Scotty Stephens

Book 2

MARY'S MANSION

ANDREW McDERMOTT

PRESS

Mary's Mansion by ANDREW McDERMOTT
www.andrewmcdermott.com.au

First published in Australia by X Press Publishing 2025
P.O. Box 395 Coolangatta
Queensland 4225 Australia
mail@andrewmcdermott.com.au

 A catalogue record for this
book is available from the
National Library of Australia

ISBN: 978-0-6453709-8-0 (pbk)
ISBN: 978-0-6453709-9-7 (ebk)

Cover design by X Press Press © 2025
Cover background image: © KinoMaster (Shutterstock)

Typesetting and design by X Press Press © 2025

For Tallebudgera Valley

BOOKS BY
ANDREW M^CDERMOTT
(see samples and more details at back of this book)

Gold Coast Detective Scotty Stephens series:
X'posé (X prequel)
Book 1 – X
Book 2 – Mary's Mansion
Book 3 – Tarnished
Book 4 - INSEXT

Detective Joe Dean series:
Hidden Moon (Flirting with The Moon prequel)
Flirting with The Moon

The Tiger Chase

Speculative fiction:
Quest of The New Templars series:
Birthright (prequel)
Book 1 – RESURRECTION

Children's books:
The Last Tiger

The Murphys

1886 – Tallebudgera Valley

'You said you'd do it and you did,' Mary Murphy said as she gazed over rolling hills and rich pasture. 'Rejoice in your achievements, husband. You're a great man!'

'Not so great, Oy think,' Callum said.

'You've put food on the tables of many a family, including your own. This valley would be a den of inequity if it wasn't for you.'

'Aye, but at what cost?'

Standing side by side on Callum's lookout, Mary rested her head on her husband's shoulder. 'You're a righteous soul in a world of heathens.'

'Oy fear the land is cursed.'

'Aye … cursed by the name of Fenton.' Mary turned and took Callum's hand. 'But we can put it right.'

Callum sighed. A righteous man, he knew he wasn't. He'd been guilty of many a bad deed over the years. Although he'd worked hard to put all that behind him, a pending day of retribution hung over his success. And today was that day.

'Oy'll fix it. Oy owe the community that.'

'*We'll* fix it.'

'No.' Callum squeezed Mary's hand. 'Oy'll love you till the day Oy die, Mary Murphy, but this is something Oy need to do alone.' He pulled his hand away, then marched down the hill.

A gust of wind tore through the trees, causing the leaves to swirl and hiss.

Mary crossed herself. 'Watch over him this day, dear Lord. Bring him home safely.'

Kathy Brown

2018

The ancient door of the logger's cottage creaked, but Kathy Brown didn't stir.

Like a silent shadow, the figure crept through the tiny house, heading straight for the bedroom.

Death would be swift.

The secret would be safe.

She had to die.

B.A. Fisher

2022

The penthouse in Santa Monica, the apartment on Sydney Harbour and the house in the wealthy Brisbane suburb of Teneriffe, were all long gone. His beloved classic Porsche was the only luxury Ben Fisher had retained after the divorce. A modest advance from his publisher had taken care of the rehab bill. His new literary agent had paid the bond on a small, rented cottage in Tallebudgera Valley. It was time to earn some money, time to get back on his feet.

According to his agent, Mary's Mansion, although tiny, would suit Ben's needs while writing his next book. The first thing he noticed when he pulled up at the front of the cottage, turned off the engine and climbed from his car, was the absence of man-made noise. The warble of a magpie, the *whoosh* of a gentle breeze teasing the trees at the back of the property, immediately made him feel uncomfortable.

While in rehab, he'd learned the importance of putting aside time for himself, time to clear his thoughts, time to just think. Apparently, this simple luxury was lost to him when the lock to his soul finally broke and the demons ran havoc through the corridors of his mind. So far, he wasn't buying any of that crap. He'd never been the sound-of-silence kind of guy. In fact, he liked the demons—needed them. They were the guardians of his creativity.

The reason his active mind kept turning.

Of course, there was still much doubt, though. He hadn't felt this insecure since he'd written his first novel twenty years ago.

Although he'd signed a three-book deal with Random House, the imposter syndrome that dogged him meant he wasn't even sure if he had another book in him. Fortunately for him, he did, but even after twenty-two more books, the uncertainty lingered. It wasn't until the first movie deal that he felt comfortable with his abilities. The fortune and fame were an added reminder of the words of encouragement from his wife when they were young and still in love. 'You can do this, Fisher!'

Ironically, it was that same feeling of doubt that humbled him somewhat as he glanced over his temporary lodgings. Nicky Lee, his new agent, had prepaid the rent for two months. 'See it as an investment in our future,' she'd said on the phone after giving Ben the address. 'You better not let me down, big shot!' How dare she speak to him like that? Four years ago, he'd started a bidding war among the top publishers who were fighting over his contract. He was also signed to one of the top literary agents in the world. How quickly all that had changed. Now Nicky was the only agent willing to take him on. Luckily, he'd signed a fresh five-year contract with Random just prior to him going off the rails. But now he was in breach. So far, he'd returned a big fat zero for the one book a year deal. Random was threatening to sue him, so too was his ex-agent. But none of that really mattered because his ex-fucking-wife had taken everything, anyway. Apart from the Porsche, all he had left was his talent. His debts were growing, so he needed to buckle down and write another bestseller.

'Of course, I can do it!' he'd told his publisher after being summoned to their headquarters in Sydney and grilled by a group of directors. The outcome of the meeting had been clear. He either produced a new book in the next three months, or they would not only terminate his contract but make sure he never worked in the industry again.

Ben reached into his jacket pocket and pulled out a small tin. His beloved baccy. Inside was a dozen or so cigarettes that he'd pre-rolled before leaving Brisbane. Tobacco was a luxury he couldn't really afford, but it was a hell of a lot cheaper than the booze and drugs he'd come accustomed to over the last few years.

As he lit a cigarette and watched a wisp of smoke swirl into the breeze, a feeling of déjà vu suddenly engulfed him. Had he been here before? Of course not. Retrieving his bag from the boot of the car, he fumbled in his other jacket pocket, produced a wad of keys and made his way toward the cottage.

A sign over the door, crudely chiselled into a piece of ancient timber, read, 'Mary's Mansion'.

'A mansion, eh?' Ben mumbled to himself. 'I'm back in the big time already.' He unlocked the door and pushed it open. Before stepping inside, he peered into the dark interior. 'Mary? Are you here?' He wasn't sure why he'd said that. It was almost as if there were a need to ask permission to enter the property. *And who the hell was Mary?*

The tiny living room and kitchen were modern and comfortable. There was a small dining table by a side window which would have to double as a desk. If Ben were the kind of man who cared about such things, he would have sat for a moment at his new workstation drinking up the amazing view it offered of the horse stud next door. But he wasn't much of a stop-and-smell-the-roses kind of guy either. A tree is a tree, a mountain is a mountain. So what? And the silence? It was deafening him.

Wasting no time, he set up the tools of his trade. First, he retrieved his beloved Breville barista coffee maker from the car and fired it up. It wasn't as good as the Lelit Giulietta he used to own, but it was all he could afford now, and it did a decent job. Then he produced a small cylindrical music player from his case, scrolled through the playlist on his phone, chose The Prodigy and hit play.

The manic intro to 'Firestarter' exploded from the speaker, and the psychotic confession of Keith Flint banished the uncomfortable silence from the room.

The third, and most important, tool was his laptop. He set it up on the table by the window and while it booted up, he poured his first cup of fresh coffee. Then, placing his baccy tin and lighter by his new workstation, he was ready to start work.

Ben Fisher wasn't interested in the natural wonders of the countryside. Nicky was excited when she'd told him all about the small valley community, the two-acre property nestled between the Fenton horse stud and the Patterson's dairy farm. 'You don't look too impressed,' she'd commented at his lack of interest.

'You're sending me to a shed in a field. Is this what my life has come to?'

'You need to get your arse in gear, buddy. No distractions. You'll thank me for this later.'

'*Pfff*…'

Sitting at the table, Ben took a sip of coffee. He'd been off his meds for two days now. *To hell with doctors, what do they know?* Movement from outside the window caught his eye.

There was a young woman riding a horse on the property next door. She was blonde, late teens, early twenties perhaps. She reminded him of someone, but he couldn't place who.

Smoking and sipping coffee, Ben stared out the window, watching the mighty horse gallop. Heaving muscles expanding and contracting, nostrils flaring. The girl's thighs throbbed and gripped the animal's torso. Resembling light sensitive panels turning and searching for the incoming signal, the creative receptors at the back of Fisher's head began to open.

Like visitors from the other side lining up behind a medium to send messages to their loved ones here on Earth, characters appeared. First, a young woman stepped forward. Her name was Kate. She looked not unlike the young girl on the horse next door.

Perhaps that's where the muse harvested his inspiration for the protagonist. Kate seemed at home in the cottage, like she owned it. Although pretty, Ben sensed a dark side to her. With copious amounts of coffee, smokes, pork scratchings, and an endless wave of electric punk and heavy metal music, Kate's story revealed itself to him over the next two months.

Although he'd never admit it for fear of ending up back in rehab—or worse, the looney bin—it was Mary who had relayed Kate's story to him. He still didn't know who Mary was, he wasn't aware that she lay just a few metres away under the ancient cedar tree. All he knew was that she was a strong woman, Irish, no nonsense, but cheeky at the same time. Her husband, Callum, was different. He was a hard man.

As his fingers scurried across the keyboard like a concert pianist, Ben didn't stop for a single minute to wonder who these people were. They were just there, like the characters in his book. It wasn't until later, when the first draft was in the bag, that he vaguely remembered them as uninvited guests visiting him every day. Then a realisation hit him. Perhaps they were characters. Perhaps they were also a part of this story. But how could they be?

They'd lived over a hundred years ago.

After a second and third draft, the manuscript was finally ready to go to Annie Shaver, Ben Fisher's long-time editor. Annie had worked on all his previous books. She was familiar with his style of writing and was well practiced in the art of turning his shabby prose into a commercially acceptable product.

'Are you sure you wrote this, Ben?' Annie asked during a Zoom call with the author. 'It's different from your usual style.'

'What can I say? I guess I've evolved.'

Annie shrugged, nodded and puckered her lips at the same time. 'I suppose you could say that.'

'But did you like it?'

The head shake changed to a wobble and a slight frown. 'It's adequate.' Annie was a true pro when it came to assessing her clients' work. 'You've written better, but this will get you back on the horse.'

'Thanks.' Ben was used to his editor's doubled-edged compliments.

Nicky Lee's reaction though was completely different. 'Whoa hoo! Well done, mate. I knew you could do it.' It was their first meeting in Nicky's office since Ben had finished the book. 'This is going to put you right back on the top where you belong,' she declared, popping the cork on a bottle of non-alcoholic champagne.

And it did. A year after leaving Mary's Mansion, *The Valley of Kate* raced to the top of the bestseller lists worldwide. B.A. Fisher was the champion of the murder mystery genre once more. And life was looking good.

That was until Lindy Williams, a member of the Brisbane chapter of the Sisters in Crime writers group, asked a question while attending the Byron Writers Festival. A Q&A session was opened at the end of a discussion with best-selling author B.A. Fisher and Candy Lawson of the ABC. Ben spoke of his time in Tallebudgera Valley and his process for writing the new book.

'How can you sit there accepting all the adulation, the fame and the fortune, when you know you stole the story?'

The record crowd, packed into the festival's largest marquee, fell deathly silent.

'Excuse me?' Fisher said, seated comfortably on the stage.

'The story you wrote,' Lindy continued. 'It's not actually *your* story, is it?'

Fisher remained silent, staring at the middle-aged woman.

'All you've done is plagiarise the murder of Kathy Brown!'

The crowd bubbled with a wave of gasps and whispers.

'I can assure you, I never—' Fisher was in the middle of a denial when a man seated next to Libby Williams stood and interrupted him.

'I'll sue you for this, Fisher!' Wearing a tweed cap and a waxed jacket, he was tall, squared jawed, and possessed the air of a wealthy farmer. 'You won't get away with it.'

The news spread quickly after the media jumped on the story.

> Bestselling author B.A. Fisher a fraud?
> Fisher used actual murder for own story!
> Author sued by thoroughbred breeder!

Each of the tabloids followed up releasing archived articles on an unsolved murder that had taken place in Mary's Mansion five years earlier.

'Is it true? Did you steal it?' Nicky Lee asked after requesting a meeting in her office.

'Of course, I didn't steal it.'

There were newspapers strewn across the agent's desk. She held one up. The headline said, "James Fenton vows to have his day in court." 'Do you even know this guy?'

With an air of nonchalance, Fisher shook his head.

'But he owns the property next to Mary's Mansion. The Fenton horse stud. You were there for two months. Surely you knew who he was?'

The slow head shake continued. 'Nope.'

'For God's sake, Ben. The wealthy landowner, Jack Finlay. The man you reveal in the book as the killer. It's obviously Fenton.'

'It isn't, I can assure you.'

'Did you ever meet him?'

'Nope.'

'And Kate Bowen? Sounds an awful lot like Kathy Brown. The list goes on. You could end up with half of Tallebudgera suing you for defamation of character!'

Fisher shrugged.

'You don't seem to realise how serious this is.' Nicky slumped back in her office chair.

'I'm innocent. How bad can it be?'

Nicky leaned forward on her desk. 'The thing is, Ben. If this Fenton guy takes you to court and wins, Random House will come for you too. It won't just be the advance they'll want back.'

'Fickle bastards.'

'Fickle indeed. You know the publishing industry as well as I do.'

'What do I need to do?' For the first time, there was concern in Fisher's voice.

'You … *we* need to get some help.'

'What do you have in mind?'

1

'His genius manifests for around two hours a day. During that time, characters are born and scenarios crafted. Subplots, distractions and twists are embroidered with precision, then woven together to form the patchwork quilt of another bestselling novel.'

'He's a self-centred, arrogant prick!'

These two comments were by the same person but two years apart. On both occasions, literary agent, Debbie Noonan, was referring to her former client and best-selling author, B.A. Fisher. The former was when he'd received the Ned Kelly Award for best novel. The latter was just after the agent had dumped him for breach of contract.

I'd been researching the writer since receiving a phone call from him earlier in the day. He seemed surprised that I didn't know who he was when he announced his name—like he was expecting a verbal fanfare or something. He'd heard of me of course. Few people in Australia didn't know who Scotty Stephens was—the novice police detective who brought an end to the reign of terror by the infamous serial killer known as X. At the same time, he ripped apart an intricate web of corruption and deceit by the Gold Coast mayor and Queensland commissioner of police. It was certainly widespread and the fame didn't seem to be dissipating—even three months later. And quitting the police force seemed to endear me to the public even more.

I must admit, a part of me was hoping my notoriety would help me in my new business venture. But another part of me still cringed when people stopped me in the street to shake my hand and take selfies or insist on footing the bill in restaurants. But who am I to complain? I can't say I haven't milked the situation for all it's worth. After starting my own private detective agency, I knew I'd need the necessary funds. My personality was the type that would usually shun the spotlight, so at first, I was knocking back the offers from all the media outlets, including *60 Minutes* and *The Sydney Morning Herald*. But they kept coming and the bids continued to rise. It was my best mate, Elvis, who finally made me realise I was in the best position of my life. I could either start a business with nothing or set myself up financially so that I didn't have to worry about money for a while. And all I had to do was tell my story exactly how it happened.

My new office was a shabby dormer loft above the Nicholadas Papageorgiou Accountancy firm on Griffith Street, Coolangatta. It was nothing flash, just one room. The view from the window was of the street below and the back of The Strand shopping centre across the road. The Amart furnishing was sparse—a desk, a couple of chairs and a bed for my four-month-old Staffordshire terrier pup, Romeo.

Elvis had presented me with a framed front page of the *Gold Coast Bulletin* that read, 'The Man who Restored the Shine to the Gold Coast'. There was a picture of me receiving the keys to the city from the new mayor, Tim Taffer. Against my better judgement, Elvis had insisted on hanging it on the wall at the top of the stairs so it would be the first thing potential clients saw before entering the office.

There was a window seat under the dormer window. I liked to sit there looking down at the busy street below, contemplating. Unfortunately, since starting my business only two days earlier,

I'd done little else. In fact, the call from Ben Fisher was my first potential lead.

We'd arranged for him to come to the office that afternoon. He'd be travelling down from Brisbane, which meant I had a couple of hours to learn as much about the bloke as I could.

I was sitting in the nook with my laptop on my knees. Romeo stirred and padded over.

There was room for us both so I budged up, allowing him to join me.

Ben Fisher's Wikipedia page told me all I needed to know about his career. He was the author of twenty-four bestselling crime novels, two were made into movies. By typing his name into Google, hundreds of articles and interviews filled many pages. And although I read as much about the guy as possible, it was the recent allegations against him of plagiarism and fraud that were most current—and the reason for his visit.

I soon found myself quite intrigued, but I was growing tired of reading, so I switched to YouTube. There, I could sift through numerous news reports. An extended commentary from the *ABC* summed it up.

'I'm standing outside the 19th century logger's cottage where the murder of Kathy Brown took place five years ago. This is also where best-selling author, Ben Fisher, stayed for two months last year while writing his latest novel, *The Valley of Kate*.' Over the right shoulder of the young female reporter was the cottage, which was little more than a shack. But over her left shoulder, and on the other side of a low fence, were sprawling horse paddocks.

The image switched to the cottage. 'It was here in Mary's Mansion …' the reporter continued, '… that Fisher, who, returning to writing after a four-year hiatus and a much-publicised divorce, allegedly learned of the unsolved Kathy Brown case from the locals and used it for his book.' The view panned across the adjacent paddock to reveal an arena and stables housing thoroughbred horses.

'But it's the climax of the book that is causing the author most harm where he reveals the killer as Jack Finlay, who has almost certainly been based on James Fenton, the owner of the Fenton horse stud next door.' The camera panned back to the reporter. 'It was Mister Fenton's complaint to the police that brought the focus on this case.'

Romeo's ears shot up. Rising to his feet, he barked with his focus on the door. Someone was climbing the stairs. The dog jumped down from the nook and rushed towards the door just as it opened.

Nicholadas Papageorgiou (aka Elvis, my best mate) entered and immediately dropped to his knees. 'Hey mate,' he said, fussing the dog. When the mandatory minute—the minimum Romeo allowed those fortunate enough to fuss him—was up, Elvis climbed back to his feet. 'Hey, bud. What's happening?'

I'd never get used to seeing him in a business suit.

'Not a lot.'

'Got much on?'

'Maybe.' I closed the laptop, stood and stretched.

'What does that mean?' His eager expression was genuine. 'You've got a case?'

'Maybe.'

'You have!' His eagerness grew to excitement. 'You've got a case. Tell me all about it.' I checked my watch. I still had about half an hour before Fisher was due to arrive.

Elvis had been my best mate since kindergarten in Victoria. We'd grown up together, played Aussie rules together, and apart from a five-year gap when my dad brought me and my brother to Queensland when I was fourteen, we'd been inseparable. We'd shared the same house at Kirra Beach for the last twenty-odd years.

'You're kidding. B.A. Fisher is coming here? *The* B.A. Fisher?'

'Yep, should be here pretty soon.'

'I've read all his books.'

'The new one?'

'My oath!'

'Any good?'

He wobbled his head as if appraising the question. 'Not as good as *The Lang Park Slasher* or *Moreton Bay Bite*, but not bad.'

'What's it about?'

He stroked his chin with the forefinger and thumb of his right hand and squinted.

'Just the *TV Week* rundown.'

'It's about this chick who comes down to the Gold Coast hinterland from Bris-Vegas. She's a nasty piece of work. And uhm … that's right, she's got this vendetta against the wealthy landowners in the area. She's actually blackmailing them. Then her body is found one morning by a young stable hand. She's been strangled. Turns out the owner of the horse stud next door killed her because she was threatening to expose him as a child molester.'

'Is that it?' It was a mediocre story or Elvis' powers of review left a lot to be desired. I suspected the latter.

'Well, there's a lot more to it than that, of course, but you wanted the abridged version.'

'I did, thanks.'

'Can you introduce me to him?'

'Later, perhaps.'

'Yeah, yeah right. You need to get to know him first.' He ran a hand over his close-cropped head that once sported the famous Elvis quiff. 'All right, I'll bugger off but tell me everything tonight, yeah?'

'We'll see.'

'Don't be a dick. I'll see you later.' He gave Romeo one last pat then bounded back down the stairs.

Returning to my laptop, I wanted to read more about the case.

Unfortunately, no longer being in the police force meant I couldn't just pull the official police report. So, for now at least, I'd need to rely on the Internet.

Kathy Brown was thirty-five years old when her strangled body was found in a small historical house in Tallebudgera Valley. She'd purchased the property a few months earlier and moved down to Tallebudgera from Brisbane only two weeks prior to her killing.

Sixteen-year-old Matilda Derby, who lived with her parents in the gatehouse of the Fenton horse stud next door, found the body. Kathy had befriended the girl not long after her arrival in the Valley. The coroner's report declared an open case. The cause of death was by asphyxiation at the hands of an unknown assailant. There had been no clues at the scene, and no sign of a scuffle. Kathy's attacker struck at night while she was sleeping.

There was obviously a lot more research for me to undertake. I needed to know everything about the woman and the complete ins and outs of the case. Getting my hands on the police report would be a big help. And I had an idea how this could be achieved.

Romeo stirred once more. The door to the street at the bottom of the stairs opened and closed. I was trying to train the dog not to go apeshit every time someone arrived. It could be bad for business. Placing a hand on the back of his neck and squeezing gently, I said, 'Shhh, that's all right mate …'

He continued to stare at the door, a low growl reverberating. Someone was climbing the stairs.

2

I'd never met a writer before. My first impression of the tall, slim man that walked into my office may have been a product of the body language that echoed the words of literary agent, Debbie Noonan, when she'd said, 'He's a self-centred, arrogant prick.'

Romeo dashed towards him, barking.

As if momentarily stunned, he scanned the walls as if he were looking for an escape route. 'Get away, get away,' he hollered.

'Romeo!' I called off the killer puppy. Ignoring me, the dog looked up at the visitor expectantly with the same expression I'd associate with the writer. *But I'm special, nobody ignores me.*

Ben Fisher didn't even offer him a pat, he just stepped over the little bloke and approached my desk.

'Scott,' he said, holding out his hand.

'Mr Fisher.' We shook hands. His grip was firm and somewhat intimidating.

'Ben, call me Ben.'

Romeo had followed him and was circling his feet, wagging his tail wildly. *Me, me, I'm down here.*

'It's good to meet you.' I gestured with my hand to the vacant seat.

'And you.' Still ignoring the dog, he took a seat.

'Can I get you anything? Something to drink perhaps?'

'No, I'm fine.'

Thank God for that. I had nothing anyway.

There was an awkward silence for a moment. Thankfully, Romeo supplied a distraction as he nudged up against the man's legs.

'In your bed, boy!' The tone was one I'd been practicing with him over the last few weeks and one he was beginning to understand. I had to repeat it before he finally gave up and retreated to the Barney Bed in the corner.

'Sorry about that,' I said, taking my seat at the desk facing Fisher.

'That's okay. I'm assuming you know who I am?'

'Yes, since your call this morning, I've been … catching up.'

'Right, right, so you know all about the allegations against me?'

'I do. Did you do it?' I was talking to my first potential client as a private detective. I didn't feel the need to beat about the bush.

'Do what?'

'You know … nick the story?'

'No, I *did* not!' He fluffed up like a defensive emu. 'There is more to it, though.' Leaning forward, he lowered his voice. 'Do you have an open mind, Mister Stephens?'

'Scott, call me Scott.'

'There's a lot more to this than …' He diverted his eyes to the ceiling. 'I … I may have been the victim of a paranormal event.'

'A what?'

'Are you familiar with spiritualism?'

'As in séances and clairvoyants, you mean?'

'Sort of. I think it was the spirits in that house that guided me.'

'Really?' My fruit loop antenna was beginning to rotate. 'You mean with the writing?'

'Yes. I had absolutely no knowledge of the terrible things that had occurred in that place before I moved in. Then, strange things started to happen.'

'Strange as in …?'

'At first there were voices. In my head, but definitely there.'

Rather than repeat everything he said for clarity, I remained quiet and let him continue.

'And when I began to write, it was as if something … someone, took over me. Like I was channelling, you know?'

I didn't know, but I offered an encouraging nod.

'Then she appeared to me!'

'She?'

'Mary. She was guiding me.'

Remembering from my research that the dead girl's name was Kathy Brown, I didn't have a clue who Mary was. Before I could ask, Fisher continued.

'There has always been an element of what I call, spiritual creativity, whenever I write. It can be like channelling, and I know other writers experience the same feeling, but this … this was different. It was as if Mary was actually writing the book through me.'

I'd been hoping this would be my first case. High-profile writer being accused of something he hadn't done, not dissimilar to the way I'd been publicly accused during the *X* case. But now I was feeling a little disappointed because the guy sitting opposite me was clearly a crackpot. Shuffling uncomfortably in my seat, I asked, 'So, you think the ghost of this Mary wrote the book?'

'That's right.'

'Right … so you're guilty then!'

He slumped backwards into his seat and seemed to shrink a couple of inches. 'What do you mean?'

'Well, the allegations against you are that you didn't write the book.'

'Oh, for goodness' sake.'

'You've just told me you didn't write it.'

He jumped to his feet, prompting Romeo to do the same. 'Forget the stupid book. That's not why I'm here.'

'It's not?'

'I'm sure you already know, but I've been charged with defamation of character.'

I'd written some notes earlier. Looking down at the scribble on my pad, there was a list of names. 'A mister James Fenton.'

'The characters in the book are all fictional of course. I didn't know there was a man living next door who matched the description of the killer.'

I'd probably need to read the book to know the full story. Apart from the footy news on the back pages of the *Bully*, reading wasn't one of my strong points.

'I need you to prove James Fenton killed Kathy Brown.'

'Right, and how do you think I'm going to do that?'

'Oh, that's the easy part. I have all the proof you need.'

My frown was enough to prompt him to continue.

'And Mary will help us, because Mary knows!'

'Mary?'

'Mary Murphy, and her husband Callum.'

'And they are?'

'The original owners of the land. They just about owned the whole of Tallebudgera Valley over a hundred years ago.'

Alrighty then. The antenna was spinning out of control. 'So they're … deceased?'

'Look, I know it sounds crazy.' He slumped back into his seat and ran a hand through his thinning hair. 'James Fenton killed Kathy Brown, yet I'm the one being dragged over the coals.'

I knew that feeling only too well. 'And you can prove he did it?'

'Absolutely. Will you help me, Scott?'

'Just one more question.' It sounded ridiculous before I even said it. 'Why wasn't it Kathy Brown who helped you?'

He quickly sat up straight. 'That bitch? Oh, she was there, but she wouldn't help. In fact, I felt quite intimidated by her, even threatened somewhat.'

'Look, mate, I don't know if this case is for me.'

Fisher stood and leaned on the desk. 'Please, Scott. You're my only hope. I'm not crazy. I didn't steal this story, and I'll make it very much worth your while if you help me.' He held out his hand.

Reluctantly, I shook it. 'Okay. When would you like me to start?'

<h1 style="text-align:center">3</h1>

With a rucksack over his shoulder and a head full of dreams, the sixteen-year-old lad waited patiently while giving as good as he got from the line of brawling Irishmen. Only yards now from the gangplank, he looked up in awe at the mighty ship and tried to imagine the journey that lay ahead.

'Name?' the weary steward asked, looking up from a trestle table.

'Callum Murphy, sir.'

'Date of birth?'

'5 July 1840.'

'Occupation?'

'Timber getter.'

The steward handed him a quill and pointed to a line at the bottom of the sheet. 'Make your mark.'

Callum signed his name with a firm hand.

'Impressive,' the steward said, looking at the neat signature. 'A Mick who can write.

Next.'

'Thank you, sir.' Callum almost skipped onto the gangplank.

The *SS Great Britain*, built by Isambard Kingdom Brunel, was launched in 1843. Callum knew this because his Uncle Dermot, a merchant sailor who'd sailed aboard her in '49, had shared with the young boy his experiences of the first, iron-hulled, steam-powered passenger liner that was once the biggest ship in the world.

Marvelling at the three mighty masts and the single steam funnel, Callum had never been on a ship before. In fact, he'd never been outside his hometown. And now, here he was in Cork about to embark on a three-month voyage and a new life in Australia.

Once aboard, weary from his journey down from the northwest coast, Callum wandered the deck. 'Is this seat taken?' he asked a giant of a lad who sat alone in the mainmast's shade.

'No.' Eyeing the rucksack over Callum's shoulder, he added, 'You should find a cabin first, otherwise you'll end up in steerage.'

'Isn't it all steerage?' Callum was forewarned it was six to a cabin.

The lad smiled. 'It's one big shit hole, that's for sure, but there are levels of shit where you don't want to be.'

Apart from the steward, Callum had never heard an accent different to his own. 'English?'

The lad nodded and frowned warily.

Callum held out his hand. 'Oy'm Callum Murphy.'

A large hand enveloped his. The grip was tight and strong. 'Jimmy Page.'

'Jimmy P?'

Jimmy shrugged. 'If you like.' Looking around at the deck that had now cleared substantially, he said, 'I think you're fucked, Callum.'

'Why's that?'

'You'll be lucky to find a bunk in the engine room now.'

'Aye, Oy'm sure you can help with that, though.' The mischievous grin ignited a sparkle in his blue eyes.

'And why would I want to do that?' Jimmy said. 'I've got my cabin.'

'Because once we reach Australia, Jimmy P, you and Oy will do great things together.'

Jimmy smirked. 'Yeah, like what?'

Although hundreds of Irish lads had boarded in Dublin and Cork, Callum had very little in common with them. Most were workers with few aspirations, heading for a brief life of hard labour, whereas Callum had ambitions to achieve great things. He put down his kit bag, sat down next to Jimmy and told him all about his plans to work hard for the next couple of years, save his money, buy land and open his own sawmill.

'A couple of years?' Jimmy's smirk widened into a patronising grin. 'And how are you going to do that?'

'With the help of good men like you.'

Nobody argued with the tall lad from Lincolnshire when he had taken the best cabin on the top level of the ship. Two years older than Callum, from the moment he'd boarded in Southampton, his pure size had demanded respect from his fellow migrants.

Bill Jarvis, a snide character from Kent, tried to put up a fight as the larger man lifted him by the scruff of the neck and threw him into the passageway, but he was no match for Jimmy Page.

Vowing revenge, Jarvis crawled off to the lower decks, cussing and swearing.

'There you go, Callum, you can have the bunk next to mine.'

'Thank you!'

There were bunks, three high, on either side of the tiny cabin. Jimmy had the lower one on the left. Callum threw his bag onto the now vacant one on the opposite side. Four men sat nervously silent at a card table.

'Don't let me interrupt, gentlemen,' Callum said.

After two days at sea, Callum realised gambling was by far the most popular pastime among his fellow passengers. There seemed to be card games happening everywhere on the ship. Although he found this odd, because most of the rag-tag men wouldn't have owned a pot to piss in, there seemed to be plenty of money exchanging hands. Thankfully, gambling didn't interest Callum. A daily regime of physical exercise, boxing and engagement in deep conversation with like-minded fellows would be his choice of pastime.

Jimmy P was suffering from seasickness. He hadn't returned to his cabin the night before, so Callum headed up to the deck in search of him. As he marched along the corridor, he side-glanced through open doors into smoke-filled cabins where men sat around tables aggressively engrossed in games of Poque. *Poor souls*, Callum thought.

When he reached the end of the corridor, the exit door opened and in stepped a group of men. Blocking his way, there were four big lads, and one smaller, skinny man. The latter, holding an air of authority, stood ahead of the group. His chin was high. An intense beady stare, combined with an arrogant smirk, immediately grabbed Callum's attention.

'Well what 'ave we got 'ere then? Another Mick. Where you been hiding, Paddy?' His accent was Cockney.

'Oy'm sorry, sir?'

The man raised his eyebrows and glanced over each shoulder at his entourage. 'Well, I never did, a polite one. Where you from, lad?'

'Sligo.'

'What's your name?'

'Callum Murphy.'

'Murphy, the Mick from Sligo, eh?'

'If you don't mind, Oy need some air,' Callum said, attempting to pass them.

'Oh, but I *do* mind.' The wiry man stepped forward, his grin turning to a broken yellow smile. He grabbed Callum's hand and shook it. 'Ron Fenton. *Mister* Fenton to you.'

Callum pulled his hand away.

'Oh dear,' Fenton said, shaking his head. 'And 'ere I was just trying to be friendly.' Side glancing at his men once more, he gave a slight nod.

The men eagerly stepped forward and tried to grab Callum.

Callum swung and caught one of them on the chin, sending him bowling into Fenton. But in the confined space, the other three grabbed his arms and rammed him up against the corridor wall, holding him firm.

'It didn't 'ave to be like this, Mick,' Fenton said, moving in close. 'Now, my boys are gonna let you go, but when they do, you behave yourself, yeah?'

Callum, realising he was overpowered, nodded reluctantly. The men released their grip.

'There you go. There was no need for all that was there?' Fenton said.

Callum moved away from the wall.

'Before you go, Mick, I've got something for you.' Fenton reached into his pocket and produced a roll of bank notes. Licking his fingers, he pulled out three pounds, and offered them to Callum.

'Oy don't want your money,' Callum said.

'Oh, it's not a gift or a loan or anything like that.' The grin slid from his face. 'It's survival money.'

'What the hell are you talking about?'

With the speed and skill of an experienced pickpocket, Fenton stuffed the notes into Callum's jacket pocket. 'There you go. There's three quid. You owe me four now, and I want it back by the end of the week.'

'No feckin way, man!' Callum pulled out the money from his pocket and threw it in Fenton's face.

'Wow, did you see that, lads?' Mocking surprise, Fenton joked with his men. 'He's just paid back eighty per cent already. How good is that? You just owe me a quid now.'

Callum lurched forward and stood toe-to-toe with Fenton. 'Oy owe you nothin'.'

'You owe me one pound an' I wan' it back tomorrow.' The grin was now a sickly sneer. 'I suggest you get yourself into a game as soon as possible. Oh, and there's a players' fee you'll need to be aware of. Fifty per cent of your winnings comes to me. That'll be on top of what you already owe me. Got it?'

Overwhelmed with anger, Callum grabbed Fenton by the throat and squeezed hard. 'You'll get nothing out of me, you feckin rat. Do you hear *me?*'

The four men grabbed Callum once more and slammed him back up against the wall. 'Sort him out, boys. Let him know who's boss around 'ere.' Fenton leaned in towards Callum. 'I know it's hard for you thick potato heads, but you'll soon learn. My boys here'll give you your first lesson.' He swaggered off along the corridor.

Callum was dragged into an adjacent cabin and beaten mercilessly until he passed out.

When he finally regained consciousness, he was alone and unsure how long he'd been comatose. Painfully, he made his way back to his cabin only to find Jimmy P in a similar state to himself.

Looking up from his bunk through bruised swollen eyes, Jimmy painfully sat up when Callum hobbled into the cabin. 'I see you've met Fenton.'

'Aye.' Callum lowered himself onto his bunk, nursing sore ribs.

'Do you even know how to play Poque?' Jimmy asked.

'No. You?'

Jimmy shook his head then winced with pain. 'I've heard some of the men call it Poker.'

'So, Oy guess we're going to have to learn,' Callum said.

'Surely you'll not bow down to him?'

'Hell no.'

'What are we going to do then?' Jimmy asked.

'Whatever it is Fenton's got going on, we're gonna take it from him.'

Jimmy's nod was high in support but low in confidence. 'How do you propose we do that?'

'First, we learn how the system works, then we take it over and send The Rat scurrying to the bowels of the ship where he belongs.'

'Sounds good to me.'

'Right then. Would you be havin' a pack of cards?'

4

Recently, I'd decided that the changes I needed to make to my life would be gradual and under my control. Perhaps this was another product of my inner arrogance to think that while I went about improving Scotty Stephens, everything else would remain the same. In reality, things were changing all around me, and at a much faster rate than I could comprehend. My other best mate, an English lad we called Tetley, had gone on an indefinite trip to the UK. This meant my life would be void of the English banter he'd introduced me to on my first day at Palm Beach Currumbin State High School all those years ago. His wicked sense of humour would be sadly missed.

But there was something else, something even more important. Tetley would come back, but the biggest cause of our heartache never would.

It might not have seemed much of a big deal to some. But to us blokes who'd shared a house in Kirra all these years, and did whatever we liked, the scene that Elvis and I witnessed that fateful morning just may have been one of those epic events that blitzed all bridges. And this meant there would never be a way back. Life had changed forever.

The roof had already gone when the claw of the JCB backhoe took purchase in the centre of the iconic Art Deco facade. With support no longer there, the front wall fell inwards. The machine continued grabbing and pushing, moving along, grabbing and pushing until the last remaining part of our second home vanished forever in a pile of dust. The Kirra Beach Hotel was no more.

I tried to wipe a tear away without Elvis noticing, but I needn't have bothered. When I glanced at my mate, he was blubbering like a baby.

'That's it,' Elvis said. 'She's gone.'

As I inhaled, my breath quavered. 'She has, mate. Gone forever!'

That wasn't entirely true, there would be a new pub on the site as part of a new multi-million dollar resort. But that was two years away, and regardless of how nice the recent development would be, it would never be as good as our scabby old pub.

We were sitting across the road, beachside. I'd just been for a surf. Wearing my half wetsuit and with my board under one arm, it had surprised me to see Elvis waiting for me holding two takeaway coffees.

'Everything all right, mate?'

'No, nothing will ever be right again.'

I stepped into the outdoor shower, cleaned the board, peeled back my wetsuit to the waist, then let the cool water rinse away the salt and sand from my hair. When I'd finished, Elvis thrust a coffee into my hand.

'You and Sandy?'

'No, mate. Nothing like that.'

For Elvis, Sandy was by far the biggest change to happen in his life in recent times.

This was something neither of us would ever have thought possible. She was a lovely girl. Of Greek heritage, like Elvis, she was two years younger than him. They met, funnily enough, in the beer garden of the Kirra Beach Hotel during a Sunday arvo session. She was up here on holiday from Victoria. They hit it off and Elvis fell in love. Before anybody knew what was happening, Sandy quit her job and moved up to Queensland which, at first, I thought would be great. I was happy for my old mate. But what I hadn't anticipated was the inevitable fact that she'd be moving into our house. I say our house, although I'd lived in it for over twenty years, I was only a paying tenant. The property belonged to Elvis. His parents had bought it for him when he moved up here to study at uni.

Although I liked Sandy a lot, being the third wheel in a new relationship was proving difficult. The house changed almost overnight. The female touch should have been a welcome reprise to our lazy, bachelor lifestyle, but we'd been living our way for so long, it was like suddenly having to fall in line.

To be truthful though, I'd been secretly planning to move out prior to Sandy's arrival. The only thing that had been stopping me was the impact it would have had on Elvis. Now I didn't have to worry about that, in fact this would make my task a lot easier— less emotional.

We continued to stare at the space where our beloved pub once stood. There were others there too—locals, regulars from the bar and a few surfers. It was kind of like being at a funeral. We all stood in silence as if recollecting fond memories of a dear lost friend.

'Okay, I've got to go,' Elvis said.

'Me too.'

We walked home along Miles Street, side by side in silence Before we reached the front gate of our house, we slowed our pace as if knowing that stepping over the threshold meant we'd be entering a place where we could no longer talk openly and express ourselves.

'So, what have you got on today?' Elvis asked.

'Got to go out to Tallebudgera. Check out the cottage.'

Elvis nodded thoughtfully.

'You?'

'Ikea.'

'Ikea?'

'Yeah, Sandy wants to get a few things for the house.'

'What about work?'

'Having a day off. I'm the boss, remember?'

This was unusual. Although we partied regularly like teenagers, Elvis took his accountancy business seriously. Even when suffering from the worst hangover, I'd never known him to take time off work.

Padding up the garden path, we both seemed to brace ourselves before entering the front door. I knew exactly what awaited us on the other side. We'd be met and showered with kisses as if we'd just returned from battle. For me, of course, I'd be the sole object of attention from one little puppy dog. For Elvis, it would be Sandy. Yes, life was changing big time on Ruby Street.

5

It was still early, but I retired to my room leaving Elvis and his sweetheart to their lovey-dovey ways. I rarely read fiction—too fidgety—and I wasn't sure if reading Fisher's novel would be of any help or not. Elvis had loaned me his copy of the book. Logically, the fact that so many people pointed out the similarities between the real-life event and the story meant it would probably be worth my while having a look. Lying on my bed with a bowl of cornflakes and a daft dog licking his balls beside me, I opened the pages to Chapter 1.

The Valley of Kate Chapter 1

1997

It was twenty years since Jack Finlay's last encounter with Kate Bowen. If only he'd known then that those weekly business trips to Brisbane would end up costing him dearly for the rest of his life, he would have been more discreet. Back then he'd have been very much in charge. Finlay was the prized wealthy punter, the kind of client that Madame Céleste, aka Brenda McFee, would term as a VIP, a guest that her girls were instructed to look after at all times. After only their first encounter one Friday afternoon, Finlay became besotted with a girl called Kate Bowen.

'He's our best client. You look after him, Katie, and there'll be a nice bonus in it for you,' McFee said after calling the new girl to her office. 'They all seem to like you. Keep up the good work, eh?'

'You know I'm only fifteen, don't you?' Katie said later as Finlay was pulling on his pants. 'No, I didn't know that. Don't want to know.' He hastened his actions, buttoned up his shirt, and put on his socks and boots.

'Well, I am. Now you know.'

Finlay's face reddened and his hands began to shake. 'Why are you telling me this now? What do you want?'

Still naked, Katie sat up, covered herself with the sheet and pulled her knees to her chest. 'I don't want anything. I just wanted you to know because I care about you. This can be our little secret.' The innocent smile she used on all her clients was well-practised.

Aroused, Finlay smiled. Slowly, he reversed his actions, removed his clothing, and climbed back into bed. 'You can be my special girl.'

'So, you don't mind? Even though you know it's illegal?'

'Mind? I'll pay you double. Half for your boss and half for you. Our little secret!' He mimicked Katie's words and grinned.

Making sure that Finlay was on the correct side of the bed so that he was facing the dresser in the corner, Katie pulled back the sheet and straddled the older man.

Back then, mobile phones were still relatively new, and without the cameras and the recording capabilities like the models of today. Secretly setting up the video camera on the side dresser, with the barely visible lens poking out of a neatly folded pile of lingerie, had been a simple task for the industrious young girl.

In no time at all, she'd built a library of tapes, all labelled with the names of her VIP clients, which she stored in a safe in her apartment.

2017

Jack Finlay was no longer in charge. The woman that fronted up to him now was a strong-willed, successful businesswoman. Jesus, how he wished he could turn back the clock. Had he really been that stupid?

Yes, he had, and he'd been paying for it for twenty years. Back then, he'd foolishly believed he'd been in charge, living his dream of having a subservient underage prostitute at his whim. The rougher he'd been with her, the more she seemed to like it, spurring him on until the last of his inhibitions were banished. On regular occasions, Katie would be beaten and strangled as he enacted his evil fantasies. But every act, every indecent assault on her body that was secretly recorded, became down payments for the life Katie Bowen was striving for. And she'd done it.

'You want more?' Finlay snapped.

'A single payment of five million and that will be the last of it. You'll never see or hear from me again.'

They were standing on the front verandah of the cottage that Katie had recently purchased next to Finlay's farm in Tallywood Valley.

'Five million? I don't have that kind of money.'

'Oh, but you do, Senator Finlay, I happen to know that just one of your many thoroughbred horses is worth twice that.'

'You'll not get a penny more from me, you conniving bitch.'

'Oh dear, that's a shame. Whatever will your constituents say when they see your tapes on YouTube? And your community, your family. I've got some lovely shots of you I'd be happy to share with them.'

'You won't.' Finlay lunged forward and grabbed Katie by the neck. Clasping his hands around her windpipe, he squeezed with all his might.

Katie tried to fight back but her efforts were useless against the stronger, more determined man. Kicking and punching, her blows had no effect.

Finlay leaned in and, using all his strength, he continued to squeeze.

Katie's knees buckled.

Instead of allowing her to fall, Finlay rammed her back against the wall of the cottage without releasing his grip.

A mournful sigh escaped Katie's body along with her last breath.

When Finlay was sure she was dead, he released his grip and let her lifeless body fall to the floor. 'You won't!' He spat at the body before marching away.

'So, he tells us who the murderer is in the very first chapter. I don't need to read the rest?' I said, holding up the book in front of Elvis' face.

'Oh, you do, mate. There's a lot more to the story—a real whodunnit—And there's a juicy twist at the end.'

'I think I've just about got the gist of it. I'm just wondering how close it is to the real episode.'

'That's for you to find out, PI Stephens,' Elvis said, grinning.

'It is. And I bloody well will!'

6

My old VW Beetle, aka the Dub, trundled its way along the Gold Coast Highway as far as Burleigh Heads. Minutes later, the scenery had completely changed from beachside playground to lush green countryside. Tallebudgera Valley is the stretch of hinterland skirting Palm Beach, Elanora and Burleigh.

Ben Fisher had scribbled down the address for me during our meeting, but he said it would be easier to look for the Fenton horse stud. The cottage was to the right of it at the end of a short dirt track.

It wasn't hard to find. A clichéd wrought iron gateway with rendered white posts capped with bronze horse statues was a dead giveaway. Just inside the entrance was a modest brick and tile home I guessed belonged to the groundsman or caretaker. At the side of the property was a narrow track, and a mailbox made from galvanised iron. Instinctively, I checked the street number with the scribbled note, and they corresponded.

I was an hour earlier than the planned meeting with Fisher. I wanted to have a good look around on my own first. Pulling into the open gateway, there was a short drive until I came to what could easily be mistaken for a garden shed. But from the news report I'd watched earlier, I already knew this was the house—Mary's Mansion.

I'd done a bit of research on the place. The cottage was built in 1869 by an early pioneer from Ireland. The land that was originally 320 acres but is now just over two and part of a densely covered forest, a parcel of which remained at the back of the house, had been subdivided over the years. To the right of the property was a 200-acre dairy farm, and to the left was the horse stud that covered over a hundred acres.

I pulled up alongside the building and climbed out of the Dub. The sights and sounds of the countryside immediately took purchase of my senses—a whipbird cried from somewhere deep in the rainforest covered hills behind the property. The aroma of horse manure drifted on a warm, gentle breeze. A cow mooed long and slow from the vast paddock to my right.

The building was not much bigger than a double garage. It was made of timber weatherboard with a corrugated iron roof. There was a small verandah at the front and two outdoor chairs. Peering in through a window, I could see the interior had been tastefully updated but was still very simple—a small kitchen, a sitting room, and two doors that I guessed led to the single bedroom and bathroom.

My plan had been to get a feel for the place prior to Fisher arriving, so I walked around the back of the house. There was an identical verandah to the one at the front, with matching outdoor chairs. I stepped up onto the deck and the aged timbers creaked beneath my feet. From here, I had a good view of the surroundings. A trail through the trees—a mixture of pine, iron bark and eucalyptus—about fifty metres from the back of the house, led up into the hills beyond. But it was the rolling paddocks on either side that demanded my attention.

To my right, a herd of black cows spread out, grazing across the same green undulating land. There were no buildings on that side that I could see from where I stood.

I took in a deep breath of fresh, warm air. A kookaburra laughed in the distance. Closing my eyes, I continued to breathe deeply, the way my former assistant/partner, Bradley Foster, had shown me. The sounds of the horses' hooves slapping the dirt. The whipbird calling out as if swiping the cheeky kookaburra around the back of the head. Boy, I could get used to this.

The sound of a car approaching interrupted the serenity. I headed back around the front of the house just as an old silver Porsche pulled up. I immediately made a note of the rego—'Fright 1'. There were two occupants in the vehicle. The driver I recognised as Ben Fisher, but in the passenger seat was a young woman. Even though Fisher had spotted me, they didn't immediately climb out of the car. They seemed to be having a heated discussion. Eventually, Fisher got out, slammed the door behind him and approached me. The woman got out slowly.

'Scott, thanks for coming,' Fisher said, holding out his hand.

'No worries.' We shook hands and he introduced the woman as Nicky Lee, his literary agent.

Her handshake was a lot more forceful than I'd expected. 'Scott, it's great to meet you.' She blushed slightly but her eyes probed mine intensely.

'Good to meet you too, Nicky.'

Thrusting a business card into my hand, she said, '*The* Scotty Stephens, eh? When you're ready to write that autobiography, let me know. I'll get you six figures.'

'Thanks, I will.' I was being polite. I had no intention of writing a book.

'So …' Ben reached into his pocket and pulled out a bunch of keys. 'I got these from the real estate agent after telling her I was interested in renting the property again. Luckily, it's vacant at the moment.'

'And are you?'

'What?'

'Interested in renting the place again?'

'God no.' He stepped onto the verandah and placed the key into the lock. The door opened and he stepped inside.

When I gestured with my arm for Nicky to follow, she took my hand and stepped onto the deck. The perfume she wore smelled expensive. I followed them inside.

Although the living room, slash diner, slash kitchen, were contemporarily furnished, the tongue-and-groove walls and open vaulted ceiling made it feel as if you were entering a historical museum exhibit. The temperature outside was around thirty degrees, but inside the house was quite cool. And there was a sweet smell, like a mixture of honey and pine needles.

'Do you feel it?' Fisher said as he closed the front door behind us.

Nicky and I shared a glance.

'Feel what, Ben?' Nicky said.

'The energy. It grabs you as you enter.'

'Can't say I do.'

'Scott?'

'Uh … not really, what does it feel like?' I didn't want to admit it, but the truth is, there was something. I was experiencing a tightness in my chest, kind of like the feeling when you're waiting in line to go on a roller coaster.

'It starts as a tingling, but the longer you spend here it's as almost as if you get high.'

'Are you on medication, Ben?' Nicky asked.

'No, well. But that's not it. There's an energy here that gradually takes over you. It's like it's charging your battery, energising you. Then once you're fully charged, you feel as if you can do anything you put your mind to.'

'Is that what you're feeling now?' Nicky asked.

I was glad she was there. Her slightly patronising tone gave me the impression that she would have no reservations about sounding Fisher out. It saved me from doing it.

'Yes … she's here!'

There was another glance between me and the young literary agent, but we remained quiet.

'She's trapped here until justice is achieved.'

'She?' I'm not sure why I felt the need to whisper.

'Kathy!'

'Kathy Brown?'

'Yes. And Mary wants her gone!' Fisher sat down at the table. 'This is where it all happened. The channelling.'

'Right, the channelling.'

'Well, Scotty doesn't want to hear about any of that,' Nicky said. 'We're here to discuss what we're going to do to make these allegations against you go away.'

'I do actually want to hear all of that. If I'm going to take on this case, I'll need to know everything.'

'Yes,' Ben said quietly. 'Everything.'

'Mister Stephens, could I have a word with you in private please?' Nicky asked.

Shrugging, I looked around the tiny property.

'Outside.' She led the way.

Fisher rolled his eyes as if to say, 'It's okay, just humour her.'

Once outside, we strolled towards the fence line between the shack and the horse stud.

'I just feel the need to tell you that Ben has been through an awful lot. He's ... he's changed considerably.'

'Since the breakdown you mean?'

'Yes. The divorce, the drugs, the breakdown, and now this.'

'In what way has he changed?'

'I didn't know him that well before, but since coming here, he's gone from being a bona fide atheist to kind of spiritual. Not religious, but spacey.'

'You think he's gone fruit loop?'

The corners of her mouth turned upwards briefly. 'He's going through intensive therapy.'

'Do you think he used the Kathy Brown case for his book?'

'As much as I'm defending him one hundred per cent, it certainly looks that way.'

'Has he confided in you in any way?'

'Oh yes.' She turned and looked out over the horse paddock.

'And?'

'He keeps talking about this Mary character. Says it was her who helped him write the book.'

'Really?'

'Yep. He's a fucking fruit loop.'

7

When we returned to the house, Fisher was waiting for us.

'She's here,' he said, mysteriously.

'Kathy?' I was definitely whispering now, as if I were in church.

'Yes. She's always here.' It only took the tall stringy man three steps to reach the bedroom door. Opening it, he stepped inside.

We followed.

'This is where she first appeared to me,' he said as the three of us stood somewhat snug in the tiny room. There was a door on the side wall that led to a small bathroom.

'Are you saying she physically appeared?' Nicky said wide-eyed and not in a whisper.

'Oh yes, all the time.'

The bedroom door suddenly slammed shut on its own.

Nicky, accompanied by a high- pitched yelp, almost hit the ceiling and I have to admit, I just about jumped out of my skin too.

Fisher didn't flinch, he just smiled and nodded knowingly. 'She can have a bit of a temper.'

'Let's go outside and talk,' I said, leading the way out of the room.

We sat out on the back verandah. I'd pulled one of the chairs around from the front so we each had a seat. The shade from the iron lean-to was surprisingly cool.

'So, what do you think, Scotty? Can you help me?'

The investigation would be a lot bigger than I first expected. To enable me to disprove the claims against Fisher of plagiarism, I'd need to find out what really happened in the house.

To do that I'd have to find out who the real killer of Kathy Brown was, but in doing that would I be proving the case against Fisher? Had he also done his research, then put two and two together in that clever way only a bestselling author could? Or was he receiving help from beyond the grave as he claimed? Neither option was a win-win situation for him. 'I'd like to take on the case.'

'Yes!' Fisher jumped to his feet and shook my hand. 'You won't regret it. This will give your new business a massive boost.'

'But I need you to know that my findings could harm you either way.'

'What do you mean?' Nicky interjected.

'Well, will finding the real killer help Mister Fisher's case?'

'Oh, I see what you're saying. By doing that, you could actually prove plagiarism against Ben.'

'That's right. Is that really what you both want?'

'It's irrelevant, Scott. I just need you to prove that it was James Fenton who killed Kathy,' Ben said.

'So, Jack Finlay *is* based on James Fenton?' As far as I knew, Fisher had yet to acknowledge or deny this.

'Of course he is. That bastard killed Kathy in this very house.'

'But what makes you so sure? What evidence do you have?'

'You obviously haven't read the book.' Fisher slumped back into his chair.

I had to admit, although I'd read the first chapter, I hadn't continued reading.

'Read the book and you'll have all the facts.'

'That could take some time. How about you tell me?'

'Wait!' Nicky suddenly said, almost jumping out of her seat. 'I've had the most amazing idea.'

Our wide-eyed silence prompted her to continue.

'I need to make sure I can organise it first.' Her gaze was on the hills but her mind was way beyond them.

'Organise what?' I asked.

She rose from her chair. 'I need to get back to Brisbane. Let's go, Ben.'

Fisher stood and the two of them stepped down from the verandah.

'What's happening?' I asked, also standing.

Nicky grabbed my hand and shook it wildly. 'This is going to be amazing!'

'What is?' Ben Fisher asked, following her back to the car.

'Not now. I've got a lot to do to make this happen. Thank you, Scott, we'll be in touch.' She climbed into the passenger side of Fisher's Porsche.

Fisher also thanked me then climbed awkwardly into the low 911. The engine burst into life, the car did a quick three-point turn in the narrow drive then kicked up a cloud of dust as it sped away.

8

Suffering from their wounds, Callum and Jimmy laid low in their cabin. The next day, however, Fenton came knocking.

'Mister Fenton, it's good to see you again,' Callum said, as Fenton and his entourage stood in the open doorway.

'You owe me money, Mick,' Fenton growled.

'Aye, that Oy do.' Callum produced a one pound note from his pocket and handed it to Fenton. 'There you go, sir.'

'Good lad.'

Jimmy did the same.

'Get yourselves in a game. My boys will be back next week for payment. Minimum return is a quid. Got that?' There was no sign of the grin. Fenton was all business, intimidating and harsh.

A quid? Thought Callum. This would seriously eat into what small savings he had. 'Aye, Mister Fenton. Will do.' He held out his hand for Fenton to shake.

The sickly grin returned as Fenton took Callum's hand.

Callum squeezed it tightly, pulled Fenton in close and bore into him with a rock solid stare.

Fenton pulled away. 'You be careful, Mick. You know what'll happen if you cross me.'

'Aye, that Oy do.'

Fenton turned and pushed through his entourage.

'I don't know about you, Callum, but I haven't got a quid to spare,' Jimmy said, after closing the cabin door.

'We won't be paying him a penny. He'll be the one paying us.'

'I hope you know what you're doing.' If Jimmy had been expecting a confident reply, he didn't get it.

'We need to rest. Heal. We can't do anything while we're banged up like this.'

Although bruised and sore, two days lying in a bunk, venturing out only for food, gave Callum plenty of time to think. 'What do you reckon?' he asked Jimmy after sharing with him his newly hatched plan.

'We only have five days.'

'Aye, so we need to start work right away. Are you with me Jimmy P?'

'I am.'

They shook hands.

With close to four hundred passengers crammed into a ship that was designed to carry around half that number, the conditions aboard the *Great Britain* soon fell to the level of squalor found in any 19th century slum. If this wasn't hard enough, the pressure Fenton was exerting was taking its toll on the men. Over the next two days, Callum and Jimmy split up, looking in on around a hundred games, not joining in but listening and watching. The men weren't happy, of course they weren't. This would be Callum's weapon.

'Has anyone tried standing up to Fenton?' Callum asked a group of fellow Irishmen as the next hand was being dealt.

'Aye. Michael McFee,' the youngest of the four men said. 'He'd had enough. Lost all his money and was getting deeper in debt.'

'What happened?'

The older men's eyes narrowed at the younger man in caution.

'He went to confront Fenton.'

'Was he beaten?'

'That was almost a week ago, shortly after leaving Dublin. We haven't seen him since.'

'Thrown overboard you think?'

'Aye. Fenton didn't actually say as much but he's using Michael as an example of what happens to anyone that crosses him.'

'The feckin rat!' 'Aye.'

Callum leaned out of the cabin, checked the corridor then closed the door behind him. 'So, listen to me now,' he said, lowering his voice and addressing the group. 'Moy name is Callum Murphy, and Oy'm going to put an end to this torment.'

'And how the hell will you be doing that, young Callum Murphy?' one of the older men asked.

'Oy'll be asking you to invest in your future.'

'You want money from us?' The same horrified expression appeared on each of the men's faces.

'Aye, but only one shilling.'

'And what will you be doing with me shilling?'

'Saving you at least the two quid Fenton will be demanding at the end of this week, plus the fifty per cent of your winnings. He won't be bothering yous again. Yous have my word.'

'For just one shilling?'

'Aye.'

The older man slid a coin across the table. 'I don't have enough to pay Fenton, so I've got nothing to lose.'

To Callum's surprise, the rest of the men followed suit.

By visiting each group throughout the ship, using caution and discretion, Callum and Jimmy P amassed eight pounds between them in only three days. Most of the men were behind them. Some willingly threw in more than a shilling, and those that either couldn't or wouldn't were told to keep quiet. It didn't surprise Callum that Fenton had few supporters aboard the ship. At the end of the week, the kitty, or the 'survival money' as Fenton had put it, sat at a whopping twenty pounds.

'I hope you know what you're doing, Callum Murphy,' Jimmy said after counting the last of the coins and notes.

Callum grinned. 'We'll remember this day for a long time.'

'The rest of our lives,' Jimmy added. 'However long that might be.'

Fenton's cabin would have once been a presidential suite or the premium first-class berth. Although the fine fixtures and fittings were long gone, a hint of elegance remained in the wood-panelled walls, and the size of the room was impressive.

'Well, if it ain't me old mate, Mick Murphy,' Fenton said as Danny Flynn—one of Fenton's thugs—led Callum into the cabin. 'You saved me the job of looking for you.'

Bill Jarvis sat at a desk in the corner, busily writing entries in a ledger. It appeared he'd taken over the role of Fenton's accountant. The rest of the thugs, who had brutally beaten Callum only a few days earlier, were sitting casually around the room like punters waiting in a brothel. When Callum approached Fenton, they stood and crowded around him.

'You 'ave something for me?' Fenton squared up to the shorter man.

Callum shook his head. 'Nothing Oy'm afraid, sir.'

'Nothing? Oh dear. Did you hear that, boys?' Fenton said, glancing at each of the men. 'That's very bad for you *and* me, Paddy. Good for these geezers, though. They like it when a punter defaults. Gives them a bit of exercise.'

'Oy have ne defaulted, sir,' Callum said. 'Oy would never do that.'

Wily and suspicious, Fenton moved in closer. 'What you playin' at, Mick?'

'Oy don't have a penny to me name. Oy've given all me money away.'

There was no humour in Fenton's laugh, only dangerous malice. 'You're even stupider than you look.'

Callum's laugh mimicked Fenton's.

Fenton grabbed him by the throat. 'Who did you give it to? Somebody trying to start their own syndicate?'

'Not that Oy know of.'

'Who then?'

'Me new employees.'

Fenton narrowed his eyes. 'Don't you fuck with me, Mick.'

'Okay … boys.'

Two of the thugs grabbed Fenton, one arm each, lifting him into the air.

Bill Jarvis jumped to his feet, not in defence of his boss, but more as an attempt to escape.

Danny Flynn blocked his path.

'What the hell are you doing?' Fenton demanded, kicking wildly.

'Takin' over your little operation, mate.' Callum's attempt at a cockney accent brought smiles to the faces of his new entourage. 'Let him down.'

The two men did as they were told.

Fenton dropped to the floor and rushed at Callum.

Now it was Callum's turn to grab his attacker by the neck. Holding him at arm's length, he said, 'It's over, rat!'

Cussing, Fenton fought to break free.

Callum released his grip.

Fenton hit out with a half-hearted right hook to Callum's jaw.

The thugs stepped forward.

Callum waved them back with one hand while he gently massaged his chin with the other. 'As Oy expected. Weak as piss.'

'Fight me you fuckin' Irish cunt!' Fenton yelled, dropping into a southpaw stance.

Callum shrugged. 'Okay, one last chance to redeem yourself, Ron Fenton, then you're off to steerage where you belong.'

'You'll never keep me down.' Fenton lunged forward, swinging wildly.

Callum, easily dodging the punches, stepped back, then swung with a mighty open-handed slap.

Dazed, Fenton stumbled sideways.

Callum followed through with a backhander, knocking his assailant in the opposite direction before finishing him with what would become his signature uppercut.

Fenton's legs buckled, and he slumped to the floor in an unconscious heap.

Callum was pumped and primed. Although he'd handed all the money over to the four thugs, allowing them to divide it among themselves equally, he'd made it clear that the payment was a debt.

He also hadn't forgotten the vicious beating he and Jimmy had received at the hands of these men. He turned to Danny, who seemed to be the leader of the group.

'Step up, Danny Boy. It's time to make your first payment.'

'Huh?'

'Oy said step up.' Callum held up his fists. 'Unlike your old boss, Oy'll be keepin' you in your feckin place.'

Danny frowned whimsically at his associates and strutted forward confidently. 'Are you sure you want to do this?'

'Aye. If you're going to be working for me, Oy need to be sure you're up to it.'

Danny shook his head and laughed. 'All right, if this is what you want?' He swung with a right.

Callum ducked and followed up once again with that right uppercut, but this time to the man's ribs.

The air bellowed from Danny's lungs.

Callum followed up with a left to the opposite side.

Danny leaned forward. Clutching at his torso and dropping his guard, leaving himself wide open.

Callum lunged forward and headbutted the larger man in the nose. There was an audible crack and a shower of blood.

Danny lifted his hands to his face.

Callum, well aware he needed to keep the advantage, kicked his assailant in the groin with all the strength he had.

Danny immediately fell to his knees and vomited.

John Mince was the largest man of the group.

'You're next, sweetheart,' Callum said, pointing to a spot on the floor.

Displaying the same confidence as Danny, John stepped forward. Although a hard man with a reputation around the docks of Southampton for being a brawler and a thug, he was no match for Callum's boxing skills. In no time at all, he was sitting on his arse on the floor alongside Danny.

Tom Sugden didn't fare any better.

Joseph Bailey was the last of the group to take his place in front of his new boss.

Meanwhile, Fenton had regained consciousness and was slowly rising to his feet. 'We don't have to do this, boss,' Joseph said.

'You didn't have to do what you did to me the other day, big man. But you did.'

'You have my allegiance now. I give you my word.'

'Good man. Now shut the hell up and hit me.'

With no one noticing, Fenton moved around the room until he was behind Callum. Reaching down to his ankle, he produced a knife and leapt forward.

'Look out, Mister Callum,' Joseph cried.

If Callum hadn't turned, the blade would have embedded between his shoulder blades instead of his left shoulder.

Joseph rushed towards Fenton and punched him in the solar plexus.

Fenton hit the wall hard.

Callum casually pulled out the knife from his shoulder and walked over to Fenton. 'So, you'd kill a man from behind, would you? Of course you would.' He held up the blade to Fenton's throat. 'Oy should slice you up and throw you overboard. Do you hear me, rat?'

Fenton remained quiet. His glare was full of hatred.

'Oy said do you feckin hear me, rat?' He pushed the blade until it cut into Fenton's skin.

'I 'ear ya!'

'That's good.' Callum lowered the knife and turned to Danny and his men. 'Take him down to the engine room. Beat ten barrels of shit out of him the way you did me. Find him a little spot suitable for a rat's nest, then report back to here.'

During the three-month voyage, Callum and Jimmy became a team. Still only sixteen years of age, Callum was the brains and became known as 'The Gaffer'. Jimmy was the muscle and was his second in command. Danny Flynn and his boys remained on the payroll. Callum took over the card syndicate that had spread through the ship like a virus. Dropping the fifty per cent fee to only a one per cent stake from all winnings. Although the mindless thuggery that had become Fenton's signature was no longer required, all unsolicited games were still deemed illegal and policed by a team of handpicked hard men. A firm hand was still required among some of the men, but they weren't forced to play as before. If they didn't like the new regime, they didn't have to take part, but if they wanted to play and didn't toe the line, there would be consequences. Callum wasn't proud of the heavy-handed tactics he'd been forced to apply, especially in the early days, but he'd always remember something his da had told him the night before he'd left Sligo. 'The road to a heavenly civilisation is paved by powerful men and bad deeds.' And although Callum was a good man, he was aware of the bad things required to reach his goal.

9

We always met in the waves. Whoever arrived first would paddle out. That way neither of us would stand around waiting. For me, it was just a stroll across the street. Jenny would come down from Burleigh Heads, so I was usually there first. I'd already caught a couple of sets and was sitting on my board out the back when I saw her MINI pull up in the surf club car park.

'The Mrs is here, mate!' Chilly, my barber, who was also a regular at Kirra Point that time of the morning, yelled across to me.

Smiling, I nodded. It was the kind of banter the boys were proficient in.

I watched as Jenny unstrapped her board from the roof of her car, then took off like a gazelle with it under her arm, heading for the groin. Within minutes, she was bobbing up and down on her board by my side.

'Hey,' I said.

'Hey, how's it going?'

'Good.'

We surfed for an hour and said very little between sets. When we finally emerged from the water, we bought two takeaway coffees from the surf club kiosk and sat on one of the park benches by the beach.

'How's life treating you at Queensland Police, Mam?' I jokingly called her 'Mam' these days because she'd been recently promoted to detective inspector. And rightly so too, not just for her role in the *X* case, but because she was a bloody good copper.

'Not too bad. How's being a PI treating you?' There was a slight smirk when she said 'PI.'

'Pretty good, actually. Just taken on my first case.'

'You have? Congratulations!' She gave me a hug.

Even after an hour in the surf, she still smelled good. I have to admit, I was still sexually aroused by Jenny Radford. We'd had a bit of a thing that lasted a couple of weeks during the *X* investigation when we'd been forced to go into hiding together, but it didn't work out. We both realised we were too alike, and that the relationship could never work.

'So, what kind of case? Lost pet? Cheating husband? Stolen library card?' Jenny was also up for a bit of banter. I guess it was indicative of a female surviving in a male dominated career, where she needed to give as good as she got. And she did. Even though she was only five-foot-four, nobody messed with Jenny Radford.

Sitting back on the bench I stretched out my legs. 'Do you remember the Tallebudgera killing about five years ago?'

'The Kathy Brown case?'

'Yeah, that's the one.'

'Sure do. I was still in uniform back then. I was actually the WPC who had the job of breaking the news to Kathy's sister, Abigail.'

'That's what I wanted to talk to you about.'

'Oh, so you didn't just invite me down here for a surf then.' She turned to me and scowled. 'You have a motive.'

'That's right, now I'm a PI I need to capitalise on any contacts.'

'So, I'm just a contact now?'

'Yeah, pretty much. What else would you be?'

'You're such a dickhead!'

We shared a giggle and sipped our coffees.

'So, tell me about the case. Who hired you?'

'Ben Fisher.'

Jenny nodded. 'Makes sense.'

I didn't have a great deal to tell Jenny, apart from my initial meeting with Fisher, and then again at the cottage with him and his agent. Everything else I knew had come from my research on the internet. I was hoping Jenny could supply some inside information that hadn't been made public.

'I did go out to the cottage when the murder happened but didn't get very close. DI Des Williams was in charge of the case. I was just one of the PCs assigned to guard the entrance and stop unauthorised personnel from entering,' Jenny said.

'Do you remember anything unusual?'

'No. Well, not at the scene because I wasn't privy due to my rank, but later when I travelled up to Brisbane to meet with the sister, I initially got the impression she wasn't that upset when I broke the news to her. In fact, I detected a suppressed smirk. Then, as if realising I was scrutinising her, she started to cry.'

'Fake tears?'

'Possibly.'

'You think the sister could have been involved?'

'Not at the time but looking back now and realising the killer was never caught, maybe.'

'Did you tell anyone? Des?'

'I mentioned it, yeah. I'm not sure if anyone followed up on it, though.'

'Fancy some breakfast?'

'I thought you'd never ask. I'm starving.'

We showered and changed at my place then strolled around to the café on the corner of Haig Street. It was still only 7.00 am. Jenny could sometimes go into work later, making the odd morning free for a surf. This was one of those days.

'So, what was it like to meet Ben Fisher?' Jenny asked after we'd ordered two full Aussie breakfasts.

'Pretty uninspiring to be honest.'

'Oh, the self-centred writer type. I thought that was just a cliché.'

'Smug comes to mind.'

'So, he obviously wrote the story from the real-life events. That's plagiarism.'

'It's not the plagiarism that I'm interested in. To be honest, I don't care if he's guilty or not. It's the unsolved murder case that got me in.'

'Cold case.'

'Absolutely. And the beauty of this is I can take my time and do a full investigation while Fisher foots the bill.'

'Here's to that.'

We chit chatted as we waited for our food to arrive. Jenny filled me in on all the gossip at Surfers Paradise Police Station. I was glad to hear that she was enjoying her new role. As she spoke, I was remembering my short stint as a detective inspector, but that was completely different. Jenny had earned her promotion, I hadn't. I was a low-ranking detective constable plucked from obscurity by the then Gold Coast Mayor, Julian Munro, and ex-Police Commissioner, Edward Singleton, to be used as their puppet.

'Jenny, I wondered if—' Bugger, the food arrived just as I'd built up the courage to ask her what was on my mind. When the waitress retreated to the kitchen, I continued. 'I wondered if you wouldn't mind, now that you're a high-ranking detective and all, if you could look into the official investigation for me. See if there's anything relevant that might help with the case.'

Her jaw dropped, and her eyes bore into me like hot coals. 'You're not seriously asking me to …' she lowered her voice … 'to be your bitch, are you?'

'No, nothing like that.'

'You are. You think you've got an inside contact who'll share whatever information you need when you need it.'

'No, honestly—'

She sat back in her seat. 'You cheeky bastard.'

'What?' The heat was rising in my cheeks.

'You think I'm going to be your little snitch.'

'No, I don't.' I was trying to play it cool, industriously cutting a piece of bacon.

'That's the only reason you asked me here this morning.'

I shrugged and filled my mouth with food.

Jenny leaned forward and scooped up a fork full of beans into her mouth.

'So will you do it?' I asked when I'd finally stopped chewing.

'Of course. What do you need?'

10

By mid-morning, the official police report was sitting in my Dropbox account. Although I was keen to study the suspects and their reasons for being under scrutiny, I decided to begin with the victim, so flicked straight to the victimology report. To learn as much as possible about a murder victim, detectives research their pasts. My old mate, Dale Mason, had done a good job which would help shed some light on the mystery woman.

Kathy Josephine Brown was born in Adelaide on 13 November 1981 to parents, Edmund Brown (civil servant) and Gillian Brown (nurse). She had a sister, Abigail, two years younger. When Kathy was twelve, her mother died of breast cancer. Six months later, the girl was expelled from school. The reasons listed were unruly behaviour, bullying, truancy, and finally aggravated assault on a teacher.

Edmund Brown, already struggling with the responsibilities of bringing up two girls as a single parent, sent his delinquent daughter to stay with his sister in Sydney. He hoped that getting her away from Adelaide and into a new environment would help her through the grieving process, which he was sure was the reason for her behaviour.

Unfortunately, sending her away had the opposite effect to his expectations. Two years later, Kathy ran away from home and was officially listed as a missing person until she was eighteen when she signed on for social security in Brisbane, Queensland. There was

47

no record of Kathy's whereabouts or movements between the years 1995 and 1999, but from the findings of Detective Dale Mason's research, the following information was obtained:

When Kathy Brown ran away from home, she hitchhiked to Brisbane. Still only fourteen but easily passing as an eighteen year old, she got a job as a barmaid at a strip joint, slash brothel, called The Panda Club in Fortitude Valley. Shortly after her arrival, she caught the eye of Maeve Morrison, who ran the brothel over the club, and offered her full-time employment as a sex worker.

In 2000, there was another period where Kathy seemed to vanish from the record for an entire year. Once again, through the detective work of Dale Mason, he'd tracked her down working as a stable hand at the Fenton horse stud in Tallebudgera for three months. But after that time, she went missing again and didn't reappear in Fortitude Valley until the spring of 2001.

In that year, and up to the time of her death in 2017, Kathy's financial situation seemed to change dramatically. Her assets included a house on the river in East Brisbane, The Panda Club, which she'd purchased from Maeve Morrison in 2010, and the property in Tallebudgera where she was murdered, called Mary's Mansion.

I flicked back through the police report to an interview, conducted by DI Des Williams and DI Dale Mason, with James Fenton. Skimming through the transcript, I found the question I was looking for. 'Were you aware that Kathy Brown worked at your establishment as a stable hand in the year 2000?'

'No. I was not,' was Fenton's reply. He then explained that the stud employed a variety of backpackers throughout the year, and that this wasn't part of the operation he oversaw. When quizzed about employing underaged workers, he passed the buck to his then manager, and now deceased, George Nicholson.

The last part of the victimology report covered Kathy's time when she arrived back in Tallebudgera twenty years later. Unfortunately, there was little in the report because the only testimonies were from the Tallebudgera locals, most of whom knew little of her or weren't willing to share their experiences of her. The consensus was that Kathy Brown was disliked. One resident, a Mrs Daisy Patterson, went as far as to say, 'If it were possible to combine the terms cunning, resentful, vengeful, merciless, and evil into a single word, that word would be branded on the soul of Kathy Brown!' When asked to elaborate on her statement, the elderly lady refused to comment further.

All 1,300 German cubic centimetres of my 1967 VW Beetle, aka The Dub, whistled and shuddered as I turned into the Tallebudgera driveway, kicking up a cloud of dust. As I passed the gatehouse just over the fence of the property next door, a woman looked up as she pegged washing on a Hills Hoist. I waved, and she offered a forced smile. Paula Dalby, no doubt. Heck, I'd only skimmed through Fisher's book, but was already familiar with the characters. It would be interesting to learn how close Fisher's 'fictional' characters—and I use the word 'fictional' with inverted quotations—were to the real people.

I didn't have a key, so couldn't enter the cottage. In fact, I was probably trespassing just being on the property. I parked the Dub in front of the house and strolled over to the fence. There was a young woman working a horse under a wide, lowset arena.

Walking along the fence line, it didn't take long to get back to the road. The woman I'd seen earlier must have retreated after hanging out the last of the washing. There was no pavement, just a grass verge. The gate to the horse stud was only a few metres away, but it was closed. There was an intercom on the right-hand gatepost. I pressed the bell icon on the keyboard.

'Hello.'

I guessed it was the woman from the gatehouse. 'Oh hi, I've got an appointment with Mister Fenton.'

There was no reply, but the gate clunked then slid silently open.

When I entered the driveway, the woman appeared from the house and approached me. 'How come you left your car over there?' As soon as the words left her lips, her expression changed from mildly annoyed curiosity to surprise. 'You're Scott Stephens.'

Bugger, although being famous and infamous had its advantages, it also meant that everyone on the Gold Coast knew who I was. Part of being a good detective was the use of anonymity, but that was impossible for me in this town. 'Guilty as charged, I'm afraid.' I held out my hand. 'And you are?'

She blushed as we shook hands and inadvertently ran the other hand through her hair as if trying to fix it up. 'Pam, Pam Derby.'

Bloody hell, Fisher. Apart from the similarity in name, his description of Paula Dalby, the groundsman's wife, was spot on.

'What brings you to Tallebudgera, Mister Stephens?'

'Call me Scotty.' I wasn't flirting, just being friendly. 'Ben Fisher has hired me to clear his name.'

Her expression reverted to the one she'd displayed earlier. 'Fisher?'

'Yes. Have you read his book?'

'No, I haven't. Did you say Mister Fenton was expecting you?'

'I did. Where can I find him?'

'He'll be up at the house.' Another facial change, this time to caution. 'Perhaps I should come up with you.'

'No, that's all right, I'll find my way.' Heading off along the sweeping bitumen driveway, I called over my shoulder, 'See you later.'

Pam rushed back into the house, no doubt to call Fenton.

Of course, I didn't really have an appointment with the big man. I'd never met him and the only details I had were what I'd read on the internet. The horse stud had an impressive website. The 'About us' page gave an outline of the current business and the Fenton's history back to the 1800s.

The place was stunning. There were paddocks either side of the private road where horses frolicked in the sunshine. When I reached the outdoor arena, the girl I'd spotted earlier was patting down her horse and rubbing its legs. She looked up as I approached. 'Hi.'

'Hi.'

'You here for the job?' she asked.

'Uhm … yeah.'

'It's a waste of time. Tom will be back tomorrow. He always comes back.'

'Tom?'

After gently patting the horse, she strolled towards me. Strands of blonde curly hair were plastered to her forehead with sweat, and her cheeks were rosy. 'Tom Partridge, my coach. They're always arguing. Tom storms off and every now and again he quits. But he always comes back.'

So far she hadn't seemed to have recognised me, so I continued. 'Is Mister Fenton a hard bloke to work for?'

'Oh yes.' She opened the gate, stepped out of the paddock and closed the gate behind her. 'He's always nice to me, but he gives everyone else a hard time, especially Tom.'

'Why is that do you think?'

'Oh, it's just his way. He's Mister Fenton, you know?'

'I'm Scott by the way.' I didn't offer my hand. For some reason, it didn't feel like the right thing to do with a young woman.

'Tilly, Matilda Derby.'

'Oh, was that your mum at the gatehouse?'

'Yes. I'm afraid I have to go, though. I've got Uni.'

'Right. What are you studying?'

'I'm doing a postgraduate degree in veterinary science.'

'You're training to be a vet?'

Tilly nodded. 'It was nice meeting you, Scott.'

'Yeah, you too.'

'Good luck with the job interview,' she said, taking the horse by the reins and leading him away.

As I continued along the driveway, the imposing homestead soon came into view. An enormous Queenslander with a full wrap around verandah, nestled between undulating fields.

The first thing I noticed was the figure of a man standing on the verandah. Before I reached the house, he'd descended the steps and was marching towards me.

'What the devil are you doing here?'

'Uhm, I'm here about the stable hand job.' It was a long shot.

'Save your lies, Stephens. You're not welcome here. I want you off my property immediately.' He was a big man, very authoritarian in his manner, mid to late sixties perhaps. His face was ruddy and a little bloated; his eyes were fierce and probing.

'Mister James Fenton, I assume.'

'I've got nothing to say to you. The last thing we need around here is you stirring up the past.'

'But I'm here to help, sir.'

'Help? *Phh*. Help yourself you mean.'

'Well, the thing is, I've been hired to find out the truth, and that's exactly what I'm going to do.'

'The truth?' His smirk was a bitter jab. He lurched towards me as if he were about to extricate me like a nightclub bouncer.

I stepped backwards and held up my hands. 'There's no need for violence, sir.'

'Get off my fucking property. NOW!'

'Okay. I'm going.' I continued my retreat backwards, slowly without breaking eye contact. 'You obviously have a problem with the truth coming out.'

He stood there silently with his arm raised and his hand pointing towards the gate.

'That's a real shame, mate.' I dispensed of the term, sir. 'See you around no doubt.' Turning, I headed away, looking back over my shoulder intermittently to see him standing in the same spot, watching me.

11

A text message from Jenny simply said, "Heading back from Tweed. Call in shortly." The bikie case she was working on had her travelling back and forth over the border.

There was no need for a shop doorbell or a buzzer to tell me when anyone entered the building at the bottom of the stairs. My little bloke heard everything. I was sitting half asleep, still skimming through Fisher's book, when Romeo shot to his feet and raced towards the door barking and growling.

Before I could restrain him, the door to my office opened and in came Jenny, already bending her knees as if she were approaching a sacred shrine.

Romeo jumped into her arms, yapping and whining.

'G'day, mate,' Jenny said, digging her fingers into his fur. 'Oh, he's weeing on me.' She quickly put the dog down.

'Yeah. He does that.'

It surprised me to see there was someone else with Jenny—a tall, stocky figure. Romeo knew who it was before I did and raced towards the man.

'Bradley!' I yelled.

Bradley Foster had been my assistant during the X case. Mid-twenties, openly gay, I'd really grown to like the lad during the time we'd worked together.

53

'Hi Scott,' Bradley said without looking up. He was having *his* moment with the esteemed dog.

'Detective Constable, eh? Congratulations! Romeo that's enough.'

The dog either ignored his master or was just too overwhelmed to hear me.

'Romeo!' My raised voice was enough to catch his attention. 'In your bed.' I pointed to the Barney.

The dog reluctantly retreated, a remanent of a wag still controlling his little tail.

'Is that what happens every time someone comes up here?' Jenny asked.

'Pretty much, yeah.'

'What do your clients think?'

'Haven't had too many clients yet.' I kissed her on the cheek then shook Bradley's hand. 'How are *you*, mate?'

'Good thanks, Scott. Yourself?'

'Getting there, buddy. Come on in and take a seat.'

Unfortunately, there was no time for chit chat, they were just passing through, so literally had only minutes to spare. I'd need to arrange another time to catch up with Bradley.

Jenny reached into her bag, pulled out a memory stick and slid it across my desk. 'The rest of the files from the Kathy Brown case are all on here. Interviews, everything.'

'Awesome.'

'I don't need to tell you how risky this is for me, do I?'

'Of course not.'

'Nobody must ever know I've given you these files.'

'I know that, and I really appreciate you getting them for me.'

'Now here's the thing.' She side glanced Bradley and lowered her voice. 'It looks like they might reopen the investigation.'

'Bugger.'

'We're taking Fenton's allegations very seriously.'

'Who'll get the case?'

The side glance again. 'It's open, but I'm going to put myself and Bradley up for it.'

This could be a real game changer. Having Jenny and Bradley working the case rather than coppers I didn't know, meant I'd be privy to first-hand information, but it would also be a two-way street. We could work together. Another important advantage would be the fact that I could gain access to the people I'd already alienated myself with—Fenton and Pam Derby. These were bridges I'd need to mend. Hopefully having the Queensland Police working with me, in an unofficial capacity of course, would give me some credibility.

'Although I was still in uniform at the time, I got to know people involved in the case quite well,' Jenny continued. 'Even Fenton warmed to me.'

'The charm of a WPC, eh?'

'Ok, got to go,' Jenny said, jumping to her feet. Bradley followed suit.

I padded around the desk and followed them to the door.

Romeo did the same.

'Listen, I really appreciate this, Jen.'

'I know you do,' Jenny said, turning. After a quick peck on the cheek for me and a cuddle with Romeo, she was heading back down the stairs.

'Catch up soon, Scott,' Bradley said after a brief hug.

'Absolutely, mate. Ruby Street is always open.'

After transferring the files from the memory stick to my laptop, I spent the rest of the day reading about the original investigation. It was interesting that everyone listed as potential witnesses were also suspects. Even the Derbys and their daughter, Tilly. The list wasn't in chronological order, so I had no way of knowing if the names were in order of importance, most suspect, or merely in the order that they'd been interviewed. The list looked like this:

James Fenton–widower, owner of horse stud
Jake Fenton (James's son)
Tom Partridge–horse trainer
Matt Derby–groundsman and caretaker
Pam Derby–house cleaner and assistant to the Fentons
Matilda Derby–sixteen year old who found Kathy Brown's body
Reg Patterson–owner of dairy farm neighbouring Mary's Mansion
Jan Patterson–wife
Daisy Patterson–elderly mother
Ron Patterson–eldest son, 39

There was also a list of young stable hands who came and went, mostly youngsters looking for temporary work—backpackers, travellers. Although they may have seemed unimportant, I realised there'd still be a need to check up on them.

12

From the moment he'd disembarked the *Great Britain* in the Port of Brisbane, Callum had relished the challenge of bettering himself in what had been described to him as one of the harshest environments in the world. Even at that young age, he was a hard drinker, but he was a man with a mission. His da was a timber cutter, and so too had been his granda and his da before him. But although Callum was a grafter, he'd known from the very first time he'd wielded an axe, that his destiny was not that of just another Paddy migrant, working hard, spending his money on the ale and horses and never getting ahead in life. He had a mission to make a better life for himself and those around him.

Along with Jimmy P, Danny Flynn and his men, plus an entourage of followers who Callum had recruited from the ship, he found work as a cedar-getter in the Tweed Valley. The bosses, most of whom were Irish or English migrants themselves, soon recognised the potential in the strong young lad who stood out as the leader. In no time at all, Callum moved up from cutter to foreman.

Thirteen years later, after working hard and saving every penny he'd earned, Callum was finally able to purchase a plot of land. But it wouldn't be just any land. Not a small house block by the Coast that he could buy for around £2.00. Instead, his sights were set on the cedar rich corridor that lay just over the border of the newly formed state of Queensland, called Tallebudgera.

At that time, the hinterland was only accessible by trails blazed through dense subtropical rainforest. Callum knew the area had massive potential and that if he were to make this happen, he'd need to act quickly, use every penny of his life savings, and secure a loan from the Australian Joint Stock Bank.

On 10 June 1869, 320 acres came up for auction. With limited funds in place, Callum bid confidently against only two other men—Fergal Keegan, the owner of a sawmill he'd spent a short time working for in Tweed, and an Englishman named Charles Stanley. Callum, still only twenty-nine years of age, was not intimidated by the two gentlemen. In fact, he unnerved them as he aggressively stared them down whenever they placed a bid.

The price had risen to a little over what Callum had hoped to pay. Stanley dropped out, so it was just him and Keegan now.

'By Christ, haven't you got enough man?' Callum called over to his advocate.

Keegan, ignoring him, raised a finger to the auctioneer, increasing the bid by another three pounds.

Callum approached the tall spindly man and lowered his voice. 'Oy'll do you a deal. You can build a sawmill on the property and you'll have a hundred per cent of the work.'

'That's what I'm going to do, anyway. Why would I need you?'

If Fergal Keegan had known Callum Murphy better, he would have realised the red-faced snarl the young man now exhibited meant trouble. Callum had gained a reputation among the local taverns after displaying on many occasions, and usually after a few pints of stout, a talent for beating the crap out of anyone who crossed him.

'So, you think you can just push me out, do you?'

Fergal ignored him.

Callum leaned in close. 'Oy'll slit your throat from ear to ear, you feckin prosy.'

There was no security at the auction, just a few blokes in a wooded clearing on the edge of the block. Keegan however had brought a couple of heavy weights with him. One was a ruddy-faced Scotsman. The other, a heavily tattooed Māori from New Zealand.

The two men stepped forward and glared down menacingly at the shorter man. Keegan held the bid and was gesturing to the auctioneer to bring down the gavel.

'Does your Mammy know where you are?' Callum asked, meeting the Scotsman's glare.

There was no verbal comeback. Instead, he grabbed Callum by the throat with one enormous hand and drew back his other into a fist.

Callum raised his knee into the man's groin.

The Scotsman released his grip and doubled over in pain.

Callum followed up with an uppercut to his nose, splattering it across his face.

The Māori swung with a mighty right hook.

Callum ducked, but only slightly, and the fist caught him on the top of the head, momentarily knocking him off balance. In an instant, he recoiled from the waist and sprung upwards with his own right hook hitting a solid jaw.

The Māori's head shot backwards. His eyes rolled, and his body wobbled before it fell in on itself like a felled chimney.

Callum moved over to Keegan, stood in front of him with his back to the auctioneer and raised a finger to increase the bid by one pound. His eyes bored into the very soul of the older man, as if daring him to bid again.

Keegan, physically shaking now, broke eye contact and lowered his head.

'The current bid is with Mister Murphy,' the auctioneer called out. 'Do we have anymore takers?' He enquired looking around the group of men.

Stanley was already retreating.

Keegan remained with his head bowed as if he were in prayer.

The group of men, mostly workers and foremen, remained silent.

The auctioneer brought down the gavel. 'Sold to Mister Callum Murphy. Congratulations, sir!'

'You had to be greedy, didn't you, yee old bastard,' Callum said, leaning into Keegan once more. 'You could have been me partner but now you're me enemy for life.'

Keegan shuffled backwards without making eye contact.

13

By late afternoon, the surf was calling to me once more, so I was about to call it a day, when my phone rang. The name on the screen said Ben Fisher.

'Hi Ben.'

'Hi Scott. Can you meet us at the cottage in say an hour from now?'

'Sure.' I was assuming the *us* was himself and his agent, Nicky. 'Is everything okay?'

'Yes it's … it's fine. Bring an overnight bag.'

'An overnight bag?'

'See you there.' He hung up.

Now I was intrigued. Were they planning on the three of us staying overnight in a one- bedroom cottage?

Romeo stood, stretched and yawned as if he knew it was time to go home. Before leaving, I called into Elvis' office downstairs and let him know I may be out all night, and that I'd have to leave Romeo at home.

'No worries, bud,' Elvis said, hardly looking up from his computer. 'I'll be a bit late myself, but I'll let Sandy know.'

The house was empty and quiet when I got home. Sandy didn't finish work until 5.30 pm, and it would take her around thirty minutes to travel from the pharmacy she worked at in Broadbeach.

After changing into a pair of board shorts and a T-shirt, I took Romeo out for a run on the beach, leaving myself just enough time to get back, shower and change before heading out to Tallebudgera. I'd be longer than an hour but wasn't too worried. Whatever Fisher and his dippy agent had in mind was intriguing, while at the same time a bloody nuisance.

Feeding Romeo a little extra, hoping it would pacify him, I also gave him a fresh bone from the fridge. 'Now you be a good boy for Uncle Elvis and Aunty Sandy, do you hear, mate?'

His focus was now solely on the bone as he dragged it over to his bed in my room.

'Good boy. See you later.' My overnight bag was a Woolies shopping bag containing a change of clothes, a bar of soap, my toothbrush, and a comb.

In no time at all, I was trundling north in the Dub along the highway towards the West Burleigh exit. When I turned into the driveway in Tallebudgera, something immediately caught my eye. At first, I thought it was a coach, like the ones that did the overnight haul from Brisbane to Sydney and back. It was silver with blacked-out windows. Then I noticed there was an identical one by its side. Both were parked just in front of the cottage. As I drew up beside them, I realised they were high end RVs. On the other side of them, there was a white van.

Fisher and Nicky were standing on the verandah. Next to them was another woman, middle-aged, with a shock of black hair. She wore a shiny, golden sequin jacket as if she'd just stepped from a variety club stage. There was also a younger man with a beard, and a girl. He was setting up a TV camera, the type that I'd become very accustomed to during the *X* case when I was followed around by the media. The girl was setting up a microphone at the end of a boom. My spider senses were tingling.

'Hi Scott,' Ben said, coming to meet me.

'Hi Ben. What's going on?'

'Nothing to do with me, I'm afraid. It's all Nicky's doing.'

'What is?'

'You'll see. Come on.'

'Scott,' Nicky said, shaking my hand as I stepped onto the verandah.

'Nicky.'

The older woman stepped forward, her face beaming as she too offered her hand. 'Scott Stephens, it's good to meet you.'

'Scott, this is Kea,' Nicky said.

'Hi Kea.' As soon as I said it, the schoolboy inside me wanted to fall about laughing. Cheap furniture came to mind.

'Kea is a medium,' Nicky said.

Looking the woman up and down, I could agree she was somewhere between a small and a large, but failed to understand the relevance.

'She's going to conduct a séance tonight.'

'Oh.' The penny dropped. That kind of medium. 'A séance?' It all suddenly made sense. The RVs, the film crew. 'What, here?'

Kea had moved in closer and was staring up at me with scrutinising eyes.

'Yes, we're all going to stay in the cottage tonight,' Nicky said.

One thing I knew for sure was that Nicky Lee and this little woman who looked like a fairground fortune teller wouldn't be staying in no shack, hence the RVs.

Nicky introduced me to the film crew couple. They were Carlos and Jasmine.

'It's great to see you again, Scotty,' Carlos said.

'Have we met?'

'Yes, we were at most of your press conferences last year. We work for the *ABC*.'

Kea was sticking close to me like Romeo did when he knew I had a treat for him.

Looking down at her, I nodded while she continued to stare up at me. 'All right, love?'

'She's with you always, Scott.'

'What's that?' Lowering my head, I cocked my ear.

'I said she's with you always.'

Ben and Nicky were watching quietly. Then I realised Carlos was filming. 'Hey.' I put my hand up to block the shot.

'It's okay, Scott,' Kea continued. 'She wants you to know that she's proud of you and that she loves you very much.'

I wasn't going to encourage the woman. I knew exactly what she was doing. 'Turn off the camera, mate, eh?' My tone was more of a growl.

Carlos did as he was told.

'She wants you to know she doesn't blame you, Scott.'

I remember reading once how these charlatans work. They research a person, then throw it back at them in a cleverly orchestrated way. I wasn't having a bar of it. Directing my attention at Ben, I shook my head and said, 'I'm out of here.'

'No Scott, please?' Nicky pleaded, 'We need you here.'

'You need me to be a part of this circus, you mean.'

Kea finally stepped away from my side.

'*I* need you, Scott,' Ben said. 'I need you to see what I saw. It'll all make sense after tonight. Trust me.'

'And how do you work that out, mate?'

'It's hard for me to explain without sounding like a complete madman. It's best you see for yourself.'

'See what?'

Kea stepped forward again. 'She doesn't blame Gladys either.'

Whoa, get the fuck out of here, I almost yelled. How the hell did she know about Gladys? It wouldn't be too difficult to dig through my history. Since the *X* case, my life story was pretty much in the public domain. I even have my own Wikipedia page. And although the details of the circumstances surrounding my mother's car accident, which resulted in her death, were public, I was pretty sure no one else knew the real reason why I'd missed the bus that night and forced my mother to come pick me up. I was losing my virginity to Gladys Fay, who would later become the wife of the infamous ex Gold Coast Mayor, Julian Monroe. My mother had a phobia against driving at night. I was an arrogant, selfish, teenage AFL player with a big future in the game. That night when we thrashed the Hawthorne Hawks, I'd missed the team bus back to Essendon because I was having it off with the blonde cheerleader in the Hawks Club women's toilets. I was the selfish shit who pleaded for my mother to come pick me up. It was me who sent her to her death on a dark Melbourne road when a truck ploughed into her car. The guilt has remained with me all my life, and I never played footy again after that night.

Trying to remain cool and not react, I realised this woman was as good at reading body language as I was so I turned my back on her. 'I'll see you later.' Heading for the Dub, Ben and Nicky followed me.

'Please Scott, we really need this,' Nicky said.

'You need the publicity, you mean.'

'No, we need this to not only save Ben's career, but to prove to you who the killer really is.'

'And how do you think you're going to do that?' I asked, turning when I reached the car. 'Have a little chat with Kathy Brown, perhaps?'

The agent's expression said, *Well yes, that's exactly what we're going to do.*

Ben Fisher placed a hand on my shoulder. 'I'll double your fee, Scotty. If you stay.'

14

Nicky Lee had planned the night out. I was to sleep in Mary's Mansion. Fisher would be in one of the RVs. Nicky and Kea would share the other one. The film crew were staying at a hotel in Burleigh.

Although I'd reluctantly agreed to stay, my involvement would be to remain quiet and observe. Nicky, on the other hand, had different ideas. She gave me a run-sheet of how she'd planned out the evening. First, there would be on-camera interviews with each of us seated separately out on the back verandah. Nicky would ask the questions. When it was her turn, she would be answering from a pre-written list she'd memorised.

Fisher went first. To my horror, this meant I was alone on the front verandah with Kea.

'It's okay, Scott. I just want you to know that you don't have to talk about … you know …' She leaned over from the other chair and touched my hand. Her tone was gentle, kind of like a caring grandmother. 'I never have time to think about the messages that come through. Just tend to blurt them out.'

In my mind there were two possible scenarios, but as yet I couldn't work out which was the more plausible. Was this woman an outright charlatan who had honed her skills to perfection? Or was she suffering from some kind of mental health issue that led her to believe she really spoke to the dead? A part of me wanted to believe the latter, but my logical detective instinct was screaming the former. I remained quiet, staring straight ahead.

'There are more messages for you, lots in fact. Your father—'

I jumped to my feet. 'Look, can we not do this?'

'Okay, okay.' Her expression softened. 'I just want you to know that if you ever want to talk, to me, to them—'

'I'll be right, thanks.'

'I understand.'

Returning to my seat, I asked, 'So, how do you do it?'

She smiled warmly. 'I don't actually do anything more than answer their calls.'

'What, like you've got a mobile phone to the after world?' I was fascinated to learn more, purely as a cynic of course.

Kea chuckled. 'That's a good way of putting it. Have you ever been under water in an indoor swimming pool?'

I nodded. 'Yeah.'

'You hear the high-pitched echo of people shouting and children yelling from above the water, but it's really hard to make out their words. Well, that's how I receive the messages from the other side. They sometimes take a bit of deciphering because they can be hard to understand. That's why I sometimes only pick up the first letter of a name, but once I focus, the messages become clearer.'

'And how long have you been doing this?'

'I haven't been doing anything, remember? I've been reluctantly receiving messages from past loved ones since I was a toddler.'

After pondering this for a moment, I asked, 'But what do you say to people who think you're a phoney? Praying on vulnerable people in their time of grief?'

'I don't say anything. I stopped trying to justify myself a long time ago. I've been put on this earth to help bring a little relief to those grieving people in this world. That's why God gave me this gift.'

'You're making a good living from it too, I bet. Would you be here if there wasn't a film crew involved?'

She shook her head slowly and looked down at the floor as if to say, *You haven't listened to a word I've said.*

To my relief, Nicky, appeared from the back of the house. 'Okay. Kea. It's your turn.'

Kea stood, offered me a sober smile, then followed Nicky.

It was around twenty minutes when they reappeared. 'Your go, Scotty,' Nicky said.

'I don't think so.'

'What do you mean?'

'I'm not a fan of reality TV. I'm just here to observe.'

'But I've got a list of questions for you.'

'Not happening, I'm afraid.'

Nicky deflated with a mighty sigh and stormed off back around the house. It was obvious she was used to getting her own way.

I remained on the front verandah while the film crew set up the camera inside the house and checked the sound, all supervised by the dynamic trio.

Nicky reappeared and gestured with her arm for me to enter the cottage. 'We're almost ready.'

You would have been struggling to get five adults into the place at the best of times, having the small round dining table in the centre of the room with the camera equipment set up in one corner made it almost impossible.

Kea was already seated at the table, Ben and Nicky took the seats on either side of her. I sat on the one opposite. In the middle of the table was a short, fat candle with a large flame. It was getting dark outside. Carlos, the cameraman, closed the curtains, and the candle flame was suddenly the only light in the room.

Then it flickered and went out.

15

Like most people, I'd seen séances in the movies and on TV. I'd never actually been to one, but it was exactly what you'd expect. We're sitting around a table in a dark room holding hands, and all eyes are on the dodgy old girl in the sequin jacket. The camera was rolling, the sound boom was hovering overhead at the end of a telescopic pole, and the only sounds we could hear was a growing wind outside and the gentle flicker of the candle flame.

With eyes closed, Kea raised her face towards the ceiling and inhaled deeply.

Nicky and Fisher stared at the medium expectantly.

Kea breathed in again, only this time louder. The rapid eye movement was quite prominant, those little suckers were racing from side-to-side beneath her eyelids. I was half expecting her to say, 'Is there anybody there?' This would have almost completed my idea of a séance, followed only by a loud knocking on the underside of the table. The candle did flicker again but I'm pretty sure that was from the draughty doorway.

Kea's breathing wavered as she inhaled loudly once more, then her voice rode the outward breath as a whisper. 'He is here!'

He? I'd expected to be talking to Kathy Brown. Who's this bloke?

'His name is …' She cocked her head to one side as if she were straining to listen. 'His accent is very strong, Scottish or Irish perhaps. His name is C … Ca … Co … Colin …'

Colin? G'Day Col. How are you, mate?

'It's Callum,' Nicky said. 'Callum Murphy.'

It had taken me very little time on the internet to find out who Callum Murphy was. Kea could easily have done the same. So far, I wasn't impressed.

'Aye, it's Callum Murphy.'

Oh my God, she'd slipped into a very poor Irish accent.

'He's welcoming us to his home. Can you help us, Callum …? Aye.' As well as having a two-way conversation with herself and addressing us at the same time, she was flicking from Aussie to Irish like one of those old-time actors who played numerous roles in a radio play. 'Is Kathy there with you …?' Silence. She rolled her head slightly from side-to-side and took in another deep breath. 'Ahhh …' The heavy exhalation again. 'I see a woman.'

Now we're getting somewhere. Come on, Kathy girl, tell us what you know. I was also having a conversation with myself, only mine was in my head.

'She is a mother.'

Uh, oh. My hackles rose. *I hope you're not going where I think you're going.*

'She wants to say she is sorry. Sorry for leaving her child.'

Okay, I'm out of here. I pulled my hands free, rose from the table and stumbled towards the door. *I told her not to go there and what did she do?*

'She says it was all her fault,' Kea continued regardless. 'She wished she could go back to that night.'

The camera was aimed directly at me now as I slammed the door behind me.

Nicky followed me onto the verandah. 'Scott, what's wrong?'

'What's wrong? I'll tell you what's bloody wrong. Me allowing myself to be a part of this ridiculous charade. That's what's wrong.'

'But we've just started. It's Kathy. We've made contact with Kathy.'

'Of course, you bloody well haven't. Can't you see what's happening?'

Her expression hardened. 'Why don't you tell me what's happening, Scott?'

'It's a bloody farce, and you know it. If she thinks she can get me onside by pretending to talk with my mother, she's got another thing coming.'

'*Your* mother? That was your mother in there?'

'No, of course it wasn't. It's just that unscrupulous old bat doing what she does, manipulating people's weaknesses and using them to her advantage.'

'But how could she know about your mother?'

I didn't think it necessary to give her an answer.

'So, what about Gladys then?'

Shocked, I turned around to face her. Either Kea had told her about our conversation earlier or she'd overheard us. I guessed the latter. 'Gladys?'

'I'm guessing Gladys Monroe. Would I be right?'

'You're not even close. I'm out of here.' I headed towards the Dub. 'I'll come back for my bag in the morning. Leave it on the porch, eh?'

'But Scott, please.' She was following me. 'Don't go. We need you to stay.'

'Yeah right. I guess the ratings won't be as good if I'm not here.'

'No … don't you see? We're so close to finding out who killed Kathy Brown.'

Swinging around, I was struggling to to control my temper. 'No, we're not. That woman is just wasting everybody's time. I'll find out who the real killer is, and in doing so I may or may not prove what a lying cheat your famous author is. But I'll do it my way, that's what I've been hired to do.'

'Okay, you're fired.' She dropped her arms to her side and deflated like a person who had given up trying to see reason.

Looking up to the stars, I inhaled, then lowered my eyes back to hers slowly. 'You can't fire me. I'm working for Fisher.' Then I noticed Carlos was filming us from the porch.

Turning back towards the Dub, I called back over my shoulder, 'I'll be back in the morning. 'Make sure you guys are long gone, eh?'

'You can't tell me what to do.'

'I just did.' Climbing into the car, I started up the engine and drove away. Through my rear-view mirror, I could see her standing there watching me. Turning out of the driveway and onto Tallebudgera Creek Road, I couldn't wait to get back to Kirra.

16

Callum Murphy stood on the top of a tall ridge, proudly surveying his land. He decided there and then that this would be a pilgrimage he would undertake every morning to witness the birth of the new day. As the sun rose from the east, a sea of red cedar swayed in a westerly breeze, slowly revealing itself for as far as the eye could see. The Perry River, a key reason for him purchasing the land, snaked from the mountains down to Burleigh, sitting on the fringe of the Jellurgal headland that jutted out into the glistening ocean. To the west and across the border to the south was the McPherson Range. The unmistakable peak of Mount Warning was also clearly visible. This truly was a magical place.

After inhaling the sweet fresh air, Callum marched down the hill. Although there was an abundance of material all around him, he still needed money to build a sawmill, hire a gang and get to work. Purchasing the land had been an achievement, but it had taken every penny he'd saved over the last few years. So, for the next stage of his plan, he needed a partner. He needed Patrick McCarthy.

McCarthy was a wealthy sawmill owner and cedar-getter from the Tweed Valley. Originally from Dublin, he was a hard businessman, but he knew Callum and respected his tenacity and hardworking spirit. They'd arranged to meet at the Rose and Crown in Maybree at midday. Callum set off on foot at daybreak, so he'd be there early.

Maybree, the small township southwest of Burleigh comprised a post office, a general store, a boarding house, and a pub.

McCarthy would arrive with an entourage, no doubt.

Callum strolled into town alone. He'd arrived in plenty of time to speak to the owners of each of the establishments and pass them handwritten signs that read:

Sawyers and getters wanted, apply within.

For each man sent to him, the owners would receive a small spotters' fee.

When he arrived at the tavern, he was surprised to find McCarthy already waiting for him. There was no entourage, as Callum had expected, only a young woman sitting with her head down.

Patrick McCarthy, a pox-faced, bear of a man, stood as he watched Callum approach. 'Callum Murphy,' his voice was deep, his accent, unapologetically Irish.

The two men shook hands. 'Mister McCarthy.'

'I always knew you'd make a name for yourself,' McCarthy said heartily.

Callum had worked for the man when he'd first arrived on The Tweed. He side glanced the young woman sitting by his old boss's side.

'This is my daughter, Mary,' McCarthy said.

Avoiding eye contact, Mary stood and curtsied. She was petite, with dark hair, fair skin, blue eyes, and rosy cheeks.

'It's good to meet you, Mary,' Callum said, taking her hand. He went to kiss it, but it was snatched away.

'Don't mind her,' McCarthy said. 'She's shy.'

'I'm not feckin shy, Daddy!' The demeanour of the fragile little woman instantly disappeared. The scowl that flicked momentarily between her father and the young man had the deliverance of a warning slap.

McCarthy, ignoring his daughter, continued to speak.

Callum hardly heard a word. Mary captivated him.

'So now you've bought it, what do you think you're going to do?' McCarthy asked.

'Why Oy'm going to log it and build a sawmill of course,' Callum said, finally dragging his eyes away from the young woman.

'You'll need a lot of money to start up an operation like that.'

'Aye, Oy know that.'

'I'm guessing you've got no money left. Would that be right, young Callum?'

Callan shrugged. 'This is why Oy wanted to speak with you, Mister McCarthy.'

'You're looking for a partner?'

'Aye, Oy am, sir!' Callum trusted Patrick McCarthy, but he also knew he was a shrewd businessman. He doubted he'd get exactly what he wanted, there would be a need for negotiation. But if Callum got half of what he needed, it meant he'd be able to start up his business. He also knew that he could learn a lot from the older man.

'I won't ask what you need,' McCarthy said, 'because I already know … pretty much everything. Am I right?'

Callum nodded reluctantly. This time, Mary met his side glance. A shiver rose through his body.

'Okay, I'll tell you what I'm prepared to do,' McCarthy said, 'but first I need a drink.' He raised his hand to the bartender.

The young man came straight over.

'Three pints of stout,' McCarthy said, 'And, he's paying.' He pointed to Callum.

Still, Callum wasn't grasping the words. He barely had enough money on him to buy food from the general store, but he nodded anyway. His mind was elsewhere, he couldn't help stealing glances at Mary McCarthy. Could this little thing really drink a full pint of stout, or were two of them for McCarthy? Like most loggers at that time, McCarthy had a reputation for being a hard drinker.

When the barman returned holding a tray of three black pints, Mary took them from the tray and dispensed them—one to McCarthy, one to Callum and one for herself. 'Cheers!' she called out, holding up her pint.

'Cheers!' McCarthy and Callum repeated in unison.

They clinked their glasses together, then each took a slow sip.

McCarthy stood. 'I'll be back.' He padded away towards the latrine.

Mary took another swig of her beer.

Callum followed suit. Feeling a need to break the awkward silence, he looked at the young woman. 'So do you live in The Tweed, Mary!'

'Aye.'

'Oy wouldn't have thought there'd be much to do there for a nice young woman like you.'

'I wouldn't know about that.' Her blush seemed to mask a hint of anger.

'Oy've known your da for a long time.'

'I know.' She wasn't going to make this easy.

Callum persevered. 'Do you ever go dancing?'

'Maybe.'

'Would you come dancing with me one time?'

Mary shrugged and took another sip of beer.

'Oy'm a good dancer, that Oy am.' Callum put down his drink, stood, and did a little Irish jig.

Mary smiled and blushed some more.

'Oy call this the Tallebudgera Tickle.'

Mary lifted her hand to her mouth to stifle a giggle.

'By Jesus, what are you doin' lad?' McCarthy said as he returned from the toilet.

'Oy was just showing young Mary how good a dancer Oy am, sir.'

'You're wasting your time, son. Mary's not … not much of a dancer.'

'I can so dance, Da,' Mary spat back with Gaelic venom.

McCarthy smirked then gulped his beer.

'In fact, I'm going dancing with Mister Murphy,' Mary added.

Callum's eyebrows just about shot to the top of his head.

Mary met his stare and held it.

'We're here for business,' McCarthy said. 'Let's get down to it. I'll build your mill and give you all the labour you'll need for fifty percent!'

Fifty per cent? Callum couldn't believe what he was hearing. The offer was beyond his expectations. He'd anticipated McCarthy to begin with an offer of something like 70 – 30 in his favour, allowing Callum to negotiate the figure down to 60 – 40. But 50 – 50, although still high, meant that Callum could begin his business right away. He was about to shake McCarthy's hand when Mary intervened.

'Don't be so damn greedy, Da.'

McCarthy lifted his drink to his lips, unphased, almost as if he'd been expecting the challenge. 'Fifty per cent is a good offer, right Callum?' He finished the rest of his drink.

Callum's eyes locked onto the young woman.

Once again, she met his eyes as if prompting him to negotiate further.

What did he have to lose? If he'd thought about it later, he'd realise the answer was *everything*. 'Oy can't hand over fifty per cent of me business, Mister McCarthy.'

'You don't have a business. You've got a little piece of land that you paid too much for.'

'Daddy!' The word came out more as a growl.

'Okay,' McCarthy said, placing his empty pint on the table. 'I'll loan you whatever you'll need, to be paid back monthly, but I'll require one hundred per cent of your business as equity should you default on the loan. Do we have a deal?' He held out his hand for Callum to shake.

Callum grabbed the hand and shook it.

'Marvellous! Three more of these please, barman,' McCarthy called towards the bar.

Mary stood, leaned over the table, and offered her hand to Callum. 'I'm looking forward to seeing the Tallebudgera Tickle again!' She said, grinning.

17

The dulcet tones of Elvis Presley singing 'Love Me Tender' wafted through the house as I entered the front door of Ruby Street. It was coming from the man shed, so I knew the volume must have been on high for me to hear it at the front of the property. But it was odd, because although my best mate shared the name—an alias granted—with the 'King of Rock 'n' Roll', he wasn't actually a fan. It was Sandy who was heavily into the great man's music. I couldn't imagine her sitting out in the man shed alone with the music cranked up high. That wasn't the Sandy I knew.

Romeo came bolting out of my bedroom, his tail wagging excessively as usual, but his head was low as if he'd done something wrong.

Uh, oh. 'Hey Boy, what's up?' I said as I knelt and fussed him.

A series of short whines sounded as if he was almost saying, 'I'm sorry, I'm sorry, I'm sorry!'

'What have you done, Boy?' Apart from my early morning surfs—he's usually snoring when I leave and still snoring when I return—I very rarely left him on his own for too long. On one occasion when I did, the little bugger had taken a liking to the TV remote, which I'd left on the arm of the sofa, and he'd chewed it. I quickly had to buy a new one, but the incident didn't go down too well with my housemates, especially Sandy. Crikey. Had he chewed something else?

Tiptoeing through the house and out to the man shed. I noticed Romeo didn't follow. Instead, he retreated to the sanctuary of my bedroom.

Elvis was sitting at the bar with his back to me. There was a glass of Scotch in front of him, but it was the LP sleeve lying next to the glass that caught my eye.

'Hey mate,' I said, gently placing a hand on his shoulder.

Inevitably, he almost jumped off the stool. Deep in thought, he hadn't heard me enter. 'Hey bud, how's it going?' he replied, returning his gaze to the glass.

'What's up?'

'We're in deep shit, mate!'

'Why, what's happened?' He reached over and passed me the album cover. It was an Elvis Presley LP, and although it was obviously very old, it was in great condition, except for the left-hand side that is, that no longer existed.

'Shit! Romeo?'

'Yep.'

I studied the cover further. There was a black-and-white picture of Elvis in his military uniform. By his side was a young Pricilla. It was a recording of a TV special entitled, *The Frank Sinatra Timex Show. Welcome home Elvis.* The recording included performances from the Rat Pack and Elvis himself. 'I've never heard of it.' This was a lame response because I knew very little about Elvis' records.'

'Of course you've never heard of it. It was never released. That's one of only a handful of original acetate recordings made specially for the industry release in 1960.' Elvis took a long swig of whisky. 'It's officially the rarest 12" Elvis Presley record ever produced.'

Romeo had bitten right through the cover and into the vinyl. The black grooved disk inside was no longer round and flat, it looked more like a discarded piece of chewed liquorice. 'So, what the hell was it doing lying around here?' I immediately regretted my defensive tone.

'Oh, hell mate. I don't know. She usually keeps it under lock and key. We were looking at it last night, she's supposed to be lending it to the organisers of this year's Cooly Rocks Festival.'

'Can we replace it?' 'Nope.'

'What about Dougie?' Dougie ran a huge vintage store in Coolangatta and sold just about everything from the last century.

'Already rang him. Pissed himself laughing when I told him what had happened. When I mentioned the title of the record, the laughter immediately turned to a stunned silence.'

'So, he hasn't got a copy?'

'No, he hasn't. Nor has anyone else. Got any idea how much he reckons it was worth?'

Shaking my head. I didn't really want to know.

'Five, six thousand dollars!'

'What?'

'Six grand?'

'Shit, mate. I'm so sorry. Is it insured?'

'It's not the money, mate. This record means more to Sandy than anything else in this world. It's a family heirloom. Her old man picked it up in the States years ago. How the hell am I going to tell her?'

I sat down on the barstool next to him. This was a horrible situation and one that I could only blame myself for. Leaving the bedroom door open meant that I'd given Romeo the run of the house, but I couldn't have left him locked up all night. The arrangement had been for Elvis to look after him once he got home from work. He actually loved the little bloke as much as I did. Sandy, though, she wasn't too keen.

'It's my responsibility, my fault. I'll tell her.'

There was no argument from Elvis. 'Thanks, mate. It won't be pretty, though.'

Perhaps now was a good idea to tell him about the plan I'd hatched while driving back from Tallebudgera. I hoped that me being the cause of this trouble may have softened the blow. I was wrong.

'You what?' Elvis cried. 'Moving out? Why?'

'It's just temporary,' I retorted and although the accommodation I was moving into would be temporary, I suspected that the move from the Ruby Street house would be a permanent thing. Especially if Sandy had her say, which I was pretty sure she would have.

'Where are you going?'

'Tallebudgera.'

'Tallebudgera?'

'Yep. I'm going to have a stint out in the Valley.' The idea had come to me as I was driving through Burleigh. It would be much easier to work on the case if I actually moved into the cottage. I knew the property was vacant at the moment, but it wouldn't be long before a potential tenant found it. So, I'd swung the Dub into James Street hoping the Burleigh Heads real estate office would still be open. To my surprise, it was. Of course, the girl behind the reception desk already knew me. I was kind of getting used to this. 'Scotty Stephens. What brings you here this evening? I was just about to close up.' Her name tag read 'Melissa'.

'I'm enquiring about a rental you have listed.' The vacant sign outside the property told me it was this agency that was handling the rental.

'Sure, which one?' 'Mary's Mansion.'

She blushed. 'Okay, yes it's still vacant.'

'Had much interest?'

'Uhmm … not really, but the market's pretty slow at the moment.'

'Is it?' We both knew the market was booming.

'It's a niche property. I could take you out there for a viewing … tomorrow morning, perhaps?'

'No that's fine. I've already seen it. Where do I sign?'

18

I didn't shun my responsibility by avoiding Sandy. It was me who met her at the front door when she arrived home from work. And it was me who broke the news. At first, she was silent, possibly numb.

'The Timex Show? Not the Timex Show?' Her voice was low. Her lips were quivering. She lifted the destroyed album from the bar. Her eyes were wide and searching. 'No.'

Elvis and I remained quiet watching her every move while my mind was trying to picture Romeo's afternoon. There was no carnage and no signs that he'd even touched anything else. It was almost like he'd gone directly for the LP. Although the door to Elvis' bedroom was closed, like a lot of the doors in this old house, it opened with a simple nudge. How did Romeo know this? Why would he have gone directly for Elvis' room when he could have gone into the living room and continued his previous meal with the remote, or the kitchen where he could have helped himself to the full bag of dog biscuits that stood near the back door? Then, once in Elvis' room, surely there were more appealing objects to get his gums around? Elvis' footy trophies, Sandy's hairbrush, underwear, anything but … anything but one of the rarest vinyl records in the world.

It was usually locked away in her father's safe at his house in Kingscliff. He'd allowed Sandy to take it from the family home because she'd offered to loan it to the organisers of the annual rock 'n' roll festival that was held in the streets of Coolangatta. It was to be displayed in a glass case alongside other Elvis Presley memorabilia. The loss would not only be devastating for Sandy's family, but it would be mourned for many years to come worldwide by the EP fraternity.

Sandy was trembling as if volcanic magma was slowly rising from her toes. Then she let rip. And rightly so. 'WHAT THE FUCK, SCOTTY …?'

My battle shields were up and ready. Standing with my head low, allowing her verbal attack to batter my defences. I should have locked him in my bedroom. I could have put him in the backyard. Or I could have taken him with me. Should have. Could have. Would have. Didn't.

The tears rolled down her face as she held the chewed vinyl disc in one hand and the sodden half-eaten cover in the other.

'THAT DOG. THAT FUCKING DOG!'

As I continued to stare at the floor, a corner of the cover caught my eye. It was lying by the sofa. I almost pointed to it, but then decided not to.

'WHAT'S MY DAD GOING TO SAY? OH MY GOD, HOW WILL I TELL HIM?' The attack went on and on. Even when it swayed towards a personal attack on me, my irresponsibility and my don't-give-a-fuck attitude towards other people—her words, not mine—I let it ride. Finally, she stormed off to their bedroom, crying uncontrollably.

'Fuck, mate,' Elvis said.

Normally after a tragic event, the three of us—myself, Elvis and Tetley—would either retreat to the pub, or more likely hit the booze hard in the man shed. Neither option was open to us at this point. The pub had gone, and the man shed? What with Tetley away in the UK and Sandy now a big presence in Elvis' life, it almost felt like the man shed was no more. Just a dwindling memory of a past life.

'I'm sorry, mate,' was all I could manage. But I truly was sorry.

'I know you are.'

As if by instinct, we wandered back out to the shed. Elvis took two beers from the fridge and we sat side by side at the bar.

'Is she going to be all right?'

Elvis exhaled through shaky lips. 'I guess.'

19

When driving out to the Valley, once you emerge from beneath the M1 overpass on Tallebudgera Creek Road, you instantly leave the Gold Coast to find yourself driving through pleasant countryside. We'd had some good rain this past year, so everywhere was green and lush. It was still early. The sun was sitting just above the trees behind me as I drove west. With the windows rolled down, I could take in the crisp, country air.

Romeo sat uncharacteristically quiet in the back. Looking back at him through the rear-view mirror, I realised he was enjoying the jet of air that was gushing through the front windows. The backseats folded down like a station wagon, so there was plenty of room for him. This was *his* space. Since his arrival in my life a few months ago, the seats had been permanently down and covered with a patchwork blanket that was donated by Tetley's mum.

Everything I owned fitted easily in the Dub's boot. Apart from my surfboard, that is. That was strapped to the roof. Thankfully, Mary's Mansion came fully furnished and would be a huge upgrade from the decor I was used to.

I'd purposely taken the long route. Jumping on the M1 at Tugun and exiting at West Burleigh would have been much quicker, but I was in no rush. I'd taken the coastal road through Currumbin, then continued along through Palm Beach until

I reached Burleigh Heads. Once I'd navigated the chaotic road system there, I was heading out to the hinterland in no time.

Romeo seemed reluctant to climb out the Dub. Until now, his life was split between Ruby Street and Kirra Beach.

'Come on, boy. Out you get.'

He whined, wagged his tail and surveyed the surroundings from inside the car. 'Come on, you're not in trouble.'

He wasn't going to move.

Leaning in, I lifted him into my arms. 'What's up with you, eh?'

He nestled his head into my chest. When I placed him on the ground, he sat on his backside and looked up at me with pleading eyes, so I suddenly bolted towards the side of the house, continued around the back and headed for the trees.

Romeo followed in hot pursuit but instead of overtaking me and wigging out as he usually would, he stayed by my side.

I rolled onto the grass, scooped him up and playfully threw him a little way. Normally he loved to wrestle, but he was having none of it today. A thought suddenly struck me. Maybe he was feeling sick from his vinyl chow down the day before. That was it. 'Hey, buddy. You feeling a bit crook, mate?'

Instead of diving all over me as he usually would, he nudged his nose into my side as if to say, 'Come on, let's get out of here.'

Picking him up, I headed back towards the cottage. 'Poor old Romey. This country air will fix you up in no time.'

It only took a couple of trips to carry everything I owned from the car to the house, and a big part of that was Romeo's stuff—his bed, bowls, toys, blanket, and food. When packing the car that morning, the realisation that a six-month-old puppy had almost as many belongings as me, a forty-three-year-old bloke, hit home.

I'd need to do a shop, but that could wait until later. After plonking my clothes on the bed, I headed back outside. 'Come on, boy.' I didn't have to call over my shoulder, my little mate was sticking to my side like a Siamese twin. 'Time to do a bit of exploring.'

We exited by the back door. I stood for a moment surveying the property from the verandah, but my attention was drawn to the activity on the horse stud next door. A group of school kids surrounded the arena. Tilly was in the centre of the circle, leading a pony at the end of a rope. One of the kids was on the pony's back. I couldn't hear the words, but I could hear her voice as she tutored over the excited chatter.

Pulling my attention back to this side of the fence, something else caught my eye to the left of the tree line, just under the shade. It appeared to be some kind of structure. 'Come on, boy,' I said to the dog and stepped down from the verandah.

As we approached the shaded area, I realised the building was an old chook house.

Checking the strength of the chicken wire that surrounded it, I realised it would be a perfect pen where I could leave Romeo when I had to go out.

Once under the trees, the land inclined. I decided to go up and see how far it went. But there was something else on the other side of the track, something half hidden in the trees. Pulling back bracken and low branches. I suddenly realised what I was looking at. Side by side were two ancient, moss covered gravestones. The inscriptions were very simple. The one to the left read:

Here lies Mary Murphy Tragically taken
October 9th 1886

And on the right:

Here lies Callum Murphy Tragically taken
October 9th 1886

'Hi. I'm ...' *What was I doing? Was I really about to introduce myself to a couple of dead people?* Mary Murphy was obviously the Mary I'd heard mentioned a few times. She must have been Callum's wife. It was interesting to note that they both died on the same day. An accident perhaps? I'd be keen to find out more.

Continuing along the worn path with Romeo in tow, the incline increased considerably and I realised we were heading up the mountain. There was no boundary fence, so I kept going. About ten minutes later, the trees thinned until we entered a clearing. There was a rocky knoll in front of us. Beside it were crude steps made from sandstone boulders.

After venturing away from the house, Romeo seemed to return to his old self. Running off in front, picking up sticks and diving into piles of leaves. When we reached the steps, he bolted up them. Finding the exploration quite exhilarating, I followed.

At the top was a lookout and a bench seat made from rocks. I turned towards the view, then gasped. 'Oh my goodness!'

The outlook truly was amazing. I could see as far south as Byron Bay and the curving coast of NSW beyond. Mount Warning to the west seemed like it was only a stone's throw away, and the Gold Coast, including Surfers Paradise and beyond, lay to the east.

Sitting on the bench, I planted my hands on either side of me, gently massaging the rough texture with my fingers. Often I'd use the breathing technique that Bradley Foster had taught me when the X case was at its most stressful. Now was a great time to put it to practice, but there was no need to close my eyes and visualise a tranquil scene. Nothing I could imagine could be better than what was right there in front of me.

Continuing to breathe deep and slow, in through the nose and out through the mouth, my whole body, even my aching legs from the climb, began to relax. Inadvertently, my right hand had made its way along and down the side of the large boulder that made up one side of the bench. As my fingers continued to probe the rough surface, I realised my index finger had found a pattern and was tracing its path. After more probing, I finally became conscious that something was carved into the rock. Opening my eyes, I stood, then knelt at the side of the bench. At first it was hard to make out, but as I wiped away a surface of sand and dirt, there were three distinctive words.

Callum loves Mary!

20

The land was cleared into two distinct areas. A smaller one that would be the site of a temporary cottage for Callum, and a larger one close to the bank of the Perry River where he intended to build his first sawmill. It was here that Callum saw his future, milling and transporting thousands of tons of quality logs down to the Coast.

With the lumber from the clearing, he built a small cottage for himself while his men built a series of workers' huts closer to the sawmill site. There was also a contingency of Aboriginal workers who built and lived in small shelters called humpies.

The sawmill, although by far the largest structure, was merely a shingled roof atop a series of posts. In the absence of walls, the air would pass through the building while the roof would keep the workers and the equipment in the cooler shade, as well as dry when the rains came.

Callum had been lucky with the skilled labour he'd attracted since arriving in Queensland.

Jimmy P was his foreman and the twenty or so men he'd recruited aboard the *Great Britain*, were all still with him. The workforce had expanded to forty now after recruiting more men from the Tweed.

The only cost so far had been the labour. This came from an advance that Callum had received from McCarthy. Although the

91

wage Callum could afford to pay was measly compared to the large sums of money a successful getter could earn, his promise to his loyal men of better times ahead was something Callum would die for rather than renege—and his team seemed to understand this.

Leaving Jimmy P to oversee the construction of the sawmill and the workers' huts, Callum built the tiny cottage with his own hands.

Today was a big day, it would see Callum's first business meeting with his partner and benefactor, Patrick McCarthy. Wanting to appear busy when he arrived, Callum continued putting the final touches to the cottage. It was a very simple structure—one room, with lean-to verandahs at the front and back.

When the work was finished, Callum stood on the front verandah, admiring his new abode.

'Oh, that's lovely.' The voice was female with a distinct Irish bite.

Callum turned to see Mary McCarthy looking up at him. 'Well bugger me backwards, Mary McCarthy.' He stepped down and greeted his guest with a peck on the cheek.

'Callum.' Her tone was all business.

'So, where's your da, over at the mill already?' There were still a few trees between the mill site and the cottage. These would be cleared soon so that Callum would have a clear view of the operations.

'My da's in Brisbane.'

'What?' Callum felt his stomach sink. *Surely this didn't mean that McCarthy was pulling out of the deal, sending his daughter to break the news?* 'But we're supposed to be having our first meeting.'

'That's right.' Mary was giving away nothing. She remained poised and calm.

'But he's in feckin Brisbane?' Callum was struggling to contain his fiery temper.

'Aye …'

'Mary … what's going on?'

'Your meeting is with me.' Mary grinned. 'Come on. There is a lot to do today.' She headed through the trees towards the sawmill.

Callum, feeling for the first time since boarding the *Great Britain* that he was no longer in charge, followed.

When they'd walked the short distance from the cottage to the construction site of his new sawmill, it surprised Callum to find the area a hive of activity. An army of workers was unloading machinery parts from wagons, while another group was assembling them in the mill.

Mary immediately threw herself into the middle of the mayhem and was shouting instructions like an experienced gaffer.

Jimmy P was overseeing the positioning of what looked to Callum like a small steam train. 'Fifty-five horses, Callum,' Jimmy proclaimed. 'Have you ever seen anything so beautiful?'

Callum's saws were to be powered by the latest steam powered technology. His heart was lifted as he realised the last piece of his master plan was coming together. He made his way into the shade of the mill. Four pits had been dug in preparation to house the heavy rip saws. He watched on as the engineers positioned the steel bases side by side that would carry the huge, six-foot diameter blades. The experienced men knew exactly what they were doing and as much as he wanted to be involved, Callum could see no reason to intervene.

'Mister Callum, sir.' The eldest of the engineers approached him holding out his hand. 'I'm Bob Merriman. My son, Joey, was aboard the *Great Britain* on the same voyage as you.'

Callum remembered young Joey Merriman. He was not much more than a boy. 'Aye, young Joey. How is the lad?'

The man lowered his gaze to the ground. 'I'm afraid he was killed last year.'

'By Jesus, Oy'm sorry to hear that. What happened to him?'

'He was working under Ron Fenton.'

'Fenton?' Callum hadn't heard that name since disembarking the *Great Britain* in Brisbane.

'He was a good lad, Mister Callum, sir, but as we both know he would never have amounted to much more than a labourer.'

Callum nodded respectfully. It was true, an abundance of enthusiasm was lacking as much in common sense.

'I had a lifetime of employment organised for him with McCarthy, but we had a falling out not long after his mother died.'

Callum remained silent.

'He turned his back on his family and got work with Fenton. I never saw him again.'

'Was there an accident?'

'We never learned of his true fate, only that Fenton was involved.'

'That bastard, Fenton. I'm sorry for your loss, Bob Merriman.' Callum retreated from the mill in search of Mary.

The wagons were unloaded, and the last of the machinery was standing outside the mill, waiting to be put in place. Under the watchful eye of Mary, Jimmy P had organised the men into groups who were carrying components into the mill as the engineers needed them.

Callum watched on in awe as Mary skilfully supervised the finely tuned operation. By late afternoon, everything was in place. Machinery was tested, tweaked and tested again. The highlight of the day was when sample logs were run through the main saws.

The Murphy sawmill was ready for business.

An enormous bonfire was lit and the carcases of sheep appeared, as well as a dozen kegs of beer.

'Where did that lot come from?' Callum asked as Mary's men organised the feast. 'Lesson one, Callum Murphy,' Mary said. 'You're to look after your workers at all times.'

'Aye, Oy already know that.'

'I know you do,' Mary said, smiling.

'Would you stay and have some dinner with me, Miss McCarthy?'

'Aye, we'll eat here with the boys.'

Callum shook his head. 'No, no, no. Come back to the cottage with me.'

'Have you a bath?' Mary asked.

'Aye.' There was a tin bath hanging on the back door of the cottage.

'And what will we eat?'

'Uhm … potatoes and cabbage.' He was kidding. Anticipating the arrival of her father, he'd ordered fresh oysters and steak from Burleigh and a bottle of the finest Champagne the day before.

Mary grinned. 'Draw me my bath, Callum Murphy.'

'Okay.' Callum returned to the cabin and lit a fire to boil water for the bath. 'By Christ, are you moving in?' He said later, wide eyed as Mary, with the help of one of her men, dragged a large trunk up the driveway.

'You're going to need help for a couple of days while you get off the ground.'

'Oy am?'

'Aye.'

'So … you're going to be sleeping … here?'

'Aye.' She was watching his face closely. 'But don't be getting any funny ideas, Callum Murphy. You'll be on the couch.'

'Oy know that,' Callum replied innocently. He relieved the men of the trunk and lifted it into the house.

Mary ushered him out of the room. 'Call me when the water is hot.' She closed the door behind her.

'Aye, your ladyship. Oy will.'

After a gentle knock on the back door, Callum announced that the water was hot and suggested he set up the bath at the foot of the bed, to which Mary was agreeable. After a few trips, the galvanised bath sat invitingly filled with steaming hot water.

'Oy'll have the water after you,' Callum said as he backed out of the door.

'Aye,' Mary replied. It was a common practice for families to share the same bath water. Twenty-five minutes later, Mary finally emerged and allowed Callum to enter the cottage.

Gone was the dirty, sweaty, worker wearing jeans, boots, flannel shirt, and Akubra. In her place stood a beautiful young woman with flushed cheeks, wearing a lace-covered dress.

'By Christ, you're a sight for sore eyes, Mary McCarthy.'

'Get yourself clean, man. You stink.'

'Aye, but first.' Callum led her out onto the back verandah. Thanks to Edna P, Jimmy's wife, there was a magnificent dinner table set up, and Champagne cooling in a silver ice bucket. He showed Mary to a seat, opened the Champagne with a satisfying *pop*, and poured her a glass. 'Okay, Oy'll be right back.' This was all lovely, but there was no way he was going to miss out on the opportunity of a hot bath. True to his word, though, he came straight back, clean and wearing his best suit.

They ate beneath a clear star-filled Tallebudgera sky. Mrs P had prepared the oysters and cooked the steak and vegetables to perfection. All Callum had had to do was serve.

'So, how come you haven't married yet, Callum?' Mary asked as they tucked into their food.

'Too busy, and as you can see, there are not that many girls around here.'

'Aye.'

'What about you?'

'The same, but I haven't been looking. Too busy like you.'

'Aye.'

Mary gently probed him about his life.

Callum was more than willing to share what he considered a very boring past.

'Your team of getters left quite the reputation in the Tweed.'

'Aye.'

'Why'd you give it up?'

'It was always temporary, a way of getting to this.' Callum waved a hand over his surroundings.

'Word has it you're a fair man.' Mary was weighing him up as she spoke.

'Aye.'

'Not like Fenton.'

Callum frowned. This was the second time he'd heard the name that day. 'What do you know of Fenton?'

Mary took in a deep breath and exhaled slowly. 'Where to begin.' She finished her glass of Champagne. 'He worked for my da for a while, but he didn't last long. A troublemaker right from the start.'

'Aye, that's the Fenton Oy knew,' Callum threw in.

'Da heard whispers he was plotting, stirring up the men against him.' Callum nodded knowingly.

'There was a …' She looked away and blushed. 'There was an incident …' 'What kind of incident?'

'He asked me out. I detested the man, but I wanted to find out what he was up to, so I accepted his invitation, and he took me out to the Cock & Bull Tavern.'

'A drinking man's pub?'

'Aye. We had dinner there and a few drinks.' She reached over, lifted the Champagne bottle from the ice, and topped up their glasses. 'It wasn't as bad as it sounds until …' She took a sip of her drink. 'Until he offered to walk me home.'

Callum moved a piece of gristle around on his plate with his knife as he listened.

'About halfway home, he suddenly pounced on me!'

'What?'

'Aye, he grabbed me and said I'd been asking for it all night.'

'My God. He didnae?'

'He did,'

'Did he … rape you?'

She burst into laughter. 'By Christ no, I kicked ten barrels of shit out of him!'

Callum joined in with her laughter. 'You defended yourself?'

'I did more than that. I wiped the floor with the little shite!'

Callum fell backwards into his chair, holding his stomach. He hadn't laughed like this for a long time. It soon became apparent that one bottle of Champagne wasn't enough. Of course, it wasn't, but luckily, he had plenty of malt beer and because Mary was a Dublin girl, the black liquid was just as good.

Mary told Callum about her life, and how her father had brought the family of six over from Ireland when she was four years old. 'I remember little of Dublin, unfortunately. My strongest memory was watching her disappear as the ship sailed from Dublin Port.' She held up her beer bottle and said, 'Here's to Ireland.'

Callum joined her in the toast. 'And here's to Australia and a bright future!'

'I'll drink to that,' Mary said, holding his stare.

21

I'd set up my office in the bedroom, just so I could shut the door on it if anyone came to visit. This meant I could have the whiteboard set up and have everything I needed at hand.

So far, I only had one photograph. It was a headshot of the victim, Kathy Brown. At a distance she was a good-looking woman, but not a preened beauty. She had a hard edge to her stare. On close inspection, her blonde hair was quite thin, her eyes were a little bloodshot, and there were tiny pot marks on her skin. I'd had plenty of time to study the picture—her face, her features, her angry blue eyes that said, 'What the fuck are you looking at?'

I'd placed her picture top centre of the board and written her name underneath it. Then beneath this, and to the left-hand side, I'd listed the names and notes of those I intended to investigate:

James Fenton (met, hostile) Jake Fenton (yet to meet) Tom Partridge (yet to meet) Tilly Derby (met, friendly) Matt Derby (yet to meet) Pam Derby (met, defensive)

I was also aware of likely players I hadn't met yet—stable hands, neighbours, etc. I had a lot to do, so it was time to get out there and get some answers. So far, Tilly had been the only person I'd spoken to properly. She was friendly, so using her as a possible way *in* was my first option.

My mobile rang. It was Nicky Lee. 'Hey Nicky, how's it going?'

'Why did you leave last night?' She was far too important and busy to have time for casual preamble.

'Because it was a complete waste of time.'

'How do you know? You weren't there.'

'I'd heard enough.'

'You didn't.' She paused as if contemplating what she was about to say. 'She said things, Scott. Kea I mean.'

'Things?'

'Things that no one else knew about.'

I was ignoring the fact that she seemed to know about my quick fling with the future mayor's wife when I was a teenager.

'After you'd left, she kept mentioning a mother figure again.'

'Even though I'd left?'

'It wasn't about *you*, Scott.'

'Who then?'

'Well that's why we hired *you*, mister detective!'

There was a pause I didn't feel the need to fill.

'She said the killing was in the writing.'

'Meaning?'

'It's in the book.'

Was this just an agent trying to market her client's book? I played along with it to see where it was heading. 'The Valley of Kate, you mean?'

'Yes, it was … co-authored.'

Was she saying that someone in Tallebudgera helped Fisher with the book? I wondered who on the list it could have been. Tilly perhaps? 'By whom?'

'Mary Murphy.'

'Oh, for goodness' sake, Nicky. Really?'

'I know, I know. It sounds ridiculous, but there's more.'

I remained quiet allowing her to continue.

'Ben has owned up. He broke down and admitted that Mary was channelling through him.'

I couldn't help but chuckle. 'This'll boost sales no doubt!'

Nicky snapped back at me. 'Don't you see? This could be the end of Fisher's career if this gets out.'

I did see and now I understood the urgency in her voice.

'I need you to find the real killer, Scott. This will take the emphasis off Ben. And if there is a similarity between the real-life events and the fiction of the book, we can work around it. We're willing to double your fee again.'

Sweet!

'We need results quickly without the police getting involved.'

'Sounds good. Leave it with me.'

'Good.' She hung up.

This brought a whole new meaning to working with a ghost writer. I obviously wasn't buying any of it.

I was about to spend the first night alone in the cottage. Tomorrow would see the beginning of the investigation proper. There were some bridges I needed to mend. Pam Derby would be the first. I was hoping I could use my charm to bring her around. James Fenton would be another matter. If he was hiding something, which I suspected he was, I doubted I'd be able to get close to him, and it would be difficult to even get on the property without his permission.

It was getting late, so I decided I'd pay Pam Derby a visit first thing in the morning. While I'd been setting up the office, Romeo had been lying underneath the bed. It was unusual for him to be so quiet. I worried if he might still be crook from chewing Sandy's LP. *Could he have some kind of poisoning?* I opened the back door, and he shot out into the garden.

'Go, boy, go,' I yelled after him as he tared around the block totally disproving my theory that he was sick. It was as if he just wasn't digging the house.

22

As I was finishing breakfast the next morning, there was a knock at the door. Romeo barked. Opening the front door, I was surprised to find James Fenton standing there.

'Good morning,' he said, civilly. 'May I come in?'

'Sure.' I stepped backwards into the house, allowing him to follow me.

Romeo continued to bark.

'Back you go, Boy,' I commanded, pointing to his bed. I had to physically scoop him back with my arms like a human bulldozer. 'Calm down, Romey. It's all right.' Gently guiding him into the bedroom, I closed the door behind him.

Fenton stood just inside the front door. 'Feisty little bugger, eh?' he said, friendly. 'He'll make a good guard dog, that's for sure.' He wore a dark tan Akubra, which he lifted from his head then turned in his hands nervously. 'So, I just wanted to uhm ... to apologise for yesterday.'

I couldn't believe what I was hearing. The one person I needed to get onside, and here he was apologising to me after I'd trespassed on his property. 'That's all right, mate.'

'I've just been, under a bit of pressure lately.' Without making eye contact, he rocked slowly from side to side. 'What with these allegations and all, doesn't look good, you know?'

'I do Mister Fenton, and I want you to know that I'm here to help you any way I can.'

'You are?' He frowned and lifted his gaze until our eyes met.

'Absolutely.' Sucking up wasn't beneath me. 'We both know that this writer bloke is full of shit.'

'We do, yes we do.'

'I guess having an overactive imagination is a big part of his job description. Can I get you anything, coffee, tea?'

'No, no, that's okay. I've got to get back.' He lifted the hat and placed it back on his head. 'Just wanted to clear the air, that's all.'

'Well, you've done that, sir. Thank you.'

'Good, good.' I could tell by his vacant expression that his mind was in multiple locations. I guess being the owner of a successful horse stud had untold pressures. He turned and lifted the latch on the door. 'You're welcome over at the stud anytime. And if there's anything I can do to help, just ask.'

'Thank you I will.' He marched away. *Well bugger me.* I'd been awake half the night wondering how I could get back onto the property next door and build the bridge with Fenton. I needn't have worried.

The lack of sleep was a worry, though. Although quiet during the day, the Valley seemed to come alive at night with the sounds of the local critters. The fact that Romeo didn't settle—whining and pacing—didn't help either. Nor did the knowledge that there was a graveyard out the back. At one point during the night, the image of the two gravestones sitting side by side in the dark brought an icy shiver to my skin.

Keen to start the investigation, I began at the Derby house.

Pam opened the door on my knock. 'Ah, Mister Stephens. Good morning.' Her demeanour had also changed and I wondered if Fenton had anything to do with it.

After deciding to emulate the same tactic I'd witnessed earlier, I stood wringing an invisible hat in hand. 'Good morning. I … I just wanted to apologise for yesterday.' It was Apology Day.

'Oh, don't be silly. Come on in.'

I followed her into a typical beige painted hallway with matching floor tiles, that led to a decent sized kitchen diner with the same colour scheme. There were cream coloured sliding doors across the back with the familiar honeycombed security screens. The décor was very 1990s and typical of your average rental property.

'Nice place,' I said.

'Is it?' Her reply wasn't really meant as a question.

'Been here long?' I knew exactly how long they'd been there but needed to make conversation.

'Almost ten years. Tea or coffee?'

'No, I'm good, thanks.'

We went out through the sliding door and onto a paved patio with an aluminium roof.

'So …' Pam said after we'd taken seats at the glass table.

'So … I met Tilly yesterday.'

'Yes, she said. She likes you. Tilly doesn't make friends easily.'

'I'm surprised. She's a lovely girl.'

'She certainly is. Too busy though for a social life.'

'Uni?'

'Yes, she also gives riding lessons here most afternoons, and then she has her own equestrian training to keep up with.'

'Competition?'

'Yes. Maybe even the Olympics one day.'

'Crikey. She is a busy girl.'

'A little too busy for my liking,' Pam said, displaying that universal expression of a concerned mother.

'I haven't met your husband yet.'

'Matt? Oh, Mister Fenton keeps him very busy. He's up and out at the crack of dawn, back for a quick lunch at midday, then hard at it again until early evening.'

'Sounds like he works long hours.'

'He does, seven days a week most weeks,' she sighed then added, 'But we can't complain.'

'I think I'd be pushing for a bit more down time.' I needed to keep the conversation going.

'Mister Fenton has been very good to us.'

'So, are you guys locals or …?' I already knew from my research that the couple was from Toowoomba.

Pam continued to tell me how her husband had been a cabinetmaker running his own joinery shop, and that she had worked in hospitality. Their life changed drastically though, after a chance meeting between Matt and James Fenton. Fenton commissioned Matt to build an extensive timber wall cabinet for his study. At first, Matt wouldn't even consider taking on the job after pointing out that the three-hour distance between his joinery shop in Toowoomba and Tallebudgera would blow out the cost. Fenton had insisted and offered to pay double what Matt had reluctantly quoted. He also offered him the use of the gatehouse so he wouldn't have to travel back and forward while he did the refit. 'With a young child in tow and the chance of a change of scenery for me, we came down for a week. While Matt worked at the big house, I fell in love with the Valley.'

'And you stayed.'

'We did, thanks to Mister Fenton. He offered Matt a full-time job as manager.' There was an excited glow to her face now.

23

As my second night in the Valley approached, the lack of fresh information on the whiteboard told me I had nothing. I needed a way to get to know the locals and was trying to work out how when there was a knock. Romeo barked as I opened the front door.

'Tilly, how's it going?'

'Good.' She was wearing a pair of those tight horsey trousers, boots and a hoodie.

I stepped onto the verandah. 'What can I do for you?' I asked as she underwent the mandatory puppy dog welcome.

'I'm selling tickets for the rural fireman's ball.' She held up two tickets after the dog had calmed down.

'Great stuff, when is it?' I asked, taking the tickets from her hand.

'Tomorrow night.'

'That soon?'

'Yep, I've been selling them for the last couple of weeks. Numbers are a bit down. There's a few left, so I thought it might be a great way for you to meet the locals.'

'Indeed, indeed.' I retrieved my wallet from the house and paid her the $10 each that was displayed on the tickets.

'It's always a great night—live music, a bit of bush dancing.'

'A hoedown?'

'Absolutely.' Her grin was as wide as the Valley.

'Well, thank you. Take a seat. Can I get you anything to drink?'

'Got a coke?' She sat on one of the outdoor chairs and stroked Romeo's head.

'Uhh … no.'

'Soft drink?'

'Uhh … no.'

'What have you got?'

'Tea, coffee, water.'

'I'm good, thanks.'

'Sorry, I need to stock up,' I said, also sitting.

'That's okay. So how are you getting on?'

'With the investigation, you mean?' I was assuming word had spread regarding my real reason for being in the Valley.

Tilly nodded.

'Not too good at the minute. In fact, I was just thinking of a way to meet the locals, and bugger me, these little beauties came from nowhere.' I held up the tickets.

'Have you spoken to Mister Fenton yet?'

'Kind of.' There was a pause as we stared out at nothing in particular. I sensed this was making her uncomfortable, so I broke the silence. 'While I've got you here, do you mind telling me what you know of Kathy Brown?'

'Sure. I got to know her quite well. She was … nice, but she was a troubled soul.'

'In what way?'

'She was a recovering alcoholic. And angry if you know what I mean?'

'Angry with anyone in particular?'

'Just the world it seemed.'

'Did she have anything against Fenton?'

'Oh yes. She hated him, but she …' Tilly frowned in thought. 'She seemed to have a power over him.'

'A power.'

'Yeah, and Jake. Almost like she had something over them.'

My mind was buzzing with questions, but I needed to be selective with the ones I threw at Tilly, remembering she was also a suspect. The revelation that Kathy Brown may have had something over the Fentons was an important piece of information. Could she have been blackmailing them, perhaps? 'What makes you say that?'

'Just a feeling I got. They avoided her at all costs.'

'Did she fit into the community?'

'No. She was always nice to me and Tom, but horrible to everyone else.'

'Even your mum?'

'Especially my mum!'

Hmm, interesting. 'Did she ever say anything to you, about anybody or …?'

'She said she was going to get even with the bastard that ruined her life!'

I'd studied the police reports and read all the interviews, but I didn't recall Tilly mentioning this in her statement. 'Did you tell the police about this?'

'No … I didn't think it was important at the time.' The slight blushing of the cheeks, the uncomfortable shuffle in the chair, the lack of eye contact were clear signs to an old detective that she was lying.

'Did you ever see her in an altercation with anyone in particular?'

'She was stirring the pot all the time. It was as if it was her mission to piss everyone off.'

'And was she? Pissing everyone off, I mean?'

'Oh yes. Even my dad.'

I'd yet to meet Matt Derby, so I hadn't had the chance to form an opinion of him yet. 'How did she do that?'

'She came to the house. I'd opened the door and immediately noticed that she was drunk or high. Some recovering alcoholic.'

'Was she aggro?'

Tilly nodded. 'Big time. Actually, can I get a drink of water?'

'Sure.' I rushed into the house.

Romeo jumped to his feet and wasn't sure whether to follow me or stay with our guest. He chose the latter.

I handed Tilly a glass of water then returned to my seat. 'So, she was angry about something. Was it directed solely at your dad?'

'No, she was going off at both my parents. She kept yelling that they owed her and that she was here to take back what was rightfully hers.'

'Do you have any idea what she meant?'

'No. Dad sent me to my room. She was still shouting, then it was suddenly Dad's voice that rose above hers. "Get the hell out of my house!" he yelled, and I heard a commotion as if he was physically throwing her out. She was screaming and shouting, "I'm going to get you for this!" She was swearing and carrying on.' Tilly took another sip of water.

'And when was this?'

She was shaking now and appeared to be close to tears. 'The day before …' A large tear suddenly rolled down her cheek. 'The day before I found her!'

Romeo whined and shuffled close to Tilly's legs as she cried.

Reaching into my pocket, I retrieved my handkerchief and handed it to her. 'Here you go, it's okay.'

'It's not okay.' She blew her nose. 'It's not okay because I didn't mention any of this to the police.'

'And why was that do you think?'

'I was protecting my dad.' She quickly finished the glass of water, placed it on the table and stood. 'I need to go, got a heap of assignments for uni.'

'Tilly, is there anything I should know about your dad?'

'What do you mean?' There was a defensive tone to her voice.

'I just need to know the facts, that's all.'

'My dad is the gentlest, kindest man you'll ever meet.'

'So, it was unusual for him to raise his voice the way he did against Kathy?'

'I'd never heard him shout like that before!'

'Do you have any idea what the argument was about?'

'No.' Shaking her head, she stepped off the verandah.

'Okay, sorry, I didn't mean to upset you. Thanks for the tickets.'

'That's all right. Who will you bring?'

'Uhm … good question.' Jenny immediately came to mind, but I recalled her telling me she was working late nights on the bikie case.

'Let me know if you can't get anyone and I'll set you up with one of my friends.' There was a slight grin, and I was glad to see she was no longer sad.

'Cool. See you tomorrow.'

My mind was whizzing as Romeo and I watched Tilly leave from the verandah. Although I knew it was Tilly who had found Kathy's strangled body, I purposely didn't press her about that specifically. There was no need. The police report had been quite thorough. But the altercation between Kathy and the Derbys was the first real information I'd received that wasn't included in the police reports. I understood she may have been worried about how this would have looked against her parents, but why was she telling me? Had she been carrying the guilt since the murder? Whatever had caused the altercation? And was it enough to have made Matt Derby go to Mary's Mansion in the dead of night and strangle Kathy Brown? I headed to the whiteboard. An update was required. I still only had the one picture—the headshot of Kathy. After studying it so closely, purely because I had nothing else to ruminate on, her troubled eyes seemed to follow me around the room.

It was a red-letter day in the life of Callum Murphy. There were three elements that woke him early that morning—the excitement of the first day's production at the mill, a need to rise from the wooden two-seater sofa he'd slept on, and the smell of frying bacon.

'Tis a big day, Callum Murphy,' Mary said when Callum joined her outside. She was carving doorstep slices from a loaf of bread.

'Aye,' Callum said, rubbing his eyes and yawning.

'We might need to build you up a bit, lad.' Using a makeshift table from a couple of planks, she spread a thick layer of butter on four slices of bread, threw on the bacon, dripping fat and all, and created two enormous sandwiches. 'Come on. Billie's already boiled.' The copper kettle was hanging over the fire that she'd stoked up from the night before.

They ate their breakfast in silence, swilling down strong Yorkshire tea.

Oy could get used to this, Callum thought as he sipped from his cup.

When they'd finished eating, Mary rose, stood at the edge of the verandah and gazed over the land as if she were surveying it. 'So, where will we build my digs?' she asked, thoughtfully.

'What's that?'

'My place. I'm going to need a place of my own.'

'You're moving out here?' Callum joined her.

'No ... I already have!'

'What?'

'Oh, was I forgetting to tell you?'

'Tell me what?'

'I'm your new partner. The McCarthy in the Murphy & McCarthy Sawmill, well that'll be me.'

'But your da is me partner.'

'Was … well, briefly.'

'You bought him out?'

'Na …' She returned to her seat, grinning. 'He gave it to me.'

Callum couldn't believe what he was hearing. His debt now belonged to Mary McCarthy. Was this a good thing, or a bad thing? He couldn't decide at that moment, but the thought of Mary sticking around excited him. 'So, he just gave it to you?'

'No.' She casually sipped her tea as if enjoying his confusion. 'I took it.'

Mary was a hard woman who could control a crew of rough sawyers like children at a Sunday school picnic. She was beautiful too and Callum suspected she'd be comfortable in any environment, whether it be buying land or livestock at an auction, making a speech at the local land titles office, or telling filthy jokes while downing pints of malt with the workers. Yes, all these things excited Callum Murphy, and he liked the feeling. Rising to his feet, he leaned in and whispered, 'Who said Oy need a partner?'

'I do.' She put down her cup, stood and stepped so close to him that their noses almost touched. 'Now, where are you going to build me feckin house?'

There was a pause as they looked into each other's eyes as if they were both searching for a higher ground. And then it happened. Their lips touched.

Callum put his arms around her waist and gently pulled her in closer. They kissed, long and slow.

'About time you made a move,' Mary said as their lips parted. 'I was beginning to think you was a pansy!'

Callum chuckled and went to kiss her again, but she pulled away.

'There'll be time for that later,' Mary said. 'But for now, we've got a sawmill to run.'

'Aye, but we've already completed one task.'

'And what might that be?'

'We've found you a hut.' He pointed with a nod to his cottage.

Mary grinned. 'Didn't you know I'd already moved in?'

Callum reached up, cradled her chin, then kissed her again. 'Oy bloody do now.'

More minor tweaking to the machinery, mainly adjustments to pulley tensions and steam pressure, didn't hamper the first day's production. Callum's ambitious target was reached easily and made him realise he'd underestimated the output. This was a significant result. Logs had been cut and stacked ready for ripping for a few weeks now, so there was plenty of work. Fresh ones were arriving all the time via the river. It meant the business hit the ground running from day one.

Callum hadn't expected to be sharing his office at the side of the mill with anyone, but he gladly made room for Mary. From the moment she stepped into the small shack, she was all business. As too was Callum. They would oversee the running of the operation together. Once more, the anticipation of what was to come excited Callum in a way he'd never experienced before. He'd always known that running his own sawmill would be hard work, but it was as if the burden had been lifted, or at least eased before it even started, thanks to Mary. As they worked together side-by-side, he couldn't help but keep side glancing to steal a look whenever he got the chance. After years of hard work to get to this point, the future had always been a positive place in Callum's mind, but now it was paradise.

On that first day, the sawmill remained operational until dusk. Men returned to their huts after a twelve-hour shift, hot and weary but with a sense of being a part of something great. Callum had also built a canteen area that was an open-walled structure, like the mill itself but only smaller. There, his workers could enjoy a cold beer after work and were provided with a good hearty meal. Callum knew the mill was nothing without good reliable men to run it. Mary was right when she'd said they were their biggest asset, so he'd do everything in his power to look after them.

That night, Callum and Mary strolled back to the cabin in silence, exhausted, not from physical work, but from the mental strains of the day. Callum was nervous. He'd never actually been with a woman that he cared about, and he wasn't sure what was required of him. Because of her uncharacteristic reserve, he sensed Mary was a little nervous too.

'So, Oy've changed my mind. Oy'm thinking we'll build you a cottage over there in the trees, as far away from me as possible,' Callum said, breaking the awkward silence.

'No that's where the chicken house is going,' Mary replied matter-of-factly. 'Perhaps if we build a doghouse on the other side, *you* can sleep there.'

When they reached the cabin, Callum took charge and held out his hand. 'Come, my lady.'

Mary took it and allowed him to lead her into the house.

25

The Friday night footy was a tradition that was ingrained in us blokes as much as surfing was. The fact that sitting on the couch in the man shed, feet up on the coffee table, cold beer in one hand, and scooping up Nobby's nuts with the other was a thing of the past, hadn't quite sunk in yet, and I doubted it would for some time. It was strange not being able to just waltz into the house on Ruby Street, kick off the work clothes and relax in a pair of boardies and thongs. They say you should be careful what you wish for. I'd been thinking about changing my ways for the last couple of years, but whether I would have actually done it or not was another matter. I guess the universe decided for me—or at least Sandy Fullerton did. But regardless, the footy would remain, it would just need to be the venue that changed.

I'd arranged to meet Elvis at Burleigh Town Tavern. The one thing I didn't like about living out in the Valley was that you couldn't walk anywhere. Living at Kirra Beach, I'd been used to the luxury of strolling to pretty much anywhere I wanted to go—the pub, the movies in Coolangatta, the supermarket, and of course the beach. So now I had to drive, which meant there wouldn't be too much drinking involved. Perhaps that was a good thing.

I'd spent the afternoon cleaning out the chicken coop. It looked as if it hadn't housed any chooks for quite some time. It was clean, just dusty, and the chicken wire run was sound.

Romeo's bed fit nicely inside the coop. As I laboured, he watched me with mournful eyes as if he knew exactly what was happening. I spoke to him as I worked. 'You're going to love it in here, mate. Your own little penthouse.'

Later, when I was ready to go out, Romeo reluctantly followed me into the back yard. My arms were laden with his toys, his water bowl and another fresh bone from the butcher. 'Come on, mate,' I called to him from the coop after putting everything in place.

He sat down in the middle of the yard.

'Look at what I got you.' I held up the juicy marrow bone. Normally, the dog would kill for his favourite treat. 'Oh, righto then, if you don't want it, I'll have it.' Holding up the bone in front of my face, I pretended to tear at it with my teeth. 'Hmm, lovely.'

He still didn't budge.

'What's the matter, Romey?' I asked after climbing from the coop and kneeling beside him.

He nudged up close to me and whined.

'If you weren't such a destructive little bugger, you could stay in the house.' I lifted him and carried him to the coop. As if realising he was doomed, he went limp in my arms. 'There you go. Look how good this is,' I said, placing him on his bed.

He scanned his surroundings then sniffed the bone.

'Lord of the manner.' Backing out of the tiny shed, I left the door ajar. There was a smaller opening in the wall, which he could enter and exit into the run at will, but I didn't want to lock him in. Was I experiencing the same feeling a parent does when leaving their child at kindy for the first time? 'See you, mate.' I waved, but he ignored me. 'Won't be too long, buddy.'

The carpark at Burleigh Town Tavern was huge, so even though there were quite a few cars and tradies' utes, it wasn't full. I turned in off the side street and swung the Dub into a spot close to the public bar entrance. As I walked towards the glass doors, I could already see Elvis sitting alone at the bar, nursing a beer. For some stupid reason, the sight of him made me feel a little sad. 'G'day, mate,' I said, coming up behind him.

He swung around on the bar stool, jumped down and hugged me like he hadn't seen me for years. 'Scotty, me old mate. How the hell are you?'

'I'm good, champ. What's up?'

'Nothing, why? Just happy to see you. Two more of these please, darl,' he called out to the barmaid, pointing to his half empty beer.

'You look like somebody just died,' I said, taking the stool next to his.

'Feels like that at home.' He finished his beer in one gulp. 'It's not the same, eh? What with you moving out and Tetley being in the UK.'

'You've got Sandy.' My attempt at reassurance sounded lame.

'Yeah, I know.' This brought a little smile to his face. 'It's just not the same though.'

'I know.'

The waitress placed two schooners in front of us.

We chit chatted but had little to say. That usual Friday night excitement for the footy, and the anticipation for the weekend ahead, was gone. I shared with him my lack of progress with the case. He told me about a new client he'd snagged, and the Tuesday night trivia at North Kirra Surf Club that Sandy had insisted they make a weekly event. Elvis didn't seem too enthusiastic.

Kick-off between the Gold Coast Suns and Collingwood was still fifteen minutes away. Then something happened that I'd never experienced before with my best mate, Elvis. An awkward silence.

There was a tap on my shoulder. Turning, I was greeted by the smiling faces of Jenny and Detective Inspector Dale Mason. 'Hey, guys, how's it going?' I said sliding from my stool. 'Good to see you, Dale,' I said, shaking my old police buddy's hand.

'Good to see you too, Scotty.'

'You remember Elvis?'

Elvis shook Dale's hand. They knew each other well after many a night's drinking in the man shed.

'Listen, I'll get seats over there, Scotty,' Elvis said, also sliding off his stool and heading for a table closer to one of the TVs.

'Yeah, no worries.'

'Is he okay?' Jenny said as we watched him mope away.

'Yeah, he's good.'

'He doesn't look good. I've never seen him look this flat before,' Dale said.

'He's become a product of domestic bliss,' I said, half joking. 'Anyway, this is a surprise, you two showing up.'

'We can't stay, still on duty, but I thought it might be good for you two to get together,' Jenny said. 'Dale worked the original case with Des Williams.'

'Great!' I was genuinely excited. A chat with Dale was on my 'things to do' list. Jenny had saved me a trip to Surfers Paradise.

'I'm going to see what's up with Elvis,' Jenny said, leaving us.

'So, I've been meaning to come and see you, Dale.'

'Thought you would.'

'As you probably know, I've been asked to look into the Kathy Brown case. Can I get you a drink?'

'No, that's fine, mate. Look, to be honest, everything was pretty much in the report.'

We stood at the bar, me with a beer in hand. 'So, you worked on the case with old Des?'

Dale nodded. 'Yep.'

'But there was never a conviction?'

'Never any proof.'

'But you know who did it?'

'Oh yeah, well. We narrowed it down to two prime suspects.'

'Who?'

'Fenton or his son!'

'Really?'

'They're slippery characters, mate. You'll need to keep a close eye on them.'

Jenny and Dale left as the game began. I was distracted by Dale's comments. Side glancing Elvis, I could see he was distracted too. 'Are you sure you're all right, mate?'

He tried to brush away my question with a not so reassuring shrug, 'Yeah.'

'I don't think you are!'

'Leave it, Scotty, eh?'

Unlike a cat, dogs cannot control their emotions, and as much as Romeo was pissed off with me for leaving him, and would have liked to have played the 'oh you're home then' card, his excitement let him down badly. When I opened the gate to the chicken run, he dived into my arms and covered me in puppy kisses.

We settled down to our second night in Mary's Mansion. I have to admit I wasn't looking forward to it. Lying in my bed, I could see the whiteboard in the corner, more specifically the picture of Kathy Brown, looking back at me. Seeing it every day, the face had become very familiar.

Surprisingly, Romeo settled straight down and fell asleep. He had this cute little snore and every now and again, he'd bark and whine as if he were dreaming.

It equally surprised me when a sudden noise outside didn't wake him. I sat bolt upright in bed. The sound I'd heard was as if someone had stepped onto the front verandah. Climbing out of bed, I crept to the front door and listened. There it was again. Definite footsteps on the creaky timber deck. Wearing only my jocks, I opened the front door and was immediately riveted to the spot. My body froze, my chest constricted, and my eyes bulged wide. Then I realised I must have been dreaming, because I was standing face to face with Kathy Brown.

<h1 style="text-align:center">26</h1>

It was the face I'd studied every day for the last week. Blonde hair, blue eyes, chiselled cheek bones. We stood in silence, just staring at each other. If I had been capable of logical thought at that moment, I would have deduced that I was dreaming or I'd lost my mind. When I'd opened the door, the night had fallen silent as if every critter was watching. I realised I was still shaking. Was I about to have a conversation with a ghost?

It was Romeo who broke the silence. They say dogs are intuitive and capable of seeing things that the human eye can't. Well, he saw her too. He'd woken, pushed past me, bounded out on to the verandah and jumped up her leg.

Kathy's icy stare broke into a smile as she leaned down and made a fuss of him. 'G'day, mate!'

Incapable of forming words, my brain was struggling to comprehend the situation.

Kathy looked up at me and casually said, 'I'm sorry to bother you so late.'

'Uhm …'

'He's a lovely fellow but I don't recall you mentioning a pet on your lease application.'

'Uhm … what's going on?'

She stood up and held out her hand. 'I'm Abigail Brown. Abi.'

I shook her hand. It was still warm from the friction of Romey's fur.

'I'm your landlord.'

'Abigail?'

'Abi.'

'Landlord?'

'I realise I shouldn't have just shown up, but I didn't think you were moving in until Sunday.'

'But you're …'

'I'm what?'

'You're Kathy Brown!'

'Oh bloody hell, I'm sorry. Now I understand why you look like you've just seen a ghost.

I'm Kathy's sister.'

I suddenly realised I was holding my breath and exhaled with a burst of air. 'Fuck me dead, I thought I was losing my mind there for a minute.'

Abi laughed. 'I can imagine, I'm so sorry.'

'Why would you be here so late?' I checked my watch it was 11.30 pm.

'I've come down from Brisbane. Didn't get away until late. I didn't expect you to be here yet. The plan was to give the old place a bit of a clean before you arrived.'

'Right, well, you better come in, I suppose.' I opened the door and stepped backwards.

'No, that's okay. I'll find a hotel in Burleigh for the night.'

'That's probably a good idea, but I'm awake. Did you want a coffee or something?' I'd forgotten Kathy had a sister. I needed to talk to this girl.

'Okay, that'll be nice.' She stepped cautiously into the house and closed the door behind her.

Romeo was jostling for her attention, which she gave to him while I slipped into the bedroom and put on a T-shirt and shorts.

'Tea or coffee?' I asked after flicking on the jug.

'Tea, please. Black, no sugar.'

'So, you own this place?' I asked as I industriously went about my task.

'Yes, Kathy left it to me in her will.'

'Right. I'm sorry for your loss, by the way. It must be hard.'

Abi sat on the sofa and continued to fulfil Romeo's desires. 'Yes, it was a terrible shock.'

The jug boiled. I made two mugs of tea and handed one to Abi. 'That's enough, Romey. He'll have you doing that all night.'

The dog was lying on the floor with his back legs in the air, allowing his tummy to be massaged.

'That's okay, he's a cutie.' She attempted to sip her tea but realised it was too hot. 'So, you're Scotty Stephens.'

'Guilty as charged, I'm afraid.'

'And why are you here?'

Should I be open and upfront or claim that I was just here having a break? The latter option sounded lame, and it was. 'I'm here to investigate Kathy's death.'

'Right, I thought so.' She hazarded a small sip of hot tea.

'Does that bother you?'

Abi shrugged. 'No. The opposite actually. But didn't I read that you'd quit the police force?'

'Yeah, that's right. I'm a private detective now.'

'Wow! How's that going for you?'

Did I detect an air of cynicism in her tone? 'This is actually my first case, but—'

'Your first case?'

'Yep.'

The tea was cooling and allowing her to take longer sips. 'So, what are you going to do that's so different to the police?'

'Keep an open mind for a start.'

'And what have you found so far?'

My face grew hot and I realised I was blushing. 'Not a lot. But I'm only just getting started.'

'Right.'

There was an awkward pause and we both looked into our cups.

Abi placed her mug on the coffee table. 'I didn't know my sister that well. She was sent away from home at fourteen. She never got on with my father.'

'Would you say she was a bit of a rebel? Or …?'

'Oh yeah, always was. Mum died when we were young. Dad provided for us girls well, but it was like Kathy was just a lost soul, you know? She was never happy.'

'Did your dad ever hit her?'

'God no, nothing like that. It broke his heart to see how she'd turned out.'

'Turned out?'

'After a year of her living in Sydney, we went up to visit and boy had she changed.'

'Changed in what way?' I was using a gentle, friendly tone— pure detective textbook.

'Her appearance mainly. She'd always been the angry victim, but it was as if her physical appearance had adapted to match her mindset.'

My mild frown was a prompt for her to continue.

'Homemade tattoos. Dyed red hair, growing out at the roots. The clothes, her attitude. She looked like a cheap prostitute.'

Perhaps she was a cheap prostitute, my inner voice said.

'But she was so angry, picking fights with Dad.'

'But you two were close?'

'Not really. I was surprised when I learned she'd left me everything. She'd only changed her will the day before she died. Did you know that?'

I didn't know that. 'When was the last time you saw her?'

'A couple of months before her death. We reconnected after all those years and I travelled up to Brisbane to meet her.'

Also on my list of things to do was a trip up to Brisbane to speak to the people who knew Kathy. I checked my watch. 'It's late. Why don't you stay here tonight?'

'No, I couldn't impose.'

'I insist.' Looking down at my dog, who was still lying on his back with his legs splayed, I added, 'Romeo insists!'

She finally and reluctantly agreed to stay the night only if she could sleep on the couch, and only if Romeo remained with her for protection.

'Protection?'

'Of course. You do know this place is haunted, right?'

I wasn't sure if she was joking.

'You know the ghost of Callum Murphy paces the house at night?'

'That's ridiculous!'

'Is it?'

27

I woke the next morning to find the house empty. No Abigail, no Romeo. There were two possible scenarios—a woman I didn't know, whom I'd let stay in my place overnight, had taken off with my dog, or she'd woken early and gone for a walk, taking Romeo with her. I suspected the latter, hoped for it anyway. Finally, I had an opportunity to learn more about Kathy, so after pouring a bowl of cornflakes and planting myself down on the back verandah, I waited patiently.

Ten minutes later, I heard the unmistakable sound of Romeo's bark. A little time later, he came tearing through the trees with a giggling Abi not far behind. When he hit the open patch of ground, he saw me and bolted towards the verandah.

'Steady on, boy,' I said as he greeted me.

After a quick fuss, he dived into the bowl of water I'd placed in the shade.

'Good morning. I didn't want to wake you, so I took Romeo for a walk. I hope that's okay?' Abi said, stepping onto the verandah.

'Yeah, no worries.' Although she was the image of her sister, but with smoother edges, she also reminded me of someone else, someone more familiar. 'Fancy a cuppa?'

'Sure. Thanks.'

Before I entered the house, I said, 'I've got some bacon left over if you want a butty?' I'd done a shop the day before.

'No thanks, I'm vegetarian.'

'Oh right. Cornflakes.'

'Toast?'

'No worries.'

I filled the jug and dropped a couple of slices of Tip Top into the toaster. 'So, how long have you been a veggie?' I asked, returning to the back verandah.

'Ten years, give or take.'

'Don't you miss bacon?'

She shrugged and pulled a non-committal face.

The sound of the toaster flipping lured me back into the house. I returned momentarily, laden with a mug of tea and toast on a plate. 'Seeing as you're a veggie, I'm guessing *Veggie*-mite is okay?'

'Sure.'

I produced a small jar of the stuff from my pocket. 'Go for your life.'

As Abi spread a generous layer of the bitter-tasting brown stuff on her toast, I returned to my seat. 'So, as I was saying last night, Ben Fisher has hired me to look into the case.' I wasn't sure what kind of reaction I'd receive from her. I'd only kind of mentioned it the previous night, but she hadn't shown too much interest.

'That's good, I'm glad.' Her worried expression told me otherwise. She took a bite of toast and looked away.

'Are you though?'

'I am but …' She continued to chew while peering out at the trees. 'I'm just a bit concerned you're working for Fisher.'

'Concerned why?'

'I'm worried that him and his bullshit will distract your focus.' She rose from her chair and continued to avoid eye contact. 'I mean, who cares if he stole the story or not? Is that really more important than finding Kathy's killer?'

It was a line of thought I was adopting myself since first meeting Fisher. After studying the case, I was surprised it was so easily put on the back burner before eventually being closed all together. The mystery of the crime was attracting more attention from my inquisitive detective mind than whether or not Fisher nicked the story for his book. 'I know what you mean, and that's exactly what I've decided to do.'

'What?'

'Find out who killed Kathy and bring them to justice.'

She swung round to face me. The solemn expression was gone. In its place was a wide smile. 'Really?'

'My oath.'

'Oh, Scott, you don't know what this means to me.' She sat back down and lifted her mug of tea. 'It's been so hard over the last five years knowing that the person who killed my sister is still out there.'

'I bet.'

'Nobody seemed to care about Kathy, you know?'

'What can you tell me about her?'

'Well …' She took a sip of tea then continued to nibble on a slice of toast. 'She was two years older than me. She was smart, very smart. So much so that she was unruly throughout her school life. The school psychologist determined that this was because she was actually more intelligent than the teachers, so her lack of stimulation was having a negative effect on her.'

'In what way?'

'At first she became rebellious, but as she got older her behaviour manifested into delinquency and even self-harm.'

'I see.'

'But she was a beautiful person deep down. Only I knew that though. She was very protective of her little sister, always looking out for me, but when she was expelled from school and sent to Sydney, it was as if she forgot all about me. Then she ran away.'

'So how often did you see her since then?'

'Just the once, a few months before she died. I came up to Brisbane to stay with her for a couple of weeks.'

'You tracked her down or …?'

'No, it was the other way around. She called me out of the blue.'

'And how was she?'

'Unbelievable. Not what I'd expected at all. Successful. She owned the nightclub and the house in Brisbane. But there was still that underlying sense that she could explode. Like a sleeping volcano, you know?'

I did know. I'd come into contact with enough addicts during my time in the police force to know how they operated. They could be experts at making people think everything was okay when there was really a raging tempest inside, and everything was far from okay. 'Was she ever aggressive towards you?'

'No. She was charming, smart and funny. She lived in a house on the river in East Brisbane.'

'Sounds expensive.'

'It was.'

28

'So, when will you build me my house?' Mary said as she watched from the back verandah.

'What?' Frowning, Callum turned from the fire. He had insisted on making the breakfast that morning. 'But Oy thought...?' His body ached, and not completely from the previous day's labour.

'You thought what, Mister Murphy?'

'Well, Oy thought we said you'd stay here with me.'

'Aye.'

Callum carried over a plate of black crispy bacon and slices of hardened bread from yesterday's loaf.

'Bloody hell, man. So, you need a cook, is that what you're asking me?'

'Aye … no … no Oy thought you'd be moving in here.'

'Aye. But this isn't a house befitting the owners of a profitable sawmill.' She laid a couple of rashers of bacon between two slices of bread and took a bite.

'You want a new house?' Callum asked. It made sense. He'd never actually thought that much about settling down before but if he was going to be the squire, he'd need a homestead. And if he was going to be a husband to Mary McCarthy, then in the tradition of a good Catholic family, there'd be lots of children.

'Of course. I've already picked out the block.'

'You have?'

'Aye. I'll show you later today.'

'So, will you then?' Callum lifted a rasher of bacon and took a nervous bite.

'Will I what?'

'Will you be me missus?'

Mary laughed. 'By Christ, Callum Murphy, you're going to have to work on your romantic approach.'

'Aye. Will you be me cook then?'

Mary threw down her sandwich, put her arms around his neck and kissed him. 'Aye … I bloody well will.'

Even with the trees cleared, the raised site that Mary took Callum to was just out of view of the mill. The block was flat and would take advantage of the southerly breezes. The house would be built with a northerly aspect enjoying not only a 360-degree breathtaking view of the Valley, but also a glimpse of the ocean.

Callum admired Mary's intelligence and gusto. This was the exact spot he'd earmarked for a possible future home when he'd first purchased the land. 'You picked well, Mary,' Callum said, peering out at the view.

'Aye. Mary knows. I've already spoken to Jimmy P. He's going to organise the work right away.'

'If Oy'd be thinking with me head instead of with me balls, Oy'd be thinking you came here with an agenda, Mary McCarthy.'

Mary laughed. 'The things a girl will do to get a house of her own, eh.'

'Aye, you're a wee hussy, that's for sure.'

The nearest Catholic church was a day's ride away in Beenleigh. Worship in the Valley was usually short private ceremonies carried out by families at their homes. Callum, although not a religious man, and certainly not game to point out the fact that they were living together was a sin, respected his future wife's beliefs and joined her in prayer on Sunday mornings.

Later, with the sawmill closed for the day of rest, they sat out on the back verandah. 'Oy have a little job to do,' Callum announced.

'On a Sunday?' Mary quizzed.

'Aye, nothing to do with work though. Shan't be long.' Callum kept a bag of tools under the house. He retrieved it and disappeared into the trees.

Over the next hour, Mary, allowing the sun to caress her face and legs, heard some light hammering, what sounded like hand sanding, and a little bit of cussing.

'Keep your eyes closed,' Callum said, appearing from the trees. Mary did as she was asked but continued to listen.

Callum went around the front of the house and stepped up onto the verandah. After more hammering, he reappeared around the back. 'Okay, Madam. If you'd like to come this way.' He held out his hand.

Mary took it and was led to the front of the house.

'Close your eyes again, Mary McCarthy,' Callum said before they reached the front. She did as she was told, allowing Callum to guide her onto the verandah.

. 'Okay, you can open your eyes now.'

Mary's face lit up when she beheld the object of Callum's labour. 'I feckin love it!' she exclaimed, threw her arms around his neck and kissed him.

'Tis befitting me thinks,' Callum joked. Over the front door hung a handmade sign he'd fashioned from a plank of iron bark timber. Chiselled into it were the words, 'Mary's Mansion'.

A month later, they were married on the cleared site that would become their future home. Father Michael McGuinness had travelled down from Beenleigh to conduct the ceremony. The workers were given the day off to attend the wedding, after which they would enjoy free beer and food supplied by their bosses.

When Patrick McCarthy and his wife had arrived the day before the wedding from Murwillumbah, Callum had insisted they stay in the cottage with Mary. After an evening entertaining his guests, he retired to Jimmy P's house on the other side of the property where he would spend the night, remaining out of sight of the bride, until the ceremony.

On the morning of 10 August 1869, blue skies and sunshine with a slight chill heralded a typical winter's day in South East Queensland. Being careful to remain out of sight of the cottage, Callum began the day with a trek up to the highest point of the property—the ridge that would later be known as Callum's Lookout. Carrying a bucket of water, a shovel and a large hessian sack over his shoulder, he was on a mission. Secret pre-preparation had insured that his task only took about an hour. He was back at Jimmy's in time for a hot bath and his last hearty breakfast as a single man.

'You're a lucky man, Callum Murphy.' Jimmy said as he sat on the verandah smoking a clay pipe.

Callum was in the tin bath rubbing soap into his chin ready for a shave. 'Aye. Oy know it.'

'Always have been.' Jimmy gazed into the distance as if it were the stage of a theatre. 'I remember when I first met you on the *Great Britain*. You told me then that you were going places.'

'Aye.'

'And you was right. Look at what you've achieved, Callum. And this is only the beginning.'

'Aye.'

'In only a matter of weeks we're already one of the largest producers of sawn cedar in the southeast.'

Although the southeast industry of the relatively new formed state of Queensland was still small in comparison to the more established Northern New South Wales region of the Tweed Shire, the rising cost of lumber, due to the declining availability of red cedar, meant even Callum couldn't have predicted his rise in fortune.

'It's as much down to Mary as me though. Mary knows.'

'Mary is a massive asset; I'll give you that. But it was your vision, Callum. And you're the one the men look up to.'

'Thank you.'

Jimmy tapped his pipe on the arm of his chair, then leaned in. 'There is something I need to discuss with you, though.'

Callum frowned as he gently ran a cut-throat blade over his chin. 'Fenton.'

'Ron Fenton, The Rat?' Callum remembered Fenton's vow of revenge aboard the *Great Britain*. 'What about him?'

'He's on the Coast.'

Callum shrugged and continued to shave. 'Aye, Oy heard. Runs a team of getters in the Tweed.'

'More than that. Much more. He's got a huge crew together by all accounts.'

The information was of no interest to Callum.

'Apparently, he's made a large purchase in Currumbin.'

This made Callum physically jolt, almost cutting his cheek. 'What?'

Jimmy lowered his voice. 'Word is he'll be opening up a sawmill too.'

'But how?' Oy've been trying to purchase that land for the last year.' The 400-hectare parcel of cedar rich high ground in the adjacent valley had been up for tender for some time.

'I know. It's just a rumour, but you know what they say about rumours.'

'Aye, but if it's true, how the hell did that snide little weasel get his hands on that land?'

'I'm sure we'll find out very soon.' Jimmy stood and handed Callum a towel. 'Come on or you'll be late for your wedding.'

The ceremony was a beautiful occasion. The bride and groom stood side-by-side atop the house clearing surrounded by an army of Sunday-best scrubbed workers, family and friends. When Father McGuiness finally said, 'I now pronounce you husband and wife.'

The men gave a loud cheer and as the couple kissed, they hip-hip-hoorayed then threw their hats into the air. It would be a memorable day for everyone present, that was for sure.

The festivities continued long after the couple left the party. Bidding farewell to their guests, Callum and Mary strolled back to the hut, hand in hand.

'Are you kidding me, Callum McCarthy?' Callum grinned as he shook his head.

'You want me to climb up there in me wedding frock?'

'Aye, come on.' He took her hand and led her through the trees and up towards the bluff. At the top, the full moon shone like daylight.

Mary smiled when she saw the object of Callum's secrecy. In the centre of the small clearing was a bench made from stone boulders and held together by cement. 'You made this?'

'Aye.' Callum led her to the side of the bench, knelt and pointed to an inscription he'd etched into the cement. *Callum loves Mary!*

'Arr, you're a big softy, Callum Murphy. Do you know that?'

'Aye …'

29

We sat on the verandah for most of the morning, just talking. And although I had an agenda, I was actually enjoying Abi's company. She told me about her parents. Her father worked for Adelaide City Council. She remembered little, or the memories were too painful, about her mother who had died when Abi was only ten. The information she shared about her sister was mostly from their childhood, because she didn't get to know the adult version of Kathy. But it was their meeting later in life that interested me the most. According to her ATO records, Kathy Brown had been working as a barmaid in a club in Fortitude Valley. She was earning a minimum wage, but then her situation changed almost overnight around twenty-years ago when she became the owner of the Panda Club and purchased the house in Brisbane. Without backers, there was no way she could have managed this transition on her barmaid salary.

I needed to squeeze as much information from Abi's memory as possible about the last time they met because I'm sure there was something there that everyone else had missed. 'Would you say Kathy was bitter?'

'Oh yes, her entire life,' Abi replied. 'Right from an early age. Our upbringing may have been quite strict, but we had a good childhood. Kathy was never really happy, though. Even on those Christmas mornings when we were spoiled rotten, she'd sulk as she nonchalantly opened her presents, uninterested, showing no thanks or excitement. She'd just kind of play the whole thing down as if being happy was beneath her. She was the same at birthdays and any other time that would usually bring excitement to a young girl.'

'Was she depressed?'

'I suppose so. We didn't really know about such things back then.'

'Tell me about your dad. You said he was quite strict.'

'Strict yes, but he loved us girls. He became kind of religious after Mum passed.'

'And this made Kathy … angry?'

'Kathy was angry at everything.'

'How was she towards you?'

She replied slowly as if she were choosing her words. 'Protective. She cared about me, that was for sure.'

'Was she ever jealous of you?'

'No! It was me that was jealous of her!'

By the time lunchtime arrived, I'd not only learned a great deal about Kathy and her family, but I got to know Abigail Brown too. She was a Year 8 teacher in Brisbane, recently out of a long-term relationship, but never married. I didn't push too much regarding the details of her past love life, but I was happy to hear she was currently single.

Then I had an idea.

'Hey, do you have to rush back to Brisbane?' I asked with a little more excitement in my tone than I'd expected.

'Not really, why?'

'It's the fireman's ball tonight and I've got two tickets!'

Abi laughed out loud. 'The fireman's ball?'

I nodded eagerly.

'Are you asking me out?'

'I'm inviting you to the ball, Princess.'

'Then I accept. Only … bugger I brought nothing to wear.'

'It's a bush ball, darl, flannel and jeans, I'm guessing.'

We chuckled, and it felt good.

'Don't even have that, though. I was expecting to head back to Brisbane today.' 'No worries, we could always go to Robina this arvo.'

She thought about this for a moment. 'Means I'd probably have to stay another night.'

'Cool. I was thinking of getting an inflatable bed for guests anyway. May as well get one today.'

'Are you sure you don't mind?'

'Positive. It'll be a pleasant distraction.'

We wandered around Robina Town Centre, an expansive shopping centre that was built during the nineties on what was once the vast Kerrydale dairy farm.

The first stop was lunch in the food court. We enjoyed authentic Mexican tucker from Guzman y Gomez. This was followed by at least three circuits of the mall, which included me waiting outside every woman's clothing store in the place, while Abi browsed the racks inside. After a couple of hours trying on clothes in every store, we ended up in the first one we'd visited. Abi purchased a pair of Levi jeans and a flannel shirt.

As we drove home in the Dub, Abi suddenly declared. 'I need boots!'

'Boots?'

'I can't go to a hoedown without boots.'

She had a point. The beige sandals she wore would hardly go with the tough cowgirl look, but I wasn't about to turn back and do another lap of the mall. 'What do you want to do?'

Abi frowned deeply for a moment then her face suddenly lit up. 'I know, I'm sure Tilly will have a pair I can borrow.'

'You know Tilly?' The traffic was chocker at the roundabout just before the M1 entrance, and I guessed the highway would be the same down to the West Burleigh exit.

'Yeah, she's a lovely girl. I met her the first time I came to look at the cottage, and on consequent visits we got to know each other.'

'And the parents?'

'Standoffish towards me for some reason, but they've certainly brought up a level-headed young woman.'

I was right. Because of the upgrade between Varsity Lakes and Tugun, the highway was bumper to bumper. The usual trip of fifteen minutes took around thirty. When we finally got back to Mary's Mansion, it was late afternoon. I'd brought more groceries while we were out too, as well as an inflatable bed from Kmart. When everything was put away, we retired to the back verandah and while I inflated the bed with a foot pump, Abi got a couple of cold beers from the fridge and joined me.

'So have you ever been to a fireman's ball before?' She asked after taking a swig of beer.

'Can't say I have, you?'

30

I didn't have any boots either, so my Adidas runners would have to do. And neither of us had an Akubra. I guess I hadn't given the occasion much thought. While I showered and dressed, Abi was out the back talking on her phone. About fifteen minutes later, Tilly appeared bearing gifts.

'Here you go.' She skimmed an Akubra in my direction. 'But wait, there's more.' From behind her back she produced two pairs of cowboy boots. 'I'm thinking you're about a nine?' She handed me the largest pair. 'They're my dad's, so I'll need them back.' Then she gave the other pair to Abi. 'And these are my spares.'

I put on the hat, pulled on the boots, and stood.

'Bloody hell, it's Alan Jackson!' Abi declared.

'The Jackson Five?' I knew absolutely nothing about country music.

Tilly excused herself and dashed away.

It was just about impossible to get a cab out in the Valley, especially on a Saturday night. Neither of us wanted to drive, so I called an Uber. Ten minutes later, we were sitting in the back of a Toyota Camry getting the life story of the semi-retired driver called Ray. The trip to Tallebudgera Community Centre was literally two minutes. By the time we arrived, the car park was already full, the lights from the building were blazing, and we could hear music from the live bush band.

'Cheers, Ray. I hope everything works out for you,' I said as I climbed from the back of the car.

'Thanks Scotty.' He knew me and I was grateful that he talked about himself instead of asking me about the X case, as most people did.

Abi placed her arm in mine as we approached the entrance. 'Ready partner?'

'Yee haa.'

The building was a simple hall. The swirling laser lights, bouncing and exploding, meant there was no longer a need to decorate a room. There were no garlands, just a disco ball and strategically placed lasers aimed at it from the four corners. The band looked as if they'd been shipped in from Tennessee. Wearing the mandatory flannel shirts, jeans, cowboy boots, and Akubra hats, the lead singer, who also played the banjo, sported a lumberjack beard and John Lennon style glasses.

Just inside the door was a table. Seated behind it were two women, one I recognised as Pam Derby. 'Hey, look at you two,' she said, smiling as she took our tickets.

'Hi Pam,' Abi said. 'You've met, Scotty?'

'Yes I have,' Pam said.

I tipped my hat John Wayne style. 'Ladies.'

Pam introduced the other woman as Jan Patterson. She and her husband owned the dairy farm on the other side of Mary's Mansion.

There was a queue behind us, so we didn't linger at the doorway for too long. When we entered the hall, Tilly came straight over to greet us. 'Hey guys, thanks for coming.' She was holding a wad of raffle tickets and a pint mug a quarter filled with coins and notes.

'Thanks for inviting us,' I said. It felt good to be a part of a community. The night was in aid of the State Emergency Service (SES) and the great work this bunch of volunteers do year-round, protecting the hinterland from the threat of bushfire. They were bloody legends, and I didn't mind putting my hand in my pocket and purchasing a full book of tickets.

'Thanks Scotty, that's very generous,' Tilly said, taking my money and throwing it into the glass.

Not to be outdone, Abi also purchased a book. 'Right, where's the bar?' she said. The question was rhetorical, the bar was at the end of a long queue to the side of the room.

We joined the line. The guy in front of us turned and broke into a smile. 'Scotty Stephens, it's an honour to meet you.'

I shook his hand.

'I'm Matt, Matt Derby.'

'Oh right, Tilly's dad.'

'That's right.' He completely ignored Abi.

'This is Abi.'

His expression cooled as he side glanced Abi. 'Yes, we've met.' There was a forced smile and a nod.

Abi's reaction was almost identical.

The queue was moving slowly. There was only one girl serving behind the bar.

'So, what brings you to this neck of the woods, Scott?' Matt asked. 'I thought you were a beach bum.'

'I am, mate. Got salt water in me veins.'

'Just fancied a break?'

'No, I'm actually working.'

Matt frowned and tilted his head to one side. 'I thought you quit the police force?'

'I did. I'm working as a private detective now.'

The line moved forward but Matt remained planted to the spot. He frowned and squinted in my direction. 'So, what would there be to do out here?'

'I'm working for Ben Fisher.'

'The writer?'

Part of me wanted to remain on the good side of Matt Derby but I if needed to press some buttons to get answers, then so be it. 'I'm here to find the killer of Kathy Brown.'

Abi looked away.

Matt's expression hardened. 'Why?'

'Justice of course. Why wouldn't anyone want that?'

'Because you're going to be opening up old wounds. We've already been dragged through the wringer.'

'But surely you'd want to know the truth. There is a killer still out there after all.'

He leaned in close and lowered his voice. 'We just want this whole situation to go away.' He was glaring at Abi now.

I wasn't going to let it go. I needed to see what kind of temper this mild-mannered man really had. 'Well, that's why I'm here, mate.'

'Is it?' Although his voice was still low, it was a yell none the less.

'My oath it is. And as long as you've got nothing to hide, you'll be fine.'

He puffed out his chest and drew back his shoulders. 'What are you saying?'

'I'm not saying anything.'

Abi intervened. 'Matt, Scotty's just here to find the truth.'

He was shaking with anger now, which I found very interesting because I'd actually said nothing that was incriminating or aimed in his direction.

We reached the bar. Matt turned and ordered two beers. When the barmaid placed two stubbies in front of him, he paid her, took the beers and swanned away without saying a word.

'That's a first,' Abi said.

'What is?'

'I've never seen Matt Derby lose his temper before. He's usually quite calm.'

'I can have that effect on people. Two beers please, love.' My order was an automatic response, and I was relieved when Abi took one of the stubbies. I'd inadvertently assumed correctly. She preferred beer over wine. My kind of girl.

31

The hall was filling up. Kids chased each other around the perimeter of the dancefloor, teenagers congregated in small groups, while adults danced as if momentarily freed from the responsibilities of parenthood.

While casually chatting with Abi and Tilly, I'd been scanning the room for quite some time. The Fentons were hard not to notice. James held centre court among a group of locals. On the dancefloor, I recognised his son, Jake, from the news articles and pictures I'd seen online. With the typical handsome features that you would expect of an ageing polo player, he was smooching cheek to cheek with a tidy young blonde woman. Matt Derby stood with a group of other men. He was constantly glancing my way.

Tilly wasn't drinking. She told us she had to be up early the next morning because she was competing in important trials in Murwillumbah.

'Did you want to dance, Scotty?' Abi asked.

'Not bloody likely.'

'Ah, come on,' Tilly said, grinning and grabbing my hand.

Abi took my beer, placed it on the table along with hers then took my other hand.

My protests fell on deaf ears, and it surprised me how strong Tilly was.

The band was playing, 'The Gambler' by Kenny Rogers. I wasn't a big fan of country music; in fact, it was right up there with heavy metal as an all-time no no. But this song wasn't too bad. Kenny was probably the only country artist who had infiltrated the man shed on Ruby Street, with a song called 'Ruby, Don't Take Your Love To Town'.

Tilly was obviously used to this kind of music and knew how to dance to it. Abi and myself, not so much. We watched her as she leaned forward and lifted her feet like she was stepping over them on the spot. I'm sure our attempts at emulating her moves looked much more comedic.

The last of the ticket holders must have arrived because Pam Derby joined us on the dancefloor. 'Look at you guys,' she yelled over the noise. Her dance was more contemporary, kind of like a slow 1970s wiggle.

When the song ended, the tempo increased dramatically as the fiddler launched into 'The Devil Went Down to Georgia'.

Tilly and Pam immediately followed the beat. I took Abi by the hand and we headed back towards the table.

We sculled our beers. I jumped back into the queue to get two more while Abi went to the loo.

'So, you're that detective chap from the telly, eh?'

I turned around to see a stout elderly gentleman wearing a white Stetson. 'That's me.'

He held out his hand. 'Reg Patterson. I own the Patterson Dairy Farm.'

'Ah, Mister Patterson.' We shook hands. 'It's good to meet you.'

'Likewise. Although I hear you're not here for pleasure.'

I leaned in melodramatically and lowered my voice. 'What have you heard?'

'She was a wild thing. Caused a lot of hurt.'

'Kathy?'

'Yep, my missus took a bit of a shine to her. Wanted to help her, you know?'

'Help her?'

'She's a true Samaritan in every sense of the word, my Jan. Always helping folk out.'

'Did you get to know Kathy very well?'

'We did.'

The queue was moving and I found myself with my back to the bar. Turning, I ordered the drinks then turned back to Reg. Being a true pro and not buckling under the pressure, the girl serving retrieved the bottles from a large esky and plonked them down on the bar before I could resume my conversation.

'Twenty bucks, mate.'

I handed over the cash and took the drinks. 'Nice to meet you, Reg. I'll see you around.'

Yeah, no worries. We're sitting over there. Come and say G'day to the family later.'

'Will do.'

Tilly had joined Abi when I returned. 'I just met Reg Patterson.'

'A lovely old boy,' Tilly said. 'If you want to learn all the gossip, speak to Reg and Jan.'

'I might just do that.'

'Listen, I've got to go,' Tilly said. 'Early start tomorrow.' She kissed us both on the cheek before ducking away.

The band announced that they'd be taking a short break and the music was replaced by a recording of various artists about ten decibels lower. Abi and I headed over towards the Pattersons.

They were a big family, all seated around a table. Four generations of dairy farmers. I introduced myself to the group. Abi already knew them. Reg introduced me to Jan and the rest of the family. He had four strapping boys—the youngest was twenty-five, and the eldest, Ron, was thirty-nine. They were all married, and a sizeable portion of the kids tearing around the hall seemed to belong to them. Daisy Partridge, Reg's mother, was ninety-four years old.

Although she was in a wheelchair, her eyes danced with energy and darted as if missing nothing. When I shook her gently by the hand, she said, 'Have you met Mary yet?'

'Mary?'

'Oh Mum, don't be silly,' Jan said. Her grin was more of an apologetic gesture aimed at me.

'Silly? It won't be silly when Callum finds out.'

'That's enough, Mum. Reg?'

'Here's your drink, Daise,' Reg said, handing a stubby of XXXX Gold to his mother.

'There'll be trouble again. You see if there won't,' the old lady continued.

'And how are you, Abi?' Jan asked. Her tone was sympathetic.

'I'm good thanks, Jan.'

'You're a wild one you are!' Daisy continued, raising her voice in Abi's direction.

'Mum, that's enough,' Jan said, her eyes drilling into Reg.

'This is Abi, Daise, Kathy's sister.'

'I know that. I ain't senile you know.' She scowled at Abi. 'She's just as bad. Mary told me.'

'How about we get some air?' Reg said, gently touching Abi's arm.

He led us out through the door and into the car park where all the smokers had congregated. 'Don't mind, do you?' he said, retrieving a half-smoked cigar from his shirt pocket.

'No, not at all,' Abi and I said in unison.

'Sorry about Mum,' Reg said through a cloud of grey smoke. 'She gets a bit confused.'

'I can understand her mistaking Abi for Kathy,' I said.

'She won't forget Kathy Brown, that's for sure.' There was a bitter edge to his tone.

'Why's that?'

'She reckons Kathy stole from her.'

'Really?' Abi, said.

'Yep. When she was last here. Jan had taken Kathy under her wing. She used to come to the house quite a lot. Daisy wasn't too keen but tolerated her.' He took another big drag on his cigar and continued to speak as the smoke slowly escaped from his mouth. 'Then Daisy claimed her jewels were stolen, and she blamed Kathy.'

I didn't recall reading any of this in the police report. 'Were the police brought in?'

'No … as far as we knew, there *were* no jewels. Mum had hocked them years ago. But she gets confused.'

'She definitely sold them?' I asked.

'Well, we don't know for sure if she did, but we weren't going to involve the police. It would have been too embarrassing for the family, only to find out that there *were* no jewels. And what with Jan befriending Kathy. She stuck up for the girl and said the whole thing was nonsense.'

'And what did you think?'

'Doesn't matter what I thought. It divided the family though.'

'In what way?' I was trying to remain casual but an inconspicuous nudge from Abi told me I had inadvertently slipped into detective mode.

'Well, the boys mainly. While they were growing up, Daisy had regaled them with stories of the treasure chest that she kept under her bed. And I think they wanted to believe it existed.'

'And Kathy Brown took it from them.'

'Hey, now wait a minute, don't you be thinking my boys had anything to do with that girl's death.'

'They'd be pretty pissed off if they thought Kathy had stolen their inheritance.'

'There were no jewels. Daisy doesn't have a cent to her name. Their inheritance is the dairy farm and they're happy with that.'

'Would you mind if I spoke to the boys?'

Reg's jolly expression shifted. 'I can't stop you, but I'd prefer it if you didn't.'

32

When we returned to the hall, I was sad to see Reg Patterson rounding up his family. A few minutes later, they left and the empty table they had inhabited got swallowed up by other guests. I hadn't meant to get Reg offside and felt the need to make things right, so I decided I'd visit the dairy farm the next morning to apologise.

While I was standing in the queue once more at the bar, I noticed Matt Derby approach Abi. The band had returned from their break. The music was pretty loud so I couldn't hear what was being said but I could tell by Matt's body language that the discussion was heated. I was about to step out of the queue and return to Abi's side when she suddenly reared up on the balls of her feet and threw her arms in the air. Matt stepped backwards. Abi pushed forward. She was yelling at him. Matt suddenly looked as if he was about to turn and run away. My instinct was telling me I needed to intervene, but before I could, Pam Derby appeared from nowhere and stepped in between them. Her expression was calm and in control like a mother breaking up a scuffle between two children.

Abi continued to shout beyond her in Matt's direction. Boy, I wish I could have heard what she was yelling. I couldn't take it any longer, so I left the queue and rushed over.

'What's going on?' I asked above the music.

Luckily, the band was so loud, and the dancefloor was so packed that nobody noticed the commotion. All except, it seems, for James

Fenton and his son, Jake. They were watching from the other side of the room. James caught my eye and frowned. Jake was smirking.

Ignoring them, I placed a hand on Abi's shoulder. 'You okay, Abi?'

'I *was*.'

'Just stay away from my daughter, do you hear?' Matt yelled.

Abi lunged forward. 'Why don't you fuck off, eh?'

'Now then, it's okay,' Pam said, still standing between them. 'Let's all just calm down and go back to enjoying the night.'

'I was, Pam, until he came over and started having a go at me.'

'Why the hell are you here, Abigail?' Matt demanded. 'Don't you think your family has caused us enough pain?'

Anticipating the arc of the launched right hook, I grabbed Abi's arm before it rounded Pam on course for Matt Derby's chin. 'Take it easy, Abi,' I said, inadvertently pulling her towards me.

People started to notice. The dancers closest to us stopped dancing.

James Fenton waded through the crowd and approached us. 'What the hell's going on here?' he demanded.

'Nothing, Jim,' Pam said, turning and attempting to usher her husband away.

'It doesn't look like nothing.'

'Really, it's just a misunderstanding, that's all.'

Jake Fenton appeared and stood behind his father. The smirk still present.

'He started it,' Abi said. 'I was having a good time until he came over and started abusing me.'

'That's bullshit,' Matt spat back.

'But that's what it looked like to me, mate.' I couldn't help myself. 'You seemed to wait until Abi was alone.'

'That's because none of this is your business!' Matt's temper was on show for all to see.

'Matt, please, let's go home.' Pam had her hands on his chest and was physically pushing him backwards.

'We don't need your kind around here.' His eyes flicked between Abi and me. 'Look what happened last time, eh?'

'Okay, I'm going to have to ask you both to leave,' Fenton said, turning to me and Abi.

'What?' we said in unison.

'You heard me. I think it would be better for everyone if you both left.'

Abi immediately hurled abuse at the older man, and as much as I wanted to join her, I remained calm. Like the Pattersons, I needed to keep the Fentons onside.

'Please accept my apologies, Mister Fenton. And I'm sorry for any embarrassment we may have caused.'

Jake Fenton was watching my every move, analysing me perhaps. The wild stare mixed with the arrogant smirk was making my blood boil. He had said nothing all this time, but I could tell he was itching to get involved. I wasn't about to give him or anyone else in the room the satisfaction. Just about everyone was watching us now. Thankfully, the band played on.

'Come on, Abs, we're going.'

'No, *we're* not. Why should *we* have to leave?'

'We don't *have* to. We just are.' A soft frown was a signal to indicate I knew what I was doing.

She looked around the room wide eyed as if she'd only just realised everyone was looking at her.

'Seriously, Abi. Let's just go.' I was still holding her arm, and I felt the tension suddenly drain from her body like a prizefighter realising the fight was lost.

'Okay … we'll go. But you stay the hell away from me, Matt Derby.'

'That's easy. Go back to Brisbane. Nobody wants you here,' Matt yelled back. Calmly, we made our way towards the exit.

Pam stroked Abi's shoulder as she passed. 'I'll see you tomorrow.'

We didn't have to look back to know that every pair of eyes in the room was still on us.

When we got outside, the cooling air was a welcome relief.

'What was all that about?' I asked working my fingers over the Uber app.

'I don't know. He just went crazy.'

'Has he ever had a go at you like this before?'

'Never. I've always got on really well with them, well Pam and Tilly at least.'

'What was he saying to you at first?' The Uber app was scanning for the nearest ride.

'He just came marching up and said I needed to stay away from Tilly, and that I was a bad influence on her.'

'Why?'

'I don't know. He's obviously had a bit too much to drink.'

The app was taking longer than usual. 'Have you done anything to piss him off?'

'No.'

'So why is he so against you spending time with his daughter?'

Abi sighed. 'Look, she is under a bit of pressure, what with the training and all. They have high hopes for her to make the next Olympics.'

'Right, so they think you might be a distraction, perhaps?'

'He went way beyond that.'

'Was that when you flipped?'

Abi smiled, and I was glad to see that the episode hadn't upset her too much. 'Yeah. That was when I nearly put him on his arse.'

'What did he say?'

'He said I'm just like my whore sister and that he didn't want me infecting, Tilly.'

'Wow. No wonder you arced up.'

'Why would he say that? I just don't understand it.'

Hmm, it was odd I had to admit. Abi was due to be going back to Brisbane the next day anyway, so why would Matt Derby cause a scene in front of everyone? Perhaps he didn't know, perhaps he thought she'd be staying in Mary's Mansion for longer. Either way though, I know a scared man when I see one. The alcohol was definitely a factor. It can have that effect on even the quietest of people, like releasing a genie from a bottle. Perhaps his fear was purely because he was worried about his daughter, perhaps he too was feeling the pressures of the impending Australian championships. Either way, I'd need to keep a close eye on him.

33

'You're a good man, Ron Fenton.' Sawmill owner, Charles Harrigan, said as he placed a coin in Fenton's hand. 'You've worked hard, and I want you to take this as a sign of my appreciation.'

Fenton looked down at the gold piece, the anger seething beneath his calm exterior like boiling water. 'Thank you, guv'nor.'

'Ahh, it's the least I can do. You deserve more.' Harrigan's smile was warm and friendly.

Fenton nodded in agreement. 'It is. And I do.'

'Come again?' Harrigan sat back in his expensive office chair as if expectantly waiting for the punchline.

'It *is* the least you can do. And I *do* deserve more!' Fenton's menacing stare had become his trademark among his peers. It was something he used to unsettle his opponents on his way up the ladder of success, just before he crushed them.

'What are you saying, man?' Harrigan leaned forward in his seat. A quick glance towards the adjoining room to where his legion of loyal fighting men were, reassured him and reinforced his bravado.

'I'm saying you're a lying, thieving old bastard!'

'Davide,' Harrigan called out to the next room. The warmth in his face had dissolved into a veneer of fear and uncertainty.

Davide Williams, a tall stocky Welshman, entered the room and removed his hat.

'Yes, sir.'

Harrigan's confidence returned. 'I'd heard you were a rat, Fenton. In fact, isn't that what they called you on the *Great Britain*?' His chin was in the air and his upper-class English accent held an unmistakable air of authority.

'I'll be the rat that'll take your daughter down the aisle.'

Harrigan's laugh was without humour. He looked at Williams for backup.

Williams stood with his head down.

'Not before I slap her around a bit first, though. Then fuck her bandy!'

'Davide, deal with this piece of dirt, will you?'

Davide remained motionless.

'This is my fuckin' mill now.' Fenton stepped forward. 'And that's my desk you're sitting at.'

'Davide …' There was panic in Harrigan's voice as he rose from his desk. 'Jones, Miller.

Come in here at once.'

None of the men from the other room made a move.

'Oh, and they're my men now,' Fenton said, circling the desk. He skilfully grabbed Harrigan by the throat and squeezed with two powerful hands.

Harrigan, shorter, older and overweight, tried to pull away, but he was no match for Fenton's strength. He gasped, fighting for air.

Fenton squeezed tighter and leaned over the weaker man, forcing him down onto his knees. 'Just another one of them unfortunate accidents that seems to plague your mill at present, Mister Harrigan.' Fenton's eyes danced with excitement as he squeezed the life from his victim. 'Very unfortunate indeed.'

It didn't take long for Harrigan to lose consciousness and even when he was dead, Fenton didn't release his grip until he was completely sure. When he finally did, Harrigan's corpse fell backwards with a thump on the polished timber floor.

Fenton calmy straightened his crumpled jacket, stepped over the body and sat in the expansive office chair.

'Take him out the back and burn him,' he instructed Davide. 'Make sure there's nothing left, all right?'

Davide nodded. 'In here, boys,' he called to the next room.

All ex-getters, four burly men entered the room and under Davide's supervision, lifted the body of their former boss as if they were undertaking a simple everyday task.

Fenton watched them patiently until they'd left the room, then he reached into an ornate wooden box that sat atop the desk, took out a cigar and lit it. Not only was he running the getters who were feeding the sawmills in Tallebudgera and Burleigh, but he now owned his own mill, had increased his workforce tenfold and recruited an army of hard men to his growing entourage who would do anything he asked. And to top it all, he'd also gained a future wife, although she didn't know it yet. But more importantly, he was only a hog's breath away from achieving his ultimate plan of bringing Callum Murphy to his knees and making him beg for his life. Yes, Ron Fenton had worked his way back up from the bowels of depravity once more. This time though he would not be going back down.

'But where is my father?' asked Dorothy Harrigan, concern exaggerating her usual rosy complexion.

'He's buggered off and left you,' Fenton said. 'Ran off with the Abo tart he was pokin'.'

'No, that's not true. He would never—'

'Of course, it's true,' Fenton said, edging up to the fly screen on the front door of Harrigan's homestead. 'It's well known that a couple of them coffee-coloured kids running around here are your siblings. Surely you knew?'

Dorothy stood behind the screen looking back at Fenton and the group of men behind him. 'No, it's not true!'

'Well, where is he then?' Fenton said, holding out his arms. 'Truth is, he's abandoned you and the business.'

'Davide, tell him that isn't true.' Dorothy trusted Davide. He'd worked for her father for many years and was a friend to the family.

Davide took off his cap and kneaded it in his hands. 'It's true, Miss Dorothy. All of it.' He didn't make eye contact. Instead, he stared at a point on the floor. 'Your dad wasn't the person you thought he was.'

'But he would never leave me or turn his back on what he's built here in the Valley.'

'That's part of the problem.' Fenton didn't address her as Miss Dorothy or Miss Harrigan like the workers did. Instead, he spoke to her as a subordinate or the next victim he was about to crush. 'The business is on the brink of collapse.'

Dorothy Harrigan's laugh was more of a nervous response to the uncertain possibly of Fenton's claims. 'That's ridiculous. We're one of the biggest sawmills in Queensland!'

'That's true,' Fenton agreed. 'But it's been mismanaged. Your old daddy's been a bit of a naughty boy, I'm afraid.'

'No …'

'Yep. Gambling. Women. A bit too much of the old opium. Not to mention the booze.'

'My father is an upstanding law-abiding member of this community. I'll not hear anything said against his character.'

'Thought you might say that. Understandable of course.' Fenton stepped to one side.

Davide and his men parted, allowing a path between them.

A young Aboriginal girl approached carrying a baby.

'This is Milly,' Fenton said.

The young girl lowered her head and almost bowed.

'Milly, tell the missus who the father of your son is.'

Milly lifted her chin defiantly. 'Boss, him dad.'

'No!' Dorothy cried out.

'Him like black fella girls,' Milly said. She held out the baby for Dorothy to see. He was a strong-looking boy with black curly hair, but his skin was at least two shades lighter than the ebony tone of his mother's. 'Him give me 'nother kid. Then buggered off, eh.'

Fenton pushed in front of the girl. 'And she's not the only one. He was a randy old bugger.'

A distinct shade of grey had replaced Dorothy's rosy complexion.

'It's okay.' Fenton warily opened the fly screen. 'This is why I'm here. To look after you. To make sure you're all right.'

With unsure eyes searching for answers, Dorothy stepped back and allowed him to enter.

Fenton's smile was part grin and part snarl. Like a vampire, he'd been invited in. Now he was over the threshold, the homestead belonged to him and everything in it. Including Miss Dorothy Harrigan.

34

Abi didn't stick around the next morning. She left for Brisbane quite early. My soft probing during the Uber trip back to Mary's Mansion the night before probably didn't help. I needed to know why Matt Derby, a usually gentle, caring chap, was so angry with her.

It was Sunday. I had a whole day in front of me. Abi had said very little before she'd left.

I was hoping she'd call me once she calmed down. Sitting out on the back verandah with a mug of tea, watching Romeo chase everything that moved—a butterfly, a grasshopper, a cheeky wagtail—Abigail Brown dominated my thoughts. She was an intelligent young woman, a schoolteacher. Why would Derby see her as a bad influence on his daughter? I would have thought the opposite would be the case, a role model perhaps. But then something struck me. I actually knew nothing about her. The only mention of her in the police report was when she flew up from Adelaide to identify the body of her sister.

Everything else was what *she'd* told me about herself. What was the school she said she worked at? Saint Andrews? Saint Anthony? Saint Wally Lewis? I'd need to find out and do some digging.

My agenda for the day was to build some bridges. After a bowl of cornflakes and a shower, I headed over to the Pattersons' place. The weather was overcast and a little cooler than the day before, so I walked. The house and the dairy weren't visible from Mary's

159

Mansion, but it wasn't far. And Romeo would enjoy the walk across the fields.

There were quite a few cows in the Patterson paddocks. Some grazed but some lay on the ground in little groups. I remembered my mother telling me when I was a little boy that this meant it was going to rain. The grey sky overhead seemed to agree with the old wives' tale and I wondered if it had any scientific validity. Romeo had never seen a cow before, so he gave them a wide berth. I knew absolutely nothing about the animals myself, only that you got milk, steak and leather jackets from them. Something struck me when we were halfway across the paddock. *Would there be a bull in the field? Shit!* I hadn't thought of that. I quickly scanned my surroundings, but the cows all seemed—to my eye anyway—identical and passive.

The house was quiet when we approached it, so too was the large state-of-the art—to my eye again—dairy farm behind it. The Patterson dwelling certainly wasn't a homestead like Fenton's place. It was a working farmhouse—large but basic, an off-white, fibro building on concrete stumps. There were the mandatory verandahs at the front and back. As I circled the front of the building, I suddenly realised I was being watched. Sitting on a rocking chair on the front verandah was Daisy.

'There's nobody here,' she called out as I scaled the half a dozen front steps. 'They're all at church. Except for Roy that is. He'll be about somewhere.'

The thought of almost an entire family going to church on a Sunday morning was totally alien to me. In fact, anyone going to church at all was something I'd never really contemplated. But three generations of the Pattersons taking time out from their busy life, rounding up the kids and going to a place of worship together, seemed somehow endearing. But I couldn't help wondering why Roy didn't go. 'Will they be long?' I asked.

'Depends. Sometimes they stick around and let the kids have a play in the church grounds.'

'Which church would they be at?' 'Tallebudgera Community.'

I remembered the little colonial style church on Trees Road. The building was cute in the same way Mary's Mansion was, but with white timber sidings and a green tin roof.

'May I come in, Mrs Patterson?' I asked, standing on the top step.

'Depends on what you want.'

'I'm Scotty Stephens, I'm staying in the place next door.'

She contemplated me with narrowed eyes.

'We met at the dance last night.'

'Don't have to be a goose to have a long neck, do you?'

'I'm sorry?'

'I know who you are.'

'Oh, right.' I gestured with my hand for permission to step onto the verandah.

She acknowledged this with a nod.

'I'd love to talk to you if that's okay,' I said, taking the vacant seat next to hers.

'Yep, Jan said you might come snooping around.'

'She did?'

The old lady nodded. 'But I already knew you'd show up.'

'Did you?' I was talking to her kind of like you would a child.

'Mary told me you were coming. She said you were here to help.'

'Mary Murphy told you that?'

'You think I'm crazy.'

'No … not at all.'

'They all do. I reckon they're planning to put me in Saint Andrew's nursing home.'

'But Mary Murphy is …'

'Dead, I know. Long dead. But she visits me, always has. I'm a Murphy you see.'

'Really?' I wasn't aware of this.

'Yep, Mary was my great grandmother.'

'Right.' Rather than questioning the woman's mental state of mind, I went along with everything she said.

'She tells me everything that happens over at that place.'

'Mary's Mansion?'

She nodded, but she was looking past me over the paddock. 'And the Fentons.' Her face screwed up like she'd just bitten into a jalapeño.

A cow close by gave out the loudest moo I'd ever heard. It was a welcomed distraction, allowing me to bring the conversation back to this century.

'Did you ever meet Kathy Brown?

'That bitch stole my jewellery.'

'How do you know it was her?'

'Who else could it have been? She used to come around here on a Sunday morning when everyone was at church, just like you have.' She looked at me suspiciously.

'I didn't realise everyone would be at church,' I reassured her. 'I actually came over to apologise to Reg for last night.'

'What have you got to apologise for? I heard it was the Brown girl that was causing all the trouble.'

'No not at all, she—'

'She's trouble, just like her sister. I'm telling you!' Daisy was getting worked up.

In an attempt to calm her, I tried changing the subject. 'How many cows do you have here?'

She ignored this. 'I see it in your eyes. It's a spell those girls have over men.'

'Those girls?'

'Them sisters. I saw that same look in the eyes of every man in this family whenever that hussy was mentioned, and the Fentons too. And now I see it in your eyes when you talk about her sister.'

'I really don't think—'

'She's trouble! Nobody believed me when I said it about the sister, nobody believes me now.'

'But she seems really nice.' For some reason I felt the need to defend Abi.

Daisy chuckled. 'Of course, she does. You've fallen right into her little trap.'

My nonchalant shrug was my only defence, remembering that I knew very little about Abi Brown.

Daisy sat up straight, lifted her chin and said, 'Mary knows!'

After thanking her for her time, I left Daisy sitting on the verandah. Roy was on my mind. After a quick peek around the back of the house, I saw him through the open doors of a large barn. He was tinkering with the engine of a tractor.

'G'day, Roy,' I said, stepping into the shed.

Roy looked up. There was oil on his hands and smudges on his face.

'Hi, Scott.' He pulled his head out of the engine and stood up straight. He was a big lad with gentle eyes. Wiping his hands on a rag, we touched elbows instead of shaking. Romeo got a quick pat. 'What can I do for you?'

'I just came around to apologise for last night.' 'They're all at church I'm afraid.'

'Yeah, just saw Daisy. So you're not into all that stuff?'

'Nah.' He threw the rag onto the tractor. 'Someone has to stay around here.'

'I seem to have put the cat among the pigeons last night bringing Abi to the ball.'

'You did. Not good.'

'What has everyone got against her?'

'Not her, her sister.'

'Did you know Kathy well?'

'I've got to keep moving, mate. Things to do.' His expression told me he'd suddenly lost interest in chatting.

'I'm just trying to find out what happened to her.'

'She got what she deserved if you ask me!' This wasn't delivered angrily, more matter of fact.

'Did she give you guys a hard time?'

He leaned back into the tractor engine and picked up a shifter. 'You'll be able to show yourself out, eh?'

'Yeah sure, no worries. I'll catch you later.'

Ignoring me, he tightened a hose on the engine.

35

It would have been nice to have relaxed, being Sunday and all, but I had work to do.

When I got back from the Pattersons' place, I decided there was another bridge I needed to rebuild.

Wearing a wide-brimmed hat, Pam Derby was on her hands and knees in the front garden, digging out weeds from a bed of roses. 'I'm afraid they're not back yet,' she said, wearily standing and approaching me at the gate. 'It depends how far Tilly goes in the competition, but I'm not expecting them back until teatime.'

'Oh right, the trials,' I said.

'I'm really sorry for what happened last night,' Pam said, leaning on the gate. 'Matt's such a gentle man usually.'

'He was pretty fired up.' Arriving fully laden, I'd taken the opportunity to return the two pair of boots and the Akubra.

Pam continued to speak as she took them from me. 'He's not a big drinker, and it can sometimes bring the worst out in him when he has too much.'

From my years with the police force, I was familiar with domestic violence and how a lot of women not only put up with abuse from their partners but actually defended it. I suspected this wasn't the case here, but I couldn't be sure. 'Is your husband ever violent towards you?'

Pam swatted away the question. 'No, nothing like that. He's a sweetheart.' She leaned forward, and although there was no one else present, she lowered her voice. 'I think you'll find Abi's presence upsets a lot of people in the Valley.'

'Why is that?'

'It's because she looks so much like her sister. She fires up bad memories.'

I enjoyed Pam's company. If she was lying about her domestic situation and covering up for her husband, she was doing an amazing job. I'd learned a thing or two about body language during my years as a detective constable, and Pam was showing none of the telltale signs—nervous sideways glances, facial tics, uncontrolled twitching, etc. But I wasn't ruling out the possibility of a domestic violence scenario. 'Would you mind telling Matt that I'm really sorry for what happened last night, and I'll call back later because I'd like to apologise properly face to face?'

36

Jake Fenton's late model red Ferrari was parked somewhat askew on the gravel driveway in front of the Fenton homestead. The house was quiet as I approached the front verandah, tiny white pebbles crunching underfoot. Climbing the front steps, I suddenly realised Jake was watching me from a two-person hammock.

Sprawled out like a sailor on shore leave, he said, 'Scotty Stephens, to what do we owe the honour?'

Late forties, he wore a pair of dark boardshorts. His tanned body was hairy and muscular. The black receding hair, possibly dyed, and the mirrored aviation sunglasses gave him a 1980s vibe. In the words of Tetley, he looked like a twat.

'Jake Fenton?' Of course, I already knew who he was. Apart from being one of those annoying celebrities who popped up on the local news from time to time, usually for the wrong reasons, we *had* actually met before. I wondered if he remembered the young, uniformed copper that arrested him outside a Surfers Paradise nightclub fifteen years ago.

'That's right.' He sat up but didn't climb out of the hammock. Instead, he held out his hand for me to approach and shake, or kiss, like he was some kind of medieval lord. 'It's great to meet you at last.'

'Like wise.' I shook his hand.

Interestingly, during my research of the Fentons, I'd learned that Jake's mother and James's wife, Moira Fenton, had died giving birth to Jake. The boy was raised by a nanny.

A sign over the front door suddenly caught my attention. It read: 'Mary's Shack'. 'Do you live here with the old man?' I asked, friendly.

'At the moment, yeah. Got a new place being renovated.'

The young blonde woman who Jake had danced with at the fireman's ball came almost skipping out of the building carrying two tall glasses of what appeared to be Coke, as well as a family sized bag of Doritos.

'Look who's here, Hun,' Jake said as she approached. 'It's the saviour of the Gold Coast.'

'Wow!' The girl, wearing a yellow bikini under a white lacey dress, passed one of the drinks to Jake, placed the other on a small wicker table at the side of the hammock and offered me her hand. 'I'm Jemma, you can call me Jem.' There was a slight slur in her voice and her eyes had what I called the ganja glaze.

'It's good to meet you, Jem.'

'Can I get you a drink, Scotty?' Jem asked.

The last thing I wanted to do was socialise with these two over privileged potheads, but ... 'Yeah, why not. What are you drinking?' I decided on the spot to get to know them on their playing field—keep them on side.

'Bundy and Coke.'

'Cool. I'll have one of them then.'

Jem skipped back into the house.

'Nice girl,' I said, plonking myself down in one of the wicker chairs and kicking off my thongs.

Jake bobbed his head from side to side as if he were evaluating Jem's worth. 'Yeah, she's all right.' He took a sip of his drink. 'So, what can we do for you, mate?'

'Ah, you know. Just trying to get to know the neighbours. Is your dad in?'

'No, he's at the horse trials.'

That made sense, Tilly was his protégé, why wouldn't he be at the event? 'Oh well, I get to meet you at least.'

Jake smiled and I could tell he was partial to having his ego stroked. 'Thanks to you, mate. The Coast is a safer place.' He held up his glass just as Jem returned.

She handed me my drink then unceremoniously climbed into the hammock next to Jake. Still holding up his glass, Jake frowned as a little of his drink spilled.

I stood, leaned over and touched his glass with mine. 'Cheers!'

'Cheers,' Jake said.

'Oh wait, wait.' Jem reached out of the hammock and grabbed her glass from the side table, causing more of Jake's drink to spill. 'Cheers,' she yelled, clinking both of our glasses with hers.

'Cheers,' I repeated, returning to my seat and taking a mouthful of my drink, which contained a little more rum and a little less Coke than I would have liked. I began my campaign of getting to know Jake Fenton the only way I knew how. 'So, do you follow the footy, mate?'

'Sure.' Then he frowned. 'AFL?'

'Yep.'

His expression told me he was relieved when he realised we both followed the same footy code and not the rugby league. 'Who do you follow?' he asked.

'Essendon all the way.'

'What? *Bullshit!* Go the Magpies, mate!'

'Collingwood? Jesus, you'd go for the Suns or the Lions, surely?'

'Nah.' He lounged back into the hammock. 'As much as I'm a Queenslander, Rules is a Victorian game.'

I nodded in agreement, and although our teams made us lifelong enemies, we'd found some common ground. 'Here's to that,' I said, raising my glass and taking another sip.

'So, is it true you're here investigating the murder?' Jem asked, changing the subject.

'No, I'm working for Ben Fisher.' The reason I was in the Valley and the person responsible seemed distant all of a sudden.

'The writer?'

'Yes.'

'The plagiarist you mean,' Jake said. His layered expression was a nasty grin and a scornful frown.

Wanting to keep on side with him, I shrugged and nodded. 'That's what I'm here to find out.'

The atmosphere had suddenly changed and I could sense tension in the air. 'That idiot's stirred it all up again.'

To remain on his good side, I nodded in the way I imagined the sycophants who usually surrounded him would. 'You think he stole the story?'

'What story?' There was a definite edge now to his tone.

'Yeah, I know. I've tried reading it. Bloody garbage if you ask me.'

'So, what does he expect *you* to do?' Jake asked, his eyes cold now and fixed on mine. I needed to play down the situation and act dumb. 'I wouldn't have a clue, mate.' 'How much is he paying you?'

'Uhhh … not a lot.' I wasn't about to share that information.

'I'll double it if you go back to the Coast and forget all about the Valley and Ben Fisher!'

I was trying; I was bloody trying but he was getting under my skin. 'And forget about Kathy Brown, you mean?'

'Especially her.'

Settle Scotty, bring it back. You need to keep him on side, remember? 'No worries, I'll be happy to consider it.'

'Good man.' Jake had been taking nervous gulps of his drink since I'd mentioned Ben Fisher. 'He emptied the last of his glass and thrust it into Jem's hand. 'Get Scotty another one too, eh?'

I was about to protest but decided against it. Sculling my drink, I handed the empty glass to Jem.

'Bloody Collingwood, eh?' I said, bringing the conversation back to the footy after Jem had disappeared into the house. 'You're having a shit season.'

'*Pff.*' That annoying smirk again. 'Early days, yet.'

'We've got you blokes next week at home.'

'Do I look worried?'

Footy aside, he did actually look worried. Worried and a little angry like I was poking him with a stick.

37

As was usually the case between two Aussie blokes, a bit of gentle footy banter brought the conversation back to a relaxed familiar playing field, if you'll pardon the pun. The very mention of Kathy Brown had instantly altered the atmosphere, and I nearly lost that tiny 'in' that befriending Jake Fenton could allow me.

His girlfriend had different ideas though. Interrupting our analysis of the AFL season so far, she continued right where she'd left off on her return. 'So, who do you think killed her, Scotty?'

'Do you mind, Hun? We're having an intelligent discussion here,' Jake said, taking his drink from her.

'I'm curious, that's all. An unsolved murder in the Valley. It's mega scary!'

During my years as a police officer and a detective, I'd learned early in my career that first impressions are not to be trusted, as widely assumed. They can be derived from the impression a person wants to portray. We can only achieve an accurate representation of someone by getting to know them and taking a mental note of their idiosyncrasies, their beliefs and their behaviour patterns. If relying on the old adage, I would have written off Jem as a dumb blonde who was only with Jake Fenton because of his wealth and fame. And as much as this evaluation may have had some credence, my experience told me otherwise. The questions she was asking were very simple, but straight to the point. There was no beating about the bush. This could quite easily have been mistaken for inquisitive curiosity, but I suspected there was more to this girl. She genuinely wanted to know the answers to her questions, and she'd keep digging until she got them regardless of the discomfort they may cause to those around her. She'd make a good detective.

If I satisfied her interest, would I lose what little ground I'd just made up with Jake?

Probably. But in truth, I had no idea who the killer was anyway, so I was able to give her an honest answer. 'I haven't got a clue!'

'You must have a theory?' She wasn't about to let it go. 'What about Jake's dad? Too obvious?'

'For fuck's sake, Jem!' Jake raised his voice.

'What?'

'Leave it, will you? Scott and I were talking about the footy—'

'Don't you want to clear his name? And yours for that matter?' She suddenly appeared completely sober, and I wondered if the tipsy bimbo had all been an act.

Jake frowned and slowly swept his head from side to side as if he were searching for the words.

'Of course you do, Jem continued. 'Well, don't you see?' She placed a reassuring arm on his shoulder. 'Scotty can help you. That is, of course …' She withdrew her arm and picked up her drink. 'That is if you're both innocent.'

Jake struggled out of the hammock, mumbling as he slipped his feet into his thongs. 'You just can't leave it, can you?'

'I'm only trying to help, hun!'

'You should probably leave now, mate,' Jake said before heading towards the front door.

If I'd lost him, I had nothing else to lose. 'Did your dad kill Kathy Brown, Jake?'

He hesitated at the door.

A scenario was forming in my mind and without thinking, I threw it out there. 'Or was he covering up for someone else …? You perhaps?'

Jake turned back to face me, and he also seemed to suddenly be sober. 'Why the hell would you ask that?'

'It's a simple yes or no question.' It wasn't. It was far more than that, but it was the only recourse I could think of at the time.

'You seriously need to leave.'

'Mate, I was just being honest when I said I don't have a clue.' I rose to my feet. 'Any help you can offer would be awesome.'

Jake padded back towards the hammock. 'This has been hard on my dad.' 'I understand that.'

'You being here isn't helping.'

'I get that too. He's been accused of murder, not officially of course but still.'

'My dad is a bastard. I hate him, but he's no killer.'

Whoa, I wasn't expecting that. 'Who then?'

'Have you spoken to Tom Partridge?'

I'd seen him industriously going about his work on the property and Tilly had given me a bit of a rundown, but I hadn't had the chance to speak to him yet. I shook my head.

'You might want to.'

'Why's that?'

'Because he was obsessed with Kathy, the same way he is with Tilly.'

'Obsessed in what way?'

'Fuck me, Scotty, you're the detective. Work it out, eh?'

Tom Partridge, the farmhand, would have been about the same age as Kathy Brown. He certainly hadn't been on my radar until now. Jake knew something, I was sure of it, so I needed to prize the information from him.

Jem stroked Jake's arm. 'Might be good to talk about it, Hun. Get it off your chest.'

Jake kicked off his thongs and climbed back into the hammock. 'You know he's not a full quid?'

'In what way?' My question was delivered casually with a bit of a friendly chuckle thrown in for good measure. Sitting back down, I lifted my drink and took a sip.

'He'd have to be somewhere on the spectrum.' Jem nodded vigorously.

'Autism you mean?'

'Yeah. He's a genius with the horses. That's why dad hired him. Got the social skills of a bucket, though.'

'What, he's like some kind of horse whisperer or something?' I'd brought the conversation back to a friendly chit-chat level.

'Dad reckons that our competition success is down to thirty per cent talent of the riders and seventy per cent training that Tom puts into the horses.'

'So, he and Kathy were close?' 'Inseparable. Just like he is with Tilly.'

'Right. Is he around?'

'No. He's at the trials of course.'

I detected disdain in his tone and wondered if there was jealousy. The next comment confirmed this.

'You would think *he* was the son of James Fenton, not me.'

I needed to add a little kindling to the flame. 'They spend a lot of time together?'

'My bloody oath. Every day!'

'But your dad's super proud of *you*, I bet?'

Jake shook his head. 'He hates polo.'

'But you're an international star,' I said, gently fanning the flame.

'Means nothing. All he seems to care about is Tilly Derby these days. And before that it was some other potential protégé. There's been many. Right back to …' The sip he took from his drink was a nervous one.

'Right, back to Kathy Brown!' I finished the sentence for him.

38

He could feel the heat of galvanised iron through his boots as he precariously scaled the front apex of the roof. This was a task he'd insisted on keeping until the very end of the build. But it was more than just a celebration marking the end of construction, it was a ceremony for Callum Murphy, a rite of passage. His empire was established, and he was the king of his castle looking down over his domain.

The six-foot long turned flagpole fit tightly into the pre-drilled hole. A single nail in the back was all that was required to hold it in place. The crowd of workers cheered as the Union flag unfurled and flew for the first time over the Murphy homestead.

'Speech,' cried Jimmy P.

'Aye,' Callum said, quietening the crowd, 'Would only be fitting to say a few words.' He gazed over the sea of faces looking up at him.

Mary, heavily pregnant, stood at the front with Jimmy P, his wife, Edna, and their two young boys.

'First, Oy'd like to thank each and every one of you for standing by me and making this business what it is today. Without you all, Callum Murphy would be nothing.'

There was more applause from the crowd.

'Jimmy P. Mate, you believed in me since that very first day we met on the *Great Britain*.

Oy'm forever indebted to you and honoured to call you me friend!' More applause and some patting on Jimmy P's back.

'There are too many names to mention, but you all know who you are. And Oy thank you all. And last but not least, Oy'd like to thank my beautiful wife, Mary Murphy. Not only were you instrumental in helping me set up this business, but you became my life partner. You give purpose to my days, and Oy can't wait to meet our first baby in a couple of weeks' time.

Thank you, my dear. Oy love you with all my heart.'

When he finally climbed down from the roof, Callum insisted on carrying his wife over the threshold.

'A hard man, my arse, Callum Murphy. You're as soft as downing, are you not?'

'Aye. A bit soft in the head, perhaps.'

The house was a six-bedroom mansion, built in the typical Queenslander style, sitting on top of sturdy hardwood stumps. An open area beneath would allow the cooler air to circulate, while the galvanised steel roof would reflect the heat of the sun, maintaining a comfortable temperature inside the house. A deep wrap-around verandah offered the all-important shade and shelter from the rain.

'Tis a fine house you designed, Mary Murphy,' Callum said.

'Tis a fine house you've built, Callum Murphy.'

'There's only one more thing to do,' Callum said, grinning.

'One more?'

'Aye, come on.' Callum led Mary out onto the front verandah. 'Close your eyes.' Leading her back to the top of the front steps, he turned her to face the front door. 'Keep them closed.'

Mary did as she was told, listening with puzzled ears.

Callum had everything pre-prepared and within a minute he said, 'Okay, you can open your eyes now.'

Mary did as she was told and burst into laughter.

Hanging above the front door was a sign. It was carved into wood like the one at the cottage, only not as crudely. The machined timber was finished and sealed. The words simply said, 'Mary's Shack'.

Keeping a tight rein over the comings and goings of the household, Edna Page was hired as housekeeper overseeing a cook and a scullery maid.

It was another day off for the workers. An afternoon of drinking and bush music would continue well on into the night. At dusk, Callum and Mary wandered hand in hand back to the old cottage.

Looking up at the crude sign that hung over the door, 'Mary's Mansion', Mary smiled. 'How on Earth did we live in this place for over a year?'

'My ma and da lived in something not much bigger for all of their lives. And with seven children,' Callum said.

'Aye, mine too. We've come a long way.'

'That we have.'

This close to the end of the pregnancy, Mary was no longer working at the sawmill. Her mother stayed with them until the baby was born, and Mary was grateful for the help of Edna P. She was ready for the baby to arrive, more than ready in fact, she was tired of waiting. Two days later, she gave birth to a girl. They named her Mary Amelia Murphy.

More settlers arriving in the Valley saw the need for more resources in the form of roads and schools. Alterations in the names of places also took place. The Perry River was recently changed to Tallebudgera Creek. In 1876, the little township that was originally called Maybree was officially changed to Tallebudgera (a mispronunciation of an Aboriginal term meaning 'good fish') after the Cobb and Co coach line chose it as a stop. The Coast was also opening up and changing to match the growing white population.

Originally called Jellurgal by the traditional landowners but changed to Burleigh by the early white surveyors who refused to recognise the traditional names, the recently renamed Burleigh Heads was quickly becoming a destination for holidaymakers and picnic goers.

Changes in the Murphy household saw three more children, and the family was prospering in more ways than Callum could ever have imagined. As Springbrook continued to open up to the west, more and more logs arrived via Tallebudgera Creek. After recognising a need, Callum had also purchased boats and more bullocks to increase the movement of timber from the Valley to the Coast.

Land sales also increased the Murphys' fortune. Pasture that was once rich with cedar but now cleared and suitable for agricultural use, was divided and sold to graziers and maize farmers for a tidy profit. Keeping only a hundred acres that surrounded the homestead and the sawmill, Mary had shown some reservation towards her husband's eagerness to sell off his assets, but she was too busy bringing up their children to have a say in the business as she had before.

The work was demanding and taking its toll on Callum. With Mary no longer working by his side, he was running the growing business on his own. With another child on the way, all Mary could do was offer him support and make sure his time at home was as relaxing as possible.

39

The cloudless star-filled sky hung overhead like diamonds captured in a chiffon net. A full moon sat high over the Coast to the east, casting a shadow behind the man and his dog who stood atop Callum's Lookout. I say cloudless, but that wasn't exactly true. When I turned to the north, I noticed blackness on the horizon. Was there a change in the weather imminent?

Heading back, my phone rang just as we reached Mary's Mansion. It was Abi. 'Hey how's it going?'

'Good ...'

I reached into my pocket for the key and unlocked the door. Romeo rushed inside ahead of me.

'I just wanted to apologise for last night and this morning,' Abi said. 'I was a brat.'

'No, not at all. You were upset.' Fumbling for the light switch, I turned it on and entered the house.

'I was, but that's no excuse.'

'You seemed to piss off Matt Derby.' I kicked off my shoes and slumped down onto the sofa. Romeo immediately jumped into my lap.

'I piss them all off just being in the Valley.'

'Why is that?'

Abi sighed and I pictured her sitting alone somewhere in Brisbane. 'My presence just stirs up bad memories for them, I suppose.'

'I'm thinking of coming up to Brisbane.' I'm not sure why I shared this with her. I'd been considering the idea, more specifically, Fortitude Valley where Kathy had lived for twenty-odd years. If I was going to find out who the real Kathy Brown was, I'd find the answers there from people who really knew her.

'Great, you can stay with me if you like.'

'Really?'

'Well, on one condition.'

'What?'

'That you bring Romeo with you.'

'Done. Text me your address and I'll let you know when I'm coming up.'

'Cool.' She was about to hang up.

'Abi?'

'Yes?'

'Can I ask what the argument with Matt Derby was about?'

There was that sigh again. 'Like I said, he thinks I'm a bad influence on Tilly.'

'Why would he think that?'

'Because I'm Kathy's sister. He probably assumes we're tarred with the same brush.'

'I sense there's more to it, though.'

'Kathy wasn't a nice person, Scotty. She didn't treat people well.'

'Was she uhm …' it was a punt, but I threw it in anyway, '… was she capable of blackmail, do you think?'

Abi laughed. 'God yes! And she'd be bloody good at it too.'

'Do you think she could have had something over Matt Derby? Or his wife? Or Fenton?'

'Hmm. It would make sense. What makes you ask?'

'They're all just so guarded.'

'I think it's a good idea to come up here. I did a bit of digging around myself after Kathy died. Tried to speak to some people she knew. I'll be able to guide you in the right direction at least.'

'Are the people you mention still up there?'

'They certainly are. I got little out of them, though.'

I already knew, but I asked anyway. 'What kind of people?'

'Sex workers, nightclub bouncers. I couldn't bare it. This was a world a million miles away from mine.'

I made my mind up there and then. I needed to get up to Brisbane as soon as possible. 'Would tomorrow be okay?'

'Sure. I'm working from home so anytime that suits you.'

'Awesome. Probably be mid-morning. I'll call you when I leave.'

One minute after we ended the call, a text came through from Abi with her address. I made tea and topped up Romeo's water bowl.

In the bedroom, the picture of Kathy Brown was still hanging prominent on the whiteboard.

'What did you do, Kathy?' I asked out loud. I understood the Pattersons being angry with her because they believed she'd stolen Daisy's jewellery, but the mere mention of Kathy's name seemed to provoke the same reaction in everyone. Except for one person that is—Tilly. Why was that? Did she really get to know her better than anyone? If this was the case, why didn't she despise her like everyone else? Perhaps the *real* Kathy wasn't as bad as everyone thought. I needed to find out.

A shiver rippled from the top of my head right down to my toes, and the house suddenly felt cold. Romeo whined. He was on the bed.

'What is it, boy?'

He flicked his ears with a paw as if he was hearing something that I wasn't. Then he barked.

I went to stroke him but he jumped down from the bed and scuttled underneath it. Bugger me, then the lights flickered.

I was never the superstitious kind. Elvis and Tetley used to bang on all the time about conspiracies, UFOs, Bigfoot, the Bermuda Triangle, and all that crap. But not me. My mind was that of the logical detective. Without proof, it didn't exist. Perhaps that's why I never went to church.

There was a rumble overhead. I made my way out to the back verandah and looked up to what was mainly still a clear sky, except for a mass of dark cloud that was coming over the ridge. A sudden light show lit up the area as bolts of lightning ricocheted within the cloud as if they were trapped and trying to escape.

'You bloody ripper.' I loved a good storm.

I'd been warned that the slightest increase in the wind could knock out the power in the Valley, and fifteen minutes later as I lay in bed with a dog cowering beneath the doona. The power went out just as the first drops of rain thumped on the tin roof. Then, all of a sudden, the downpour hit, and a crack of thunder shook the house. Intermittent flashes of lightning lit up the interior of the bedroom like a strobe light. With each flash, I saw Kathy Brown's face staring back from the whiteboard like a headmaster about to administer six of the best. In those momentary flashes of daylight, I could have sworn she was grinning back at me. 'Settle down, you idiot,' I told myself, rolling over and pulling the doona over my head.

40

There was one person I hadn't spoken to yet—Tom Partridge.
I also wanted to get some time with the Pattersons if possible.
Leaving Romeo in the chicken coop with a bone, I'd arranged to
meet Tilly at the horse stud. It was early in the morning and for
some reason we felt the need to whisper as I met her at the gate.

'How did you go yesterday?' I asked as I stepped through the gate.

'You won't believe it.' Her face was beaming.

'What?'

'I took out the gold!'

'What? Wow!' I gave her a hug.

'You know what this means? I may be in with a chance to try
out for the Olympics.'

'Really? Wow again. You're amazing!'

While we made our way along the bitumen driveway, Tilly
told me all about the competition the day before. It sounded like
the judges were very impressed. We continued past the homestead
and seemed to walk for quite some time. This was the first time I'd
been on the other side of the property, and the landscape back there
was even more spectacular. Rolling hills, more paddocks and an
enormous billabong. In the distance, the sound of a diesel engine
undulated on the air and a cloud of dust was rising from the wake
of a small orange tractor as it navigated the outer rim of a circular

paddock. I hadn't realised the property was this big. If I had, I may have come in the Dub. But the exercise would do me good.

When we finally reached the enormous open-air arena, I was sweating.

Tom Partridge was slowly circumnavigating the paddock in the tractor, pulling a wide steel roller. Like an enormous rolling pin, it was flattening the ground and ironing out the weekend's traffic.

It took a few moments for Tilly to catch Tom's eye. He was wearing dark wraparound sunglasses and a pair of industrial earmuffs. He brought the tractor to a halt, cut off the engine and climbed down. Strolling towards us, he removed the earmuffs and, without making eye contact with me, he spoke to Tilly. 'What's up?'

'Nothing,' Tilly said. 'This is, Scott.'

Tom climbed through the copper-logged fence. There was a slight nod in my direction.

I stepped forward and shook his hand. 'Good to meet you at last, mate.'

The handshake was weak, and I could tell right away by the lowered gaze and the lack of eye contact Tom wasn't big on social interaction. 'Good to see you too.'

'Tom, Scotty would like to talk to you about Kathy,' Tilly said.

There was a definite reaction to this, a momentary frown at the sound of Kathy's name.

For a moment I thought his head would withdraw into his body like a Galapagos tortoise. 'Kathy?' His attempt at playing down the situation was doleful.

As if anticipating Tom's next words, Tilly took the earmuffs from him and climbed into the arena. 'I'll carry on here while you guys chat.' She jumped onto the tractor, started up the engine and continued the circular trek.

I stepped away from the fence. Tom reluctantly followed. 'I hear you were friends with Kathy,' I said as we strolled along the driveway.

'She was my friend, yes.'

I'd heard a lot about Tom, how he was good with the horses. He was terribly shy and although Tom was older, he reminded me of Troy Monroe, the autistic son of ex-Gold Coast Mayor, Julian Monroe.

'Do you know why anyone would have wanted to hurt her?'

We certainly weren't in one of the interview rooms at Surfers Paradise District Police Headquarters, but my method of gentle probing while reading his body language was exactly the same. Tom was extremely uncomfortable talking about Kathy. Like the tortoise once more, his neck was disappearing.

'Nobody liked her. Except me and Tilly.' His voice was barely audible.

'Why is that, do you think?'

This triggered a slight smirk, which took me by surprise. 'She was a wicked girl.'

'Wicked? In what way?' I grinned mischievously as if we were naughty schoolboys about to share a secret.

'She knew how to wind everyone up.'

'Right. Mister Fenton?'

'Oh yeah. I used to tell her not to do it because Mister Fenton is a good man.'

'And Matt Derby?'

Tom nodded.

'So where are you from, Tom? From around here?'

He shook his head. 'Brisbane. Mister Fenton gave me a job.'

I stopped and placed a hand on his shoulder. 'Mister Fenton brought you down from Brisbane?'

Tom nodded again.

Did Fenton have a penchant for giving people he hardly knew jobs and lodgings at his horse stud? There seemed to be a pattern here. First Tom, and then the Derbys. Was there anyone else? 'Did he bring Kathy down too?'

This made him smile. 'I was happy when she came.' 'And he gave her a job at the horse stud?'

'Uh-huh.'

Yes, there was a definite pattern. 'Why did she go away?' I was preventing him from walking.

'I don't know but it was just after she had a big row with Mister Fenton and Jake.'

'Jake?'

'Yeah. I heard him yelling at her one day. He said ... he said if she ever came back, he'd kill her!'

'Jake said that? Why didn't you tell any of this to the police?'

Tom shrugged and shook his head. 'I should have ... but I was scared.'

'Scared of Jake Fenton?'

There was no affirmative nod, he just continued to gaze at the ground. 'He calls me a fuck wit.'

'Why would he say that?'

'Because he's jealous.'

'Jealous of you?'

He shrugged, and I sensed he was growing tired.

'Do you know where Kathy went when she left?' There was about a year's gap between Kathy leaving Tallebudgera Valley for the first time, then showing up again in Brisbane.

He shook his head.

'But she came back, years later.' This made him smile.

'Why did she come back?'

'Because she thought someone had stolen something from her.'

'Really? Who?'

'Can't say.'

'But don't you think it could have been that person who hurt her?' I subconsciously used the term 'hurt' instead of 'killed'.

'No, Mister Fenton would never hurt anyone.'

Okay, although my actions may have seemed slow and casual, my mind was working overtime. Tom had just inadvertently informed me that Fenton may have stolen something from Kathy, and that Kathy had returned to the Valley wanting it back. I was finally getting somewhere. Although Tom's previous address was listed as Brisbane, the police didn't follow up because he had an alibi—one he shared with James Fenton and his son. They were together at a fundraiser in Byron Bay at the time of the murder.

A black Range Rover approached us from the direction of the house. Before I could make out who the driver was, I'd already guessed it was James Fenton. As the vehicle pulled up alongside us, my guess was confirmed.

'Scotty,' he said cheerfully as he climbed from the Rover offering me his hand. 'Did you hear the news?'

'News?'

'Tilly?'

'Oh yes.' He was referring to Tilly's win.

'She's going all the way that girl!'

'She certainly is.'

'I best get on,' Tom said, tipping an imaginary hat, then slipping away.

I wanted to grab him and pull him back. There were a zillion questions I still wanted to ask him, but they'd have to wait for another time.

'So how is the investigation going? I'm guessing you're starting to realise what a fraud Fisher is.'

He was right about one thing, I was swaying towards the idea that Fisher did indeed steal the story, and although it was the author who was paying for my services, his quest was the furthest thing from my mind. I used this to my advantage. 'Yes, I think you're right, sir. He completely ripped you off.'

'Good man. And will you testify to that in court?'

'Not at present, because I need to be absolutely sure. But when the time comes, I think we'll definitely have our day in court!'

'Excellent. I've got to keep moving.' He climbed back into the Rover and called out through the open window as he started the engine. 'Let me know if you need anything else from me. I'm only too happy to help.'

'Thank you, sir. I will.'

He drove onto the grass, turned the vehicle around and headed back down the driveway the way he came.

My pace heading back to Mary's Mansion was unconsciously faster. Feeling disconnected from my bodily functions, my mind churned through the information I'd just harvested. As I walked, I was making a mental list to add to the whiteboard:

1. *Fenton brought Tom to the Valley and gave him a job.*
2. *Shortly after, Kathy arrived, Fenton also gave her a job and accommodation in Mary's Mansion.*
3. *Then Kathy disappeared from the Valley for sixteen years.*
4. *In the meantime, Fenton met Matt Derby and also offered him a job and the prospect of relocating his family to Tallebudgera.*

<h1 style="text-align:center">41</h1>

Mrs Elizabeth Harrigan never adapted to the harsh Australian climate. In fact, life beyond the London social set didn't agree with her at all. From the moment the young couple and their first child of only four years old, left their stately home in Kensington and travelled down to Southampton, Elizabeth felt unwell. Bolstered with a broken heart for leaving behind the life she loved, her condition worsened during the long journey, and she suffered with what would later be termed as depression. Hardly even seeing daylight for the entire voyage, she'd remained in her cabin. Six months after arriving in Queensland, Elizabeth Harrigan was dead. Dorothy, her daughter, was five years old.

'What should I do, mother?' Dorothy asked as she knelt before Elizabeth's gravestone. 'The man is a pig, but I cannot escape him.' She paused, as if expecting a reply. Dorothy was still only nineteen. After finishing school, she'd recently started working for her father in the office of his sawmill. With no money, few belongings, and her old school friends scattered around the state, she felt abandoned and alone. Had her father really left her and done the things Fenton had said? Of course not. Charles Harrigan was a good man. He'd raised her on his own while single-handedly running his business. She knew him better than anyone else. He would never leave her. Because of this, she feared he was dead, killed at the hands of that monster Ron Fenton. 'Help me, mother.' Clasping her hands in prayer, she closed her eyes tightly.

'I thought I told you not to leave the house without seeing me first.'

The sound of his voice sent a shiver through her bones. She squeezed her eyes tightly together and prayed. 'Please Lord, deliver me from this evil, I beg—'

Fenton grabbed her hair from behind and yanked her to her feet. 'Don't you ignore me, girl,' he growled into her ear. 'So, you think you're high and mighty, do you?' He turned her around and pulled her towards him. Keeping a grip on her hair, he placed his other hand around her waist. Forcing her closer, he ran his wet lips over her cheek. 'You think you're better than old Ronny, do you?'

'No, sir. I do not.'

He pushed his lips on hers. It wasn't a kiss, more of an oral grope. His festering breath, mixed with whiskey and tobacco, made her want to vomit.

She could feel his hard body through her garments. Shaking free of him was impossible, he was far too strong. She tried to call out, but she knew there was no one around. Everything she did seemed to excite him. Her knees finally buckled as the monster forced her to the ground.

'Time to make you a woman, girl!' Fenton spat.

He was rough but thank God it was quick. The only thing Dorothy Harrigan still owned was stolen from her on top of her mother's grave. Raped by the man she suspected of killing her father. Sullied by a heathen.

Fenton marched away leaving her lying there. 'Get back to the house. You'll need to make arrangements for the wedding,' he called over his shoulder.

Wedding? Would this nightmare never end? Will she be forced to live the rest of her life under the control of this tyrant? Bruised and sore, she managed to sit up. Throwing her arms around the gravestone and openly weeping, she no longer felt like a lady, more like a dog or a thoroughbred horse that had just been broken.

***

Dorothy Fenton wanted to hate the child, she really did, but when the midwife placed little James in her arms, a feeling of joy that she hadn't experienced for a long time filled her heart. With a thatch of dark curly hair and green eyes, the little person looking back at her was forced into this world just as she had been.

Although the wedding was hastily arranged, it was, in Ron Fenton's eyes at least, the most extravagant occasion to be held in Currumbin Valley. Dorothy hated every moment but was trapped. Fenton owned her now. Memories of her past life at the private school for girls in Brisbane, and of her dreams for a bright future, were things of the past. Even the guest list reflected Fenton's will. None of her friends received invitations. She had no family, so of the hundred or so people present—businessmen and their wives, politicians, local dignitaries—Dorothy knew no one. It was as if the Harrigans were completely wiped from history. This was mostly due to Fenton spreading lies about her father.

For the nine months she'd carried the child, she'd lived in dread. For some reason, she knew it would be a boy. Fenton frequently threatened that should she give birth to a girl, he would throw it to the pigs. There was no doubt in Dorothy's mind that his threats were genuine. He was a cruel man.

So, the maternal feelings she experienced for the child, although unexpected, actually offered a glimmer of hope in a life that was quashed. She decided it would be she who took control of the boy's upbringing.

'Of course. That's why you're here,' Fenton said after Dorothy had finally worked up the courage to broach the subject. 'I don't even wanna see him till his balls drop.'

Fenton dismissed her from his office with an impatient wave of his hand. 'But don't be thinking you're gonna bring him up like a ponce,' he called after her. 'He needs to be a man like me.'

This was exactly what Dorothy had hoped for. Under her control, James would receive the best education and grow as a true gentleman like his grandfather. If this was to be her only achievement in life, then so be it.

Over the next five years, Dorothy gave birth to five more children—three boys and two girls—and although she loved them equally, it would be her first born she held closest to her heart. There was a bond as if they'd been the first inmates of a new jail, or missionaries trying to uphold the word of the Lord in a new colony. However, with a sharp wit and a cunning aptitude, little James Fenton may have had a different point of view. Time would tell.

42

My little recognisance into the world of Tom Partridge had paid off heaps. Although I'd need to talk to him again, he'd given me a whole new outlook on the case. So, fully loaded with a barrage of questions but no one yet to fire them at, I set off for Brisbane in the Dub with Romeo in the back.

There was the usual congestion on the M1 between the West Burleigh and Varsity Lakes exits due to the two-year upgrade that felt like it was taking ten, but once the traffic emerged from the boxed-off lanes and out under the Reedy Creek overpass, it was a steady run all the way to the Stanley Street exit, eighty-five kilometres north.

After exiting the M1, the mighty Gabba soon came into view. The AFL home of the Brisbane Lions. It was at times like this when I wondered how my life would have turned out if I'd turned pro like my youth coaches had predicted.

Doris, my pet name for the Google Maps girl, interrupted my thoughts. 'In four hundred metres, turn left onto Wellington Road and bear right towards East Brisbane.'

I did as I was told.

Then, 'Keep right.' Pause. 'In thirty metres, turn right onto Lytton Road and bear left.' A minute later, I got a glimpse of the Brisbane River as I cruised past Mowbray Park.

I was glad I'd entered the address Abigail had given me into Google Maps A recent mass road widening had changed the area vastly since I'd last been up there. When I finally turned off the busy road, I instantly found myself weaving along a narrow tree-lined street with rows of traditional Queenslander homes on either side.

Abi's place was quite a large example—cream weatherboard, siding, a green corrugated iron roof, a verandah out front, with a timber balustrade and matching stairs. I pipped my horn as I swung into the tight driveway. Abi's car was parked along the side of the house in front of a matching freestanding garage.

When I climbed from the Dub, Abi came down the front stairs. 'Hey Scotty, you made it.'

'Yep.'

Romeo jumped over the driver's seat, bounded out of the car and rushed to greet Abi.

After the mandatory 'fuss' time, Abi rose to her feet and held out her hand for me to shake. 'How was the traffic?'

I shook her hand. 'Not bad for this time of the day.'

'Good. Come on.' She turned and headed back towards the stairs. I ducked back into the Dub, pulled the bonnet release knob with a clunk and retrieved my overnight bag from the boot. Romeo, meanwhile, had abandoned me and followed Abi into the house.

The interior of the building was traditional just like the exterior—cream tongue and grooved walls, high ornate ceilings and polished timber floors. The furniture was mostly antique, and I suspected this wasn't actually Abi's choice. 'Nice place.'

'Thanks. This was Kathy's house.'

I had already guessed as much.

'Drink?'

'Sure.'

We headed through the lounge and into the kitchen at the back of the house. 'Coffee, tea, beer?'

'Have you got a soft drink?'

She opened the fridge and pulled out two cans of Coke. 'This okay?'

'Perfect.'

After handing one to me, she retrieved a stainless-steel bowl from one of the overhead cupboards, filled it with water and placed it on the floor for Romeo. 'There you go, mate.'

Romeo lapped up the cool liquid, splashing it all over the floor.

I'd already spied through a row of French doors, a large deck at the back of the house. It was furnished with contemporary basket weave sofas, and a huge timber outdoor table and chairs. The view over the park, the river, the Story Bridge and Brisbane City in the distance, was spectacular. 'Bags coming here on New Year's Eve,' I said.

'It's a date,' Abi said, smiling before opening her can with a loud *shpuch*.

I did the same. 'So, Kathy owned this place as well as Mary's Mansion?'

'Apparently.'

'I don't mean to be rude, but how could she afford something like this?'

Abi shrugged.

In the current market, I'd estimate the place to be worth around two million dollars. 'Did she have it for long?'

Abi shook her head. 'A couple of years before she died!'

'Really.' This was interesting. 'A year or so before she bought Mary's Mansion.'

'Yep, and there are no mortgages on either property.'

'She paid cash?'

'Looks that way. What do you want to do first?' Abi asked, changing the subject.

'Chill for a bit then head over to the Valley later.'

'Monday night's probably a good time to go. Towards the weekend it's just too crazy.'

I nodded knowingly. Every city has one. Fortitude Valley was Brisbane's answer to Sydney's Kings Cross or Soho in London. The area was somewhere between sleazy and trendy. Night clubs, strip joints, restaurants, and bars. Not much more than a couple of hilly parallel streets, the Valley seemed to have a dark energy that was probably a lingering vestige of a murky past. I wasn't familiar with the actual history of the place. My only real experience was the night when Elvis got bashed. We were in our early twenties. Elvis was at uni. I was in the process of applying to join the police force. We'd all come up to Brisbane for a stag night. Josh Palmer, an old mate from Palm Beach Currumbin High, was marrying a girl from Lutwyche, and decided he wanted to hold his big night in the Valley. The crowds of drunken revellers made Surfers Paradise look like a botanical garden. There was a small party of us and we got split up halfway through the night. When we met up again later, a gang of youths had set on Elvis—he'd suffered a split lip and a black eye.

We took seats on the comfy sofas.

'So, you were telling me you had some contacts, people who knew Kathy?' I said.

'I sold The Panda Club right away. Only set foot in the place once. Met with a girl who had worked with Kathy. She had a good memory and was happy to talk, but I wasn't listening. I couldn't concentrate in that place. Just wanted to get out of there and throw up.'

'That bad, eh?'

'It was horrible. And to think that was my sister's world. It just sickened me.'

Although I was itching to prize out the secrets that Kathy Brown took to her grave, I had to admit, I wasn't looking forward to delving into Brisbane's underbelly. But it had to be done.

43

Through Abi, I'd arranged to meet Katz in The Panda Club bar at 6.00 pm. The only information I had about the woman was that she'd known Kathy since she'd first arrived in Fortitude Valley. She'd worked beside her, on and off, for a couple of years. The meeting time was a compromise, before the rush. Johns needed servicing even on a Monday night. Katz would be at the beginning of her shift. I was her first client for the evening. I'd made it clear all I wanted to do was talk.

Abi dropped me outside the old Woolstore building. I was strategically ten minutes early.

The walk down to the bar took around thirty seconds. There was already a bouncer on the door but no queue.

'Fuck me, Scotty Stephens,' the burly lad said. His bandy legs and slight limp told me he was an ex-league player; however, his pummelled features said he could have just as easy have been a boxer. 'It's not come to this, has it, mate?'

I didn't know him. Like everyone else, he obviously knew me from my fifteen minutes of fame. The Gold Coast Suns baseball cap I'd hoped would hide my identity failed at the first hurdle. 'Afraid so, mate.' I grinned mischievously. It was always a good idea to keep on the right side of a doorman.

He grinned back knowingly. 'Bullshit! You working a new case? Private dick now, I hear.' His expression suddenly hardened. 'Shit, you're not on the trail of another serial killer, are you?'

'No, nothing like that, mate. Just meeting a friend for a drink.'

The grin returned and he tapped the side of his nose with his index finger. After years on the police force, I could spot a working girl a mile off, but none of that instinct was required here. Even this early in the evening, it was obvious the girls congregated at the far end of the bar were hookers having a drink before their shifts began. There were a couple of punters sitting in separate booths, each chatting to a girl. As I approached the bar, one girl from the group stood and swanned towards me on impossibly high stilettoes.

'Hello handsome.' Her accent was distinctly Kiwi. 'Want to buy a girl a drink?' Thankfully, she didn't seem to recognise me.

'I'm looking for Katz.'

The responsive flicker of an expression said, *'Oough!'* She leaned in close. 'You can do much better than that.' She held out her hand as if expecting me to kiss it. 'I'm Juicy.'

My smile generated the same reaction as if I'd shown her my old detective badge. Like me, years of experience had honed the skills of these girls. They knew a copper when they saw one. She immediately backed away, turned and headed back to the group.

I ordered a Coke and planted myself down on a barstool. People watching was one of my favourite pastimes. Sitting with my back to the bar, I scanned the room. Not much to see apart from the two middle-aged businessmen. One was Asian, the other overweight and balding—both were being primed by the two working girls. The décor was over-the-top-tacky and had seen better days. The carpet was stained and worn.

'There you go, mate,' the barman said, placing a tall glass of Coke on the bar. I recognised an accent.

The name tag on the young man's chest said, 'Luiz'.

'Gracias senor.'

This brought a smile to Luiz's face. *'Obrigado* … Brazilian not Espanyol.'

'Ah, *lociento*,' I didn't know any Portuguese and my Spanish was limited. I once dated a Mexican student who'd spent a year living in Rainbow Bay.

Thankfully, Luiz's English was good.

'Worked here long?'

There was that familiar expression when the penny dropped. His body stiffened. 'Six months only.'

'It's all right. I'm not a copper.' I reassured him. 'Ex copper but, so your instincts are good.'

This did little to relax him.

'I'm meeting with Katz.' I exaggerated a scan of the room with my eyes. 'Is she here already?'

Luiz blushed. 'Yes.'

'She is? Where?'

He nodded past me.

I swivelled around on the stool to find a woman standing right behind me.

'Who's asking?' she said with a deep smoker's rattle.

'Hi.' I rose from the stool and offered my hand. 'I'm Scotty.'

'I know who you are.' She didn't take my hand. 'Usual Luiz,' she said to the barman then sat herself down on the stool next to mine.

The heavy make-up did little to hide the telltale signs of a hard life. In fact, the blue eyeliner made her eyes look more sunken than they actually were, and overly applied rouge seemed to enhance the broken capillaries on her cheeks and nose. Her black, shoulder length hair was dry and parted by a sliver of grey. She wore a golden sequined jacket, a red low-cut blouse and a pink skirt. 'So, you know Abi?' she asked, placing an oversized handbag on the bar.

'I do.'

'You know the rate?'

I nodded, reached into my wallet and handed her two fifty-dollar notes.

She folded them over and placed them in her bag, but as she did; she glared at the group of girls at the other end of the bar and I realised she was gloating.

As if reading my expression, she said, 'Don't flatter yourself. I get all the has-beens.'

Right, so she had recognised me. 'I'm actually here to talk about Kathy Brown.'

Luiz returned with a large rainbow-coloured cocktail.

'Put it on his bill,' Katz said. She stood, lifted the drink in one hand and her bag in the other. 'Come on, I need a smoke.'

I followed her as she sauntered past the group of girls towards a door at the end of a bar.

This led to a balcony overlooking the street behind a screen of timber slats. There were half a dozen high tables and stools and, thankfully, no other smokers.

Katz plonked down her bag and drink on the nearest table, reached into the bag and retrieved a box of Richmond Express cigarettes. She didn't offer me one, which I obviously would have turned down. Instead, she slid one from the pack, lit it with a cheap plastic lighter and climbed onto one of the stools.

I retrieved my iPhone from my pocket. 'Do you mind if I record our conversation?'

'Whatever turns you on, I guess.' She took a deep draw of her cigarette and instantly blew out the smoke towards the ceiling. 'What is it you wanna know?'

'You worked with Kathy?'

'You don't work with anybody in this game,' she snapped back impatiently. 'It's not fucking McDonald's.'

'But you knew her.'

'Yeah.' She took a sip of her cocktail. 'She was my bud.'

'When did you first meet her?'

'Are you still a copper? I heard you got booted out?'

'I'm a private detective.'

'You're working for Abi?' There was a glimmer of interest in her question.

'Yes.' I lied.

'Good. Someone needs to find out the truth.'

'So, you knew Kathy back in the day?'

'She arrived just after me. I'd come up from Melbourne, she came from Sydney.' She lowered her chin and her voice. 'We were both runaways.'

'How old would you have been?'

'I was fifteen, Kathy was fourteen.'

Although I already knew this, the realisation that these young girls had arrived in this environment at such early ages still shocked me.

Katz seemed to sense what I was thinking and lightened the mood. 'We both had the same name. I was Kathy Booth, she was Kathy Brown. Maeve didn't like that, so she called me Katz.'

'Maeve Morrison, the Madame?'

This made Katz laugh, instigating a phlegmy coughing fit. A drag of her cigarette and a sip of her drink calmed her down. 'She certainly was a Madame. She took us newbies under her wing. At first we thought this was an act of kindness, but she was grooming us.' She leaned in. The aroma of cigarette smoke and alcohol on the breath of someone who probably hadn't eaten all day was rank. 'Protecting her investments.'

'She put you to work right away?'

'Pretty much. No such thing as underage then.' She leaned in again and whispered. 'Still isn't.'

I was fighting the urge to turn my head away from her. Instead, I held her stare. 'What can you tell me about Kathy?'

'Oh, she was a smart one. And tough as old boots.' 'She was popular?'

The reaction to my question was a high-pitched wheezy laugh. 'Popular? I guess you could say that. She was in control from day one.'

'What do you mean?'

'Well, for every trick we girls turned, she turned two. She worked seven days a week, and every punter wanted her.'

'But she was fourteen?'

'That girl was never fourteen. She was born a woman.'

'Did the other girls grow to resent her?'

Katz inhaled and exhaled another cloud of smoke. 'Not just the girls, Maeve was getting wary. Some of the Johns were complaining. Kathy had a way of manipulating people.'

'You think she might have been what? Blackmailing the odd businessman?'

'I know she was.'

'When did you last see her?'

'She's fucking dead you idiot. When do you think I last saw her?'

'I mean, did you see her long before she died?'

Katz shook her head and inhaled more smoke. 'Kathy moved up in the world. She went down to the Gold Coast for a time, but when she came back, she'd changed.'

'In what way?'

'More determined. Then fuck me, a few years later she bought the club from old Maeve, and she was the new boss.'

'Did you resent that?'

'Hell no, good on her. We're all looking for that sugar daddy. Kathy found hers.'

'Fenton you mean?' It was a stab in the dark and one that just popped into my mind.

Katz nodded. She was holding the cigarette in one hand and the drink in the other, dipping between the two. 'That bastard Fenton!'

44

I wasn't sure how long a hundred bucks would get me, but I would keep revving that engine until the tank ran dry. Katz didn't seem too worried about the time, so I pressed on.

'Did Fenton take a shine to Kathy?'

Katz had the melodramatic habit of throwing her head back when she smoked, exhaling a plume of smoke towards the ceiling. 'Oh, he loved Kathy. All the punters did.'

'Did he know she was underage?'

'Of course! That was his thing.'

'Did he take her away?'

Katz tilted her head and looked at me through squinting eyes as if to say, *What the hell? Aren't you listening?* 'Nobody told Kathy what to do.'

'So, what? She …? She went to Tallebudgera on her own accord?'

'Yep, but not for Fenton.' Her answers were delivered between inhalations of smoke and sips of drink.

'Who else would she go for?'

'Tommy!'

Did she mean Tom Partridge? I played dumb. 'Tommy?'

'Maeve's boy.' She finished her drink and handed me the glass.

When I came back from the bar with a fresh cocktail, Katz was nowhere to be seen. To my relief, she appeared a few minutes later from the ladies toilets. Before sitting back down, she lit another cigarette.

204

'You were telling me about Tommy.'

'Ahh, Tommy. We all loved him. Soft in the head, you know?' She tapped her temple. 'We all looked out for him.'

'So why would Fenton be interested in him? Was he …?' Now it was my turn to tilt my head.

Katz furrowed her brow and pouted.

'Was he into boys as well?'

She laughed. 'Not as far as I know.'

'So, what then?'

'Well, he was the boy's dad, of course.'

I shouldn't have been taking a drink at that moment because I choked and almost spewed a spray of Coke all over Katz. After a couple of hearty coughs, I regained my composure. 'Fenton was Tommy's father?'

'Yep, well at least Maeve claimed he was. Threatened to tell his wife. Milked that cow until she kicked it.'

'So, Fenton took the lad to Tallebudgera?'

'When he was about sixteen or so.' She finished her second drink at the same time as her cigarette. 'I'm hungry.'

I'd learned more in the last thirty minutes than in the entire week since I'd taken on the case. Katz suggested a Thai restaurant. I agreed, following her out of the club and down the hill. Staggering slightly, her shoes clip-clopping loudly on the pavement, I was glad it was a Monday night and reasonably quiet. It may sound harsh but being seen in an area like this with a known, and very mature, hooker wouldn't have looked good on my resumé.

Walking down the hill, Katz suddenly stopped and pointed to an expensive-looking apartment block. 'This is where we used to live. Not there, of course.' She dismissed the building with a wave of a hand. 'Before this place was built, Maeve owned a block of shithole units that we girls lived in. Kathy and I shared a room.'

'So, you knew her pretty well?'

'Better than anyone, I reckon.'

Over spring rolls, noodles and pad thai, I continued to gently probe. 'What about Kathy? Did she follow Tommy or did Fenton entice her down?'

'Don't know.'

It wasn't pretty watching Katz eat, and her speaking with a mouth full of food didn't help.

'Did Kathy ever confide in you?'

'In the early days. But that was before she went away.' She burped and wiped her mouth with a napkin, then added matter-of-factly, 'Before the baby.'

Thankfully, this time, there were no potential projectiles in my mouth. 'Baby?'

Katz continued to stuff her face as if she hadn't eaten for days. 'About six months after she left, she turned up here on her way to the Sunshine Coast.'

'Pregnant?'

'She wasn't showing at that time, but she told me.'

'Tommy's?' I immediately regretted asking the question. My instinct was to duck my head and shield my face with my hands as Katz laughed out loud, almost dumping the contents of her mouth on the table. 'Not Tommy, you idiot. Fenton!'

Although I was acting dumb to prize out as much information as I could, little parts of the puzzle were falling into place. Fenton brought Tommy down to the Gold Coast and gave him a job because the lad was his illegitimate son. And he was probably being fleeced by Tommy's mother, Maeve. But for some reason, Kathy followed Tommy. Why would she do that? Was she sick of being on the game? Or did Fenton lure her down to the Coast also? Knowing that the two of them were close, could that have been the reason Fenton took Tommy away, knowing that Kathy would follow? Like weeds in a garden; for every answer you unearthed, another question popped up. So, Fenton was not only the father of Tommy, but he also fathered a child with Kathy. 'Why did she go to the Sunshine Coast?' I already had a pretty good idea of the answer, but there was no room for idle assumptions.

'To have the baby without anyone knowing.'

I was right. 'What happened to the child?'

'It was put up for adoption right after the birth.'

'Then what? She came back here?'

'Yes, but no longer as a working girl. I don't know how she did it, but she wound up managing The Panda Bar.'

'Did you remain friends?'

'Nope. As I said, Kathy moved up in the world. Left us all behind.'

I wasn't sensing any anger in her tone; on the contrary, she spoke as if she was proud of her old friend. 'Can't blame her. She did what we all wanted to do.'

'To get out?'

Katz had finished her food and I could tell by a nervous twitch that she was dying for another fag. 'There are rooms out the back of The Panda Club,' she said before finishing her drink.

The information she was giving me was priceless. I nodded eagerly for her to continue. 'Right.'

'Another hunjy'll do it.'

'I'm sorry?'

'Another hundred. We can go to one of the rooms.' She placed a hand on top of mine and winked.

The body language as I checked my watch said, *Oh is that the time?*

'You know you want to,' she said, stroking my hand.

I stood. We were finished here. 'Would love to, but I've got to go.' I reached into my wallet, withdrew another hundred and gave it to her. 'You've been really helpful, Katz, and I appreciate your time.'

Katz rose unsteadily from the table. 'Think nothing of it. Come back anytime.'

I watched her leave then fixed up the bill. Financially, it had been an expensive exercise but in terms of information, it had been a bloody good night. And the fact that Ben Fisher was footing the bill for all expenses, somehow made it sweeter.

I called an Uber and was soon travelling over the Story Bridge on my way back to East Brisbane. After bidding goodnight to the driver, Don, a retired pastry chef who suffered with anxiety, I knocked on Abi's front door. She opened it almost immediately.

'Gee, you're back early,' she said, stepping back and allowing me to enter.

Romeo came to greet me and stole my attention for the mandatory fuss.

'I know, I thought it was later.'

'How'd you go?'

'Good. Really good actually.'

'Want to tell me about it over a beer?'

'Sure, what have you got in mind?'

45

It was a rare occasion when Callum Murphy found time to relax. But even as he sat on the back verandah watching the neighbourhood children gathering around his daughter as she blew out the candles on her birthday cake, his mind was elsewhere. The name *Ron Fenton* was not only popping up in conversation more and more just recently, but it was seeping into the infrastructure of the Valley like sewage from an overfilled drop pit. Somehow The Rat had procured land close to the mouth of Tallebudgera Creek in Burleigh Heads and built a sawmill there. Not only that, he'd offered the getters great incentives to bypass the Murphy mill and send their logs directly to Burleigh, after offering to transport and mill their lumber for almost half the cost of Callum's charges. With his existing mill and cutting operation in the neighbouring Currumbin Valley, the name *Fenton* was building in reputation.

Although he hated the man with a passion, Callum couldn't help but wonder how Fenton had gained such power in a relatively short time. It was the *Great Britain* all over again, but this time it was Fenton who was gaining the upper hand.

'I'll get you for this, Callum Murphy. See if I don't,' Fenton vowed when he was banished to the bowels of the ship. But in only a matter of weeks, he'd risen from the depths of depravity with a new following and was back in the upper decks. The man

209

was smart, cunning and tough, but he'd always be known as The Rat, thanks to Callum.

Callum knew his enemy wouldn't renege on his promise of revenge and that one day there'd be a confrontation. For the first few years in the Valley, this had been the farthest thing from his mind; in fact, he almost forgot about the ship rat completely. But as he began to hear of the rising gaffer called Fenton, it was like a timer was set within him, ticking away, counting down towards an inevitable showdown.

***

'Can you not forget the mill for just a few minutes, Callum?' Mary said, handing him a plate of birthday cake.

'Aye, Oy was watching Mare and her friends.'

Mary frowned at her husband. 'You was not. You might have been looking in that direction but that's not what you was seeing. What's bothering you?'

'Nuttin, just tired that's all.'

Taking advantage of a quiet moment while the children, seated in a circle on the grass, ate their cake, Mary knelt by his side. 'Is it Fenton?'

Although she didn't spend as much time working at the sawmill these days, Mary knew there was no aspect of the milling process her husband couldn't handle. This was purely because he'd not only experienced every situation, from workplace accidents and deaths, bushfires and floods, but he'd remained strong throughout the bad times. So, there was only one thing that could govern his thoughts this way—Ron Fenton.

'He's controlling the log flow.'

Mary shrugged. 'So?'

'So, he's slowly killing our business.'

'Worry about it tomorrow. Enjoy today,' Mary said.

***

Mary was right. There was nothing to be done at that moment but to enjoy the company of his family. Callum rose from his stupor, kicked off his boots and socks, joined the children on the grass, and ate cake with them.

'Have you finished with your sulking, Da?' little Mare asked nonchalantly.

She was ten years old, cute as a bobby pin and twice as sharp. Maybe it was because she was the only girl in the litter, or because she reminded Callum so much of his wife. But one thing was for sure, she got away with a lot more than her brothers ever did.

'Aye, no more sulking.'

'Did you meet me new friend Jimmy?' Mare asked.

'No, Oy did not.'

Sitting next to Mare was a thin lad of the same age. He had a shock of black hair and deep penetrating green eyes. 'It's good to meet you, sir.'

'It's good to meet you too, Jimmy.'

'James, I … I prefer to be called James.' He had an Australian accent with an English tone.

Mare laughed and punched him on the arm. 'That's why I call him Jimmy.'

'And do you live in the Valley, James?' Callum asked, shovelling cake into his mouth.

'Yes, sir. We just moved from Currumbin.'

'Jimmy is in my class at school,' Mare said.

A group of children sprang from the ground and, with the added high of pure sugar, they tore around the garden, screaming and yelling.

Callum finished his cake and made his way back to the verandah.

***

Mary was waiting for him apprehensively.

'What's the matter with you?' Callum asked noticing his wife's wary expression.

'I saw you talking to James.'

'Aye, seems like a nice lad.'

Mary inhaled and exhaled slowly. 'He's Ron Fenton's son!'

'What?' Callum's face raged scarlet as if millions of blood vessels were exploding at the same time.

Mary, anticipating the worse, grabbed him by the shoulders. 'Calm down, fella.'

'How could you allow a Fenton to come on this property, woman?'

'I only found out myself a few minutes ago. Mare has been telling me about her new friend at school for the last couple of weeks, but she only ever referred to him as Jimmy.'

'But he's a Fenton. And they don't live in Tallebudgera Valley.'

'They do now, it seems. Ron bought the Fowler property down by the oyster beds.'

'The bastard's moving in. Oy knew it …'

'Calm down,' Mary said, squeezing his shoulders.

A group of parents, some on the verandah, some on the grass, turned at Callum's outburst.

Now it was Callum's turn to take a deep breath until he noticed there was one woman watching him closely. He immediately knew it was Fenton's wife.

Following his gaze, Mary realised who he was looking at and physically turned him in the opposite direction. 'Aye, that's Fenton's missus.'

Callum lowered his voice into a growl. 'We need to get them off this property right now.'

'We need to ignore them and act as if we don't care who they are.'

'Have you spoken to her?' He was whispering now.

'Aye, but I didn't know who she was then.'

'And?'
'She seems like a gracious lady.'
'But—'
'I know. They're Fentons. I know.'

46

Because it was Monday night, it was also quiet at the Shafston Hotel. Abi was familiar with the bar staff, so they allowed us to sit in the back bar with Romeo, even making a fuss of him, which he loved.

I ordered two beers from the bar. When I went to pay, the barman smiled and said, 'On the house, mate.'

'Really?'

'My bloody oath. You're a legend, Scotty. My sister lives on the Gold Coast. She was a wreck while that maniac was on the loose. You put an end to it. Thank you!'

'Thanks, mate.' I held up a beer as a salute.

'The least I can do.'

When I sauntered back from the bar, one of the barmaids was chatting to Abi while massaging Romeo's fur. She'd placed a bowl of water by his side.

'This is Kelly, Scott. A good friend of mine.'

'G'day, Kel,' I said, placing the drinks on the table.

'Scotty Stephens, wow!' She wobbled a little as she rose to her feet. Wearing the black uniform polo shirt, tight black shorts and Doc Martens boots, one arm was a full tattoo sleeve. 'I never thought I'd get to meet you.'

'I never thought I'd get to meet *you*.' Grinning, I shook her hand. This made her giggle.

'Quite the bloody rock star you are,' Abi said when Kelly returned to the bar. 'I never realised.'

'I know, it's embarrassing.'

'Yeah right.' She playfully punched me on the arm. 'You love it.'

Truth is, I didn't love it. In fact, I would have much preferred that it didn't happen, but I was also grateful, because my fame could easily have been infamy if I hadn't solved the X case. There was a time there when the public, believing I'd lied and had an innocent man killed, had wanted my blood.

Romeo stood alert, eyeing up the handful of other punters and watching the comings and goings of the bar staff with great interest.

We took a sip of our drinks in that universal way and smiled with satisfaction.

'Kelly almost ended up in Fortitude Valley.'

'She did?'

'Yep. I was outside The Panda Club one day, trying to get up the courage to go in and ask some questions. Kelly was standing on the pavement outside carrying a backpack. She asked me if I worked there. I said I didn't. She was so lovely. Talkative, you know? After a bit of friendly chat, I learned she'd come up from Sydney to get a job in the Valley. She reminded me of Kathy.'

'Did she get the job?'

'No. I talked her out of it and ended up taking her home with me. She got a job here, got a place of her own.'

'Good for you!' I said, holding up my glass.

'We're a right pair of saints, aren't we?'

After clinking our glasses together, we took another drink. Not a sip this time, more of a long savour.

'When are you going back?'

'I was gonna head off in the morning but made no plans.'

'Stick around a bit if you like. I can reschedule my work tomorrow.'

It was school holidays, but Abi still had work to do from home.

'A day in Bris Vegas?'

'Why not?'

It sounded quite appealing. Plus, after parting with Katz and returning to East Brisbane, I couldn't help feeling there were more answers to be found in Fortitude Valley. If I stayed another night, I could return there and continue digging. 'All right. You can be the tour guide.'

'Cool.'

'Abi, did you know Kathy had a baby?'

Like me, she almost choked on her drink. 'What?'

According to Katz, Abi got pregnant when she was only fifteen, during her first stint at Tallebudgera.

'Are you sure?' Her question was tinged with anger.

'Apparently. She went up to the Sunshine Coast, had the baby and put it straight up for adoption.' I could tell Abi was genuinely shocked by this news.

'But …' Her eyes scanned the floor like a minesweeper. 'I had no idea. Do we know anything about the child?'

'Nope, that's all I have, but I should be able to find out when I get back to the Coast.' I was hoping Jenny or Bradley could help with this.

Abi went to the bar to order the next round. As I watched her pass across the room, I got that feeling of familiarity once more. But now I knew exactly who it was that she reminded me of.

We had one more beer, also on the house. It surprised me when Abi didn't speak again of the revelation I'd just presented her with. In fact, she'd said very little after that until we left the pub. Heading back over Mowbray Park, Abi placed her arm in mine as we strolled, Romeo pulling on his leash out front. It was a nice night for a stroll. We stopped momentarily and watched a Brisbane City Cat ferry as it docked, unloaded a couple of passengers, then continued on its way.

'We can go into town on one of those tomorrow,' Abi said.

It was only a few minutes' walk from the pub to Abi's house, but we strung it out, both enjoying the warm clear evening.

'Are you any closer to working it out?' Abi asked as we passed the rowing club.

'Who killed Kathy, you mean?'

Abi nodded.

'I have to be honest with you, I haven't, but all the signs are pointing to Fenton at the moment.'

'But he had an alibi.'

'I know but I've heard that before.' The fact that Fenton's guilt seemed obvious was making me question the case even more. It was like watching one of those whodunit movies when the story purposely focuses on a certain character, but you know that it's just too obvious for him to be the killer. I couldn't help thinking there was more to this. A lot more.

After returning to Abi's house, we had coffee and chatted more. When we finally said good night and Romeo and I had retired to the spare bedroom, I was feeling a little guilty as I lay there in bed, going over the day in my mind. For some reason, I hadn't fully shared the game-changing epiphany with Abi that hit me like a bolt of lightning as soon as Katz told me about Kathy's pregnancy. Perhaps I was waiting to see if she'd work it out too. She hadn't, so I'd let it go. Of course, it was still just a theory, but as I lay there with Romeo snuggled by my side; the pieces were falling together in my mind like a giant Tetra Puzzle.

Was I the only person who knew that Tilly Derby was Kathy Brown's daughter?

47

'But they seem like such decent people, Ronald.'

'Decent my arse. Callum Murphy ain't got a decent bone in his body!' Ron Fenton's East London accent was a stark contrast to his wife's refined Kensington intonation. An unsuspecting onlooker would be excused for mistaking the lean leather-skinned layman as the lady's servant. Underestimating the man though would be a different matter, as many had.

'New money, lacking the social graces one would expect of a wealthy family, yes, but impressive nonetheless when you think of what they have achieved.'

'They've achieved?' Ron raised his voice in anger. 'What about what I've achieved?'

'Well, you're impressive too, my love. That's why I married you.'

'Don't you patronise me, woman.' Ron's backhand blow was swift across the young woman's face. 'I'm better than all of them Micks put together, an' it'll be me driving 'em out of this valley.'

'I didn't mean to patronise you, sir,' Dorothy said, sobbing. 'I would never do that.' For as much as the act seemed painfully subservient, the woman was smart enough to know that addressing her husband as 'sir' would calm him down. It always did.

'You do it too often, Dorothy Harrigan,' Ron replied, using Dorothy's maiden name as part of the ritual. This would bolster his superiority requisite to the extent of arousal.

'I've been very naughty. Will you ever forgive me?' She put her arms around his neck and lowered her head in mock shame.

'You'll need to earn my forgiveness, you filthy slut.'

'Yes, sir.'

James Fenton, crouched at the keyhole of his parents' bedroom, watching the unfolding scene until the very end. When his father finally fell back on the bed, naked and exhausted, and his mother covered her naked sore body with the eiderdown, he snuck back to his room.

Fenton had passed on his agenda to his son and ordered him to infiltrate the Murphy family by befriending their daughter. He'd even moved the boy from his school in Currumbin to the Tallebudgera school after purchasing the old Fowler cottage.

'We're gonna drive 'em out!' Ron said one day while teaching James how to pick a lock. 'We've overtaken them in the west, now we're coming for 'em from the east and we'll cut 'em off before they get to Springwood.' He slashed his hand slowly across his neck as if he had a knife.

It was part of a master plan Ron had hatched over the years since he'd sworn his vengeance on Callum Murphy. And it was no idle threat. Under a pseudonym, he'd already purchased hundreds of acres of pastureland between the oyster beds and the Murphy homestead, and although the land was cleared of cedar, it was now sought after for grazing or maize farming. With most of the getters on his payroll, his plan was to head as far out west with the logging as he could while spreading north. Then, like a military strategy, Fenton's army would double back. Murphy would have nowhere to go. Even a retreat would only take him as far back as his homestead. Beyond that was land soon to be owned by Fenton. Not only was he looking forward to the day when he'd enjoy watching his old adversary squirm, but destroying everything that bastard had built for himself, including his home, his family, and most of all, that bitch Mary McCarthy, was the reason he got up in the mornings.

***

'But why, Da? He's my friend,' young Mary Murphy pleaded, sobbing.

'Because he's a Fenton, and Fenton's are no good!' Callum said, trying to control the tremble in his voice.

'But I like him.'

'Oy don't care. You're not to see him again, do you hear me girl?' It was useless trying to control his emotions. He was yelling now.

'Don't be beating up on the wee girl,' Mary said, pushing past her husband and comforting her daughter.

'Oy've never harmed a hair on that girl's head, but by Christ if she ever sees that boy again, Oy'll not be responsible for my actions.'

'Oh, don't be so dramatic, man,' Mary said as calm as ever. 'He's a ten-year-old boy.'

'He's a Fenton!' Callum retorted.

'It's okay, sweet cake,' Mary said, holding her daughter to her breast. 'You get ready for bed now and I'll come and tuck you in.'

The girl stood and headed towards her bedroom.

'You take heed of what Oy say, girl!' Callum called after her.

When she reached the door, she turned to face her father. 'You'll not tell me what to do, Da. I'll see who I like when I like.'

'Oh, you will, will you?' Callum was about to rush towards her when Mary jumped up and stood in his path.

'And what do you think you're going to do? Eh?' Mary said, fronting up to the furious man. 'Going to be hitting on your daughter? Just like Ron Fenton now are ye?'

This was a direct hit. Callum seemed to deflate.

'Go on, off to bed with ye,' Mary called to the girl.

Father and daughter stood glaring at one another like two prize fighters waiting for the bell to ring. Neither was going to break eye contact, both sharing that same strong-willed stubbornness.

'Get along with you, Mare,' Mary said before shepherding her daughter out of the room.

It wasn't until Mary closed the door behind her that the standoff was finally broken.

'Can you believe that girl?' Callum said as he and Mary retreated to the parlour.

'Aye, I can. She's her father's daughter.'

'Mother's daughter more like.'

Mary's expression softened and she placed a hand on her husband's shoulder. 'You were a bit hard on her.'

'Aye, but that's the effect Fenton has on me. Anything to do with that man drives me mad.'

'Aye, it does, but you need to control that, Callum.'

'Oy know.'

'You ruined the poor girl's birthday.'

'Aye.' Callum exhaled and turned to look out the window. 'Oy'll make it up to her in the morning.'

'You will that.'

'But Oy have to admit, Mary, this Fenton business has me worried.'

'I know. So, you have to do something about it.'

<h1 style="text-align:center">48</h1>

Romeo stayed at home in the back garden wrestling a fresh bovine thigh. We travelled into the city aboard the City Cat. It was the kind of morning that we Queenslanders take for granted—warm, sunny and fucking awesome.

'Don't you love Brisbane?' Abi remarked as we stood at the bow of the boat ploughing through the Brisbane River.

'I do actually.' And I did. In my opinion, Brisbane is the best city in the world. Not that I'd been to many others.

'Where would you like to go?' Abi asked, her face to the sun, the wind flowing through her hair.

'Fortitude Valley.'

'Really?'

'Yep. Before I go back to the Coast, I want to find more people who knew her.'

'No worries. I know a nice little place we can go for lunch.'

It was time to test my new theory. I needed to see what Abi's reaction would be. 'Abi, what would you say if I told you Kathy was Tilly's biological mother?'

'What?' As she swivelled on her heels to face me, the wind caught her hair and blew it across her face.

'Tilly is Kathy's daughter.'

'Don't be ridiculous. How could she be?'

'I'm pretty certain. In fact, I lay awake most of last night, and it all started to make sense.' It wasn't just that Kathy had had a baby twenty-one years ago and put it up for adoption, or that Fenton possibly staged a meeting with the Derbys after tracking down the adoptees of his child, then brought them to the Valley. The thing that made me most sure was Tilly's mannerisms. She wasn't a dead ringer for Kathy or anything like that, and I'd never actually met Kathy; it was Abi who supplied the final clue, purely because she'd reminded me of someone—Tilly.

'But the Derbys are Tilly's parents.'

'Adopted parents.'

'Really?'

'I'd bet my life on it.'

We got off the boat at Felons Brewing Co, just under the Story Bridge. From there, it was a short walk to the Valley. The place looked completely different in the day—more trendy than sleazy. We strolled past The Panda Club, which was closed at that time of the day. Continuing down the hill past the prestige car dealerships, we just strolled, window shopping, until we reached a large intersection at the bottom, then we turned and headed slowly back up the other side. Cutting across Chinatown, we headed back down the road parallel to the first. To be honest, there wasn't that much to see—cafés, restaurants, bars, a large Coles, and a few clothes shops scattered here and there. We'd been wandering for a couple of hours when we found ourselves back at the bottom of the hill. By then, the area was beginning to stir.

We entered a small dining precinct. At the entrance to a bar called The Brown Fox, Abi grabbed my hand and steered me through the front door. 'Come on, we can grab some lunch here.'

Planting myself on a barstool, I was surprised when Abi swanned around to the other side of the bar as if she owned the place. The young bartender bowed his head when he saw her.

'What will you have?' Abi asked me, leaning forward with her arms splayed across the bar.

'You work here as well as teaching?'

'Nope. Just like to pop in now and again, check the accounts.' She lowered her voice. 'Keep an eye on the staff.'

'So … you're the manager?'

'I guess. I own the place.'

Sitting tall on my stool, I raised a questioning chin. 'Kathy owned this too?'

'No, I bought it when I sold The Panda Club.' Without asking again, she grabbed a glass and flung it under the XXXX Gold tap.

Watching her as she skilfully poured the drink, I realised once again that I knew hardly anything about her. There was something niggling me about Abi Brown. 'Why would you buy a bar in the Valley when you'd loathed The Panda Club so much?'

Abi gave a nonchalant shrug and placed the beer in front of me. 'Taking a leaf out of my sister's book. This place came up for sale at the same time I sold the club. Seemed like a good investment.'

The place certainly wasn't sleazy like the club her sister owned. It was trendier and more modern, but could it be a front for something darker? I wasn't about to rule anything out.

While sipping my beer, I tried unsuccessfully to eavesdrop as she spoke to the barman just out of earshot. Pondering over her initial reaction when I'd mentioned that Kathy had a baby, there was obvious shock but also a hint of anger, which I found interesting. The fact that she'd done very well from the death of her sister may have been the governing factor that was biting at me. She'd inherited the house in East Brisbane, Mary's Mansion, The Panda Club—which she'd sold—and bought a bar of her own. Was the anger she'd briefly exhibited a reaction to the possibility that she may no longer legally be the only next of kin, and that her ownership of Kathy's assets could be challenged? It was a possibility.

49

Since deciding to stay in Brisbane for another day, it had been my intention all along to return to The Panda Club before heading back to the Coast. As we strolled up the hill, I decided to leave that afternoon. I needed to get back to Tallebudgera. I'd let Abi know later.

Although the club was a big freestanding building, the largest part of the business was a nightclub that didn't open until the evening. There was a cocktail bar, slash mini strip joint, at the front of the premises that opened at lunchtime. During my time as a police officer and a detective on the Gold Coast, I was familiar with joints of this nature. If ever we needed to speak to an informant or find one of the so-called crime lords, we'd always find them in dives like this. The very existence of these places sickened me. They were patronised by low life scum preying on young women.

When we walked into the bar, I stopped dead in my tracks. Sitting alone, nursing a beer, was a man that, in my mind, seeing him there in that environment, instantly relegated his status to that of the aforementioned scum. It was Ben Fisher.

'Mister Fisher,' I said, patting him heavily on the back.

Startled, Fisher just about jumped off his stool. 'What the hell?'

'Sorry, mate. I didn't mean to startle you.'

He blushed and looked around as if checking his surroundings. 'What are you doing here?'

'Working, of course. You know Abi?'

Without even looking at Abi, he ignored this and said, 'You should be in Tallebudgera, surely.'

'Tallebudgera, Fortitude. There are lots of answers hidden in them thar valleys. I'm surprised to see you here. A regular haunt of yours?'

'Certainly not!' Fisher said, unfurling upright in defence. 'I'm researching my next book.'

Right. Who are you plagiarising this time? I wanted to say but ordered two beers instead and instructed the barmaid to replenish whatever it was Fisher was drinking. To his irritation, we took the stools next to him.

'So how is it going? Are you any closer to proving Fenton did it?' Fisher asked.

'I'm getting there.'

His searching expression invited me to elaborate.

Something was telling me not to divulge everything I'd learned so far. As I gazed back into his shifty eyes, a volley of questions suddenly hit my brain like bullets from a machine gun. What if this wasn't just a one-off visit to The Panda Club? What if he frequented the establishment? What if this was the reason for his divorce? I made a mental note to get the court records of the annulment. There had to be a reason for his wife to walk away with everything. But above all this, there was something that was burning deep, as if a bullet was lodged in my central nervous system, rendering me paralysed if I didn't prize it out there and then. 'You're full of shit, Fisher.'

'I beg your pardon?'

'You knew Kathy Brown.'

'What?' Both Fisher and Abi said in unison.

'You met her back in the day when she worked here.' I had absolutely nothing to back up this claim. I wasn't even sure where it had come from.

'I can assure you I didn't.'

The twitch of the eyes, the uncomfortable shuffle on his stool. The sudden need to avoid eye contact were those familiar telltale signs.

'Yes, you did. In fact, you used to come here a lot. Still do, I bet.'

'What the hell are you doing, Stephens?' he asked, lowering his voice to a whisper. 'I'm not employing you to go around slandering me.'

'I just need to know the truth.'

Abi remained quiet with her eyes firmly fixed on Fisher.

'I can pull the CCTV tapes for the last however many months they keep them for. I'd be willing to bet they'll prove you come here often.' Usually, businesses only kept them about a week but I was hoping he didn't know that.

Fisher took a large swig of beer. 'I come here purely for research,' he said, averting his gaze.

'Look mate,' I said, leaning forward. 'I don't give a fuck what you do in your spare time. You're a single bloke. I get that. But I *will* find out.'

'Okay. Here's some information for you. You're fired. How about that?' His eyes were now cold and dark.

I shook my head dismissively. 'I just *need* to know the truth. Did you know Kathy Brown?'

'No, I did not!'

'Okay. Cool. Now we know, we can move on.'

'This has gone far enough. I should never have hired you.'

'But you did, and I'm doing what you employed me to do.'

'Bullshit! You're supposed to be proving that Fenton killed the bitch.'

Now it was Abi's turn to take the defensive. 'Watch your mouth, dickhead.'

Fisher shook his head and grinned nervously. It was as if he'd just noticed Abi for the first time and realised she must have been Kathy's sister. 'Something about those Brown girls, eh?'

I jumped between them, once again averting the infamous right hook.

'You don't know us,' Abi yelled.

Fisher's grin turned into a sickly chuckle. 'Everyone around here knew your sister.'

'All except you, it seems,' I mumbled, pulling Abi away.

Once outside, she was cussing at me for not letting her hit him. Perhaps I should have.

'Wait here. I'll be one minute, then we'll head back,' I said, tentatively leaving her leaning against the outside wall.

When I returned into the bar, Fisher was standing, finishing his drink, getting ready to leave.

'Listen mate. I'm sorry. That got a bit heated,' I said.

'You *should* be sorry.'

'I know, and I am. I want to keep working the case. I'm getting close, and between you and me, it's seriously looking like you were right. Fenton could be the killer.'

'Really?'

'Yep.'

'And will you be able to prove it?'

'I will. It's just a matter of time.'

'Okay, but I swear to God, if you pull another stunt like that, you're gone. Do you hear?'

I nodded apologetically.

He rushed away and out the front door.

Following him, I was relieved that Abi had moved a little way down the street and was looking the other way, so she didn't see him leave.

'Come on, Tiger,' I said, placing a hand on her shoulder. 'Let's get back to East Brisbane.'

It was a quiet stroll back to the ferry terminal and equally quiet on the journey back across the river. Another very important piece of the puzzle had slotted into place. I still don't know what brought on the sudden hunch that Fisher knew Kathy. At least he'd confirmed he didn't.

But of course, that was a lie!

50

Abi wasn't too happy that I left early, but I really needed to get back to the Coast as quickly as possible. I was bursting with questions. The timing was good, the mid-afternoon traffic was reasonably light. I was back in Tallebudgera by teatime.

With Romeo fast asleep in the back of the car, passing the Patterson's place, I noticed Reg standing at the side of the road supervising a tradesman as he scrutinised the gate to the property. I pulled the Dub over and climbed out. 'Hey, Reg, how's it going?'

He didn't seem too pleased to see me. 'Damn gate's playing up.' He spoke while staring at the nest of wires protruding from a box on the side of the post. 'I preferred the old farm gate, but no, we had to have a fancy-schmancy electric thing with a remote control. Been nothing but trouble.'

The tradesman, obviously an electrician, wearing fluro work gear, was separating the wires with his fingers.

'Can I have a word, Reg?'

He didn't seem to hear me. Thankfully, the electrician retreated to his van.

'I just wanted to say sorry for the other night. I can see that your family are good decent people.'

'We are. My family has been producing the finest milk in this valley for over eighty years.'

'You should be very proud.' I was sucking up, but I felt the need to apologise. The electrician returned with a toolbox and went about his work.

'Can I leave you here?' Reg said.

The electrician nodded. 'Yeah, shouldn't be too long.'

'That's what the last guy said, and the one before that.' He turned to walk up the long driveway towards the house.

'Let me give you a lift,' I said.

Reg, overweight, fair skinned and visually suffering from the heat, nodded.

We walked across the road and climbed into the Dub. Romeo didn't even stir. 'You've got a great business here,' I said, negotiating the winding driveway with cow fields on either side.

'It's a hard life. The bullshit bureaucracy doesn't help. We're constantly squeezed dry by the stores. My sons want to give it all away and convert the land into a golf course, can you believe?'

Looking over the enormous undulating block, I could believe it.

With numerous billabongs, pockets of forest and wide-open paddocks, the area would make a great course.

'Over my dead body, I tell them. But that's probably what'll happen. As soon as I'm gone. Wait and see.'

I pulled up behind a white Toyota Landcruiser in front of the house. We climbed out of the Dub and I followed Reg onto the verandah.

'Jan isn't here.' He gestured for me to take a seat on one of the wicker chairs. 'There's not a lot for me to do once the morning shift is done. The boys'll be getting ready for the arvo shift about now.' He checked his watch. 'My days are pretty boring.' He padded towards an old fridge, retrieved two bottles of Victoria Bitter and handed one to me.

I didn't really feel like drinking beer but took it anyway.

Reg sat down on a chair on the other side of a coffee table made from a polished flitch of camphor laurel. 'So, what have you been up to?' he asked.

'Uhm ... I've been learning a lot about Kathy Brown.'

There was a slight flinch, like I'd touched a nerve. 'No doubt you have, and I'm guessing it's not a pretty picture you're revealing.'

'No, sir, it certainly isn't. I understand she caused your family some pain.'

We swigged our beers in unison.

'That girl almost destroyed us.' The very mention of Kathy's name seemed to manifest anger in what was naturally a jolly disposition. He lowered his voice and leaned forward. 'Jan still doesn't know. In fact, apart from Roy and me, no one does.' Quickly leaning back, his expression closed as if he'd inadvertently revealed a secret he'd been bound to keep.

I wasn't about to let the moment slip away. 'Roy and Kathy, you mean?' It was a pure punt.

Reg sighed and took another drink of his beer. When he placed the bottle on the table, his hand was shaking. 'I knew it'd only be a matter of time before someone found out. And I guess with you being a detective ...'

'So ... Roy was the father of Kathy's baby.' I didn't deliver this as a question, more as if it was something I already knew. While trying to remain calm and nonchalant on the outside, my brain was working overtime. I hadn't seen this coming at all. Since learning of Kathy's pregnancy, I'd assumed that Fenton was the father. Roy Patterson, the eldest son of the God- fearing Pattersons wasn't even on my radar.

Reg nodded. 'It was a terrible time. He'd just married Kelly.'

'So, you sent her away to have the baby.'

'Yes, well no. She organised all that. Went to stay with a friend on the Sunshine Coast.'

'But you funded her.'

Nodding slowly, he cupped the bottle of beer in his hands and held it like a bible. 'And even after she'd put the child up for adoption, she demanded more money from us. Or else she'd tell Jan and Kelly.'

'Wouldn't it have been better to just come clean, let it all out in the open?'

'In hindsight, yes and no. For my soul salvation, yes, and this is something that has dogged me for these last twenty-odd years, but for Roy, no. He's happily married with three beautiful children. The secret has been worth that.'

'How did it happen? Were Roy and Kathy seeing each other?'

'No. Nothing like that. The girl was a sneak. It happened on Roy's bucks' night. Apparently, she tagged onto the group in Surfers Paradise later in the night when the boys were wasted.'

'So, when Kathy came back all those years later …'

'Even though there was still money going into her bank account, we thought it was all in the past, you know? But when she showed up again …'

'She demanded more money.'

'Yes. A lot more money.'

I'd seriously approached Reg just to apologise for Abi's behaviour the other night at the firemen's ball. What I hadn't anticipated was unearthing two possible new suspects. With the return of Kathy to the Valley and more blackmail demands, Reg could have killed her to protect his son. Or Roy could have killed her to protect his name and his marriage.

Not wanting to upset Reg or risk getting him offside again, I didn't probe too much further. Deciding instead to keep the conversation in the vein that I already knew everything, I chatted with him casually. 'She certainly was a piece of work.'

'Worst thing to happen to this valley since Ron Fenton.'

'Ron Fenton?'

'James's great-grandfather. Just about stole every inch of land you see from the original owners, Callum and Mary Murphy.'

The Murphys. I was getting to know them well.

'More blood on the hands of the Fentons than a slaughterhouse lackey.'

51

'But I paid good money for this land, Mister Fenton,' Bill Wallace said.

Fenton's thugs surrounded him like hounds waiting to be released.

'And so will I,' Fenton replied.

'You're not, though. You're offering me less than what I paid and if the land were for sale, there'd be appreciation to consider.' The smaller man spoke with rising desperation.

Fenton grinned. 'You misunderstand.' He tapped the walking cane, which once belonged to Charles Harrigan, across his palm. 'This ain't an offer, Mister Wallace. This is your last chance to walk away from 'ere alive.'

'But my family, my livelihood.' Wallace waved a hand across the vista, the half-built farmhouse, the recently acquired pastoral land fringing Mary's Mansion. 'We've worked so hard. Show some compassion, please, Mister Fenton.'

Fenton suddenly raised the heavy cane and brought it down hard across Wallace's head, its golden British lion shaped handle, pummelling the man's skull.

Wallace dropped to his knees clutching at the gaping wound, blood pouring through his fingers.

'Okay, there's your compassion, Mister Wallace. I was gonna burn you alive, but you're right, a bit of compassion never hurt no one.' Fenton turned to his gang. 'I must be getting soft in me old age.'

The men laughed.

Fenton nodded to his second in command, Bill Jarvis.

Jarvis stepped forward. In his hand was a contract of sale and the deed to the property. He handed it to Fenton.

Fenton knelt by Wallace. 'Here you go, sign this and all your troubles will be over.'

'But ...' The man was openly sobbing.

'But? Oh ... okay. Let's look at the "BUT", shall we?' Fenton spoke now as if he were empathetic to Wallace's protest. 'If you sign the contract of sale and the deed over to me, you can walk away from 'ere with your life. "BUT" if you don't, not only will I burn down the house with you in it, I'll force you to watch as I slice the throats of your family. "BUT" you can prevent all of that by signing these documents.'

Jarvis stood beside them with a quill and an inkpot.

Wallace rose slowly to his feet, still clutching his head. He took the quill, dipped it in the ink and awkwardly scribbled his signature where Jarvis directed him.

'Good man,' Fenton said when Jarvis retreated with the signed papers. 'Of course, there is still one "BUT" that we forgot to discuss.'

Wallace squinted through the pain.

'We *could* let you go on your merry way, "BUT" you'd probably go runnin' to your little mate, Callum Murphy.'

'No, sir, I will not,' Wallace pleaded.

'Well, I want to believe you, me old mucker, "BUT"...'

This time the cane smashed into the right side of Wallace's head from a sweeping backhanded ark. There was a sickly, audible crunch as the sharp edge of the lion's jaw penetrated the man's temple. Fenton immediately followed up with a forward swing, putting his hips and all his strength behind it like he was swinging an axe. The blow rendered Wallace a corpse before he hit the ground. 'No more "BUTs" eh, Mister Wallace?'

He knelt and wiped the blood from the lion's head with the jacket of the corpse. When he was satisfied it was clean, he stood and turned to his men. 'Where are they?'

'Over there behind the house,' Jarvis said.

'How old are the girls?'

Jarvis shrugged. 'About seven and nine.'

'Bring the women to me. Do what you want with the girls.'

'Yes, sir,' Jarvis said, backing eagerly away.

Within minutes, he was back, dragging Emily Wallace behind him.

The young woman screamed when she saw the body of her husband with his head bashed in. 'Oh, Jesus Christ, please help us through this day …' she prayed to the sky.

'He's not gonna help you now, love,' Fenton said, grabbing her from Jarvis' grasp.

***

Emily Wallace was raped next to the corpse of her husband while she listened to the screams of her daughters from the house. She no longer prayed. God had forsaken her and her family. When the screams finally stopped, she closed her eyes. The mantra she'd whispered as her body was violated was not a prayer, but a curse. A curse not only on the man that had killed her family and was no doubt about to kill her, but on the land on which the atrocity had taken place.

***

'You can just see the boundary of the Murphy place from here,' Jarvis said, pointing across the fields. There's a little shack there, look.'

Fenton followed his gaze. 'A shack?'

'Apparently that was the first home Murphy built.'
'And the sawmill?'
'Just yonder.'
'So, we've done it.'
'We own all the land now between here and Burleigh.'
'And the west?'
'Obtaining it as quickly as the getters are clearing it.'
'Good. I want to force him down just like he did to me.'
'We're nearly there.'
'Now we'll see who the rat is!'

Romeo was wide awake when the Dub trundled up towards the little shack I'd called home for the last few days. When he caught sight of the red Ferrari parked in my space, he growled and barked, snapping me back to the present. I wondered if Jake Fenton would mind if I nudged the back of his car the way I used to fondly kiss Tetley's Vespa outside Ruby Street, the red paint still present on my rusting chrome bumper.

Fenton was sitting on the front verandah watching me through vacant eyes. He was chewing the nails on his left hand, the twenty-thousand dollar watch he wore glistening in the late afternoon sun.

Romeo rushed towards him aggressively then stopped just before the verandah, eyeing him suspiciously.

I retrieved my overnight bag from the boot and padded wearily towards the house. 'G'day, Jake. How's it going?' Treat him like a mate. Be friendly.

'Scott.' He stood up, nervously scanned his surrounding and shuffled on his feet.

'What can I do for you, buddy?' Stepping onto the verandah, I threw down my bag and offered my hand for him to shake.

Unlike the vice-like grip he'd used on our previous meeting, his handshake was limp and spongy. 'I need to talk.' His searching eyes betrayed a nervousness I wouldn't have thought possible in the confident guy I'd met a couple of days earlier.

'Sure. What's on your mind?'

He was constantly side glancing as if making sure no one was watching. 'You look like you need a drink.'

His nod was erratic like I'd just offered him a fix of heroin. I grabbed my bag and took it inside the house, reappearing almost instantly, carrying two stubbies.

Romeo had ventured onto the verandah but sat quietly at its edge.

Jake drank slow and long, savouring every drop.

'Jeez, looks like you needed that,' I said, sitting down on one of the outdoor chairs.

He followed my lead but sat on the edge of his chair as if he were in readiness to take off at any moment.

'What's up, mate? You look like you've seen a ghost.' I was trying to calm him down by acting as if his anxiety was no big deal.

'I heard you've been to Brisbane.'

'Yeah, that's right. A few things I needed to clear up, people I needed to speak to.'

'Right.' If he edged any closer to the front of his seat, I swear he would have fallen on his arse. 'Did you, uhm … did you get to speak to anyone?'

'Oh yeah,' I said, keeping the situation at a nonchalant level while being direct.

'Okay, I didn't do it,' he suddenly blurted out.

The obvious reply to this would have been, 'Do what?' But whatever was on his mind was cutting him up. I got the impression he thought I'd uncovered some information about him. I wasn't about to lose this advantage by letting him know I didn't have a clue what he was talking about, because whatever it was, it was bloody important. 'Can you prove it?' I asked, continuing with the concerned mate approach who already knew his secret.

'Yes, yes. I can. I was away on the night of Kathy's murder.'

It was true, according to the police report. He was in Byron Bay on a fundraiser with his father and Tom Partridge the night Kathy died.

'So, what's the problem?'

He eyed me warily. 'Who did you speak to?'

'Everyone.'

'And what did they say about me?'

A subtle approach was necessary. I needed to keep him on the edge of that chair while gently squeezing his balls. 'Well, it's not looking good. You must have known it'd come out eventually.' I was flying blind, but God I was good.

He nodded again and his tense body seemed to deflate a little. He took another shaky swig of beer then continued. 'Okay, yes. But that's the essence of blackmail, isn't it? If you stopped to think about it rationally, you'd realise that all those threats, all those revelations, those things that were hanging over you threatening to be revealed, would come out in time anyway, regardless of how much money you paid and how long you paid it for.'

'So just how long has it been going on?' I had no idea what 'it' was, but he obviously didn't know that.

'Since she fell pregnant of course.'

'Right.' The penny dropped and the reason for Kathy's accumulation of wealth suddenly made perfect sense. Not only had she been blackmailing Fenton as well as Reg and Roy Patterson, but she was also into Jake Fenton for the same reason. I no longer had to wing it. Knowing now exactly what Jake was afraid of would make the gentle questioning a whole lot easier. Or so I thought.

'But hand on heart, Scotty. I didn't rape her as she claimed.'

Run with it, Scotty, run with it. 'But you were aware she was underage. That's still statutory rape.'

He shook his head violently. 'No, no, I didn't. She lied about her age. Said she was nineteen. Everybody thought she was older than she actually was.'

'Including your old man.'

'Well yeah, he gave her a job on the farm.'

The swig of beer I took wasn't from a shaking hand, it was controlled and firm—the trembling was inside. 'Like I said, mate, it doesn't look good. Especially with you keeping this information from the police during the murder investigation.'

'I know. I was obviously petrified, but ...'

'Because you knew you'd be a suspect. You'd been paying this woman all these years, then she suddenly shows up in the Valley demanding more ... a lot more ... and threatening to expose you.'

'But I was in Byron—'

'I'm sure you know as well as I do that the police'll be able to pick that to bits. That's why you're shitting yourself.'

He exhaled slowly like a weightlifter preparing to lift his personal best. 'I didn't do it, Scott. I have proof. I was in Byron Bay that night.'

I shrugged. 'Could have hired someone. You're well known in all the wrong places.

Fortitude Valley, Kings Cross.' I was ad-libbing again. 'Did you send her away to the Sunshine Coast?'

'No. she must have organised that herself. She didn't actually approach me until a year later. I was at the peak of my career. She showed up out of the blue. Said she was going to tell the police that I'd raped her and that she could prove it because she'd given birth to my baby.'

'Did you ever see the child?'

'No, she put it up for adoption as soon as it was born. Are you going to tell the police?'

'I'll have to, mate.'

His nod was the expectant kind that said, "Okay, the game's up." He inhaled deeply and lifted his face towards the last rays of sunlight. 'I understand. It had to come out sooner or later. But

I just need you to know, Scott. I didn't rape Kathy Brown, and I certainly didn't kill her. I'd paid her hundreds of thousands of dollars all these years.' He finished his beer and stood. 'When will you tell them? The police I mean?'

I joined him standing. 'There's no hurry.'

'Thank you.' He shook my hand. Some of the strength had returned to his grip. 'I won't be going anywhere. It's time for me to face this like a man. I'm innocent, that's the main thing.'

Romeo and I watched him closely as he climbed into his car and drove off.

It was another sleepless night. Romeo was wide awake too, so I took him for a walk. Passing the two moss-covered headstones, I stopped for a moment and acknowledged my landlords. They intrigued me and I was desperate to learn more about them. But for now, I had a case to solve, and for want of the correct technical term, I was approaching the pointy end.

Since leaving for Brisbane the previous day, I'd been summarising the intel in my head as it came. Now I needed to write it down, make another list, display it on the whiteboard.

Getting it out of my head and into the universe would create and record organic reference data, rather than stored cerebral data that could easily be forgotten. It was time to download, reboot and shift into the next phase.

53

Within minutes, the makeshift whiteboard in my bedroom became an external hard drive as I downloaded the latest data to it from my brain. Using my phone, I quickly found headshots of the Fentons—James from the Fenton horse stud website and Jake from his Wikipedia page. I printed them out and placed them on the board. A small shot of Tom Partridge was also available. There was even a family shot of the Pattersons from an archived article in the *Tally Talk* iNewsletter, documenting a sizeable donation they'd made towards the Tallebudgera Post Office restoration fund. Airdropping the shot to my laptop, I easily isolated the images of Reg and Roy from the rest of the family, enlarged them and printed them out. Two very pixelated shots of the Patterson men hung side by side with the Fentons, but the lack of quality didn't matter, having them in constant view was all my mind required. Beneath these I made another list summarising my findings over the last couple of days, which looked something like this:

1. *According to Katz, Tom Partridge was the illegitimate and secret son of James Fenton. I have no proof to back this up.*
2. *Fenton brought Tom to Tallebudgera Valley and gave him a job and accommodation.*
3. *Both James and Jake Fenton possibly used Kathy's services in a Brisbane brothel and became besotted with her.*

4. *Jimmy P warned Callum Murphy about Ron Fenton.*
5. *Kathy followed Tom to the Valley.*
6. *Fenton gave her a job and put her up in Mary's Mansion.*
7. *Kathy stole the family jewels from Daisy Patterson.*
8. *Still underage, Kathy fell pregnant and was sent to the Sunshine Coast to have the baby in secret.*
9. *James Fenton, believing he is the father, pays for her to go away and continues to make monthly payments to Kathy for the rest of her life.*
10. *Jake Fenton, believing he is the father, pays for her to go away and continues to make monthly payments to Kathy for the rest of her life.*
11. *Ron Fenton vows revenge on Callum Murphy.*
12. *Roy Patterson, believing he is the father, pays for her to go away and continues to make monthly payments to Kathy for the rest of her life.*
13. *After the birth, the child is immediately given up for adoption, Kathy returns to Brisbane, but not as a prostitute as before, she is an upwardly mobile young woman who amasses property and her own business.*
14. *Callum Murphy vows to put an end to Ron Fenton once and for all.*
15. *James Fenton tracked down the child to a family living in Toowoomba. He orchestrates a meeting with the child's adopted father, Matt Derby, offers him a job as the manager of his estate. The Derbys move to Tallebudgera, bringing with them their adopted daughter, Tilly.*
16. *Some years later, Kathy moves back to the Valley. She stirs up the shit in the peaceful community and demands more money from those she's blackmailing. Did she know Tilly was her daughter?*
17. *Fuelled with the recent knowledge that Kathy stole his mother's valuable jewellery, and that she has been blackmailing his eldest son for sixteen years, Reg Patterson publicly announces that Kathy will pay for her sins.*

Gee whiz, it was some list. I left room to add more to it, then just stood there silently for the next hour. If the download of information from my brain to the board was a compressed low resolution zip file, the opened file was in high-definition colour. First, I scanned each of the photographs. The deep-set, dark eyes of James Fenton would watch my every move from now on. The cocky grin of his son would irritate the shit out of me. Christian pride of the family and the community Reg Patterson loved was etched into his jolly face. Somebody once said, 'Fear the anger of a gentle man' and I wondered how far Reg would go to protect the reputation of his family. Roy's expression was different—anxiety of a good man who carried a bad secret was the impression I got from his face. He was a big guy with a gentle disposition. Quietly spoken, like his father, he was dedicated to his wife and family.

Something dawned on me, and I returned to my phone. There needed to be a place on the board for the Derbys. I couldn't rule out the fact that each of them could be involved. Once again, the *Tally Talk* provided a nice shot of the proud parents and their daughter displaying a '1ˢᵗ place' rosette Tilly had won at one of the local horse shows. Moving over the black-and-white image of Callum and Mary Murphy, I placed them next to Roy Patterson, then added the following to my list:

18. *Matt Derby is furious with Kathy after she demanded access to Tilly. Is Pam Derby protective of her daughter?*

After spending time just staring at the photographs, I went to the list and analysed each entry.

It was dark outside. The only light I had on in the house was a desktop lamp that I had shining on the whiteboard. My thoughts were interrupted by a light flickering onto the ceiling then sweeping down the wall and across the room. A car with its headlights on full beam had just pulled up outside.

Romeo barked, then rushed from the bedroom and into the living room.

I followed and opened the front door. In the driveway was a red MINI. I knew who it was immediately. 'G'day, stranger,' I said as Jenny Radford climbed from the car.

'How's it going?' Her genuine, friendly smile was a welcome distraction. The six-pack she held was a damn good sight too. I stepped eagerly off the verandah but was forced to wait as the mandatory Romeo ritual took place before I could hug her.

The embrace was much more than a hug, and the kiss was more of a snog. I knew Jenny had been working hard of late on the bikie case, that's why I had seen little of her. And of course, I'd been distracted here in Tallebudgera. When our lips finally parted, she handed the beer cans to me, ducked back into the car and produced a bottle of Champagne. 'We nailed the bastard,' she said, grinning from ear to ear.

'Brennan?'

'Yep. He caved.'

'Brilliant. Well done!'

We embraced again, and boy did it feel good. *Why did I ever let this girl go?* The inner Scotty asked, *Did I let her go?*

We entered the house. Jenny was excited. She really had been working hard—the long hours, the shit involved in a case like this. While she filled me in on the details, I poured two glasses of Champagne. Then, realising we were both hungry, we ordered Indian takeaway via Uber Eats.

It was great to see Jenny so relaxed. The last time I'd seen her, I'd sensed the stress she was harbouring, which I understood completely.

By the time the food arrived, we'd finished the bottle of champers and had started on the beers. We ate out on the back verandah.

'Bloody hell, listen to me going on and on,' Jenny said, breaking a poppadom in two and dipping it into her curry. 'How are you getting on?'

'Good, I think.' I'd specifically asked for a mild vindaloo. My mouth was tingling from too much chilly.

'So, tell me all about the case.'

It felt good to share my findings with Jenny while at the same time it made me realise I still had very little to go on.

Jenny sat there contemplating my words. 'Hmm, tricky one. But what about the writer?

Aren't you supposed to be vindicating him?'

'Well yeah, but—'

Jenny leaned forward and lowered her voice. 'Show me your whiteboard.'

Feigning shock, I pulled back. 'That's a bit personal, isn't it?'

'Come on, I know you've got one.' Even with a mouth full of dal makhani, her cheeky grin was just as infectious as ever.

After dinner, and with fresh beers in hand, we retreated to the bedroom.

'There you go,' Jenny said, stepping in front of the board and immediately locking on to the information it held. After a few minutes' silence, she turned to me with a puzzled expression.

'What's up?' I asked. She was a brilliant detective. Had she spotted something I'd missed?

She glanced at the board then back at me. 'Who are Callum and Mary Murphy?'

I looked at the vintage black-and-white image of a handsome couple wearing what looked like their Sunday best. 'What the fu—' My eyes followed the list down to their names! 'I don't recall writing this.'

'Who are they?' Jenny asked.

'They're the original owners of Mary's Mansion.'

'Are they relevant to the case?'

My reaction was part shrug, part shake of the head. 'I have no idea!'

54

Callum was sitting at his desk in his study. Jimmy P, his right-hand man, was sitting opposite him.

'How was this allowed to happen, Jimmy?'

'He used a solicitor to purchase the land on his behalf. We never would have sold it to him if we'd known what was going on,' Jimmy said.

'How much does he have?'

Jimmy shuffled uncomfortably in his seat. 'All of it.'

'All of it?'

'Yes, from the oyster beds right up to Mary's Mansion.'

'Oh, by Christ.' Callum rose from his desk and padded towards the window. 'Oy should have at least kept what we owned.'

'It was a shrewd move to sell off the land we no longer required.'

'No, it wisnae. We should have kept it and leased it to the dairy farmers. Now we've lost control.'

'Hindsight is a wonderful thing, Callum.'

'Aye.'

'So, what are we going to do about it?'

'We need to stop him. We both know what his agenda is.' Callum turned to face Jimmy and when their eyes met, their minds were transported back to the *Great Britain*.

***

'I'll get you for this, Callum Murphy, if it's the last thing I do. See if I don't,' Ron Fenton growled as he struggled to break free of Jimmy P's grip.

Callum let fly with another right, smashing into Ron's nose. 'Well, remember that one when you come looking for me, eh?'

Jimmy released his grip and let the man fall to the floor.

'Oh, don't you worry about that, I will.' Fenton wiped the blood from his face with the back of his hand.

Callum knelt and grabbed him by the collar. 'Now if Oy hear of you organising games behind my back again, Oy'll feckin kill you. Do you hear me, Rat?'

The hatred burning in Fenton's eyes spoke louder than words could.

A ragtag group of mainly Scottish and Englishmen stood nervously around the peripheral of the small cabin.

Callum stood and looked each of them in the eye. 'And if Oy hear of you lot even talking to this man again, you'll be thrown overboard. Do you hear me?'

The men nodded and shuffled from side to side.

'Now get out of here.'

They filed out of the cabin still with their heads down.

The takings weren't huge, nothing like the games Callum ran, so it didn't take Jimmy P long to stuff it into his pockets.

Although the cabin was small, it was still a cabin, and it was only one deck lower than Callum's.

'How did you wheedle your way back up here, Rat?' Callum's voice was filled with disdain.

'A good man will always come back,' Fenton said, rising to a seated position.

'A good man? You'll never know what good is. You're the feckin devil himself Oy suspect.'

Fenton rose to his feet. 'You're right to fear me, Callum Murphy.'

Callum laughed. 'Fear you? Is that what you think this is?' He was about to hit Fenton again and as much as it would have given him great satisfaction to feel the cheek bones of his adversary crunch under his knuckles, he drew back, glanced at Jimmy P and nodded.

Jimmy P grabbed one of Fenton's arms, twisted it up behind his back and yanked a handful of his hair with his other hand.

'Oy should be throwing you overboard, that's what Oy should be doing,' Callum said.

Jimmy P's puzzled expression said, "Isn't that what we're doing?"

'No, take him back down to the engine room, give him another hiding then leave him there with the rest of the rats.' Callum leaned in close to Fenton's face. 'And you'll stay down there for the rest of the journey this time. Do you hear me, Ron Fenton?'

Fenton spat in Callum's face. 'You should throw me overboard now, because you'll never keep me down.'

Callum was fighting hard to control the rage inside. 'Take him away, Jimmy.'

'I'll be back. You see if I won't, you Irish pig!' Fenton yelled as Jimmy P pushed him towards the cabin door.

'As long as there's breath in my body, by Christ, you'll never amount to nothing more than a rat. So, what the feckin hell do you think you'll ever do to me?'

'I'll be coming for you. I'll be fuckin coming for you, Callum Murphy.' Fenton's words trailed off as he was dragged along the corridor.

Danny Flynn and John Mince stood on either side of the door. 'Search this place and bring anything you find to me.'

'Aye, Mister Murphy.' The two men went about an industrious search as Callum exited the cabin.

'It's unbelievable.' Callum was seated in the mess hall digging at a bowl of boiled cabbage with his fork. 'So, we've been forced to eat this shite every feckin day because that little rat's been stealing the food?'

'Looks that way,' Jimmy P said.

Callum shook his head and threw the fork into the bowl. 'What else did we find?'

'He's horded a small fortune—cash, watches, anything of any value on this ship seems to have ended up under Fenton's mattress.'

'How?'

'I don't know but he's obviously a cunning little fucker. It's only been a few weeks since we took everything he had and banished him to the engine room.'

'But we control what little money there is on this ship,' Callum said.

'That's what we thought. Seems we were wrong.'

'And did you make him pay?'

'Oh yeah, he won't be walking for quite some time, never mind working his way back up through the decks.'

'And do we know who's been helping him?'

'We do, but they'll be working for you from now on.'

'Good, good.' Callum was about to rise from the table, but Jimmy stopped him.

'We should be rid of him now, Callum, while we have the chance.'

Callum shrugged. 'Aye, you're probably right, but we'll be in Brisbane in a couple of weeks. After that we'll never see or hear of him again.'

'I've got a bad feeling about this,' Jimmy said. 'The only way to be sure is if we slice his throat now and throw him overboard. We'll never get this chance again.'

'You worry too much, Jimmy P.'

'Do I though?'

'Aye. He's just a rat, remember?' He stepped away from the table and placed an arm on Jimmy's shoulder. 'We're moving onto bigger and better things, my friend. Bigger than you could ever imagine. Australia awaits us.'

***

We should have done away with him back then, Callum,' Jimmy said, pouring Scotch from a decanter.

'Aye,' Callum said as Jimmy handed him a glass. 'Oy know that now. You was right.'

'It's not too late.'

Callum noticed the look in Jimmy's eyes that he hadn't seen since the voyage over.

'No, we're better than that now. Fenton is still the scrawny little rat he ever was, but we've grown, my friend. We're successful, law abiding businessmen with families.'

Jimmy nodded. 'You're right, you're right.'

'We *do* need to do something though,' Callum added.

'Yes. What have you got in mind?'

<h1 style="text-align:center">55</h1>

Jenny Radford was the best mate a bloke could ask for. We didn't have sex. We made love because we loved each other. Sharing a mutual affection for the waves, we surfed together. We shared the odd beer because we enjoyed each other's company. If only we could have lived together, we'd have the perfect relationship. But then again, perhaps that's what this was.

When the Champagne and the beer was gone, we'd retired to bed. Jenny obviously had no intention of driving home. In the morning, we piled into her MINI and headed to Burleigh Heads with my surfboard strapped to the roof. I waited for a few minutes outside Jenny's apartment on Goodwin Terrace, surfboard under one arm, wetsuit peeled down to the waist. The spectacular curve of the Gold Coast laid out before me like a front yard paradise.

Jenny joined me and we hit the surf. The waves weren't that great, but the company was.

After an hour, we returned to Jenny's place and drank coffee on her balcony.

'I'll see what else I can dig up on the Infamous Five?' Jenny said, startling me from a moment of reverence.

'Huh?'

'The Fentons, The Pattersons and Matt Derby.' 'Yeah, that'd be great.'

'But what about the other two?' She looked at me warily.

'The other two?'

'Callum and Mary.'

I'd been thinking about Callum and Mary Murphy a lot since the previous night. I must have subconsciously searched the internet, found a photograph of them, printed it out, placed it on the whiteboard and included them in my summary list. How and why, I did not know.

'I'll see what I can find out about them too if you like,' Jenny said.

'No, that's okay. I don't know what happened there. Must have been tired after the drive back from Brisbane. They weren't supposed to be on the board.'

I couldn't quite tell if the slight smirk was dismissive, patronising or a product of worry. 'What are you going to do now?' she asked.

'I need to speak to James Fenton again.'

'Confront him?'

I nodded. 'Why not? I've got nothing to lose.'

'I think you're getting close.'

'Me too.' As detectives, we were both familiar with that feeling after a long investigation when nothing seemed to happen for weeks, or sometimes months, then a morsel of information could shift the whole axis of the case and push you in the right direction as if you were only metres away from the finish line of a gruelling marathon. I'd only been working on this case for a few days but there had been an intensive police investigation prior, of which I took the gauntlet. But until my trip to Brisbane, I'd had absolutely nothing.

Jenny gave me a lift back to Tallebudgera Valley on her way into work. It was out of her way but she didn't mind. The bikie case was over, she could relax and settle back into normal hours, a luxury she hadn't experienced for quite some time.

Romeo seemed to enjoy his solitude in the old chicken coop, but he still went crazy when I let him out, as if I'd been away for weeks. As he tore around the garden, the trees to the right of the property rustled, causing me to glance in their direction. The two headstones caught my eye, sitting silently side by side in the shadows. I strolled over in their direction and I remembered something the medium, Kea, had said at the séance:

'Mary knows!'

It was my imagination, of course it was, but the trees seemed to whisper. 'Mary knows ...'

'Good morning,' I said, standing before the graves. 'I'm guessing you want justice too.' My gaze flicked between the two headstones.

If either Callum or Mary Murphy had answered me, I would have run all the way back to Ruby Street in Kirra. But they didn't need to. The trees did it for them. A gust of wind whipped through the low-hanging branches. Bowes *creaked*. Leaves *whooshed*. Branches *groaned*. Romeo barked, then on the wind I heard a woman's voice calling to me.

'Scott ...'

I looked at Mary Murphy's grave, the swaying shadows falling across it like gradient pixels.

'Scott ...' The voice was getting closer.

I continued to stare at the headstone as if expecting Mary Murphy to rise from the ground and drift towards me with outspread arms. Suddenly, there was a hand on my shoulder and I almost leapfrogged the gravestones.

'Are you all right?' It was Tilly.

'Bloody hell, you scared the shit out of me!'

'Sorry.' She lifted a hand to her mouth to hide her laughter.

She had no reason to be sorry. I was the goose for being startled.

'I see you've found them then,' Tilly said, gesturing with her eyes towards the graves. 'How could I not?'

'Absolutely tragic.'

'You know what happened to them?'

Tilly nodded. 'Of course. It's local legend.' We walked back towards the house.

Romeo, not wanting to be left out, had jumped up into Tilly's arms and was covering her in kisses.

'Can you tell me about them?' I asked as he we stepped onto the back verandah.

'Sure. Not now though. I've got a class. It's a long story but I can come back later.'

'That'd be great.'

She nuzzled her face into Romeo's fur then placed him down on the deck. 'I just wanted to make sure you got back from Brisbane okay.'

'Yeah, all good.'

'Did you find what you were looking for?'

'I think so.' I wondered if she knew Kathy was her mother. They'd become close. Perhaps Kathy confided in her. Would she have known anything about the ring of blackmail that was woven into this tiny community? Would she have sided with the Derbys if she'd found out the truth? Or taken pity on her mother? I watched her as she headed back down the driveway on foot. She would have been around sixteen at the time of Kathy's death. What if she found out that her friend, who was actually the mother who had given her up for adoption as soon as she'd been born, was actually here to harm the people she loved? Would she be capable of murder? I needed to ruminate on this.

56

For some reason, the adrenalin was pumping as I marched out down the driveway of Mary's Mansion, turned right onto Tallebudgera Creek Road, covered the short distance between the two properties, and headed through the gates of the horse stud. I'd decided I was going to confront James Fenton, balls and all. Looking straight ahead, my peripheral vision remained a blur. If I wasn't so focused, I may have seen Pam Derby pegging out washing on the Hills Hoist, or Tilly working with a bunch of kids in the arena. Or perhaps Tom Partridge in a paddock overseeing a vet checking the hindquarters of a thoroughbred mare, Matt Derby discussing the replacement of a section of fencing with a tradesman, or Jake Fenton floating face up in the family pool while the pretty blonde sucked his dick. Such, I guessed, would be the day-to-day goings-on at the Fenton ranch. But I saw none of this. The sprawling homestead that grew bigger as I approached it fully occupied my vision.

On that TV screen that we all have in our heads, I was visualising the meeting. Fenton would be his usual cleanly shaven self, wearing the trademark Akubra, khaki shirt, tan chinos, and riding boots. His expression, although welcoming, carried with it an authoritarian hardness that would easily melt an assailant. I was having none of this. Thanks to Jenny, I'd managed to get a good night's sleep, possibly the first since arriving in the Valley. So, with a clear mind and time to ponder during an uneventful surf, the one person dominating my thoughts had been James Fenton.

The approach of misleading the suspects into believing I knew a lot more than I actually did had worked for me so far on this case. As I climbed the front steps to the great house, I wondered if it would work on Fenton.

'I thought I might see you again.'

The familiar voice snatched me from my thoughts.

When I reached the top of the steps, Fenton was leaning on the balustrade with a mug of coffee in one hand, surveying his land perhaps. Had he been surveying me also as I approached?

'Good morning, sir.' Keeping it civil, friendly and in control.

He didn't move, come to greet me or anything like that. He just watched me stroll towards him along the hardwood deck.

I held out my hand and he shook it.

'Good to see you, Scott.'

I almost replied with, 'Is it?' but that would break the first rule at the first hurdle. Keep it civil. 'It's good to see you too, Mister Fenton.'

'Jim. Call me Jim.'

'Jim.' Keep it friendly.

'What can I do for you?' He turned and leaned his butt against the balustrade. 'Coffee?'

'Yeah, that'd be great.' Keep in control, make him work.

We didn't go into the house, instead we circumnavigated the wrap around verandah until we reached a wide expanse of concertina French doors that were fully open revealing a huge, very modern kitchen inside. I heard a splash and a woman's giggle. Looking to my right, I saw the family pool. Almost as predicted, Jake Fenton and his girlfriend were frolicking in the water.

Without being invited, I took a seat at a large outdoor table and waited for Fenton to return. When he did, he handed me a mug and took the seat facing me.

'So, what can I do for you, son?' he said, removing his Akubra and dropping it onto the floor.

'I think you know why I'm here.' Straight to the point, remain in control. He probably had absolutely no idea why I was there, but it didn't sway me from sticking to my plan.

Fenton chuckled and lanced me with his most penetrating stare. 'Do I?' He was good.

But I was better. 'I just got back from Brisbane last night. Fortitude Valley.'

His searching shrug said, 'So?'

'Everyone said to say hi.'

'Everyone?' His lingering grin was accompanied by a puzzled frown.

'Sure. Katz. All the staff at The Panda Club.' I leaned forward and added with a grin. 'They all seem to know you, sir.'

There was a definite fluster that could easily have been missed by a lesser experienced detective.

'They? What are you talking about?' The friendly smile was back.

'Let's not waste time or insult each other's intelligence, sir, please?' Lowering my voice, I added, 'I know everything.'

He sat back in his chair like we were about to share a good old-boy yarn. 'Great. If you know everything, please continue because I haven't got the faintest idea what you're going on about.'

'Glad to.' I placed my mug on the table. A yarn it would be. 'I know you frequented The Panda Club in Fortitude Valley.'

'Rubbish. Who told you that?'

'Oh, you're quite the legend up there. It's a shame Maeve is no longer with us. I'm sure she'd have a few stories to tell, eh?' I inadvertently nudged my elbow and actually did the wink-wink routine. "Twat," Tetley would have said.

'Maeve? I'm afraid I haven't got a clue what you're talking about.' He checked his watch.

I had him cornered, and I wasn't about to let him go. 'Maeve Morrison, you know? Tom's mother.'

He narrowed his eyes.

'The mother of the boy that you brought down to Tallebudgera and took into your home.'

'Tom's mother? What on Earth has she got to do with this?' He'd lowered his voice.

Carrying on with the pretence that I knew everything, I pushed on, hoping he would fill in the gaping chasms. 'Were you horrified when Kathy followed him, or happy?'

No answer, but the iron stare was showing no sign of tarnish.

'Mrs Fenton was still alive then.' I edged closer to the front of my seat. 'Sir, I know that Kathy was blackmailing you. Nobody else knew that Tom was your son and only Kathy knew you frequented The Panda Club. She was a very clever girl, practised in the art of leverage.'

He suddenly laughed. 'Tom, my son? The Panda Club? Is this an exert from Fisher's book?'

'But she *was* blackmailing you.'

'It's not what you're thinking at all. She could have destroyed us.'

Yes! At last. A breakthrough. The manifestation of my visualisation was finally about to pay off. My instincts had been right. It was important to carry on without showing surprise, as if he were telling me things I already knew, regardless of what it was. 'So how on Earth did she end up getting pregnant?' Oops, careful. Don't be judgemental. Understanding remember?

Fenton stood and leaned on the balustrade with his back to me. 'She was pure evil!'

'So, you sent her away.' It wasn't a question.

'Yes. I found a private clinic on the Sunshine Coast where she could stay for the duration of the birth. When the baby was born, it was immediately put up for adoption.'

'But you continued to pay her.' His nod was slow and submissive.

'And then you searched for the child, found her and brought her to the Valley.'

Fenton dropped back into his chair like his legs had deserted him. 'My God. You really do think you know everything.'

With my suspicions confirmed, I needed to fill in those gaps. 'How did you do it?'

'Find her you mean?'

'No.' I'm a detective, I know how easy it is to access archives, especially if you have money and influence. 'How did you get the DNA?'

He continued to tell me how once he'd found out that it was the Derbys who had adopted the girl and that they lived in Toowoomba, he'd orchestrated a meeting with Matt. It was my theory almost word for word. He'd gotten to know him and eventually met the family. It had been hard for him not to put too much attention on the little girl, but when he invited the family out to dinner, he saw his chance and took with him the spoon the child had used. A DNA test later proved positive.

'So, everything was going good …' I detected a slight wince at this statement confirming more of my suspicions that everything was far from good. I didn't let on and continued. '… until Kathy returned when Tilly was what? Sixteen?'

Fenton nodded.

'How did she find out about Tilly?'

'She met her. They became friends. Tilly is so much like her mother. The mannerisms, identical. She also shares that same intelligence, only, thanks to the Derbys and me, she uses it for good, not like Kathy.'

'So, you think Kathy just put two and two together.'

'Yes. But whether it was just a mother's instinct or something else, I don't know.'

'*Hmm.* So now she had even more leverage over you. I'm guessing the blackmail demands increased?'

More slow nodding.

'Is that why you killed her?' "You don't sip a shot, you knock it straight back" was one of Elvis' sayings. I'd been sipping on information for the last week or so, now I needed some deep gulps.

Fenton leaned forward in his seat and lowered his voice to a defiant growl. 'I did not kill that woman!'

Still calm, still friendly and still in control, I also leaned forward, and asked in a whisper, 'So, who did then?'

57

After surfing, footy, sex, and drinking beer, standing before a loaded whiteboard teasing out missed information was my favourite pastime. Of course, Kathy still took centre stage. Even though she was the victim, she was also the star of the show. Next were the pictures of the suspects.

Almost as if deep in meditation, my mind started to storyboard scenarios for each of them.

James Fenton, long-time patron of The Panda Club. He produced an illegitimate son, Tom Partridge, with Maeve Morrison, the madame of the club. Although the bulk of the information I'd harvested on him was from the public domain, for a high-profile figure and local personality, he was also a very private man who, I sensed, was the custodian of a great many secrets. The revelation that he'd fathered an illegitimate son may have been enough to trigger a self-preservation order within him, especially as this could have—would have—prized open the real reason for his regular business visits to Brisbane.

If this wasn't enough, he'd also committed statutory rape, and secretly fathered a child with the girl, Kathy Brown—or so he'd been led to believe. James Fenton would have had the most to lose had Kathy gone ahead with her threats to expose him. Did James Fenton have a motive to kill Kathy Brown …? Absolutely!

Jake Fenton, the high profile and rising celebrity in the sporting world at that time, also fearing a charge of statutory rape, and while possibly believing *he* was the father of the child, had been paying off Kathy for sixteen years to protect the secret they shared. Would any of this have affected his reputation back then when he was a rising star in the world of polo? If Kathy hadn't been underage, maybe not. But being charged with rape would definitely have sent his life on a whole different trajectory, jeopardising his lifestyle and stature. Add to this the fact that he had been paying the victim all these years for her silence would only add fuel to the fire.

Did Jake Fenton have a motive to kill Kathy Brown …? Absolutely!

Reg Patterson was a God-fearing pillar of the Tallebudgera community. A prominent figure promoting the virtues of family life and Christian ways. He was well known and liked by just about everyone he met. The only motive, or the one I knew of, was that he could have been protecting his son and the family name. Was this enough of a reason for him to pay off Kathy for all these years? Or was there more to it? Could it be that he also feared prosecution for the same charges of statutory rape? And that he too was led to believe he was the child's father? *Hmm* … if that was the case, he was in the same position as the Fentons.

Did Reg Patterson have a motive to kill Kathy Brown …? Maybe.

Roy Patterson, Reg and Jan's eldest son, was a newly married man when Kathy approached him, likely wielding the same allegations she'd used on her other victims. Roy also had a lot to lose, but was it enough? Well, once again, it was enough to force him to put his hand in his pocket and keep doing so on a monthly basis. When Kathy returned to the Valley sixteen years later, Roy, like his father, was now an upstanding highly liked individual in the local community, with a family of his own.

Did Roy Patterson have a motive to kill Kathy Brown …? Absolutely!

I still wasn't sure if Matt Derby knew of Fenton's real reasons for giving him the job. How angry would he have been if he found out? Would his anger be directed at Fenton? Or towards the person who had stirred the pot—Kathy? It was all speculation on my behalf. The Derbys hadn't even told their daughter she was adopted. Unfortunately, there was no way of knowing what transpired between the loving father of the adopted child and the biological mother who had suddenly turned up out of the blue. Had Kathy threatened to tell Tilly and spoil their family life?

Did Matt Derby have a motive to kill Kathy Brown …? Maybe!

It was at this point that I realised I was overlooking Pam Derby. If her husband had a motive, then she did too. Had she known the situation, would she have shared the same motive?

My original opinion of Tilly Derby was that she was not only a smart, driven and beautiful young woman, but that she also had a wonderful soul to match. Delving into her personal life, I was pretty sure I wouldn't unearth anything to change this view. So, did she deserve to be on the whiteboard? Well, when you considered she was the daughter of Kathy Brown, an evil, scheming and possibly dangerous individual who, by all accounts, could be just as charming, then perhaps it was warranted to at least allow some of my focus on her.

Although a completely different personality, at the time of Kathy's death, she was in a similar position to Jake Fenton in that she was working towards a career in the equestrian sport. Had Kathy told her she was adopted, and that the Derbys had lied to her her whole life? Did she go as far as to tell her she was her real mother? Kathy was definitely capable of this.

If so, how would Tilly have reacted? If she'd suddenly learned that the two people she cared about the most had lied to her, would her anger be directed at Kathy for trying to destroy her family bond? *Hmm.* For every answer, more questions burgeoned.

Did Tilly Derby have motive to kill Kathy Brown …? Unsure at this time, but doubtful.

Tom Partridge was around the same age as Kathy. He was her friend who had known her in both valleys—Fortitude and Tallebudgera. He was a wild card for me because I wasn't a hundred per cent sure that he wasn't hiding behind the spectrum card. Once again, was this quiet individual capable of killing someone? And if so, what was it that would have turned him against his friend so much to make him want to kill her? In my mind, he wasn't really a suspect, but he *was* a part of the story.

Did Tom Partridge have a motive to kill Kathy Brown …? Doubtful.

I wasn't sure how long I'd been staring at the board when my phone rang. A mandatory eye roll followed a quick glance at the screen when I realised it was Ben Fisher. 'G'day, Ben. How's it going?'

'You tell me,' he said in his usual abrupt manner.

'Aargh, it's a balmy 29 degrees in the Valley, there's a bloody onshore hanging around so bugger all surf this morning—'

'I'm talking about the case, as you well know.'

'Oh right. The case.' I strolled back into the living room.

Romeo was sprawled out on the sofa. As if startled, he suddenly sprung to his feet, then yawned.

'Yeah, it's going good, mate.'

'I'm sensing a lack of enthusiasm.'

This couldn't have been further from the truth. I was totally pumped.

'Have you done anything? Or just been popping up to Brisbane at my expense, or spending the day in the surf?'

'No mate, no surf at the minute, remember?' For some reason, I was that arrogant school kid again with the smart mouth.

'Well, that's it. I want you out of Mary's Mansion immediately. I can see why they kicked you out of the police force.'

"They didn't kick me out of the police force, dickhead!" I wanted to say but didn't. Instead, I remained calm and professional. My opinion of this guy had changed since I'd first met him. Not drastically, because I'd pegged him as a bit of a dick from day one, but since seeing him sitting alone at the bar of The Panda Club, there was something else about him I must have subconsciously flagged. Was the reason he was in the club that day really for research purposes as he claimed? Or was he, in fact, a regular patron, just like Fenton? *Woah!* Wait a minute. There could be a link there. Did Fisher know of Fenton from The Panda Club, prior to coming to the Valley?

'I'm preparing to write a new book. Mary's Mansion is the perfect place. I'll be there on Saturday. Make sure you're gone.'

'Sure, no worries.'

He hung up.

'No worries, me old mate,' I said out loud. No worries for me that is. Although I was using Fisher's money to pay for it, the name on the short-term lease of the property rental was mine. Perhaps I should have called him back to have explained. *Nah... fuck him,* I found myself looking forward to seeing his face when he arrived to find me still here.

Returning to the whiteboard I had another name to add to the list of suspects, and after a quick Google search, another photograph was added to the growing gallery. The fact that Ben Fisher wasn't smiling on the image, I found to be quite appropriate. Like the rest of the suspects, were there secrets to be found there too? I couldn't wait to find out.

58

'What do you mean operations are slowing?' Callum demanded.

'We're losing the workforce, Callum,' Jimmy P said.

Callum stood from his desk. 'But how? We're one of the biggest employers in South East Queensland, surely?'

'Were. We *were* one of the biggest employers in South East Queensland. Not any longer though. Fenton's leaving us for dead and now he's poaching your men.'

'We need to rally the community, make them aware of what's happening.'

Jimmy shuffled uneasily from one foot to the other, looking at the floor as if searching for his next words. 'That's the thing, Callum. There is no community. Fenton's bought up all the land and evicted the local folk. Bill Sherrington, Fowler, they're all gone.'

'Gone where?'

'God only knows. Fenton and his cronies are the local community now.'

Callum dropped back into his chair. 'That bastard. You were right, Jimmy, we should have fixed him once and for all when we had the chance.'

'Yes, we should have.'

'You said there was something else?'

Jimmy turned and stepped out of the office, returning momentarily with a thickset, ruddy-faced man. 'This is Mick Flannigan.'

Flannigan removed his cap and bowed his head as if he were in the presence of Queen Victoria herself.

'There's something Mick overheard last night in the Rose and Crown.' Jimmy prompted the man to speak with a reassuring nod.

'I was in the bar with a couple of me mates, two hard working lads from Galway. Like me, they're loyal to you, Mister Murphy. You've been good to us, with plenty of work, decent pay and lodgings.'

'What was it you overheard?' Callum asked.

'Not really overheard, sir, more unable not to hear. Fenton now owns the tavern. He was in there last night celebrating his latest acquisition with his men.'

'What happened to William Downy. Did he sell out?' Callum asked, sitting forward in his chair.

Flannigan shrugged. 'Nobody knows. According to Fenton, he went back to Brisbane.' '

But Oy know Bill quite well,' Callum said. 'He never mentioned he was thinking of selling.'

'No, sir, neither did Bob Stephens, the owner of the General Store. Or Benjamin Gibson, the proprietor of the boarding house. Or Madame Du Pont, the brothel owner. But that's because nobody's been able to ask them. They've all gone. Up, scoot and left town without as much as a farewell.'

'My God, he's not just buying up all the land. He's buying the entire region!'

'Aye, sir. It appears that way.'

'So, what was it you heard?'

Flanigan was kneading his hat in his hands. He side glanced Jimmy P and swallowed nervously before continuing. 'He's said he's coming for you next, sir.'

Callum rose slowly back to his feet. 'Coming for me?'

'Aye. Boasting he was, that he was going to put you in the ground.'

'Oh, he was, was he?'

'Aye, and that Burleigh Heads would soon be known as Fenton Heads. The Valley will be Fenton's Valley.' His thick black eyebrows knitted into one as his gaze returned to the floor.

'What is it?' Callum asked. 'What else did he say?'

'He said he was going to fuck that whore you call a wife like she'd never been fucked before, and that he was going to take her in as a scullery maid.'

'Oy've heard enough. You can go now, Flannigan.'

'Thank you, sir.' Flanigan bowed his head and backed out of the room, but before Jimmy could close the door behind him, he lifted his gaze once more. 'I'm telling you this, sir, because you deserve to know. Fenton is undermining you. Even your best workers are jumping ship, purely because he's offering more money.'

Jimmy closed the door. 'We can't sit back any longer, Callum. That bastard won't just be running you out of town.'

'Aye. Oy know it. Get the men together. It's time we had a meeting.'

Jimmy's face turned a shade of white. 'That's the thing, Callum. There aren't that many men left.'

'You mean they've abandoned us?'

'I don't believe they have. They're fiercely loyal to you, you know that.'

'Then where are they?'

'Murdered I'm guessing.'

'What?'

'It's war, Callum. We need to strike back now before it's too late.'

'Not we, Jimmy. Me … it's between me and The Rat. Oy should have finished this a long time ago.' He slumped back down into his chair. 'This is all my fault. If only Oy'd listened to you and wrung his scrawny little neck when Oy'd had the chance.'

'Don't be hard on yourself, Callum. Fenton has taken advantage of you being a good man.'

Callum rose once more, only this time more determined. 'It's time Oy put an end to this once and for all.'

'What will you do?'

'Something Oy should have done aboard the *Great Britain*.'

***

Mary Murphy still liked to spend time at Mary's Mansion. She'd kept it the same as when she and Callum lived there. The place reminded her of the days when life was less complicated and filled with naïve hope. Whenever she got the chance, she'd clean the place, then sit on the back verandah with a mug of billy tea. Part of her wished that she and her husband still lived there, running a much smaller operation perhaps, keeping life simpler and stress free. Something caught her eye in the cow fields to her right.

A man was approaching. She recognised the gait right away, the cocky swagger, the arrogant self-important demeanour. 'Damn,' she cussed out loud. After cleaning the interior of the tiny house from top to bottom, she knew there wasn't a gun in the place, or even a knife.

Calmy, she looked around her for a potential weapon.

59

After calling the bluff of the main suspects with the old you-know-I-know-what-you-did routine, I'd obviously poked a stick into a hornets' nest and given it a good stir. If one of the faces that stared back at me belonged to the killer, they may have been panicking at that moment, and like a vicious rat, when you corner a psychopath, you need to be on your guard. They've killed before, so they'll kill again. Of course, there was also the possibility that a complete stranger murdered Kathy Brown—someone passing through the Valley, or someone else from her past who I was unaware of. I'm sure she had plenty of enemies.

Although Tilly and Tom were kind of on the list, until now I'd treated them gently. In fact, they were probably unaware that I even suspected them at all.

I'd arranged to meet with Tilly early the next morning, after she'd offered to give me a free riding lesson. Although I wasn't that keen, the one-on-one time with her would be interesting. We were to meet in the arena at 7.30 am. When I sauntered across the paddock, I was surprised to see Tom Partridge leaning up against the circular ranch-style fence. Tilly was already in the arena, holding the bridal of a not too spectacular black and white, rather stumpy horse. She was whispering in its ear as she stroked its face.

'Good morning!' I called over to Tom as I approached.

Tom nodded, nervously or shyly. I couldn't tell which.

'Hey, here he is,' Tilly cried, looking up when she heard my voice.

I climbed through the copper log fence and joined her. 'How's it going?'

'Good. This is Elvis,' Tilly said, introducing me to the horse.

'Elvis? You're kidding.'

'Nope. He's the king of rock 'n' roll so you're going to need to hang on.' Her attempt at suppressing a cheeky grin was pitiful.

Tom joined us and handed me a helmet. He didn't speak or make eye contact.

'Thanks, mate,' I said cheerfully, patting him on the back to relax him.

'Okay. You ready?' Tilly asked.

'S'pose. Are you sure he's big enough?' I asked, stroking Elvis' mane.

'Yeah, he's as strong as a horse.'

Tom, who had returned to his perch on the other side of the fence, laughed out loud as if Tilly's little joke was the funniest thing he'd ever heard. The metamorphosis from staid to hysterics took me completely by surprise. Then I wondered if he knew Tilly was Kathy's daughter. And if so, would his immature mind be able to keep such a secret? Especially from his best friend. *Hmm.* I needed to speak to him again.

After an hour in the saddle, my arse was as raw as a kipper. Elvis had lived up to his reputation. At times, I thought the saddle might slip around his wide girth and take me with it. We trotted, we cantered and we dashed, all within a confined circle, while remaining at the end of a rope held by Tilly. I have to say; she was a great teacher, gently calling out instructions to both the student and the horse. I learned how to use the muscles in my legs to act as shock absorbers, and how to anticipate the motion of the horse.

'Just like a pro!' Tilly called out. Was there a smidge of patronisation in her praise?

I really enjoyed the session but was glad when it was over. Now I know why John Wayne walked the way he did. I'd be adopting that easy, non-chaffing strut for at least the rest of the day.

We headed towards the stables, me leading Elvis by the reins, Tilly and Tom alongside us.

'Listen, you guys know why I'm here, right?' They nodded in unison.

'Do you think you can help me?' What may have appeared as a casual glance in their direction was actually me gauging their reactions closely.

Tom frowned and lowered his gaze to the ground.

Tilly also frowned, but hers was more of the quizzical kind.

Both reactions were exactly what I'd expected. 'I think you guys are great and I'm loving hanging out with you both, but I'm here to do a job.'

'To prove that Ben Fisher didn't steal his story,' Tilly said.

'At first, maybe. But it's much more than that now.'

'To find the killer of Kathy Brown,' Tilly added.

Tom remained quiet, but I could see he was listening.

'That's right, and ... I'm pretty sure I know who it is.' Of course, I had no idea at this point who the killer was, but I was sticking to my newly adopted method. If I was talking to the killer right now, how would he, or she, react? Out of the two, Tom was definitely the most agitated. A twitching brow joined the frown as if he were processing the information.

Tilly looked at me wide-eyed. 'Really?'

I have to admit; I have a good poker face. The slight nod and the blank grave expression were an attempt at saying without words, "That's right, and it's time to come clean. You know I know!"

'Wow!' Then, with her eyes fixed on mine, she lowered her voice. 'Who is it?'

I looked at Tom. His eyes caught mine then quickly returned to the ground. His face had turned a sickly shade of white, but his cheeks were flushed.

I narrowed my eyes.

Tilly said, 'What? You don't think Tom had—?'

'*I* didn't do it!' Tom blurted out.

'I didn't say you did, mate.'

'But you looked at him,' Tilly said.

I shook my head casually. 'No. I looked at you both.'

We reached the stables. Tilly took Elvis' reins from my hand and led him into one of the stalls, leaving Tom and I alone.

'So, is there anything you want to tell me, Tom?'

He shook his head wildly like an unruly child at a kindergarten.

'You sure about that?'

When he finally looked at me, the shy, insecure demeanour was no longer present. In his eyes, I sensed all the things I would have expected to see in a trapped animal desperate to escape. His chin rose, and I noticed he was clenching his fists.

Actually feeling a little threatened, I pushed on regardless. 'We both know what happened, don't we, mate?'

He glanced around as if it to make sure Tilly wasn't in earshot. Then, he leaned in and growled, 'You've got nothing on me, you fucker!'

Tilly returned and, as if someone had flicked a switch, Tom's engorged frame returned to normal. The aggressive yet frightened expression immediately melted back into a docile demeanour. I'd seen this before in psychiatric patients with dual personalities. If Tom Partridge suffered from schizophrenia, would this bump him up to the top of the suspect list?

'So, who then?' Tilly asked as she rejoined us.

'Well, the thing is, I want to make it easy on the guilty party. If they come forward and confess, the law will be more lenient, a lot more understanding.' My eyes were flicking from side to side like an albino rabbit's. 'I'll help them. They can be sure about that.'

Tom was staring into the distance.

Tilly's focus remained on me. 'What if the killer isn't in the Valley?'

I waved this suggestion away with an impatient shake of the head. 'The killer is here. My worry is that now they know I'm getting close, they could strike again.'

Tilly checked her watch. 'I've got to go. Got a class in five minutes.' She rushed away.

Tom went to follow her, but before he did he leaned in towards me and in a lowered voice said, 'Mary knows!'

60

It was mid-morning by the time I got back to Mary's Mansion. Too late to go for a surf. I was at a bit of a loss at what to do next. As always, Romeo was a great distraction when I let him out of the chicken coop. He greeted me like I'd been away for a month. The little bugger had done a cheeky poo in the middle of the run, but I couldn't get angry with him. 'What are you doing, mate?' He was fully house trained but not chicken coop trained. There was a rusty garden trowel hanging on a nail. Using it to scoop up the little turd, I brazenly flicked it over the other side of the fence onto Fenton's property.

We headed up to Callum's Lookout, Romeo dashing ahead, stopping to sniff a tree trunk, then falling behind before catching up again. He seemed to enjoy the freedom.

When the trees thinned out at the top of the slope, I took a seat on the old bench. Mary and Callum Murphy were on my mind. I'd done some research on the internet. There wasn't much information about the couple. Just a paragraph or two about Callum starting a sawmill in the area in the 1860s, and Mary was briefly mentioned as his wife. 'Mary knows.' I'd heard this three times now from three different people. First, from Kea the medium. Then Daisy Patterson. And now from Tom Partridge. What did it mean? Although she'd been dead for over a hundred years, Mary Murphy's influence seemed to be everywhere. Mary's

Mansion, Mary's Shack, her grave next to that of her husband's, the inscription scratched into the stone bench, *Callum loves Mary!*

'What is it you know, Mary?' I called into the air.

Romeo, assuming I'd seen someone approaching, barked and raced towards the tree line.

Kneeling by the side of the bench, I followed the letters in the inscription with my finger. 'What happened here?'

Romeo's barking increased. He was out of sight. Suddenly, he fell silent.

'Romey, what are you doin' boy?'

He raced from the trees towards me, his ears back and his tail between his legs. Then Tilly appeared, hot on his heels clapping her hands.

'Come here, you little bugger!' She called after him playfully.

'That was a quick lesson,' I said as she joined me on the bench.

'They cancelled at the last minute. Apparently, Lucy has the flu.' Lucy being the student I assumed.

'Cool, you got a bit of time off?'

'Yep. Nothing else until teatime.' She took a deep breath and looked out over the view. I got the impression she had something to say.

'You okay?'

She nodded but remained silent, her eyes fixed on the horizon.

'You sure?'

She exhaled loud and slow. 'Was Kathy Brown my mother?'

Bloody hell, I wasn't expecting that. As far as I was aware, Tilly didn't even know she was adopted, so why would she suspect Kathy was her mother? I was contemplating my answer. Should I lie? She's not a child, she's twenty-one after all. But was it my place to destroy everything she'd believed her whole life? I needn't have worried. My loaded pause answered the question.

'I knew it!'

'What makes you say that?'

'I can't explain it … just knew.'

So far, I hadn't actually confirmed her belief. I wanted to keep it that way so offered a nonchalant shrug.

'Why didn't they tell me?'

I didn't need to reply. Her questions were rhetorical now.

'It's funny but … I always suspected they weren't my parents.'

'I think you need to speak to them.'

'No, they've lied to me my whole life. Why would they tell me the truth now?'

I really wasn't prepared for this. I didn't want to lie to Tilly, but it wasn't my place to discuss her family politics. They must have had their reasons for not telling her. Perhaps they knew something of the biological parents' history. Perhaps they were afraid that if she knew, she'd try to find her mother and end up in the same situation. This made sense. 'I really can't comment.'

She began to cry.

Shuffling up beside her, I placed an arm around her shoulders and gently pulled her in for a hug. 'It's okay.'

'It's far from okay. But … I don't blame them.'

I was relieved to hear that.

'They've given me a great life.'

'They certainly have.' I retrieved my hanky from my shorts pocket and handed it to her.

Tilly took it, sat upright and blew her nose. 'She would have been bad for me.'

This was one of those important moments when you learn as a detective to keep your mouth shut.

'She was great towards me, but I could see how everyone else acted whenever she was around.' Tilly dabbed her eyes with the handkerchief. 'There's something else I didn't tell you. Or the police.'

A slight raise of my eyebrows prompted her to continue.

'The day before … the day before … I found her, Tom and I came over to Mary's Mansion. Tom was excited because he'd got a new iPhone. He wanted to show it to his friend, Kathy. At first, we couldn't find her. I knocked and called out her name but there was no reply. We went around the back. She was kneeling on Mary Murphy's grave, staring at the headstone, sobbing. I placed a hand on her shoulder. She jumped to her feet, and I thought she was going to hit me. "Kathy," Tom shouted and threw himself in between us. "It's me. It's Tommy." Kathy narrowed her eyes and looked around as if she didn't know where she was. "Tommy? Tilly?" Her brow was glistening with sweat, her fringe was matted, and her cheeks were flushed. "What are you guys doing here?" Tom held up the phone and took a photograph of her. This made Kathy giggle. Then Tom waved me into the shot. Kathy's whole demeanour had completely changed. She was smiling now.'

As she gazed out over the view, Tilly's face broke into a smile as if she were reliving the moment. 'Tom stepped back and took the photograph. Then he showed off airdropping it to us both.'

'Do you still have it?' I asked.

Tilly nodded. The outline of her phone was clearly visible in the pocket of her tight leggings, but she didn't attempt to retrieve it. Instead, she continued where she'd left off. 'Kathy suddenly became agitated. "You guys need to go. There's somebody coming over. I've got to get showered and ready." "Ohhh, a boyfriend, eh?" I said, playfully. "Yes. Something like that." She hurried us towards the house and watched as we headed back down the driveway. "I'll see you later, Tills," she called after us. I looked over my shoulder and waved. I did see her later. She was standing at the fence drinking a glass of wine. She told me she had to leave for Brisbane the next morning.' The tears returned, and she dabbed her eyes some more.

We strolled back down the hill. Romeo following in his own time.

'What will you do?' I asked.

'About my parents?'

I nodded.

'What do you think I should do?'

'Do you have to tell them? What would it achieve?' Technically, I still wasn't confirming her question.

This caused a deep furrow in Tilly's brow as she contemplated my words. 'I need to think about it.'

'I think you do.'

When we reached Mary's Mansion, I offered her a cold drink, but she declined. 'I need to saddle up Bronson and just ride. I'll be able to think clearly then.'

'Okay.' I understood this, her ride was my surf. 'Before you go.'

Tilly turned to face me.

'Would you be able to send me a copy of the photograph?'

She nodded, pulled out the phone from her pocket, then skilfully went to work on the screen with her thumbs. A moment later, my phone dinged as a message with a photo attachment came through. She turned and headed away deep in thought.

Sitting on the back verandah with a mug of tea, I studied the photograph that Tilly had sent me. It was exactly how she had described it. Mother and daughter standing side by side. Looking into their eyes, I realised how obvious it was that they were related, and I wondered when it had dawned on Tilly. Was this a recent revelation, or had she figured it out five years ago?

Something in the picture caught my eye. Kathy's left arm was hanging by her side. She was holding something. I zoomed in on the picture and squinted. 'Well bugger me,' I said out loud.

Romeo didn't follow me into the chicken coop. When he realised where I was going, he stopped about halfway between the house and the coop, dropped onto his stomach and observed.

Lifting the garden trowel from the nail where I'd replaced it earlier, I held it up against the image on my phone. It was obviously older, but the same. Backing out of the coop, I strolled over to the graves that lay in the shadows of the trees. Still using the picture on my phone as a reference, I worked out where Tilly and Kathy were standing and realised they were directly in front of Mary's grave. Kneeling, I ran a hand across the hard dirt then said out loud, 'I'm sorry about this, Mary.'

Driving the blade of the trowel into the ground, I dug a small hole and continued to work it wider and deeper. When I was only about five inches down, the blade hit something hollow. Moving from my haunches to my knees. The soil was rich with clay and chipped away like soft stone. I continued to dig carefully around the perimeter of a small box. Then, using the fingers of both hands, I gently prized it out of the ground. Although it was quite bland and was probably once finished in a shiny lacquer, it was obvious what it was right away. There was no lock, just a tarnished brass clasp, which I easily prized open with a finger. The inside looked the same as it would have five years ago when it was buried, lined with red velvet. The top layer was a shelf of compartments that held diamond rings, a woman's gold watch, and pearl and diamond earrings. Looking completely out of place, though, was an old-style computer memory card. On its plastic surface was crudely scratched, 'Kathy'. There was a similar shelf beneath the top one where a Cameo broach sat among a gold chain necklace with a heart locket, a string of pearls and various sized bracelets. There was another shelf underneath this one, but I didn't need to look at it. This was the jewellery box that Daisy Patterson had accused Kathy of stealing from her, I was sure of it. But why was it buried here?

Closing the lid, I still had the memory card in my hand. This obviously didn't belong to Daisy.

I was cursing technology when I got back to the house. My old laptop had a series of ports, one of which would have accommodated the card, but my latest one only facilitated USBs.

Retrieving my mobile phone from my pocket, I dialled Jenny Radford's number.

61

'Don't worry yourself, Jimmy lad. Oy won't be doing nothing stupid,' Callum reassured his wing man. 'Oy'll handle this in the correct way, see if Oy don't.'

Jimmy reluctantly returned to his duties running the sawmill, leaving his boss and best friend in the office.

Callum watched Jimmy trudge across the timber yard between the office building and the mill. As soon as he was out of sight, he slipped out the back door where he had his horse and buggy waiting.

Fenton was goading him now, taunting him to a showdown. Callum purposely hadn't mentioned it to Jimmy, but he'd received a note that afternoon from Fenton telling him to meet him in the Rose and Crown at 2.30 pm. And to come alone.

Callum relished the chance of standing toe to toe with the heathen one last time.

When he entered the saloon bar, Callum thought it odd for it to be so busy with working men at that time of the day. Fenton was standing alone at the bar nursing a whiskey.

Callum hadn't seen The Rat since they'd disembarked the *Great Britain* in Brisbane, but he had changed very little—those deep-set, beady eyes, hooked nose and high cheekbones.

'Fenton,' Callum said as he approached the bar.

'Murphy.' Fenton grinned revealing black broken teeth. 'I'm glad you could join me.

We're having a little celebration.'

'We?' Callum looked around and realised that more than half of the patrons were now standing around them like a band of pirates.

'That's right,' Fenton said, pushing off from the bar and fronting up to Callum. 'I'm not only the biggest landowner around here, but I've just attained my most prized trophy.'

Callum noticed a fresh scratch across Fenton's face and there was a wince of pain as he shuffled towards him. 'Oh aye, and what might that be?'

Fenton downed his whiskey and jiggled the empty glass in front of Callum's face. 'Drink?'

Callum smacked the glass from Fenton's hand sending it bouncing across the wooden floor.

There was a rumble from the onlookers, their eager faces were like expectant punters at a cock fight.

Callum, recognising how stupid he'd been to come on his own, realised that Fenton was far too much of a coward to meet him alone.

'Suit yourself,' Fenton said. Still facing Callum, he leaned back on the bar. 'S'pose you've got *nothink* to celebrate.'

'You've stolen the land you own, you feckin rat,' Callum cussed.

Reacting to the word 'rat', Fenton sprung forward. 'You'll never call me that again.' He pulled out a knife and thrust it forward, resting the blade at Callum's throat. Then he began to chuckle. 'There you go. Now we're finally gettin' somewhere. There's only one bit of land left that I need.'

'You'll never set foot on my land, Fenton. Oy'll promise you that!' 'Already have.' His sickly grin stirred the pit of Callum's stomach.

Leaning forward slightly, causing the blade to nick his skin, Callum challenged his adversary. 'Put down the knife, Rat, and fight me like a man. Or are you too scared to show your men what a coward you really are?'

'Will you scream like your whore did?' Fenton said, narrowing his eyes.

The adrenalin flowing through Callum's veins suddenly pumped through his entire body like a burst sluice gate. 'What did you do?' he demanded, knowing there was weight to Fenton's comment.

'She wasn't as good as I'd hoped. I didn't expect her to scream so much, it was like she'd never had a real man before.'

Callum knocked the knife away from his neck with the back of his left hand. The blade flew across the room, narrowly missing a group of onlookers, embedding itself in the timber floor like a dart. He immediately followed up with a thunderous headbutt, busting Fenton's nose like a ripe tomato. But he didn't stop there. Chasing Fenton's retreat, he followed through with a series of punches that any prize fighter would have been proud of.

The crowd of mill workers cheered. Fenton hit the floor hard.

Dropping to his knees so he was straddling his opponent, Callum allowed his full weight to impact Fenton's abdomen, forcing the air from his lungs. 'What did you feckin do, Fenton?' Callum demanded, grabbing him by the lapels and pulling him close.

The blood on Fenton's teeth were an improvement on the smoke stains, but the grin was even more evil than ever. 'It's too late. You've lost everythink now, you fuckin' stupid Mick.'

Callum lifted his fist and was about to bring it crashing down in Fenton's face when it was grabbed from behind. Another hand grabbed his other arm below the armpit and he was dragged backwards.

Lifting Callum to his feet, two burly men now held his arms from either side. They were big lads, fighters themselves no doubt.

'Let me go ya ediots.' Callum cussed and fought to break free, but the two men were much stronger than him. 'We need to rid the Valley of this cancer,' Callum pleaded. 'Now's our chance.'

Fenton rose warily from the floor, wiping the blood from his face with the cuff of his jacket. He glanced around as if looking for the knife, but then approached Callum with an exaggerated shuffle. 'That's right. It is time to get rid of the tumour that's been inflicting me all these years.' He drew back his right fist then launched it forward into Callum's nose. He followed up with a left to his right eye and another right to his left eye. 'Hold him tight,' Fenton ordered the men. 'Don't let him fall to the floor.'

Over the next fifteen minutes or so, Fenton hit Callum Murphy with everything he had, pummelling his head and body, and when his fists were too bloody and sore to continue, he instructed the men to let him fall to the floor, where he then proceeded to kick him.

There was a mixture of excitement and disgust in the cheers of the onlookers. When Callum's head was kicked like a football so many times and Fenton was physically exhausted. He instructed the men to pick him up again. The grand finale was afoot. He looked around for the knife again, but the wall of onlookers was concealing it. There was a large hunting knife on the belt of one of the men who held Callum. Fenton grabbed the handle and slowly slid it upwards, marvelling at the steel blade.

'At last,' he said, stumbling towards Callum. 'The moment I have been waiting for all these years is finally here.' Fenton drew back the knife, savouring the moment, visualising the trajectory of the blade before launching it forward into his opponent's heart.

62

For reasons explained earlier by Reg Patterson, the theft of the jewellery box wasn't reported to the police. Being embedded in a layer of clay for five years had actually preserved it, but the outer lacquer was cracked and blistered. I doubted there'd be any fingerprints, apart from Daisy's, on the jewellery itself. DNA perhaps, but what would that prove? That Kathy stole it? After contemplating the outcome of handing it over to the police, I decided against it. Giving it back to Daisy Patterson I suspected would be more productive, especially if she had further information about Kathy.

I'd also had an idea about the memory card. There was a copy and print shop in the Burleigh high street. In the window they advertised a video to DVD service. I suspected they might be able to transfer the contents of an old memory card to a USB stick. A quick phone call confirmed this, and I made an appointment to drop in a couple of hours later.

After taking the card out of the jewellery box and appraising it in my fingers for a moment or two, I placed it on the table.

The weekly wash was due and a bit of housekeeping wouldn't go a miss. With the ancient Simpson washing machine churning away in the laundry cupboard, Hot Tomato FM full blast on the radio, but hardly audible over the drone of the vacuum cleaner, I became aware that Romeo was barking. 'What's up, boy?' I said, turning off the vacuum cleaner.

From the back of the couch, he had a view through the window of the driveway out front. His barking intensified.

I was about to open the front door when it opened by itself.

Ben Fisher stood on the threshold.

Romeo jumped down from the couch, raced towards him and made a half-hearted fuss.

As usual, Fisher ignored him completely. 'What the hell are you still doing here?'

'What's it to you?' I said, approaching him and blocking the entrance.

'You're off the case remember?' He scanned the room over my shoulder.

'I'll be off this case when I say I am.' I'm not the aggressive type but if someone was to press the wrong buttons, watch out. This bloke seemed to possess a natural ability for winding me up.

'But you're not staying here. You need to go.'

'I don't think so,' I said, stepping closer. 'It's my name on the lease.'

'That I've paid for.'

The grin seemed to be an accessory that came with the shrug. 'That's right. Thanks.'

'You've done nothing. You've wasted my time and money. Why are you still here?'

'Oh, I'm close.'

'Close to what?' The question was a simple one, delivered with curiosity, but I also sensed something else. A sprinkle of worry, perhaps. I was still blocking the doorway. 'Do you really want everyone to think you stole the story?'

He broke eye contact and glanced over his shoulder. 'I don't care about that anymore.'

'Yes, you do. Because you're an egocentric, arrogant prick—'

'Now, just hold on a minute.' He obviously wasn't used to being spoken to this way. He'd fluffed up as if ready for a fight but then his body seemed to deflate as if he'd thought twice about it. 'What is it you've found out?'

'You might not like it.'

'What?'

'I want you to be honest with me now. You used the story of Kathy Brown's death for your book. I know it, you know it.'

'No, I didn't.'

'You knew Kathy. I saw you in The Panda Club, remember?'

'That was a coincidence. I was in there for research that's all.'

'So, you said.' To be honest I was winging it again. Although I was now certain he used the Kathy Brown case for the basis of his story, I wasn't sure if it was plagiarism or not, and I didn't care. 'You can't stay here, I'm afraid. I'm paid up until the end of the month.'

'*I'm* paid up you mean!'

I checked my watch. 'If you don't mind there's somewhere else I need to be.'

'But I've come all the way from Brisbane.'

'Bugger.' I was enjoying a facetious moment.

'You ungrateful bastard,' he spat.

Stepping forward, I wouldn't have hit him but throwing him out on his arse was definitely on the cards.

He backed away. 'You won't get away with this. Fucking has-been.'

'Ta-ta, then.' Watching him return to his little Porsche, I waved sarcastically as he drove away.

It was a quick drive from Mary's Mansion to the Patterson's dairy farm next door. They were a working family, so I suspected Daisy would be alone in the granny flat beneath the house. I found her sitting outside under the shade of a gazebo, looking out over a small rose garden.

'Hello, Daisy,' I said, standing at the gate. At first, she seemed a little confused, wary. 'Scott. Scott Stephens.'

Her face warmed. 'Ah, that's right. The copper.'

'May I come in?'

She nodded.

'What's in the bag?' she asked as I entered the garden.

I was carrying an Aldi bag. 'Oh, I think you're going to like this.' Taking the seat opposite her at a small circular table with a ceramic mosaic top, I placed the bag in front of her and gently lifted out the jewellery box.

Daisy's face lit up as I placed it on the table. 'You found it?'

'I did.'

'Where was it?'

I told her where and how I'd found it.

'See, I told you!' She tapped the side of her nose with her index finger.

'You did?'

'Yep, Mary knows.' She opened the box and was gently lifting out the shelves.

'Are you aware of anything missing?'

Retrieving the locket and gold chain, she squeezed it in her hands. 'I thought I'd never see this again.'

'Is everything there?' I asked again.

'Looks like it,' she replied, lifting out the compartments. 'Thank you so much for returning this.'

'You're welcome. Daisy. You said Mary knows. What did you mean by that?'

'Well, who's been looking after these since they were stolen?'

'They were buried in Mary's grave if that's what you mean.'

'There you go. Want a cup of tea?'

Over a cup of Earl Grey and a plate of ginger biscuits, I spent the next half hour gently probing the old lady for information about Kathy Brown. She didn't seem to know much more than she'd already told me, although she did say something interesting when I asked her why Reg didn't like Kathy.

'She was a vixen. The men around here were like bitumen on a hot day in her presence.'

'But not Reg, surely?'

'No, but his boys could easily have fallen victims to a girl like that.'

'Roy?'

'I've said enough.'

'Did Roy and Kathy …?'

She leaned forward and lowered her voice. 'It would have ruined everything.'

'So, what happened?'

'They paid the girl off and sent her away.'

'But she came back.'

Daisy nodded and sat back in her chair. 'She did. Not for quite some years though.'

'And that would have made everyone around here very nervous.'

'It's time for my nap.'

'Do you know if Reg threatened Kathy?'

'That's ridiculous. Thank you for returning the box. You can see yourself out?' She'd shut down.

I went to help her as she struggled to her feet but she waved me away.

With the jewellery box under one arm, she made her way into the house.

63

From the Patterson's place, I drove into Burleigh and found a car park on James Street. 'Copy That!' was a somewhat bland shopfront among colourful homeware stores, boutiques and restaurants. The owner, a balding, overweight young man named Ken, was cheerful and confident of the outcome as he slid the memory card into a small device that was plugged into an iMac.

'Let's see what we have here.' A message box appeared on the screen. '416 MB. Looks like photographs,' Ken said, leaning in closer to the monitor. After a quick finger shuffle on the keyboard, rows of thumb-sized photographs appeared. He plugged a USB stick into the same device and it began to flash. 'Should only be a couple of minutes.'

While the transfer took place, I also leaned into the screen. Although the images were small, I could see them clearly. They were all similar—mostly of Kathy with different men—simple snaps, selfies perhaps. At the bottom of the screen, I read '26 images'. *Shit. Did this mean she was blackmailing twenty-six people? No wonder she became so wealthy.* Then a realisation hit me. If this was the case, there could have been far more suspects than the handful I'd met so far. *Hmm.* This could complicate things.

I needed to get back to Mary's Mansion so I could load the stick onto my laptop and open up each image to a full screen. Of course, this was evidence, so I'd need to hand it over to the police, but I decided to have a good look first and make a copy.

During the drive back to Tallebudgera, I was itching with anticipation. Pulling up outside the little shack, I headed straight around the back of the house and was surprised not to hear Romeo barking. The door to the chicken coop was open. 'What the hell?' Romeo was nowhere to be seen. 'Damn!' Had I not fastened the latch properly? No, I knew I had. The memory was quite vivid. *So, who had been here?* 'ROMEO!' I called out, my voice echoing across the Valley. 'COME ON, BOY!' If he could've heard me, he would have come running. *Would Tilly have taken him for a walk?* It was possible. I rushed back to the front of the house, then I noticed the front door was slightly open. 'Hello!' Calling out slowly, I pushed open the door. 'Fuck!' I cussed. The house was ransacked. Kitchen drawers thrown across the floor. The table upended. Couch cushions ripped open; their contents scattered like artificial snow. My laptop was nowhere to be seen. Through the open bedroom door, I could see it was pretty much the same in there—the mattress was overturned and my clothes and belongings were strewn across the place. The whiteboard was leaning against the wall. The photographs were gone, my notes scrubbed into a blurry swirl.

I was careful not to touch anything. Whether I liked it or not, I'd have to call the police. But first I needed to find my dog. There were two directions for him to go—he'd either wandered out onto Tallebudgera Creek Road, or he'd gone for a walk out the back of the property and up to Callum's Lookout. Hoping for the latter, I headed up there first.

I rarely cried. Two notable occasions were when my mother died after I'd selfishly forced her to drive on that fateful night. The other was when I missed my father's passing by minutes due to me being elsewhere. I had shed tears on both occasions but not drowned in them the way I did when I reached Callum's Lookout and dropped to my knees.

The thing that struck me first was that the only time he was motionless was when he was asleep. When he was awake, he was a rocket. But he wasn't asleep. Those bright mischievous little eyes that were usually filled with the curious energy of a child were now opaque and dull. I lifted his lifeless body and held him close to my chest. Sobbing, I buried my face in the little cluster of fur at the back of his neck that we'd fondly termed as his mullet in progress.

My heart felt as if it would burst, and the tears poured like Springbrook Falls. There was no sign of a wound, but he'd been laid out on the bench for me to find.

The question of, 'Who would do such a thing?' never came to my mind. It was obvious that whoever murdered Kathy Brown had returned and killed my dog. Was this meant to be a warning? Was I getting too close to the truth? I carried Romeo's body back down to the house and gently placed him on the back verandah. It was my fault, of course. It was me who had stirred the pot. Leading the killer to believe I knew what they'd done and was about to expose them. Was it me they'd actually come to kill? It was possible.

My duty was to call the police right away and let them take charge, let them take over the case. But the thought of stepping back was not an option. I needed to see this through.

I buried Romeo between Mary and Callum Murphy's graves. The ground there was still loose from my earlier excavation. 'I'm so sorry, Romey. I should never have left you,' I said, laying him in the hole. I'd wrapped him in his blanket, placing a half-devoured bone and a toy next to him. With the realisation I would never hear his bark again, never be the reciprocate of his puppy dog kisses, I broke down.

Returning to the house, my body was heavy and numb. Then, remembering the break-in, I yelled at the ceiling, 'FUCK!' Reaching into my pocket for my phone, I called Jenny.

64

I'm not a violent man, but at that moment I wanted to tear somebody's head off. I'm not an emotional man either, but at the moment I couldn't contain the tears.

Jenny hadn't answered, so I left a message. 'Can you come over to Mary's Mansion right away please, Jen?' I wondered what she'd make of the tremble in my voice. She certainly hadn't heard me blubber this way before.

Stepping outside onto the back verandah, I took in some deep sobering breaths. It was late afternoon. Whoever had done this had done it in broad daylight. Looking over the fence to the stud, I noticed a half dozen or so parents with their children standing outside the arena, no doubt waiting for their lesson with Tilly. Would Tilly have seen who'd entered Mary's Mansion? Looking in the opposite direction, the Patterson's place was too far away. The only witnesses that side would have been a group of cows grazing in the paddock. That doesn't mean to say though that one of the boys wasn't working over this side of the property at the time.

Taking in more air, I needed to calm myself. The rational thing to do was to hand this over to the police, let them take over. But rationality was the farthest thing from my mind at that time.

The walk actually did me some good, calming me enough to at least speak without the broken waiver. 'Hello Pam,' I called over to the Derbys' fence. She was busy in the front garden of the gate house cutting back a row of lilly pillies.

'Hi, Scott. How are you?' She put down the large secateurs and approached me. 'Are you okay?'

'Yeah. I'm fine. Just a bit tired. You didn't see anybody over at Mary's Mansion this afternoon, did you?'

She furrowed her brow. 'Uhmm, yes. I saw the writer. Ben Fisher.'

'I was home then. I nipped out for a moment later though. Did you see anybody else?'

'No, sorry. Why, what's happened?'

'Oh nothing. All good. Is Tilly around?'

'She's got a group class at the arena.'

We both turned to look at the arena. It was just visible from the cottage.

Pam frowned and checked her watch when she realised the group was still waiting. 'That's strange, she should have been back half an hour ago.'

'Where did she go?'

'She rode Bronson up to the rock pools for a paddle.' Pam pulled out her phone, rang Tilly's number, then waited patiently. There was no reply.

'Okay, you check on the group. I'll drive up to the rock pools and see if she's all right,' I said.

Rushing back to Mary's Mansion, I jumped straight in the Dub and drove west along Tallebudgera Creek Road. Unlike the Currumbin Rock Pools, Tallebudgera's version was a little less commercial; in fact, most Gold Coasters weren't even aware of their existence. As I pulled into the dirt car park, I was relieved to see Bronson grazing on the freshly mown grass. Climbing out of the car, I scanned the area. There was no sign of Tilly. 'COOEE!' I called out, then waited. The only sounds were the gentle flow of the icy cold mountain stream and the steady *whoosh* between the trees. After speaking to the horse as if it were human, 'Where's

Tilly, Bronson? Eh? Where is she?' I made my way towards the only structure, a modern drop toilet at the far end of the paddock. 'Tilly? You in there?' She wasn't. Trying all the doors, I realised the block was empty.

My legs grew heavy with dread as I made my way to the water's edge. The premonition of a young blonde girl lying face down in the knee-deep water flashed through my mind. I was relieved to find that she wasn't there, but at the same time, deeply concerned. *Where the hell was she?* It was too far to walk back to Fenton's place, and I would have seen her on the drive up, but she wouldn't leave Bronson here, anyway. Something had happened to her.

Someone, perhaps the same person who ransacked Mary's Mansion and killed Romeo, had taken her.

As much as I didn't want the police here, it was my duty to call them. I'd hoped that I'd be able to keep it low key by bringing Jenny in, but she was obviously busy. I rang Pam Derby and explained the situation. She was immediately irate.

'Calm down. I'm sure it's nothing. Call the police, then get Matt to come out here. I'll wait with Bronson until he arrives.'

Pam arrived within minutes, the tyres of the white ute skidding on the gravel driveway as it screeched to a halt next to the Dub.

'Where could she be?' she yelled, running towards me. 'She would never miss a class.' She was crying heavily when she took Bronson's reins. 'Where's Tilly, Bronson? Where is she?' In the same way I had earlier, she spoke to the horse like it would answer her.

'Where's Matt?' I asked.

'I don't know. He's not answering his phone.' She was growing hysterical.

'Did you call the police?'

'Yes, they're on the way.'

I headed back to the stream. Scanning the banks on either side, I called out, 'TILLY!' First in one direction, then in the other.

'TILLY!' There was no reply. The council land was a paddock, maybe four or six acres wide. Wandering north until I reached the boundary fence, I turned back and headed south until I reached the fence at the opposite end, carefully scanning the area around me like an Aboriginal tracker.

I made my way back to Pam who was just returning from the same trek but at the roadside of the plot.

'Pam, I'm going to head back and look for her around home.'

Pam nodded. 'Okay.' Then she burst into tears. 'Where could she be?'

I put my arms around her and pulled her close to my chest. 'It's okay, we'll find her.'

Driving back towards the stud I wasn't so sure she *would* be okay. If Tilly had seen the killer at Mary's Mansion, she was definitely in danger.

Pulling into Fenton's horse stud, I drove straight to the arena. Tom Partridge was teaching the group. Blocking the bitumen drive, I climbed out of the car, caught his eye and called him over. He reluctantly left the group and climbed through the arena fence.

'Tom, have you seen Tilly?'

'No, she should be here.'

'Did you see anybody at Mary's Mansion this afternoon?'

He shook his head.

'Are you sure? This is important, Tom.'

'No. I've been working the new thoroughbred in the back paddock.'

The back paddock was way over the other side of the property, you couldn't even see Fenton's house from there, never mind Mary's Mansion.

'Were you there all day?'

'Yes. Is Tilly okay?'

'I don't know, Tom. I don't know. Can anybody vouch for your whereabouts?'

He shook his head warily. 'No.'

'Okay, you better get back to your class but don't go anywhere. The police are on the way.'

He nodded industriously then returned to the arena.

Although the whiteboard was destroyed, the gallery of suspects was still clear in my mind. I needed to account for them all.

The Fenton homestead was deadly quiet. I knocked on the front door, but there was no answer. There was also no sign of the Fentons' vehicles out front. My phone rang, and I was relieved to see Jenny's picture on the screen.

'Jenny, thank goodness, where are you?'

'I'm about five minutes away. We got a call from Pam Derby. She sounded pretty upset.

Is there any sign of Tilly yet?'

'No, I left Pam out at the rock pools. Is there a despatch going out there?'

'There is. I'll peel off and meet you at Mary's Mansion.'

'Okay, see you soon.'

65

Mare Murphy and James Fenton had been seeing more and more of each other now that they were teenagers. Mare was boarding at All Hallows' School for girls in Brisbane's Fortitude Valley. James was at the Brisbane Grammar School for boys in Spring Hill. Most weekends they would meet up in the city and spend their days window shopping, strolling along the riverbank, and picnicking in the Botanic Gardens.

When they returned to Tallebudgera for the school holidays, and now being neighbours, they were inseparable. Albeit still secret from their parents, their relationship had blossomed into one of teenage love.

It was during one of the school holidays that they happened to be wandering around the small Tallebudgera township.

James was angry, as usual, with his father's lack of interest in him. 'I'm nothing like him, Mare,' he said as they strolled along the tiny high street.

'I know you're not, my love.'

'I wish he was more like *your* father.'

Although the usual condolences would be something like, 'I'm sure he's not that bad,' or 'he's a very busy man,' or 'I'm sure he cares about you, he just has an old-fashioned way of showing it', Mare knew that none of these scenarios were true. If only a fraction of the stories she'd heard about Ron Fenton held any veracity, he was indeed an evil man.

'I promise you this ...' James continued, walking purposely. '... I will never be like him. Never in a million years. It will be me who will shovel the Fenton name out of the gutter and make it respectable in the same vein as the Murphys.'

Mare took his hand and squeezed it. 'We'll do it together, my love.'

James lifted his gaze. Their eyes met and the two lovers blushed. There'd never been mention of marriage, but they'd both been thinking about it. Silently, they continued walking, hand in hand.

'Is that my father's buggy?' Mare said as they reached the tavern, asking the question more of herself.

'I wouldn't know,' James replied.

'It is. What would he be doing here?' She knew her father never frequented the pub. There was a loud commotion coming from inside the building, men shouting, cheering, swearing. It sounded like there was a cock fight taking place.

'Let's keep moving, Mare,' James said, taking her by the hand.

'No. My dad's in there.' She broke free of his hand and rushed towards the pub's entrance.

Inside, there seemed to be a massive brawl taking place. It was as if half of the men present were trying to break through a circle of men who were pushing them back like rugby players. Fists and tempers were flying.

Fearless, Mare pushed through the crowd, walking on tiptoes, bobbing up and down, trying to get a view of what was happening in the eye of the storm.

Narrowly ducking and diving between flying fists and elbows, James grabbed Mare's hand and wrapped himself around her like a human shield, then barged through the throng.

'Father!' Mare screamed when she saw Callum propped up between Fenton's wingmen, his face covered in blood, his eyes swollen shut. But her voice was lost in the chaos.

Ron Fenton was standing in front of Callum's limp body, grasping his hair in his left hand. In his right hand was a large knife. The words he mumbled were inaudible but the hatred and content in his expression delivered his intentions as clear as a Sunday sermon.

'No!' James cried, rushing forward and barging into his father's back.

Fenton, letting go of Callum's hair, turned and without blinking, delivered a ferocious backhander across his son's face, sending him sprawling across the floor.

Mare was grabbed by one of Fenton's men and thrown towards the door.

Fenton turned back to face Callum, grabbed him by the hair once more and lifted the knife into the air.

From the floor, something caught Mare's eye—a glint of silver. It was the knife Callum had slapped from Fenton's hand, still in its resting place, sticking up from the floor. She grabbed it by the handle, jumped to her feet, and rushed back into the crowd. 'AHHHHH!' she yelled at the top of her voice, rendering the surrounding chaos to an instant silence.

James too had regained his composure and raced to aid his love. The crowd parted, allowing the two teenagers through.

Fenton, unaware of what was happening behind him, lifted the knife higher and was just about to bring it down into Callum's chest when his eyes suddenly bulged like a squashed possum.

James had reached out and grabbed Mare's tiny hand.

Momentarily, Mare had fought to keep control of it but then realised he wasn't about to stop her. Instead, he'd wrapped his hand around hers. Together, they drove the knife down hard between Fenton's shoulder blades.

Blood spewed from Fenton's mouth. He dropped the knife and stumbled forward, clutching desperately at Callum's throat as if attempting a last ditched effort to kill him.

The men holding Callum let go, and the two opponents slumped to the floor in a heap. The room suddenly emptied as the workers scrambled to get away.

With the six-inch blade still embedded in his back, Fenton was gasping for air. James pulled out the knife and rolled his father off Callum and onto his back.

Mare rushed to aid her father. 'Daddy, daddy,' she pleaded as if begging him to wake up. 'Get the doctor, man,' she yelled to the barman.

Callum, barely managing to open his swollen blood-filled eyes, looked up at her and tried to speak.

Mare leaned in so she could hear him.

'Mare,' Callum whispered. 'Where's Mary?'

Fenton suddenly spasmed. His legs kicked out, his back arched and his mouth gasped like a dying fish. He delivered a gruesome groan, followed by what appeared to be an epileptic fit, then his body deflated along with the last remnants of air from his lungs.

Callum grasped Mare's hand. 'Where's your mother?'

Mare remembered that her mother was spending the day cleaning Mary's Mansion.

'Take me to her,' Callum whispered.

The barman returned with bad news. Doctor Stewart had been called to an accident in the Currumbin Valley Sawmill. He'd be away all day.

'Help us load him into his buggy,' Mare said.

Realising they wouldn't all fit in Callum's buggy, James noticed a horse and cart standing in the courtyard. 'Who's is that?' he asked the barman.

The barman shrugged and shook his head.

Although James steered carefully and slowly, every bump in the road made Callum wince with pain. His body was badly beaten. Limbs were broken as were his ribs, his teeth, his jaw. There was massive bruising around his head and neck where Fenton had repeatedly kicked him.

Mare sat with him in the back of the cart, holding him in her arms, whispering in his ear. 'T'will be ar'right, Da,' she said, abandoning the English pronunciation drilled into her at All Hallows' and instead speaking with her parents' dialect. 'Mary will look after ya. See if she won't.'

When they pulled up outside Mary's Mansion, Callum was weak. While slipping in and out of consciousness, his breathing was shallow. During the trip, he'd constantly called out his wife's name.

'Mammy, are you there?' Mare called out. The only sound was the rustling of trees.

'Mammy?' Mare continued to call as she stepped onto the front verandah.

The door was open. She entered with James behind her. The house was empty and quiet.

They made their way through the house and out the back. 'Mammy, are you there?'

'Mrs Murphy!' James bellowed through cupped hands.

There was no reply.

'Maybe she's back at the homestead,' James said.

But Mare had caught sight of something under the trees. 'Mammy? Is that you?' She stepped off the verandah and rushed across the yard.

James followed.

'NOOOO!' Mare screamed.

Mary was lying on the ground, her eyes staring up at the canopy.

Mare dropped onto her knees beside her mother's body. Gently lifting her head and cradling it in her arms, she sobbed bitterly. 'Mammy.'

Although she was glad of James' comfort, she brushed away his hand from her shoulder without looking up.

The hand returned, but this time it was more forceful, almost as if it were pulling her away. When she tore her gaze away from her mother's eyes and looked up, it wasn't James standing behind her. 'Da!'

Barely able to see through the swelling around his eyes, Callum dropped to his knees, his bottom lip trembling in time with the rest of his body. 'Mary, my beloved,' he whispered.

'She's gone, Da. She's gone,' Mare sobbed.

'No. she'll never leave this place,' Callum said, moving closer to his wife, tears streaming down his face.

Mare helped him cup Mary's head in his lap. Then she stood and was comforted by James.

***

'Oy've loved you from the moment Oy first set eyes on you,' Callum said. Painfully shuffling off his knees, he lay down by Mary's side. 'And Oy'll love you for eternity.' He kissed his wife on the cheek.

The hard-edged beauty of Mary Murphy remained as sharp as a cedar getter's axe.

Squinting through blood-filled eyes, tears burning his shattered cheeks, Callum Murphy's sobs sent ripples of pain through his broken body. With fractured arms and ligaments torn, he held his beloved wife tightly. 'Mary ... my darling, Mary.' The barely audible words, seeping through smashed teeth and cracked, swollen lips, lingered in a dying whisper. 'Wait for me, my love. Oy'll not let ye go alone.' Like rolling thunder, his head throbbed and roared in pounding waves. Deep crimson darkness was rapidly consuming him until a long wheezing sigh carried with it his last breath.

Then there was light.

66

When I climbed from the Dub, it was heartbreakingly strange not to hear Romeo barking from the chicken coop. Once again, my heart felt heavy, like a lead weight in my chest. As I stepped up onto the front verandah, Jenny's MINI raced up the driveway and slid on the gravel before coming to a halt.

She jumped out and raced towards me. 'Still no sign?'

'I shook my head.' Then the tear damn burst its banks.

'Hey, hey, it's okay.' Jenny wrapped an arm around my waist and nurtured my head to her bosom with the other. 'We'll find her.'

I wasn't crying for Tilly, but I couldn't speak.

Jenny guided me to the front door, took the keys from my hand, and opened it. Before entering, she inadvertently dropped to her knees and held out her arms like a wicket keeper. 'Where's that boy? Where is he?' she called out playfully. When she realised Romeo wasn't there, she rose to her feet. 'Is he in the coop?'

'No.'

'Then where is …? Did Tilly take him?' She was watching my lips as if waiting to gobble up my words.

'He's gone, Jen!'

'Gone? Where?' Jenny Radford was the hardest woman I knew. A real ball breaker. Like me, she rarely showed emotion. But also, like me, she had a soft spot for that little dog. Her bottom lip began to tremble.

Taking her by the hand, I led her into the house.

Her eyes opened wide when she saw the state of the place. 'Who did this?'

'The same person who killed Romeo.'

I'd never seen her cry before. Now it was my turn to comfort her.

'How did … was …?'

'I'm not sure. There were no marks or signs. I'm guessing poison, an injection or …'

'A euthanasia shot? The type a vet would administer?'

It was a thought that had crossed my mind.

'I'll take him with me. Organise a toxicology report.'

'No, he's not going anywhere. I've buried him out the back.'

Jenny didn't protest, as I would have expected. Instead, she produced a pair of latex gloves from her pocket, snapped them on, and went into detective mode. 'I'm sorry I missed your call.'

'That's okay.'

'You haven't touched anything? Of course, you haven't, sorry.'

'I called you first because I didn't want to explain this to some young uniform.'

Jenny nodded knowingly as she gently sifted through the debris on the floor. 'Any idea who might have done this?'

'I've got a few suspects.' The vision of the whiteboard gallery came to mind.

'Were they looking for something?'

I remembered the USB stick. It was in the Dub's glovebox. I went out to the car to retrieve it.

Handing it to Jenny, I searched with my eyes for my laptop, but it wasn't there. The perpetrator must have taken it. 'Do you have your lappy?'

'I do, in the car. Where did you get this?' she asked, holding up the USB stick. I told her about Daisy's jewellery box.

Jenny went out to her car, returning a couple of minutes later carrying a beat-up vinyl briefcase. Placing it on the kitchen bench, she slid out her laptop and plugged it in.

'Are you okay?' Jenny asked, putting a hand on my shoulder.

'To be honest, mate, no, I'm not. I can't believe he's gone.'

The computer buzzed. After entering her password, Jenny inserted the USB stick. As the gallery of thumbnails came up side by side, one at a time, a question suddenly demanded my attention. If it was the memory card that the killer had been looking for when they ransacked Mary's Mansion, how did they know I had it? Nobody else knew about it. I hadn't mentioned it to Daisy Patterson when I'd returned the jewellery box. Or was she already aware of its existence? Was it she who had put it in the box before it was stolen? This made little sense, but I wasn't ruling it out. No, the only person who knew about the memory card was me and Ken at the copy shop.

Jenny clicked on image 1. It expanded and almost filled the screen.

We could have been excused for mistaking the young girl on the screen for Tilly Derby. Although the more recent pictures of Kathy Brown had shown her to be a little haggard, at this earlier age, the likeness to her daughter was uncanny. Next to her was a middle-aged man. He had an arm around the smiling girl. His eyes were heavy and his jaw was slightly drooped, as if he were inebriated or drugged. This was twenty-odd years ago, and before selfies. The image was set back a little, allowing a glimpse of the background. Although the décor was different, it was unmistakably The Panda Club.

The next photograph was almost identical but of a different man. So was the next one. So was the next one and the next. I was surprised when a picture of Tom Partridge came up.

Unlike the other shots, he wore a wide grin that matched Kathy's. It didn't surprise me to see Jake Fenton in another. There were also pictures of Reg and Roy Patterson, but these differed in that they weren't taken in The Panda Club. Interestingly, there wasn't a picture of James Fenton. The photograph taken with Roy Patterson was in front of the milking station at the dairy. They looked mischievously back at the camera as if they'd just had a romp in the hay.

Reg Patterson was seated on a couch, possibly in the family front room. Kathy sat on her hands with her shoulders high and her head forward, that ever-present grin as if she'd just been caught doing something she shouldn't.

'She sure was one clever girl,' Jenny said as we continued to scan through the images.

Like me, she'd obviously deduced the power of the memory card as evidence. It was likely that every male in the pictures had been threatened with statutory rape, each believing they had fathered an illegitimate child, each paying for their sins ever since. One other thing that had dawned on me as we continued through the files was that unless Kathy had a remote-controlled camera, someone would have had to have taken the pictures. Katz? Or Tom Partridge perhaps? If this was the case, Tom may also have been aware of the memory card.

I say the only pictures that differed were those of the Pattersons. When we opened up the final one, I realised this wasn't the case. Jenny and I both instinctively leaned into the screen and in unison said, 'Shit!'

Like the Patterson's pictures, this one wasn't taken in The Panda Club. It was an unfamiliar setting, but those cold eyes and that self-important smirk were still present.

'Is that …?' Jenny asked without expecting a reply. 'It certainly is.'

We sat back from the screen, our minds turning like the Plucka Duck wheel until it gradually slowed and stopped at the same conclusion. The familiar face in the last picture was very likely the killer of Kathy Brown.

67

Jenny got straight on her phone and rushed outside.

I remained on the kitchen stool, looking closely at the image. Kathy was standing in a queue in a bookstore. She was sticking her tongue out at the camera. At the front of the queue was a table. At the table sat a man signing books. It was a young Ben Fisher.

Could the famous Brisbane author of twenty-three bestselling novels be Tilly's father?

Although he hadn't been a suspect, I was familiar with his history from research I did prior to taking on the case. This allowed me to fill in the gaps. My thought process was churning away like this: Ben Fisher, a new and exciting author with a big future ahead of him, frequented The Panda Club in Fortitude Valley and the services it provided. His favourite girl was a young, seemingly innocent, lass called Kathy. He began to solicit her services outside of the club to the point of infatuation. The only problem was that he was married to the daughter of his publisher.

Kathy, wanting to escape her life, followed her only friend, Tommy Partridge, to the Gold Coast Hinterland. But Fisher tracked her down. Then Kathy fell pregnant. She demanded that Fisher leave his wife and marry her. He refused and turned his back on her. As his success grew, Fisher moved away from Brisbane, firstly to Sydney and then to LA, making it impossible for Kathy to contact him.

However, being resourceful and the service provider for many powerful and wealthy clients, Kathy realised she was in a unique position. Any of the men she had slept with recently—and there were many—could be deceived into believing they were the father of the child. And with the revelation that she was underage at the time of conception, she held a powerful and lucrative card. Unaware of the real situation, each of the men paid for Kathy to move to the Sunshine Coast to have the baby and put it up for adoption, as well as continuing with payments for her silence.

When Fisher finally returned to Brisbane from the US years later, he was on the brink of bankruptcy after his wife had filed for divorce. Kathy learned of his return and immediately saw her chance to confront him. Which she did.

Fearing the repercussions of the revelations this woman could incur on his pending divorce proceedings, and in a state of emotional desperation, Fisher agreed to meet with Kathy at an address in Tallebudgera Valley. On his arrival, the conversation became heated. Something snapped in the writer—maybe it was something that had been there all along, maybe it was the reason the horrendous scenes in his books were described as being so realistic and vivid. Still wearing the driving gloves that he always wore when driving his beloved Porsche, he grabbed her by the throat and squeezed until she was dead.

Four years later, and what little money he'd had now gone, his publisher, and ex-father-in-law, was threatening to sue him for breach of contract. His health had deteriorated so much that work as an extra on *The Walking Dead* could have been an option for a return to society. There was one spark of hope, though—the fact that nobody had come knocking at his door in relation to the death of Kathy Brown was a bonus. Surely, if the police had suspected his involvement, they would have at least approached him for questioning by now? Had he got away with the perfect murder? For the first time in a long while, the idea for a new story germinated. A stint in rehab, at the expense of his publisher, allowed him to clean up his act. While doing so, a plot, characters, and scenarios seeped into his mind.

Author Ben Fisher was back.

A great theory, but it could have been just as fictitious as one of Fisher's books. I had no proof whatsoever. Then I remembered Fisher's glance over my shoulder when I blocked his entrance at the door. Could he have seen the memory card on the kitchen bench?

Jenny came back in. 'I've got a full despatch on its way. A quick check with QMR confirms Fisher is driving a 1984 Silver Porsche 911, registration number Fright 1.'

Remembering the number plate, I confirmed this. 'Let's go. We'll take your car.' I felt the need to be out searching for Tilly.

'So, do you think Fisher is Tilly's father?' Jenny asked as we raced out of the driveway in her MINI.

I replied with the universal "fucked-if-I-know" shrug.

'It's irrelevant, I guess. He's been made to think he is. That's all that matters to him.'

'The important thing is his state of mind at the moment. Does he mean Tilly harm? Or has he gone into some kind of parental welfare situation?' I said.

'We're tracking the highway cams to see if he's headed back to Brisbane.'

'Good. My guess is he's still down here, though.'

'Yeah, me too. But where?'

'Where indeed.'

We hit lucky. Miss Doris Beatty of Trees Road, Tallebudgera was what we referred to in the police as a regular caller, meaning in less polite terms, she was a serial whinger or a pain in the arse.

Staff Sergeant Alex Aswell at Palm Beach Police Station took a call from Doris, screwing up his face when he realised who it was on the other end of the line. He reluctantly wrote down her complaint, then filed it away in the 'Doris' file—the wastepaper bin. This time, the elderly spinster was calling to complain about a silver sports car that had raced past her house as it reached what the locals termed as 'the top of the world'. Trees Road was a long, steep hill that eventually levelled out at the plateau of Tally Valley. The view from the top was a breathtaking 360-degree vista of the Coast and surrounding hinterland. Properties up there were premium priced dwellings on boutique acreage blocks. I once dated a girl back in the day whose parents lived up there, and although it had been some time since I'd driven the trek that always seemed to take forever, I was still familiar with it.

When he received the bulletin to be on the lookout for a 1984 silver Porsche, Sergeant Aswell retrieved the screwed up sticky note from the bin and called the number he was given—Jenny Radford's.

The little late model MINI with the BMW engine managed the steep incline easily as Jenny pushed the pedal to the floor. 'I've never actually been up here,' she said, sitting back in her seat like an airline pilot shortly after take-off.

'Most people wouldn't even know it was here,' I said. 'Why would Fisher bring Tilly here, do you think?'

Trees Road was one of those drives that once you'd done it, all the way up and back down, the thought of doing it again was probably the farthest thing from your mind. As much as the view up there was amazing, I didn't envy the residents for having to make the drive daily.

When we finally reached the top, it was like entering an enchanted village in the sky. The house blocks were flat, the architecture was a mixed bag of old Queenslanders to mid-century minimalistic structures, to modern boxes, all built to make the most of the breathtaking views. The narrow road was quiet and there was no sign of any other vehicles except for those parked in the driveways.

Doris Beatty's house was on the left just as you reached the summit and after the only other exit, Syndicate Road.

The elderly woman standing anxiously at the side of the road waving us down, we assumed was Doris. Our assumption was correct.

Jenny pulled up alongside her and lowered her window. 'Are you the police?' Doris asked.

'Yes, mam,' Jenny replied. 'And you are?'

'Doris Beatty. I would have expected a proper police car.' She looked disappointed.

'You reported a car speeding earlier. Did you see where it went?'

'Yes, I did.' She pointed towards a driveway on the other side of the street about a hundred metres away. 'Pulled up outside old Mister Dexter's place, stopped for a minute or two, then drove in.'

I climbed from the car and gazed in the direction she was pointing. I couldn't see a house, just a driveway.

'Who lives there?' I asked.

'Well, it's that famous chap. What's his name ...?' She frowned as if she were scanning her memory for the name. 'He bought it a couple of months ago, but I don't think he lives there. Just see his sports car going in and out every now and again. He never waves or anything like that.'

Jenny also climbed from the car. 'Is there another way out of the property?'

Doris, ignoring the question, was looking me up and down instead. 'You're Scott Stephens.'

'Yes, I am.'

'What you did for the Gold Coast was outstanding!'

'Thank you.' Blushing, I repeated Jenny's question.

'No. He's still in there.'

'Thank you, Miss Beatty,' Jenny said.

We climbed back into the car and Jenny requested back-up on the police radio. Then we drove slowly towards the unfenced property.

'Are you going to wait for back-up?' I asked. 'Nah. Let's go in.'

'That's my girl.'

The driveway was a discoloured clay paving. Dull, dry palms and shrubs on either side gave the impression that the gardens were once looked after, but not for some time. The house was a large two-storey brick and tile but, like the garden; it was tired and dated.

There was a double garage under the building, but the Porsche was parked out the front.

By the registration plate, 'Fright 1', we instantly knew it was Fisher's. Jenny pulled up alongside it.

Creeping like Special Op agents, we split up. Jenny followed the perimeter of the house to the right, me to the left.

A path guided me to a stairway. This led up to an enormous deck. The view of the sweeping valley below was breathtaking.

Stepping onto the deck, I immediately saw Fisher sitting on a wicker chair with his back to me. Approaching him cautiously, I called out, 'Where's Tilly, Ben?'

He didn't react or even flinch.

'What have you done with her, mate?' Still nothing.

Jenny stepped onto the deck at the opposite end. She was actually closer to where Fisher sat. It surprised me when she suddenly bolted towards the writer at full pelt.

Fisher still didn't move.

When I reached him, Jenny was kneeling by his side with his wrist in her hand, feeling for a pulse.

'Jesus!' I yelled. His head was resting back against the chair. The tweed jacket and white shirt he wore were heavily soaked in dark crimson blood. A knife was buried in his chest.

'He's dead,' Jenny said, calm and in control. She rose, pulled out her phone from her pocket, turned away and made a call.

This dissolved my theory into the wind like a stream of weak piss. My immediate concern, though, was for Tilly. Where could she be? Noticing the sliding glass door to the house was open, I cautiously entered the property. 'Tilly?' Are you in here?'

The house was open plan, mid-century architecture, with what looked like mostly original fixtures and fittings, a tiled floor and dull wallpapered walls.

To the right of the kitchen was a corridor. A sudden bump coming from its direction startled me. 'Tilly, is that you? It's okay. It's Scotty.' I crept along the passageway. There were timber veneer doors on either side, all open, and bedrooms that were tidy but dull, as if they hadn't been used in a long time. I passed a bathroom with avocado green tiles and a corner bath.

There was only one door that was closed. It was at the end of the corridor, probably the master bedroom.

'Tilly, are you in there?' Placing an ear against the dusty, grained veneer, I couldn't hear anything. Slowly, I turned the doorknob and opened the door. 'Tilly?'

It was indeed the master bedroom. There was a simple queen-sized bed and apart from two bedside cabinets, there was little else furniture in the room. Tilly was standing by the window, her eyes bloodshot with tears, her nose red and swollen. 'Tilly, are you okay?' I rushed towards her.

She lifted her hands as if to stop me. Suddenly, a searing pain shot through the back of my head.

The room went dark, and I hit the floor face down. Someone had king-hit me from behind.

Although the pain was excruciating, thankfully, I didn't lose consciousness. Rolling over onto my back, I looked up at my attacker through throbbing eyes. 'You?'

'Scott, are you okay?' Jenny entered the room.

Jake Fenton swung a nine-iron golf club towards her head.

Jenny stepped backwards just in time, narrowly missing the blow by millimetres.

As if automatically following through as any experienced golfer would, the swing continued along the full curve.

Jenny, seizing the opportunity, lunged forward and punched him in the mouth. Fenton dropped the club and was momentarily dazed.

Like a prize fighter wanting to finish the bout in the first round, Jenny let go with a combination of punches, pummelling his head and torso.

Fenton, hunching his back, lowered his head and brought up his fists to protect his face.

Jenny stepped back, took a breath, then moved in again. Jabbing first with her left, then, as if measuring up for the next punch, she dropped her stance slightly, recoiled and was about to deliver a thunderous right when Fenton, seeing an opening, pounced. Mirroring Jenny's manoeuvre, only faster, his right fist hit her square on the chin, knocking her to the floor.

It was the adrenalin overriding the pain that allowed me to get back up. Fenton was standing over Jenny with his back to me. I was about to administer a full body tackle on him when Tilly raced past me, screaming. She threw herself between Fenton and Jenny.

Using the momentum of her attack, Fenton whipped out a backhander as if returning serve on the Wimbledon centre court, sending her flying backwards in a heap.

'Over here, dickhead,' I called out.

But he'd already spotted me and was fronting up for a sparring session.

I'd been in the police force long enough to know the signs—dilated pupils, soft distant expression. My bet was that it was narcotics of some kind that were fuelling his seemingly superhuman strength. My drug of choice was the natural adrenalin pumping through my veins. Adopting the orthodox boxing stance, I was standing toe to toe with the killer of at least two people—Kathy Brown and Ben Fisher. He'd also hurt people I cared about—Jenny and Tilly—but most of all, he'd killed my fucking dog.

He led with a left jab.

Lowering my chin, and taking the blow on the forehead, I was surprised at his strength, but then remembered he was an ex-international polo player. 'It's over, Fenton,' I said, raising my chin slightly and making eye contact.

'That's right. Over for you.' His outlandish swing was a typical fully committed sucker punch.

Luckily, I managed to duck below it but then, firing upwards, I delivered a hammering right uppercut to his ribs, followed up with a left to the opposite side, and then another right, hitting the same spot as before. I was certainly no boxer but had trained at the Palm Beach boxing gym for many years during my time in the police force. The simple techniques I'd learned had got me through a few harrowing situations while on patrol in Surfers Paradise on those rare occasions when I was forced to defend myself from drunken thugs, bikies or rugby players out celebrating a win. If it weren't for the anaesthetic from the chemicals in Fenton's system, he would have doubled over in pain and taken the count. I'd cracked at least two ribs. But he continued to come forward.

Old Al, the five-foot trainer at the Palm Beach gym, wouldn't have approved, but Clive Wilkins, my old coach at Essendon Schoolboys AFL Club, would have been proud of the goal scoring right-footed kick I unleashed, counteracting Fenton's attack. The move seemed to have become my signature—using it first on the future Gold Coast Mayor, Julian Monroe years ago when he tried to beat me up in the toilets of the Hawthorn Footy Club for stealing his girl, and later when confronted by the notorious serial killer known as *X*. As on both previous occasions, the perfectly executed kick of the potential future full-forward superstar that never was, hit its mark perfectly. Another six pointer. Fenton fell to his knees, grasping his groin in both hands. The pain may have been dulled somewhat by the drugs, but the permanent damage rendered him inert.

Grabbing him by the scruff of the neck, I lifted him to his feet, then punched him in the face. 'That's for Kathy.' I punched him again. 'And that's for Fisher.' I was about to punch him again when Jenny grabbed my arm. Our eyes locked. 'And this one's for Romeo!'

She let go of my arm.

It was rare for me to lose my composure and act unprofessionally but driving my fist down into Fenton's face and feeling his nose crunch beneath my knuckles felt damn good.

Forcing his hands behind his back, Jenny cuffed him and read him his rights.

Remembering Tilly, I rushed over to her. She was sitting on the floor, a little dazed, nursing her right eye. 'You okay, Tilly?'

She nodded.

I helped her to her feet while the sound of police sirens outside grew louder. 'It's going to be all right,' I reassured her, leading her out of the room.

Jenny was kneeling on Fenton's back, keeping him pinned to the ground. She had the situation under control. Within minutes, the place was swarming with detectives and uniformed police.

As Fenton was led away, Jenny joined Tilly and me outside. We embraced tightly.

'You okay?' I asked, gently pushing her away and holding her at arm's length.

She frowned and shrugged nonchalantly. 'Of course. All in a day's work, mate.' Breaking away, she put an arm around Tilly. 'What about you, you okay?'

Tilly nodded. Her eye was swollen and red. She'd have one hell of a shiner in the morning.

'You've done it again, Scotty!' Jenny said. 'No, this is your collar.'

'I'll make sure the right people know it was you who reopened the case, taking up the leads where we left off, getting the result we couldn't.'

'That's kind but—'

'Pig's arse. Kind,' Jenny interrupted. 'You deserve this. And what a great start to your new business.'

It was a good result, but I had to be honest with myself, it was only because Fenton slipped up that we caught him. Until only a few minutes ago, I was convinced Fisher was the killer.

70

No DNA swabs were taken at the time of the original investigation because there was no physical evidence found at the scene. The killer had simply entered the property wearing gloves, strangled Kathy while she slept, then disappeared into the night. The theory that Tilly may have been the daughter of the killer wasn't approached. Even in Fisher's book, five years later, the scenario wasn't suggested.

Although it seemed likely that Jake Fenton was the father, Jenny arranged for those that Kathy had blackmailed to supply swabs. Obviously, they weren't keen. The realisation that they were no longer suspects in a murder investigation should have come as a relief, but the fact that each of them was led to believe they were the father of an illegitimate child, and had been paying for the mother's silence, wouldn't sit well with their families or their standing in the local community. Add to this a possible charge of statutory rape and I could understand their reluctance.

After explaining that the truth was going to come out anyway and the promise that the rape charge would be dropped after twenty-one years, they all reluctantly agreed to take part.

Two days later, and with Jake Fenton safely incarcerated in Woodford Correctional Centre, the results came back. Jenny rang me to say she was on her way out to Tallebudgera.

'So, we know for sure who the father is?' I asked.

'Yep!' She refused to tell me more until she arrived.

'Come on, Jen. I'm busting to know.'

She chuckled and hung up.

Traffic must have been heavy because it took her forty minutes to drive from Surfers Paradise out to the Valley. When she finally pulled up outside Mary's Mansion, I was standing on the front verandah waiting for her.

'I know something you don't know,' she sang as she skipped between the car and the house like a mischievous schoolgirl. In her hand was a yellow A4 envelope. Climbing onto the verandah, she rose on tippy-toes and kissed me on the cheek.

I went to grab the envelope, but she pulled back and hid it behind her back. 'See if you can guess who it is.'

'Ahh …' I shook my head sagely. 'Let's see … James Fenton.'

'Nope.' Her grin was quite annoying.

'Ben Fisher?'

'Nope.'

'One of the Pattersons then?'

Her head wobbled as if she were appraising my answer.

'I'm getting close. Roy?'

She shook her head smiling.

'Reg? Wow! I didn't think for a minute he was really involved.'

'No, not Reg.'

'What? one of the other sons?'

It was as if she were trying as many different ways to execute a simple head shake as possible. This one was slow and very smug.

'Come on, Jen.'

She was playing with me and enjoying every minute.

'If it's neither of the Fentons and none of the Pattersons, there isn't anybody else. Wait … no … not Matt Derby? Bloody hell, we hadn't *thought* of that.'

'Nope.' She delivered her answer slow and drawn out, popping the 'p' sound.

'Fuck it, Jen, just tell me.' I was out of names and out of patience.

Jenny opened the envelope like she was about to reveal the name of best actor at the Dolby Theatre in Hollywood. With her eyes fixed on mine, she slid out a sheet of paper and handed it to me. 'And the winner is …'

Breaking eye contact, I looked down at the sheet. Being familiar with the layout of a DNA report, I knew exactly where to direct my eyes, bypassing the superfluous findings and medical jargon. The name stuck out from the page as if it was highlighted. 'You have got to be kidding me,' I said slowly and meticulously.

'Neither of us saw that one coming.'

'You're not wrong.'

Jenny swept an arm towards her car. 'Shall we?'

'Yes. Let's.'

We climbed into the MINI and drove out of the driveway.

It didn't take us long to find him. Jenny pulled over and waited in the car. As I climbed out of the passenger side, I noticed that same nervous twitch that seemed to appear whenever I approached him.

'Tom. Can I have a word please, mate?'

When I returned to the car, I wasn't sure if Tom had fully understood the information I'd just shared with him. There was to be no arrest; in fact, Jenny doubted there'd be any further action because of Tom's age at the time of his one-night fling with Kathy. They'd both been underage.

'Do we tell Tilly?' Jenny asked as we drove back towards the gatehouse.

'Is it our place to?'

'I guess it's up to Tom to do it, but is he capable?'

I had my doubts. 'Maybe we should tell the Derbys.' Tilly had confided in me briefly the day before that she had discussed her adoption with her parents.

Jenny nodded and pulled up outside the Derby house. 'We can tell them we have the results of the test. Then, if they want to know, they can ask. Tilly's an adult too, so she has the right to know if that's what she wants.'

It was Tilly who answered the door. I was glad to see she was back to her old cheerful self, albeit sporting a black eye. She'd spent a fair bit of time over the last couple of days speaking to the police, answering questions and filling out a full statement, but thankfully, Jenny had personally handled everything and the two now greeted each other as if they were friends.

'How are you holding up, Tilly?' I asked.

'Good.'

'Are your mum and dad in?'

'Yes, we've just had dinner,' Tilly said, gesturing for us to enter.

Jenny had a natural way of being both professional and personal at the same time. After the initial greeting, being offered a cup of tea and asked to take a seat at the patio table outside, she got straight to the point and produced the envelope. Matt and Pam Derby lowered their heads and held hands. 'We just wanted to let you know, but we understand if you don't want to know who the father is.'

Matt exhaled loudly.

'It's up to you, Tilly,' Pam said. 'We'll respect your wishes, of course we will.' Her voice was shaking with emotion.

The black eye and the red bloom on Tilly's cheeks exaggerated her fair complexion, making her look a little like a circus clown. She lifted her chin into the air and said defiantly, 'I already know who my father is!'

'You do?' Pam said, tears welling in the corners of her eyes.

Side glancing Jenny, I knew we were thinking the same thing. Tilly and Tom were very close; in fact, he'd been a big part of her life. Was it possible that Tom already knew he was Tilly's dad? Or could Tilly have worked it out, or at least suspected?

Tilly approached her parents and placed her hand on Matt's shoulder. 'This is my dad!'

No longer able to hold back the tears, the Derbys rose from their chairs and pulled their daughter in to their bosoms. It was more than a group hug; it was a family hug wrapped in safety and love.

Jenny and I slipped away, leaving them there.

71

Callum Murphy and his beloved wife, Mary, were buried side by side on the very spot that they died. Both lost their lives at the hands of Ron Fenton. Callum died from a result of the continuous kicking to his head. Mary was strangled. If there was one blessing, it would be that she wasn't raped. She'd managed to defend herself by first scratching Fenton's face at his initial advance, then kicking him hard in the groin. Although the opium pumping through his veins had dampened the pain, the damage would have rendered his planned attack useless.

Enraged and with super, chemically enhanced strength, he'd grabbed her by the neck with both hands and literally squeezed the life from her. The attack happened under the trees at the back and to the right of Mary's Mansion. Fenton left her body there on the ground. When he'd limped back to the property next door, which would eventually become the dairy farm owned by the Pattersons, he sent a messenger to Callum Murphy with a note to meet him at The Rose & Crown Tavern.

The funeral was held in the grounds of Mary's Mansion. The branches overhanging the stark white gravestones had been trimmed back to give those present a clear view of the graves.

The ceremony was conducted by Father McGuiness from Beenleigh.

After the ceremony, when everyone had retreated to Mary's Shack next door, James and Mare stood at the foot of the graves holding hands.

'I'll come visit ye every single day, Ma, Da.' Gone was the refined English accent, adopting instead the soft Southern Irish tones which would act as a constant reminder of her parents.

'Aye, and me too.'

James' attempt at an Irish accent prompted an unexpected and welcome giggle to escape from Mare. She put an arm around him and rested her head on his shoulder. 'Wherever they are, do you think they're together?' she asked, staring at the headstones.

'Of course, they are. They're here. Can't you feel their presence?' James said.

Mare shivered in time with a breeze that blew through the trees making the leaves rustle and hiss. 'I do. You're right. They are here!' Her face broke into a smile. 'They'll always be here!'

'Aye.'

The body of Ron Fenton was cremated. No one attended the funeral, not even his wife. James Fenton rose to the challenge of his vow to raise his family name from the gutter and make it into a respectable one. His task was made seemingly impossible, though, when the details of his father's underhanded deeds, including murder, torture and rape, became public.

Six months later, James Fenton and Mare Murphy were married at the Tallebudgera Uniting Church. Not turning her back entirely on the Catholic faith, Mare had decided she wanted to be married not just in the Valley, but in church. It was a low-key ceremony, only family and friends were present. Jimmy P had the honour of giving away the bride.

After the death of their parents, the young couple had dropped out of school and took over the reins of their fathers' milling operations. Fortunately for Mare, she had the help of Jimmy P, but James' task was much greater. The first thing he had to do was weed out the loyal followers of his father. There was no place for men like this in the new Fenton business model.

A week later, the couple returned to the tiny church. James had approached Reverend Erwin after the wedding and asked if he could address the community. In his thirty-minute speech, he spoke of his love for the Valley, apologised wholeheartedly for his father's past deeds, and pledged to make things right again. The first task would be to give back the land and properties that Ron Fenton had procured. He also offered substantial compensation for those who had fallen victim to his father's wicked plan.

'I realise it will be a long time before the wounds are healed,' James said, 'but I stand here today as a man who is begging for your forgiveness.'

Unlike his father, James Fenton was a good man. He loved his wife and the four children she gave him. Working hard and learning the skills required to manage a sawmill from scratch, he eventually amalgamated the Tallebudgera and Currumbin mills under the name 'Callmary Holdings'. After vowing to change the dark cloud that surrounded the Fenton name, James became an upstanding pillar of the community, donating greatly to the infrastructures of the two sister valleys, creating a legacy that future generations would enjoy to this day.

72

The last time I stepped into a church was at my father's funeral a couple of months ago, and that was more of a chapel than a church. I'm not religious in any way or form, but I appreciate that a lot of people are, and I respect that. For some reason I felt nervous as I entered the tiny white church. Wearing one of the Anthony Squire suits that the Queensland Police had kindly supplied when they publicly promoted me to detective inspector, I held Jenny's hand tightly as we made our way to a vacant pew at the back of the room.

The building was tiny, with whitewashed tongue-and-groove walls. There were rows of timber pews with an aisle down the middle. There was a crude wooden pulpit at the head of the room, and an upright piano to one side. The vaulted ceiling was high, with half a dozen ceiling fans whirring full blast and creating a welcomed breeze. Even though the French windows were all open, there was little air coming in from outside.

The Pattersons were all present, as were the Derbys. Tilly smiled when she caught my eye. I noticed Tom Partridge wasn't there.

Jenny looked lovely in a floral summer dress. We made quite the handsome couple.

I'd been invited by James Fenton to attend the special service. The week prior was the anniversary of the deaths of Callum and Mary Murphy. I suspected that the occasion would also be a platform for Fenton to address his community about the unfortunate and unforgiveable acts of his son.

Reverend Alan Baker delivered a sermon about forgiveness and tolerance. He spoke of Callum and Mary Murphy and touched on the tragedy of their deaths without mentioning the name of their killer.

The reverend continued and spoke of the latest tragedy to fall upon the Valley. Once again, the themes of forgiveness and tolerance were present in his words as he skilfully interweaved the growing concerns facing the community with mental health issues troubling many families, and the importance of support and charity.

After the sermon, the congregation was invited to join in prayer. Then we stood and sang the hymn, 'The Lord's My Shepherd'. After returning to our seats, I wasn't surprised when the reverend invited James Fenton to the pulpit.

For an awkward moment, James stood silently with a hand on either side of the pulpit, his eyes lowered as if he were praying or going over in his mind what he was about to say. When he finally looked up, his expression was solemn. The only sound in the room was the whirring of the overhead fans.

'You all know me …'

This triggered a communal nodding of heads.

'You all know me as James Fenton. What most of you probably don't know is that I'm actually James Fenton the second.'

There was a flurry of whispers in the congregation.

'Today, as with every Sunday, we are here to give thanks to our Creator and to ask his forgiveness for our sins. But we are also here to mark the tragic passing of Callum and Mary Murphy who, as some of you may also not know, were my great-grandparents.'

More whispers, turning of heads.

'James Byron Fenton married Mary Amelia Murphy, the daughter of Callum and Mary, in this very church over a hundred and thirty years ago. But a week after the wedding, James stood before a congregation just like this one, the good and God-fearing people of Tallebudgera Valley, and delivered an apology for the actions of his father. What began as a heartfelt plea for forgiveness ended with a promise that, with their permission, not only would the Fenton name be redeemed but it would repay the debt it owed to the community in all ways possible.'

The congregation was silent as if they were holding on to every word James spoke.

'I stand before you now as my great-grandfather did all those years ago, begging your forgiveness. But not for the actions of my father, but for those of my son.'

The reaction in the congregation was a collective sigh.

'And I too will pledge my allegiance to the welfare and future of this valley by offering the Fenton name as a patron.'

Jenny drove us back to Mary's Mansion in her MINI. We remained silent. My thoughts were with James Fenton. No one was more surprised than me when the truth had finally come out. The upstanding pillar of the community was exactly that. He'd never even been to The Panda Club. When Katz had spoken of Fenton, my preconceived opinion averted me to assume she meant James, when in fact she'd been talking about Jake. James kept secrets from us, of course he did, but nothing as dark as we'd expected. The DNA report also proved that Tom Partridge was not his son. This had just been more speculation. But James did somehow find out that Tilly may have been his granddaughter, possibly from Kathy. And I believe because of this he'd been paying her along with all the others for her silence.

If I was going to be any good at my new career, I realised I'd need to open my mind more. There were a couple of clues I'd missed. Although I didn't believe in any of that stuff, when Kea the medium opened the séance, she spoke of the presence of a mother figure. In my arrogance, I assumed she was referring to my mum, when in fact she could have meant Kathy. At that time,

I wasn't aware of the pregnancy and the illegitimate child. Could Kea really have been in contact with Kathy's spirit? Of course not, although … *hmm.*

Doris Beatty had said the house across the street belonged to that famous chap. She often saw him driving in and out in his sports car. I assumed she meant Fisher. Once again, my assumption was wrong. She'd meant Jake Fenton driving his Ferrari. Jake had actually mentioned previously that he'd a bought a house to renovate. His Ferrari was later found in the garage.

Neither points were that important. The end result was what really mattered, but it was little things like this that would nag me, keep me awake at night, force me to improve.

Before we entered the house, it felt only right to wander around the back and pay our respects to Callum and Mary. As we approached, my eyes were immediately drawn to the small mound between the graves. Someone had placed a small wooden cross on it. There was one word chiselled into it—ROMEO. Over the top of it hung Romeo's collar.

Bloody hell, some bloke I am. The tears flowed again. I lifted a hand to my mouth to prevent the sob that was about to erupt.

Jenny put her arm around me and pulled me close to her chest. 'It's okay. Let it out.'

'Poor little bugger,' I said, releasing the sob. 'He didn't deserve that.'

'No … no he didn't.'

Before we walked back to the house, I turned back to the grave. 'Will you look after him please, Mary? He loves Red Rock chips, but don't give him too many like I did. Oh, and not the chilli flavour, they make him fart. He'll need a walk first thing in the morning and again last thing at night. Just keep an eye on him too because he's a bugger for chewing. He might want to sleep on your bed from time to time too. I used to let him …' The tears obscured my vision like a wiper less windscreen in a storm. Wiping my eyes on the cuff of my jacket, I knelt and placed a hand on the tiny cross. 'I'll see you, mate. Be a good boy for Mary and Callum, eh?'

I didn't want to go. I wasn't sure how long I'd been there, but when I finally strolled back to the house, Jenny was sitting on the verandah. On the table were two mugs of tea. Hers was empty and mine had gone cold.

After making two fresh cups, Jenny returned and joined me. 'You okay?'

'Yeah ... just had a bit of a moment, you know?' The tea was hot, but I sipped it anyway, more as a way of a distraction.

'What now?'

'*Hmm*, what now?'

'Will you stay on here a bit longer?'

'Nah.'

'Ruby Street?'

The thought of Ruby Street wasn't that appealing. The fact that Sandy had gone was a plus, and I *was* missing my mate, Elvis, but did I really want to go back to that life? 'Don't know yet. I'll stay here one more night, then decide what to do in the morning.'

'You could come back to mine!' Jenny said, raising an eyebrow.

I'm forty-three years old. Here was a girl I could quite easily settle down with, marry perhaps, start a family with. Was that me, though?

If *I* didn't know, who would?

How would you rate
this book?

I hope you enjoyed reading *Mary's Mansion*. If so, I would be truly grateful if you would consider writing a review.

Reviews are a very important way of enabling me to reach a wider audience and bringing my stories to more readers just like you.

If you have an Amazon account, you can rate this title and leave a customer review by scanning the QR code below or logging into you KDP account.

Or, alternatively, if you purchased your book from one of the online stores, you can login to your account and leave a review there.

Or if you have a Goodreads account you can post your review at:

Thanks in advance, I really appreciate your support!
Andrew

ACKNOWLEDGEMENTS

As a proud Queenslander, I'd like to begin by acknowledging the traditional custodians of this land which we inhabit, and pay my respects to the Elders past and present.

Thank you to my editor, Julie Guthrie, for your concise edits that force me to work a little harder, of which I am grateful. And a big thank you to the best beta readers ever, Carole Phillips, and Jane McDermott.

ABOUT THE AUTHOR

Andrew McDermott was born in Nottingham, England. A naturalised Aussie he has lived on the Gold Coast Australia since 1989 with his wife, Jane. He is a patron of the Gold Coast Writers Association, and currently resides at Kirra Beach.

Other books by this author...

Also by ANDREW M^cDERMOTT

THE TIGER CHASE

Dr Elizabeth Smith brings a rare Chinese tiger to the La Zoo, but the tiger is stolen on its arrival. Detective John Dean of the LAPD hates two things in life, strong willed woman, and cats. His worst nightmare is realised when he is ordered to retrieve the tiger with Dr Smith and travel back 2000 miles across America in a station wagon, with the tiger in the back, and a gang of crooks in hot pursuit.

The Tiger Chase is an action-packed story that incorporates drama and humour with a wealth of information about one of the most precious, yet most endangered, species on earth the South China tiger.

An entertaining story about the fight for survival which is sure to raise awareness about the very real threat of extinction facing the mystical and majestic South China Tiger.

Nick Rhodes, Duran Duran

For the first time in history, this most ancient tiger – the South China Tiger, is brought to the consciousness of the western public through story telling. The Tiger Chase has captured the spirit of the Chinese tiger, ancestral to all other subspecies, as well as the culture associated with it. I hope that the awareness it raises would encourage the reader to join us in our fight to save this cultural symbol and protector of nature from the fate of extinction.

Li Quan, Save China's Tigers (Charity)
www.savechinastigers.org

Purchase your copy from all good online book stores or at:
www.andrewmcdermott.com.au

Sign up at the link below to join Andrew's mailing list and receive your free ebooks, his bi-annual newsletter, be the first to know about up and coming titles, and have direct contact with the author.

"I would love for you to be part of my writing community. Your opinion is dear to me and I hope you will enjoy the books in my catalogue and all future releases."

Andrew

X'posé (X prequel)
Hidden Moon (Flirting with The Moon prequel)
Download your free ebooks here:
www.andrewmcdermott.com.au

You can also follow Andrew at:
Facebook: https://www.facebook.com/andrewmcdermottauthor/
Instagram: https://www.instagram.com/andrewmcdermottauthor/
X (Twitter): https://x.com/andymcdauthor